Never Let Go

NEVER LET GO

Based on historical events.

PAMELA NOWAK

FIVE STAR
A part of Gale, a Cengage Company

Maps: Lake Shetek Settlers' Cabins, 1862 (courtesy of Jon Isch); Presumed Route of Lake Shetek Captives with White Lodge and the Fool Soldiers (from *Minnesota's Heritage*, Vol. 4, page 8, courtesy of the Dakota County Historical Society); Southwest Minnesota and the Santee Reservation (courtesy of Pond Dakota Heritage Society, owner).
Five Star Publishing, a part of Gale, a Cengage Company

LIBRARY OF CONGRESS CATALOGING-IN-PUBLICATION DATA

Names: Nowak, Pamela, author.
Title: Never let go / Pamela Nowak.
Description: First edition. | Waterville, Maine : Five Star, [2020]
Identifiers: LCCN 2019045248 | ISBN 9781432872434 (hardcover)
Subjects: LCSH: Dakota Indians—Wars, 1862-1865—Fiction. | Minnesota—History—1858—Fiction. | GSAFD: Western stories. | Historical fiction.
Classification: LCC PS3614.O964 N48 2020 | DDC 813/.6—dc23
LC record available at https://lccn.loc.gov/2019045248

First Edition. First Printing: January 2021
Find us on Facebook—https://www.facebook.com/FiveStarCengage
Visit our website—http://www.gale.cengage.com/fivestar
Contact Five Star Publishing at FiveStar@cengage.com

Printed in Mexico
Print Number: 02 Print Year: 2021

For Bill Bolin,
my teacher and friend.
You ignited my passion for history,
taught me the value of its lessons,
and introduced me to the
settlers of Lake Shetek.
Thank you . . . more than you will ever know.

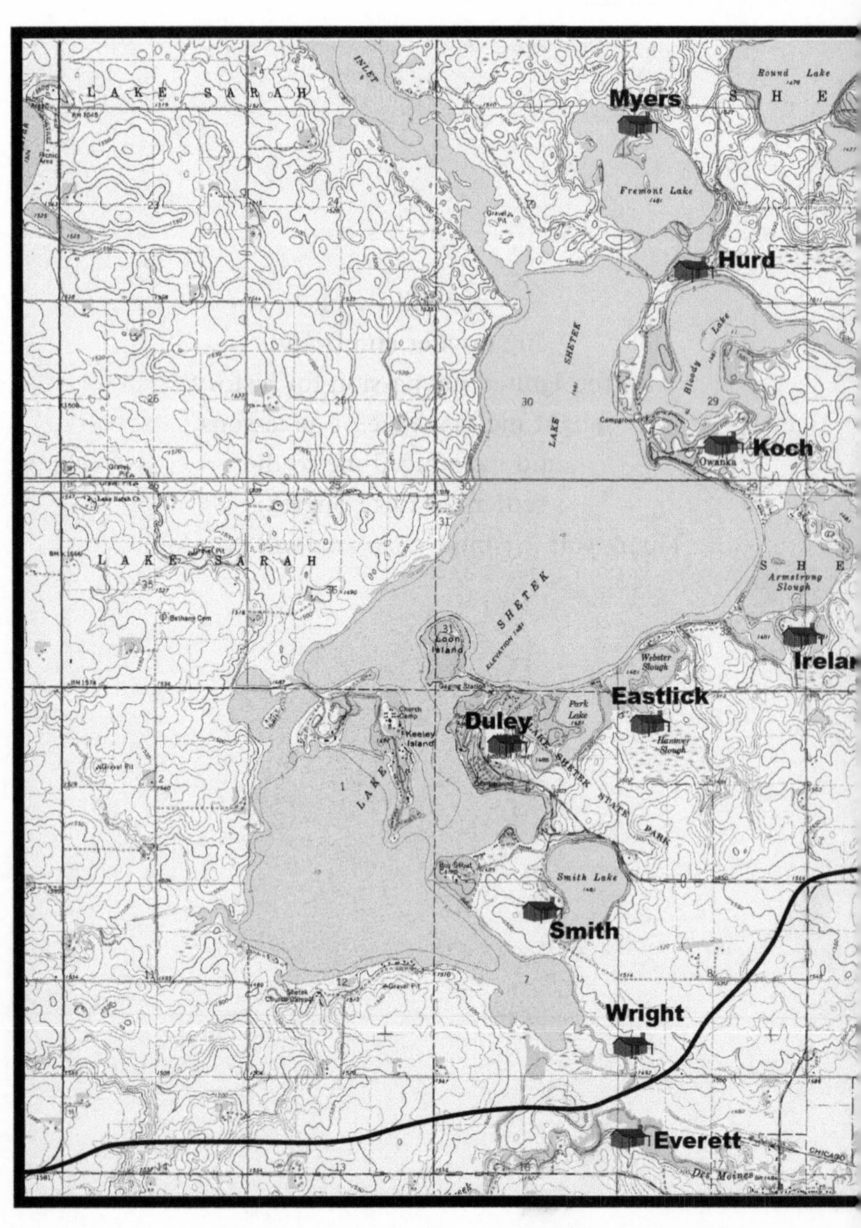

Myers
Hurd
Koch
Irelan
Eastlick
Duley
Smith
Wright
Everett
LAKE SARAH
Round Lake
Fremont Lake
Bloody Lake
LAKE SHETEK
Armstrong Slough
Loon Island
Webster Slough
Park Lake
Keeley Island
Hanover Slough
Smith Lake
LAKE SHETEK STATE PARK
Owanka
Bethany Cem

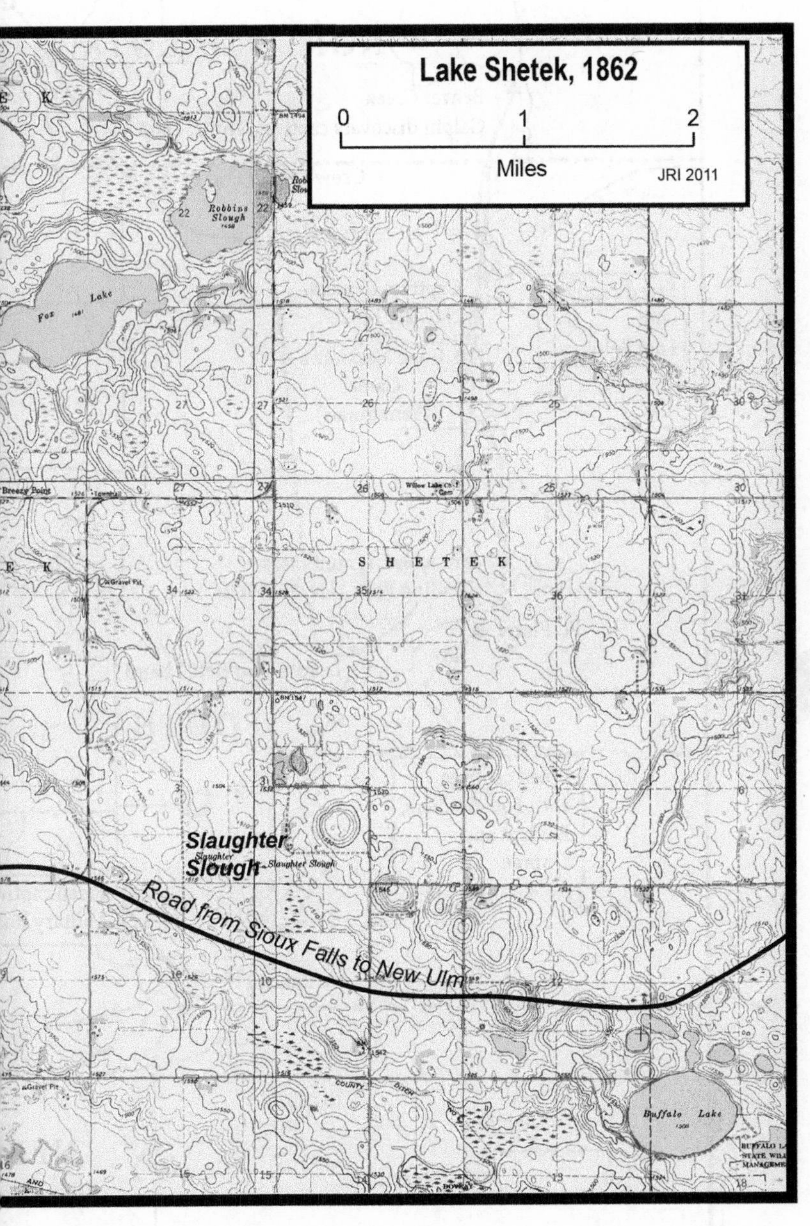

Lake Shetek, 1862
0
1
2
Miles
JRI 2011
Robbins Slough
Fox Lake
Breezy Point
Willow Lake Ch.
S H E T E K
Slaughter Slough
Road from Sioux Falls to New Ulm
Buffalo Lake

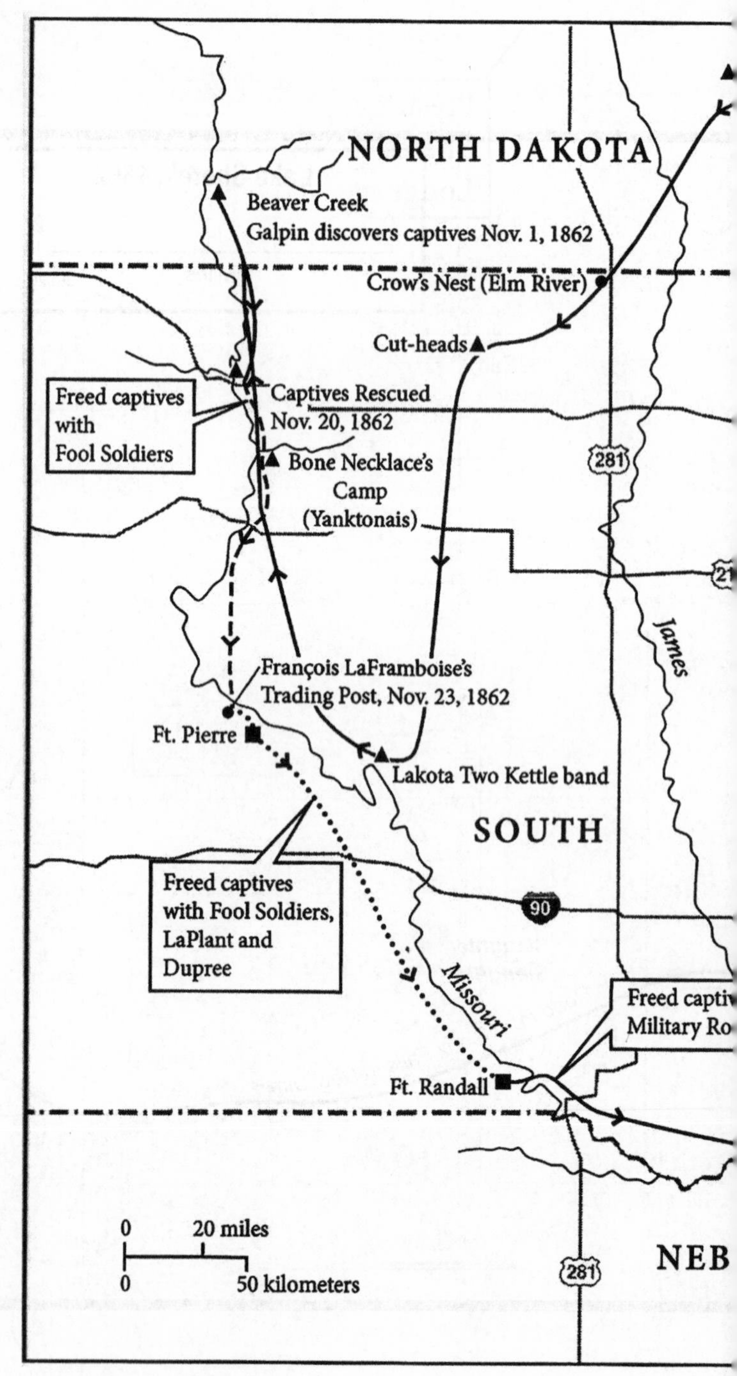
NORTH DAKOTA
Beaver Creek
Galpin discovers captives Nov. 1, 1862
Crow's Nest (Elm River)
Cut-heads
Freed captives
with
Fool Soldiers
Captives Rescued
Nov. 20, 1862
Bone Necklace's
Camp
(Yanktonais)
281
James
François LaFramboise's
Trading Post, Nov. 23, 1862
Ft. Pierre
Lakota Two Kettle band
SOUTH
Freed captives
with Fool Soldiers,
LaPlant and
Dupree
90
Missouri
Freed capti
Military Ro
Ft. Randall
0
20 miles
0
50 kilometers
281
NEB

Map by Patti Isaacs, 2011

Presumed Route of the Lake Shetek Captives with White Lodge and the Fool Soldiers
Buffalo hunter camp (Sheyenne River)
Wahpeton
94
Standing Buffalo band
MINNESOTA
St. Cloud
71
Minnesota
Montevideo
Lean Bear's Camp
Big Sioux
Upper Sioux Agency
29
Captives with White Lodge
Lake Shetek
Attacked
August 20, 1862
DAKOTA
Worthington
90
Sioux Falls
IOWA
71
Sioux City
Ft. Dodge
20
SKA

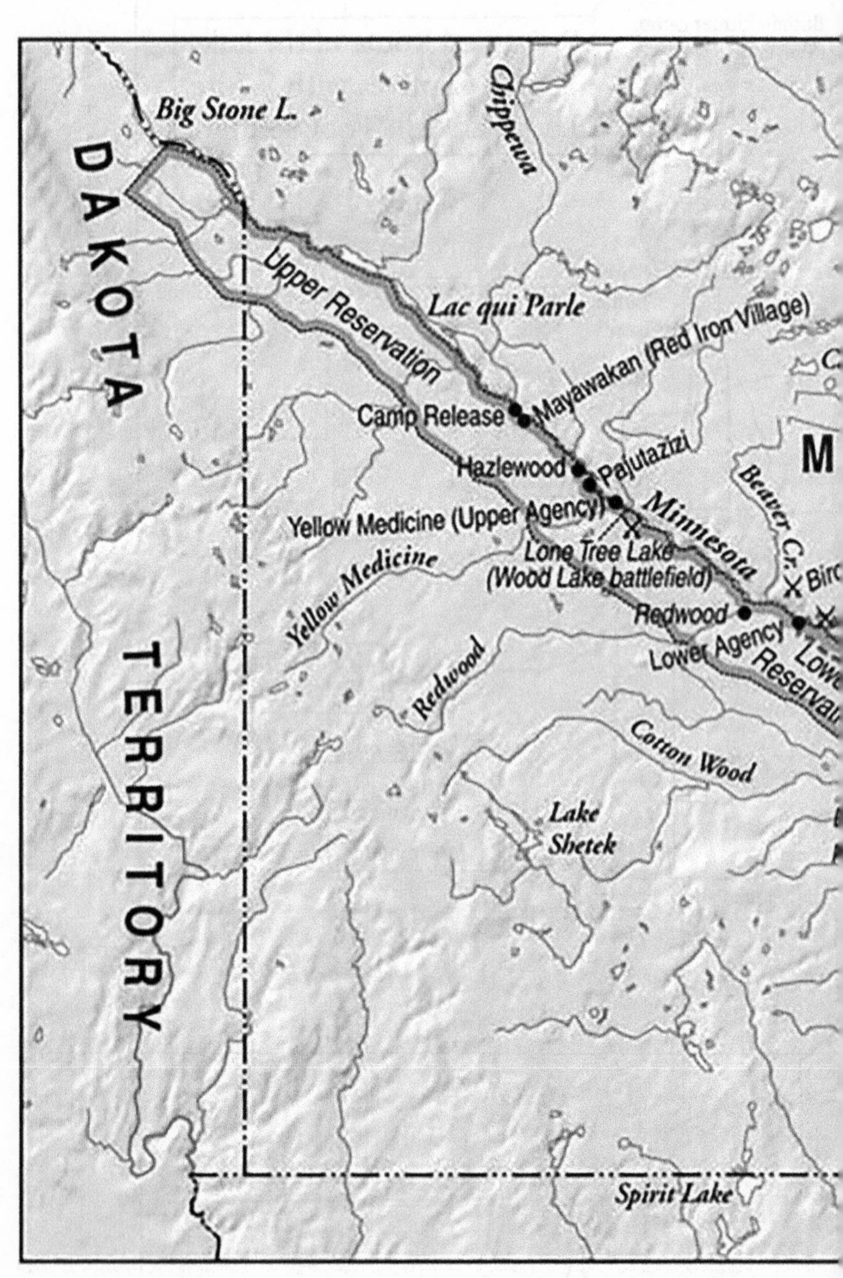
Big Stone L.
DAKOTA
TERRITORY
Chippewa
Upper Reservation
Lac qui Parle
Mayawakan (Red Iron Village)
Camp Release
Hazlewood
Pajutazizi
Yellow Medicine (Upper Agency)
Minnesota
Lone Tree Lake
(Wood Lake battlefield)
Yellow Medicine
Beaver Cr.
Redwood
Lower Agency
Reservation
Redwood
Cotton Wood
Lake
Shetek
Spirit Lake
M

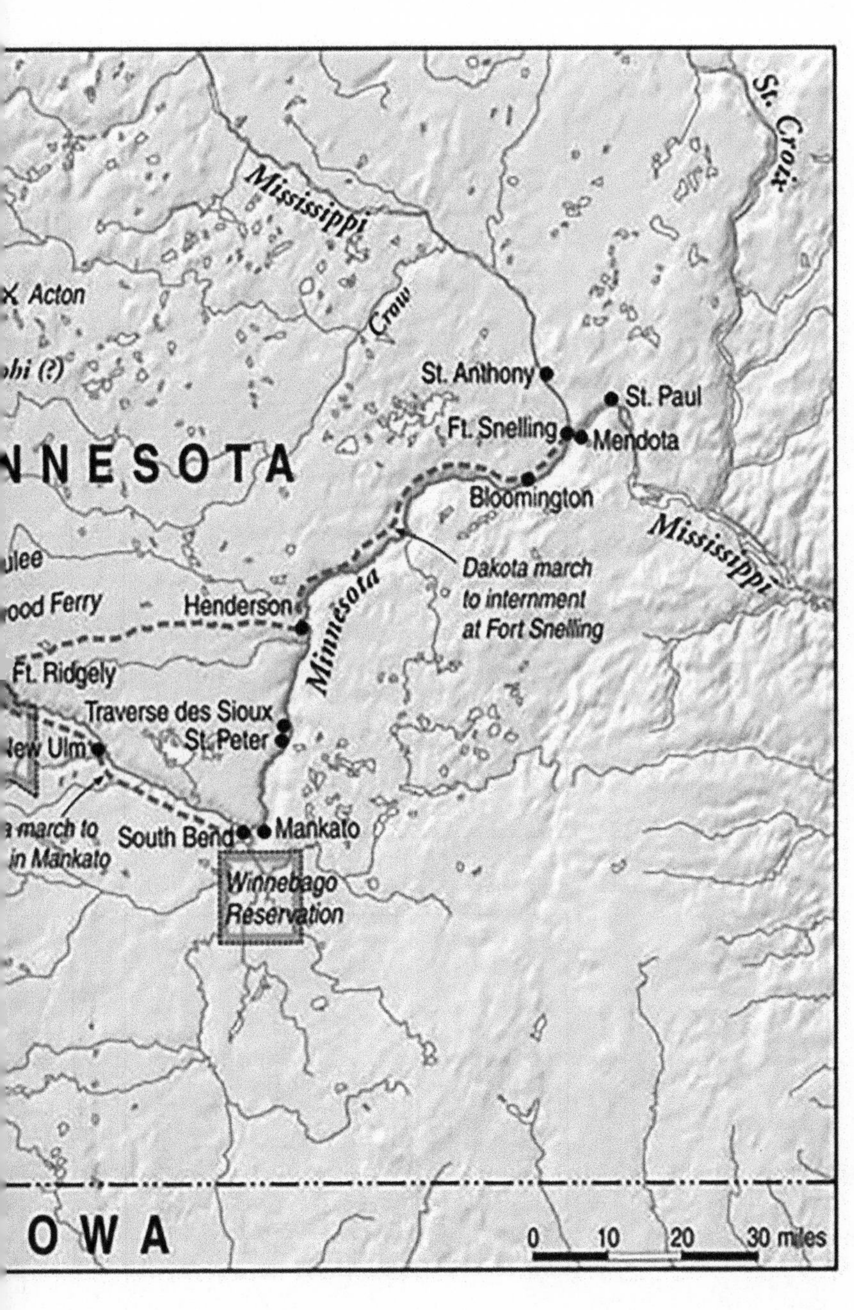

St. Croix
Mississippi
Acton
Crow
St. Anthony
St. Paul
Ft. Snelling
Mendota
NNESOTA
Bloomington
Mississippi
Dakota march
to internment
at Fort Snelling
Henderson
Minnesota
Ft. Ridgely
Traverse des Sioux
St. Peter
South Bend
Mankato
Winnebago
Reservation
OWA
0
10
20
30 miles

Families at Lake Shetek

On August 20, 1862
(by cabin location, north to south)

MYERS

Aaron (36)
Mary (36)
Louisa (12)
Arthur (11)
Olive (8), away at school
Fred (5)
Abby (1)
Edgar Bentley (30)

HURD

Phineas B. (29), missing
Almena (26), full name Alomina
William Henry (3)
Frank Elmer (18 mos)
John Voigt (??)

KOCH

Andreas (45)
Christina (??), aka Mariah
E.G. Koch (??), not related, absent

IRELAND

EASTLICK

DULEY

Thomas (50)
Sophia (??)
Roseanna (8)
Ellen (6), aka Nellie
Sarah (5)
Julianne (3)

John (39)
Lavina (29)
Merton (11)
Franklin (10)
Giles (8)
Freddy (5)
Johnnie (2)
A.A. Rhodes (??)

William (43)
Laura (34)
William, Jr. (10)
Emma (8)
Jefferson (6)
Bell (4)
Frances (2)

SMITH

Henry Watson (42), aka Wat
Sophia (37)

WRIGHT

John (27), absent
Julia (25)
Dora (5), full name Eldora
George (3)

EVERETT

William (31), called Will in novel
Almira (21), called Mira in novel
Lillie (6), full name Ablillian
Willie (5)
Charlie (2)
Charlie Hatch (25)

DAKOTA BANDS in Southwestern Minnesota, August 1862

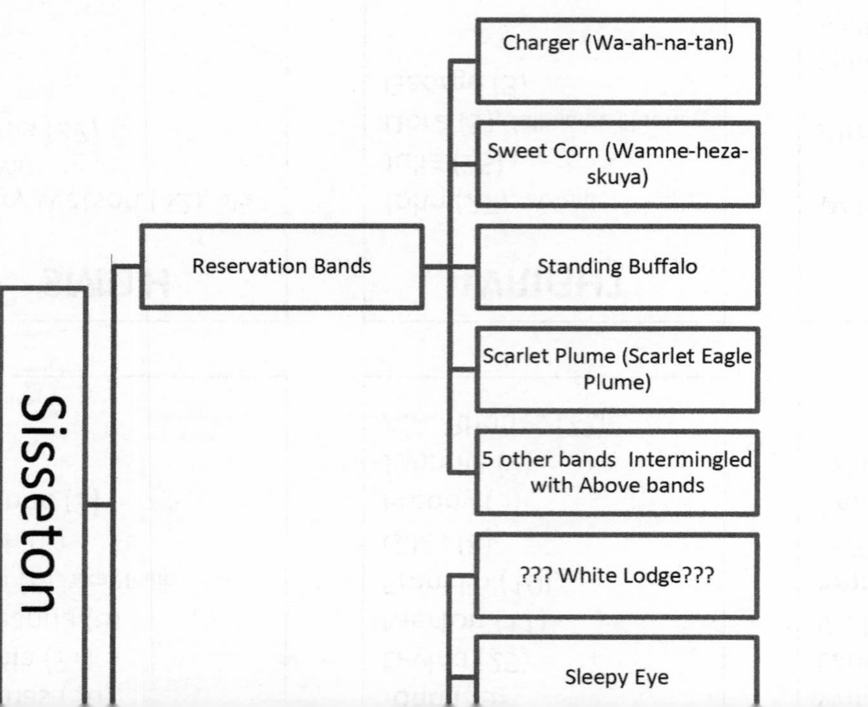

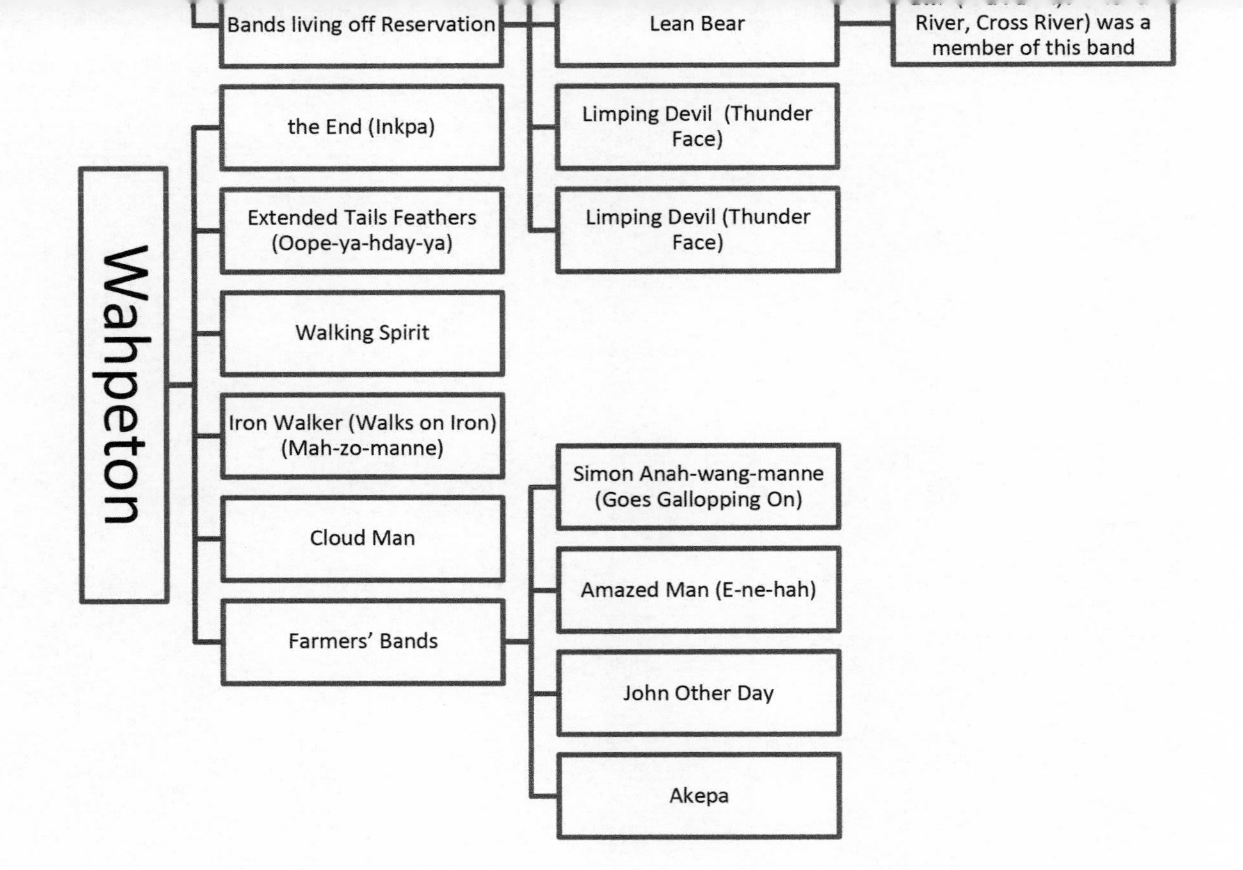
Wahpeton
Bands living off Reservation
the End (Inkpa)
Extended Tails Feathers (Oope-ya-hday-ya)
Walking Spirit
Iron Walker (Walks on Iron) (Mah-zo-manne)
Cloud Man
Farmers' Bands
Lean Bear
Limping Devil (Thunder Face)
Limping Devil (Thunder Face)
River, Cross River) was a member of this band
Simon Anah-wang-manne (Goes Gallopping On)
Amazed Man (E-ne-hah)
John Other Day
Akepa

SISSETON BANDS LIVING OFF RESERVATION

White Lodge (*Wakeska*)
This village was located 25 miles west of Big Stone Lake in present South Dakota. White Lodge's sons were Black Hawk and Chased by the Ree.

Sleepy Eye (Young Sleepy Eye)
This village was located 20 miles west of the Yellow Medicine (Upper) Agency. This was the nephew of Old Sleepy Eye and was part of Old Sleepy Eye's band.

Lean Bear (Lean Grizzly Bear, Grizzly Bear)
The village was located at Lake Shaokaton or Bullhead Lake near present day Lake Benton, MN. White Owl and Old Pawn (Cross River, Pawn, Across the River) were members of this band. This was part of Old Sleepy Eye's band, and Pawn's wife was a relative of Old Sleepy Eye. This village was to the northwest of Lake Shetek, about 30 miles.

Limping Devil (Thunder Face)
These were two bands under the same chief. The village was located at the Two Woods, not far from Lake Shetek. Blue Face was his son.

CAST OF CHARACTERS

MAJOR PROTAGONISTS are capitalized, underlined, and in bold.

Secondary characters are underlined in bold.

Tertiary characters are in bold.

Minor characters are not bolded.

Characters are grouped by association.

LAURA DULEY (nee Terry): Marries William Duley in Ripley County, Indiana, and expects a fairy-tale life. Instead, they move ever farther West, and she suffers loss and depression. Reflects common biases of her time.

William Duley: Laura's husband, a man always looking for a big break. Aspires to politics and is known as someone who always thinks he's right; has few friends and dislikes Native Americans.

William and Rachel Terry: Laura's parents.

Ellen and Hannah Terry: Laura's closest sisters.

William and (Mother) Emily Duley: Laura's in-laws.

Monroe (Washington Monroe) Duley: Laura's brother-in-law. He lived with William in Iowa before William married Laura.

Hattie Mae Tucker: Laura's neighbor in Iowa, a feisty woman who helps Laura through difficult times. (a created character)

Ellen, Emiley, William Jr., Emma, Bell (Isabella), Rachael, and Frances Duley: Laura's children, in order of birth.

Jo: a half-breed captive who befriends Laura. (a created character)

Old Hag: the name Laura calls one of her captors. (a created character)

LAVINA EASTLICK (nee Day): Goes to live with her brother in Seneca County, Ohio, where she wants to be on her own and become a teacher. Instead, she meets John Eastlick, and they anchor their hopes in acquiring their own farmland. She's practical and takes life as it comes.

Leicester Day: Lavina's older brother who, with his wife, Christine, and young daughters, take Lavina in.

Mr. Beal: an opinionated teacher in Ohio. (a created character)

John Eastlick: Lavina's husband. His goal is to own his own land and support his family.

Mr. Covey, Maggie Knowles (a created character), the

Malindy brothers, Dr. Brooks: townspeople in Beaver, Minnesota.

Merton, Frank (Franklin), Giles, Fred, Willie (William), and Johnnie (John) Eastlick: Lavina's children in order of their birth.

A. A. Rhodes: a bachelor settler who meets John in Olmstead County and comes to the lake with John; lives with the Eastlick family.

Sophia and Thomas Ireland: Friends of the Eastlicks from Illinois. They share the Eastlick dream of owning a farm and move West with them. Sophia is a confidant, and "Uncle Tommy" is a hardy man with common sense.

Roseanna, Ellen (Nellie), Sarah, and Julianne Ireland: the Ireland children in order of birth.

ALMENA (ALOMINA) HURD (nee Hamm): left home at age 14 with her younger brother in Caton, New York. She is determined to be self-sufficient and becomes an expert butter-maker; has a strong belief in the importance of family.

Seneca Hamm: Almena's younger brother, put up for adoption.

Chauncy Hamm: Almena's father. He remarries after her mother dies and adopts children out to make room for growing family.

Marilla and Christian Minier: adopt Seneca and take in Almena. Marilla teaches Almena butter-making while

Christian teaches her to read. They later have daughters of their own.

Phineas B. Hurd (Phin): Almena's husband. He works in a mercantile but dreams of owning land. He respects Almena's independent spirit.

William Henry and Frank Hurd: Almena's children in order of their birth.

Bill Jones: a friend of Phin's who travels West with the Hurd family.

Agnes Jones: Bill's ex-wife. (a created character)

John Voigt: a German trader who settles at Lake Shetek, partners with E. G. Koch. He dislikes Indians and is disliked by the Santee locals. He resides with the Hurd family while Phineas is away.

Iltimony and Bad Ox: Dakota men who often trade for cheese with Almena.

Spot: the mail carrier who travels the route between New Ulm and Sioux Falls.

Mr. Berry: an attorney who assists Mrs. Hurd with her depredation claim.

CHRISTINA (Mariah) KOCH: A hearty German immigrant who wants to have her own home within the German community of New Ulm. She's tidy and industrious.

Andreas Koch: Christina's husband. He speaks with a heavy accent and dislikes Indians.

Mr. Renicker: A German immigrant from the Lake Shetek community who travels to New Ulm for supplies. Suspected of selling whiskey to the Sioux.

Dutch Zierke (Dutch Charley): A German immigrant who, with his family, lives between Lake Shetek and New Ulm. Travelers often spend the night there.

The Browns: a family living between Lake Shetek and New Ulm. Travelers often spend the night there.

Parmlee and Hammer: bachelor fur trappers who have shacks at Lake Shetek.

E. G. (Ernst) Koch: A German trader who settles at Lake Shetek, partners with John Voigt. No relation to Andreas and Christina. Desires to settle at north end of lake.

Inkpaduta: a Dakota man who visits the Kochs.

Running Bear: a member of White Lodge's band who is responsible for Christina.

Falling Star: a Dakota woman who treats Christina well. (a created character)

JULIA WRIGHT (nee Silsby): An ethical woman who finds herself married to an unscrupulous man. Gifted with language and an understanding of other cultures, she regrets her hasty marriage but is committed to her vows. She is friends with the Dakota who camp near the lake.

Jack (John) Wright: Julia's husband. A heavy drinker, he becomes an Indian trader. He is always looking for ways to get rich without working and is easily talked into breaking the law.

Dora (Eldora) and George Wright: Julia's children in order of birth.

Lorenza (Laura) and George Lamb: Julia's sister and her husband (a trapper), who settle with the Wrights at Lake Shetek for a time. They have several children.

Bill Clark and Charley Wambau: disreputable characters who meet Jack Wright and later come to Lake Shetek.

The Jacques Brothers: horse thieves said to keep stolen horses on land across the lake.

LaBousche: a half-breed fur trapper who camps near the Wright cabin.

Mr. Annadon: an attorney from Sioux Falls.

Aaron and Mary Myers: A couple living at the north end of Lake Shetek. Aaron is known for his medical abilities, though he is not a doctor. He is well-liked by the Santee.

Louisa, Arthur, Olive, Fred, and Abby Myers: the Myers's children in order of birth.

Edgar Bentley: a bachelor who lives with the Myers family.

Henry Watson (Wat) and Sophia Smith: a couple living toward the south end of Lake Shetek.

Will (William) and Mira (Almira) Everett: a couple living at the far south end of Lake Shetek.

Lillie (Ablillian), Willie, and Charlie Everett: the Everett children in order of birth.

Charlie Hatch: Mira Everett's bachelor brother. The man who discovers the attack and warns the other settlers.

Old Scalpie: a scarred Dakota woman who cares for Lillie Everett. She was once doctored by Aaron Myers and often camped near Lake Shetek.

Across the River (Pawn/Old Pawn): A Sisseton (Santee Dakota) man who camps frequently at the lake and befriends Julia Wright. He is a member of Lean Bear's band.

Speaks with Strong Tongue: First wife of Across the River. She is prideful and resents Julia. (a created character)

Dances in Water: second wife of Across the River. (a created character)

Tizzie Tonka: a Dakota man who is often with Across the River.

Lean Bear (Lean Grizzly Bear, Grizzly Bear): Leader of a Sisseton (Santee Dakota) band located about thirty miles from the lake.

White Lodge (*Wakeska*): Leader of a Sisseton (Santee Dakota) band who is known for his cruelty. His band joins with Lean Bear's band after the conflict begins.

Black Hawk: White Lodge's son.

Redwood: a member of White Lodge's band; he and his wife adopt Roseanna.

Sleepy Eye (Young Sleepy Eye): Leader of another Sisseton (Santee Dakota) band, nephew of Old Sleepy Eye.

The Fool Soldiers Band: Eight young Yankton Sioux (Lakota) men who disagree with the actions of the Dakota bands to the east and pursue rescue of the white captives. They include **Martin Charger** (*Waneta*), Joseph Four Bear (*Mah to top ah*), Swift Bird (Alex Chapelle), Kills and Comes (Kills Game and Comes Home or *Waktegli*), Mad Bear (*Mato Watogla*), Red Dog, Bears Rib (Kills Enemy), Sitting Bear, Pretty Bear (*Mato Waste*), Charging Dog, Jonah One Rib, Strikes Fire, Big Head, Foolish Bear, and Black Tomahawk.

Major Galpin, Eagle Woman, et al: a trader, his wife, and their party who are traveling on the Missouri River and see the captives.

Little Crow: A Dakota leader who is recognized as the chief and leader of the conflict.

General Sibley: The military leader in charge of the response to the attacks.

Prologue

Murray County, Minnesota
August 20, 1862

Charlie Hatch slogged northward, up the marshy stretch of land between Lake Shetek and Bloody Lake. The mud sucked at his feet in the areas where solid land gave way to water, slowing him. Still, he was grateful for the shortcut that saved him the four-mile detour around the inlet. Already, the summer sun was creeping over the horizon. After he secured Voigt's yoke of oxen, he still had to return the six miles to his brother-in-law's place on the Des Moines River before they even began the heavy work of raising the sawmill. No doubt about it, it would be a long day.

The air filled with the sound of early morning waterfowl, a variety of greetings to the new day, and the glow of sunrise gave way to full light.

A distant shot broke the tranquility, and Charlie chuckled. *Almena Hurd, shooting at blackbirds again.*

On Shetek, the fresh sun glinted off the water, rousing the pelicans from their leisurely nap by the shoreline. Charlie watched one dive for its breakfast, then turned toward the Hurd place where Voigt was serving as hired hand during Phineas Hurd's absence. His very long absence.

Mrs. Hurd is going to have to make some hard decisions unless some sort of miracle happens.

Charlie emerged from the trees and stopped in his tracks.

Holy Mother of God!

Household goods lay strewn across the cleared land in front of the Hurd cabin, feather ticks slashed open, trunks upended.

Eerie silence greeted him. Not even a blackbird chattered. Charlie sprinted toward the cabin, past an overturned milk pail, its souring contents staining the ground. Near the door, Voigt lay on the ground, blood pooling beneath him. Not yet gelled, its coppery stench still hung in the air. Charlie turned away, swallowing against the bile rising in his throat.

Indians. It had to be Indians.

He glanced into the cabin, empty save for larger pieces of furniture flung about the room. He dashed toward the two stables and found the livestock gone. All of it, gone. Almena and the boys were nowhere in sight. Charlie's skin crawled at the implications.

There's nothing more to be done here.

Some forty others lived along the shores of Lake Shetek, most of them to the south, all of them needing to be warned. Chest pounding, Charlie turned back the way he had come and sprang toward the trees.

If the Sioux were attacking the entire settlement, he prayed like hell that he could make it back down the shortcut ahead of them.

★ ★ ★ ★ ★

Part One: Beginnings

★ ★ ★ ★ ★

Chapter One

Laura
Ripley County, Indiana
April 27, 1848

For better or for worse, my new life was about to start.

I drew a shaky breath and peered forward. William waited at the front of the church. Ellen, my closest sister, patted my forehead with a lace-trimmed handkerchief, tucked it into my hand, and bade me to follow her. I clutched the now damp handkerchief in my palm, knowing it would never fit in the tiny watch pocket of my gown, and smoothed the fine cream wool with its delicate floral pattern and pink silk striping. I took Papa's arm, my eyes on William's bright face, and started down the aisle.

The man I loved was making me his. When he'd asked for my hand, he'd pledged to provide me a secure and comfortable life. A smile tugged at my mouth as I recalled his clumsy, albeit romantic promise to make me his fairy princess. I might be leaving the sanctuary of childhood, but my prince awaited me.

The Pipe Creek Baptist Society congregation appeared ready to burst, so eager were they to make my happiness their own. Pride stretched across Mama's face, and she lifted her hands to her mouth as it formed into an "oh." William's warm gaze was firm upon me, his unruly chestnut hair freshly trimmed and tamed for the service. He reached for me, taking my arm as Papa handed me off.

We made our vows, he to love and honor, me to love and obey. From this moment forward, my life would be in his hands. Apprehension over leaving my childhood behind still prickled at me, but my giddiness chased it away. There was nothing but promise in our future. Children of the leading families of Sunman Township, it seemed as if we were destined for one another. We had grown up together, though I a few years behind him. Three years ago, our love had blossomed as if it really were a fairy tale. We turned, William taking my hand in his and squeezing it. Facing the assembly, we felt their admiration and led them out into the spring sunshine to celebrate our arrival as a couple.

Our family of relatives and friends offered congratulations as they spread out upon the church lawn. With the ladies, as a new matron of the community, I set out hams and fried chicken, cakes and cookies on plank tables that were laid across sawhorses. William and I took our place of honor at the front of the line and settled on a quilt to eat. I hardly touched my food. My thoughts were a jumbled mess . . . bliss, desire, nervous anticipation over what would come later. My pulse raced a bit with the realization that tonight I would be in his bed rather than the one I had shared with my sister for so many years.

I was a wife. Laura Duley. Mrs. William Duley.

Reluctantly, I gathered our plates as William folded the quilt. We had obligations. I took the dishes to be washed as he returned the quilt to his mother.

"So, how does it feel?" Hannah, my fifteen-year-old sister intercepted me, always curious about all things adult.

"Oh, ever so grand. I can hardly catch my breath." I exaggerated for her, waiting to see her eyes widen. When they did, I took smug satisfaction in my successful teasing. Gullible as Hannah was, Ellen and I were too often merciless with her. I would miss that.

In truth, I was no different now than I'd been in my previous score of years. I felt much the same as I had this morning, both nervous and expectant. Though perhaps a bit more of both.

I herded Hannah toward the women gathered at a wash tub. This was my place now, not giggling like a school girl with my sister. Hannah could stay or drift off with the youngsters her own age.

"Well, Mrs. Duley," Mama said as she took the dishes from me, "the Lord has gifted you with a gorgeous day."

"Almost like He is smiling on your union," piped in one of my aunts, her expression as proud as Mama's.

I responded with what I hoped was a sage and knowledgeable expression. "I'm certain He is."

"William is a fine man, of such good stock. The two of you will be pillars of the community," my aunt added, her confirmation of our roles warming me.

"Not to mention that he's already built his fortune," Mama said. "Not many young men are responsible enough to do so before marriage these days. The two of you will want for nothing. William and Monroe did a good thing."

He would be providing well for me, though I hadn't been entirely in agreement during the two years he'd been away. While William had increased his financial footing, the wait and worry had been interminable. After his proposal, he'd left Indiana in the company of his younger brother, Washington Monroe, bound for Iowa. William had preempted land there, Monroe having not yet achieved his majority; they'd cleared the claim and farmed the rich black soil together. Their first harvest had been fruitful, giving both of them a nest egg, one that would be even larger for William once Monroe bought out the claim. This, and the legacy our parents had built, would assure the perfect life he'd pledged to provide.

I looked forward to being well-established, respected, with a solid home and our own land. Few brides were as lucky as I.

Mama tucked a stray strand of my dark hair back into one of the intricate braids that framed my chignon and secured it with a pin.

"There, all beautiful again. A wife should always primp for her husband. Shoo, now. He's likely waiting for you."

I spotted him across the yard, huddled with Monroe and their parents. William and I would live with them for the first year, perhaps starting construction of our own house on the family farm by Christmas. Eventually, the land would become William's inheritance while Monroe grew a new branch of the family out West.

My husband. The strange new proprietorship filled me with warm pride.

I sensed the moment he spied me approaching in my spring-striped gown. His gray eyes softened and their conversation halted.

Halted entirely.

Glancing from one of them to another, I slid my arm through William's. "Am I interrupting?"

"No, not at all." His words came out hurried, and I knew I had stumbled into the midst of a conversation not intended to include me.

A wedding surprise?

I glanced at William and noted his now shuttered eyes. Avoidance? Not a surprise, then, but something else. I knew him well enough; he wasn't likely to say anything more, not unless I pried it from him. I turned to his mother, a woman incapable of keeping a secret. "Mother Emily?"

"I . . . uh . . ."

"Come, Mother, let's leave the newlyweds on their own." Father William raised his brow and steered his wife away.

Monroe cleared his throat, shuffling from one foot to another.

"Guess I'd better tag along."

"That would be best," William prompted. "Leave Laura and me a bit of privacy. We'll talk later."

Their unified evasiveness mystified me. I waited until Monroe was out of earshot, but still William did not speak.

"Well, what is it?"

"Now, Laura, don't get all sharp with me." Chastisement was clear, despite his light tone. A wife should not be prickly on her wedding day.

I drew a breath. Mama had warned me a thorny tongue would not be tolerated in a marriage. I searched for a more suitable way to ask. "I'm sorry. I didn't mean to snap, Husband. I sense there is something you mean to tell me, something you suspect I don't want to hear."

"Let's walk a bit."

He guided me away from the gathering, down the path leading to the river. My chest tightened. This was not good, not good at all. I waited, as should a proper wife, and twisted the handkerchief in my apron pocket.

When we were a distance into the woods, he stopped and settled on a fallen tree. He patted his leg, an invitation to sit.

My skin flushed.

"We're married. There's no shame in a wife sitting on her husband's lap, especially on their wedding day." He winked.

I perched, birdlike, thankful for the care he was taking of my gown, nervous at the intimacy.

He drew me close, kissing my eyelids, my cheeks, the corners of my mouth until I melted into his arms and surrendered to his full kiss, desire running roughshod over my good sense. It was only when his hand, greedy upon my breast, moved to the buttons of my gown that I pulled reluctantly away. We had a yard full of wedding guests waiting for us, and it would not do to return with hints of dishabille.

Besides, I knew my husband in this behavior as well. It wasn't the first time he'd distracted me with his warm mouth.

"William?"

"Please, you won't deny me today?"

"I'm not denying, merely delaying." I kissed his cheek, a promise that we would return to pleasures of the flesh later. "We've company to return to, and you've yet to tell me what needs discussing."

"Laura—"

"What is it?" I winced at my impatience.

He sighed and took my hand as if he were a schoolboy seeking a dance. The sudden formality launched my palpitations anew. "I know we discussed taking over my father's farm, making our life here in Ripley County . . ."

"Yes. We did." The words came out curt. This was the dream we shared, taking our rightful place in the community, building our home and continuing our parents' legacy. His silence frightened me. "What is it?" I said for the third time. "What's happened?"

"Monroe and I have decided he will stay here, and we will go to Iowa."

"We'll do what?" I sprang off his knee and glared at him, hardly proper behavior for a new wife, but I didn't care one whit.

He gained his feet and reached for my shoulders. "Now, Laura." His words were laced with syrup, and I was none too pleased with the condescension.

"Don't you 'now Laura' me." My hands plastered themselves on my hips. "You've no right to make such a decision without consulting me."

William drew back, as if shocked to discover a fishwife had usurped his quiet new spouse. "I have every right."

I ignored his clipped assertion. "But we agreed. We had

everything planned out."

"Plans can change."

"What earthly reason would you have to change something we discussed and agreed upon?" I fought to stay calm. It tore my heart that he would alter our dream, that he would confer with this family but fail to consult me. Hot tears stung my eyes. He'd promised me a life here. Surely I had not bound myself to a man who would make empty pledges?

"Monroe's young." William shrugged. "I don't see him doing well out there alone."

"Why not sell off the land in Iowa? You can both stay here. It was only about building up a nest egg anyway. You can both farm with Father William. There's nothing tying either of you to Iowa."

"Oh, but there is. The soil there is unbelievably rich. It puts my father's land to shame. The yields, Laura, the yields!" His eyes grew animated as the words tumbled from his mouth. "When the Mississippi floods, it leaves such fertile ground behind. Even freshly broken, the land is generous."

"And here, the land is already broken."

"Our farms there are cleared now, too. All that remains is to harvest the bounty."

"Let Monroe harvest it."

I uttered the words in a flat tone, unwilling to surrender the argument.

"Monroe is still a boy. He'll never survive out there alone. I want this, Wife. I want the land, I want the dream."

My chest tightened. This wasn't about Monroe. William had latched on to a fantasy I knew nothing about, and he was dragging me along on the chase. And what's worse, he was so enamored of it that he'd not told me, not even considered me.

"And the struggle? You're willing to give up the ease our parents have created for us?" I knew I sounded petty but he'd promised me comfort and security. I couldn't let it slip away. "We belong here, William. This is our destiny. We're the first of the second generation. The *heads* of the generation."

"And in Iowa, we will be the heads of the first generation, leaders of the entire community, not just the second wave."

"I'll be all alone." Panic seized me as I realized what the words meant. I knew *no one* in Iowa.

"We'll be together, among the founding families of Jackson County. We may not have a township named for us, but we'll form a life there, establish towns and governments, not simply carry on what our parents did. We'll create our own destiny."

"You promised me a perfect life." I laid my head on his shoulder, angry still, but it would be pointless to argue. I wasn't going to win. Not with William so excited. His mind was set, and it was a husband's decision to make, no matter what his wife might feel.

"Ah, Laura, it will still be perfect," he told me, cupping my head in his hand. "The only difference is that it will be perfect in Iowa instead of Indiana."

Two weeks later

Our departure was accomplished with more speed than I imagined possible in order to arrive in time to sow a garden. As it was, the vegetables would be late, but the truck would be too important for our winter food store to ignore it all together. Monroe had agreed to go ahead, on horseback, to sow the early crops as his wedding gift to us, and would return to Indiana once we arrived in Iowa.

We traveled lightly, with only my possessions and the household items I'd deemed necessary: rugs and curtains, quilts, and other items to which William and Monroe had likely paid scant attention. Most of what we would need was already there,

William said; the house built and comfortably furnished. Mama and I had doubts about the items that would truly make the house a home and concentrated on packing the items men tended to forget.

I mourned the loss of the life to which I was accustomed, however temporary it might be. Until we built our community, no one would come calling; I would have no need for my tea service. I would be lucky, even, to be able to purchase tea. For a while, there might be few women to gather with and compare dress patterns. Until we established society, I'd wear serviceable clothes, dark colors that would need laundering less often, and I would have little use for my silk-striped gown.

Though William professed bright hope for our future, I knew much of our early survival would depend on my abilities to grow vegetables, bake bread, and maintain our household. I'd been raised in such tasks, but my family had not relied on me. Perhaps such fright was shared by all newly-wedded wives, but the responsibility weighed heavy upon me. For a few years, there would be no other supply, no one to share the burden. I would not see Mama or Ellen or Hannah for a long time, if ever again. They would not be with me as I birthed my children, and I was terrified that I would be entirely alone with no one to advise or assist me. And I knew not at all whether natives still abounded in that country.

Anxiety pressed upon my heart, one already breaking at the loss of everyone and everything I held dear, and I clung for dear life to William's assurances that we would build that community and enjoy both its comforts and our place within it.

The early weeks were not the ideal start for our marriage with one or the other of us sullen for most of the trip. I still resented William's decision to alter the plans we'd agreed upon during our betrothal, one made without consulting me. Though resigned to his authority, I found myself sulking to convey my dissatisfaction during our first wedded days. I was not the only one, however. William complained at any complication, as if it were my fault that the garden would be late. Some days, we literally drove mile after mile in silence.

We'd not displayed such behaviors to one another during our courtship, and I wondered if every couple experienced such adjustments. I missed William's teasing. Moreover, I wasn't certain if our new conduct was part of both our natures, in which case our future would have its trials, but it seemed to me the long jostling days on the wagon seat aggravated our petulance. Each evening, despite our fatigue, we released our petty behavior. Perhaps it was our removal from the wagon, the sharing of tavern fare and glasses of ale. I cannot recall a night that we took our discontent to our bed, and I was glad of it, for Mama had advised never to sleep with anger between us. And, too, I discovered much joy in William's arms, dispelling all the disparaging words I'd ever heard about those particular wifely duties.

As we neared Iowa, William's enthusiasm for our new home finally began to infect me. Though the country became ever more untamed, my fears grew less sharp. I allowed my anger to play out, committing to his theory that we would become the bedrocks of society in Jackson County and build a comfortable life there.

Emerging from the woods onto the marshlands and sandy prairie along the Mississippi, I had my first view of Iowa. Bell-view sat on a wide plateau, surrounded by high hills and rugged bluffs. The river itself was dotted with islands that belied its half-mile width. Everywhere, it was green—bright, lush, unbelievable green in every shade. Such an echo of Indiana's own verdant landscape spurred my hopes.

"Oh, William, it's so pretty." I bounced on the wagon seat. "You never told me there would be such beauty."

"You wouldn't have listened had I done so."

Though the reminder came with a wink, I hung my head, knowing he was right.

"Our land is about two and a half miles that way." He pointed northwest.

I glanced around, trying to envision it, my gaze settling on the town across the river. An entire host of buildings ran along the shoreline and back toward the hills. This was no burgeoning settlement. William had misled me. This was a town already developed, its businesses firmly part and parcel of daily life, churches and schools raised, leaders no doubt in positions they'd long ago carved out for themselves.

"It looks already well-established," I finally said.

"It was platted in 1835."

"So we *won't* be among the founders of the community." Accusation crept into my voice.

"Not of Bellview." William patted my hand. "We'll be among the founding families in Tetes Des Morts Township."

"But not in town." I fought to keep my voice level, my newfound confidence in William's promises slipping away with most of my hope. Though pleased beyond measure that civilization existed here, I felt off balance, insecure in my trust in him, unsure what else might not be as he'd pledged.

"There's the river crossing." He pointed ahead, subtly shifting the topic, a technique in which I'd come to realize he was quite skilled.

I focused my attention on the small, flat boat. It appeared none too secure, a simple log platform bobbing in the water. With each wave, one side heaved then dipped as the other end rose. "That's the ferry?" I choked out.

"That's it."

I peered at it, my stomach already queasy, anxiety clawing at me. One sudden swell could send me into the water, where I'd most assuredly drown. “But I thought it would be a real boat, with paddlewheels, like the advertisement I saw in Rockford.”

William sighed. “We’d have to go all the way up through Galena to the Dubuque crossing.”

His stubbornness raised my dander. “I would prefer we cross there. That flat boat is little more than a raft. With the current of a river that size, I can’t imagine it being safe.”

“It rocks pretty good, but it’s safe enough.” He halted the wagon. “Guess you’ll have to spend the entire trip across in my arms.”

I ignored his wink, refusing to be teased away from my concerns. “I would prefer we cross at Dubuque.” I made the announcement with all the discontent I could manage to remind him of the discomfort of the situation, of the promises he continued to break.

“Dubuque is nearly fifty miles out of our way, and, when I left for Indiana, toll charges there were close to a dollar.”

“We can take it from the pin money Mama sent along with me.” I patted my reticule.

“I’ll be damned if I pay four times the going rate to cross the river. And I am sure as hell not going to take this wagon twenty-five miles north simply to cross the river and drive back again. That’s three or four days, given the condition of the roads.”

“But—”

“For God’s sake, Laura, it would be a waste of time and money.”

I bit my lip, knowing he was right and that my insistence rose more from anger than distrust of the bobbing flatboat. I simmered with the realization that William had misled me. We would not be founders, with the honor of leading a fledgling group of pioneers. We would be forcing our way in, interlopers within an already established society. There wouldn’t be any guaranteed prestige and no fairy-tale life.

I'd left that behind in Indiana, along with my faith in my husband's promises.

William made the arrangements for the crossing as I stewed on the hard seat of the wagon. I held my tongue, not wanting to embarrass him in front of the ferry operator, a man who would be within our circle of friends and acquaintances. The two shook hands, and William returned to me.

"They'll take us across immediately."

I remained stubbornly silent.

"Time to get down, Laura."

"I'll stay on the wagon."

At least if the overgrown raft pitched us into the water, I would have something to cling to.

"You'll feel the sway more up there. We'll be an hour or more getting across."

"I don't care. I feel safer on the wagon."

"You'll be safer standing on your own two feet." He pointed to a crude wooden rail that stood like a short fence at the center of the boat. "You can hold on to that. Or me."

"I'll stay on the wagon, Husband."

He muttered under his breath, shaking his head. He led the team down a planked incline, keeping the descent slow and steady. Workers stood at the ready as we neared the shore.

The wagon lurched as the horses pulled it onto the huge flatboat, and I choked back a yelp. The weight dipped the raft, and my hands flew to clutch the seat as the platform rose from the water ahead of me. My stomach rolled.

One of the men tugged the horses forward, speeding them across the platform until the weight was centered. The pitching ebbed much more slowly. Laborers nailed blocks in front of the wheels as well as behind. Though their placement was careless, I knew the blocks were meant to keep the wagon from rolling off should the current become troublesome. Large as the ferry was, each step, each movement, still caused it to bob. My stomach protested, and I straightened, closing my eyes as I told myself not to be sick.

"I'd git down, missus," one of the men uttered.

I shook my head and twisted my handkerchief.

The ferryman disappeared, and I thought I heard him say, "Your funeral."

Oh lord.

The men took their places at the sides of the barge where large poles were threaded through rings. One of them gave a yell, and the operator on the shore released the rope. They shoved off, the raft sliding forward into the vast lane of water. The current caught, and the barge flowed downriver. The pole-men, their feet widespread, shifted their weight with each swell and dug deeply to hold the boat on course. With the movement of the water, the wagon slipped forward, rolling until it hit the block, jerking to a stop, and rolling back again.

Acid rose into my throat, making the sour stomach I'd had these past three mornings trivial. I bent over the side of the wagon and heaved, again and again.

It was an inauspicious beginning to life in Iowa.

William lifted me from the wagon and wiped my mouth. Though I longed to simply crumple, he enfolded me into his arms and guided me to the rail, telling me to shift my weight as the boat-men did. I managed to control my nausea by the time we hit shore, but my dress was stained, and my mouth tasted bitter. I left the barge on shaky legs, thankful we'd made it safely across. A woman on the other side handed me a ladle full of water and pointed me to a bench where I waited while the wagon was unloaded from the ferry.

We stopped at the mercantile, buying supplies, and I gained

my first glimpse of life in Bellview. Well-stocked with all the necessary basics, including tea, the store would provision us with all we needed. Luxuries could be ordered, for a price. My apprehension dipped a bit. We would not want for supplies, at least.

As to our role in the community, I accepted it would not be as I'd expected. Despite William's insistence that we would be a leading family in our township, I knew how life worked. We were close to town; our community life would be in Bellview. William had placated me all this time, and I had no choice but resign myself to reality. At least, I would have a fine house to make into a home. In that, I would be able to make our dreams come true.

We trekked northward from town, toward the farm. Verdant green was everywhere. There were abundant trees and bright wildflowers blooming in welcome. I imagined looking out of my lace curtains to gaze upon the flora of this beautiful new land, breathing in the fragrance of summer blooms as I worked in my garden. I'd set the table with an embroidered tablecloth—one of the fine ones Mama said was from England, trimmed with Irish lace. I'd use my fragile china tea set, the other wives sipping and sharing delicate baked treats. Or, we might take our tea in the parlor where imported figurines would grace the side tables and a fine rug would warm the gleaming wood floor.

With town so close, I would be able to hire out laundry like Mama did. I hadn't thought to ask William about a laundress, but I was certain Bellview had one. After all, someone must have done wash for him and Monroe these past two years. I was sure I'd be able to hire a town girl to help out, as well. I'd ride one of the horses into town in the next few days to check. Glad I'd insisted on bringing my side-saddle along, I smiled to myself. We were near enough to town that I would be able to ride in often to attend social events. Never a wallflower, I would soon work my way into the fabric of the community, despite being a newcomer.

"Laura? Are you wool-gathering?"

I looked up. "I am, Husband. Daydreaming a bit."

"You're better?" His expression was soft, concerned, and I knew he loved me, despite our head-butting.

"I am, though I'll not want to do that crossing again."

"You won't need to." He grinned and patted my leg. "You seemed pleased with Bellview, once we were there."

"I was."

"And past your anger at me?"

"Yes." I paused, uncertain whether it was proper for me to lay out my feelings. In this, Mama had offered no advice. "You've been less than honest with me," I said, choosing my words and tone carefully lest I provoke another argument. "That does not bode well."

"I didn't mean to mislead you." His words were contrite, and I took solace in the apology.

Emboldened, I pressed on. "Perhaps it is time we talk about that tendency. We will not have a happy marriage if this continues. I am not a child to be mollified."

"I suspect we've much still to learn about one another." He clutched my hand, and we rode in silence for a while before he found his words. "I am discovering daily that you are a wholly different type of wife than my mother is, and that me being the type of husband my father is will not work well with us."

I thought about Father William's authoritative mannerisms, Mother Emily's quiet acquiescence. "No, it will not. I do not wish to be pacified, nor do I wish you to guide me around like a mule without regard to my opinion."

"And I don't wish to be contradicted."

I recognized his right in that desire and did not want to diminish it. Still, I'd not live with a lifetime of being shut out of planning for our future. “Perhaps if you were to ask me for my thoughts prior to making your decisions, I would not be so argumentative.”

“You would still be very vocal, I believe. This is a side of you I had not seen until we were wedded.”

No, we’d both taken great care to display only the best of ourselves during our courtship. “Nor had I seen you try to deceive me.”

“It appears we have some work ahead of us.”

“I will try to curb my tongue if you will treat me as your partner rather than as a child along for the ride.”

He offered me a wry smile. “I can manage that.”

“We are agreed, then.”

We rounded a bend in the river and emerged from the trees where William halted the wagon. A small dwelling stood in front of us, unpainted wood planks forming its sides. A step up from a log cabin, it was coarsely built all the same. Our nearest neighbor, I suspected.

“Well? What do you think?”

I was about to open my mouth with a comment about how glad I was that our home was superior when Monroe opened the door, grinning like a fool.

Where was my grand house?

I waited for the anger to erupt. Instead, I felt only oppressing disappointment. This time, I had misled myself. William had told me we had a comfortable, furnished house. I had filled in my own meaning of comfortable. Tears stung my eyes.

I wanted to go home.

Chapter Two

Lavina
Seneca County, Ohio
The same year (1848)

At fifteen, I think myself quite worldly, venturing off into the unknown all on my own.

Well, almost on my own.

My brother, rocking beside me with the steady rhythm of the wagon, is intent on the plodding horses. I ignore him, having long since decided not to countenance him; he's but my conduit to my new life of independence.

"You doing all right, there, little sister?"

I bristle a bit at the reminder of my role as the baby of the family. "Fine."

"Won't be too long now." Leicester stretches his lanky limbs and flicks the reins.

I let go of my imaginings. I'm not worldly in the least, just plain simple Lavina Day. Still, I have high hopes of making my own way, perhaps as a teacher or a milliner or a seamstress. My father is aging, as is my mother. With both of them in their sixties, I am moving to live with Leicester's family and launch my own life. I'll not be too far, but I do feel grown-up to be leaving my childhood behind me.

I adjust the skirt of my new, full-length dress and pat my inexpert bun, hoping I've used enough pins to hold my heavy tresses. Not sophisticated but definitely all grown-up.

The wagon rolls to a stop, and I recognize I've been musing again. I completely missed entering the town.

"Well, this is Tiffin."

I peer around, noting all the necessities . . . a general store, a cafe, blacksmith and livery, saloons. Board sidewalks line the street for two whole blocks. "Is there a school?"

"And a church. They're across town along with the courthouse."

Good. I file the fact away and glance up and down the dusty street again. No hat shop, but there is a dressmaker, and a bakery with aromas so delicious my stomach growls despite the fact I ate a sandwich on the road. I'm not much of a baker, or a cook for that matter, but I can learn. I don't want to live with Leicester forever, after all.

"Cinnamon rolls," Leicester comments, reading my thoughts.

"Was my nose twitching?"

"A little. Jump on down, and I'll buy you one to celebrate. It's not every day a girl leaves home."

My excitement patters to a stop. "You think Ma and Pa will be all right?"

"They'll be fine. There's enough family close by if needed."

He climbs from the wagon and hitches the horses to the rail while I scrabble down with more clumsiness than I desire. Long dresses take some getting used to. Leicester rescues me part way through, lifting me to the ground. "Surprised you didn't want to go live with our sister."

I scrunch my face. "Her boys would be the death of me. Besides, I wanted to get away from Trumbell County and make my own way."

"You're a few years away from that, little sister."

"I'm fifteen."

"Fifteen is young still," he says from his vantage point of twenty-five. He heads down the boardwalk. "You've a lot yet to learn before you're ready to be on your own."

I hitch up my skirt a bit, struggling to keep up with him under the bulk of my petticoats. "I went all the way through normal school, graduated from eighth grade. That's two whole grades more than you did."

"Pa got sick, needed my help working the forge. Else Ma would have made me stay in school."

"Well, you didn't, so you got no call telling me I'm not learned."

He stops. "There's more to life than book-learning."

"Pshaw."

"You'll see, little sister; you'll see."

He opens the door to the bakery and waits for me.

I step in, pouting. I'm always *little sister* to everyone. I want to be defined by who I am, not by my place in a long line of siblings. I'll show them all, I will.

"You want one or two?"

I eye the assortment of rolls in the case. Scents of cinnamon and maple fill the small shop along with heady vanilla and yeast. My mouth waters, and I fight a greedy urge to ask for two. One is a splurge. Only a child would ask for two. "Just one."

"One for each of us," Leicester tells the baker.

She hands us each a warm, gooey piece of heaven along with cloth napkins. Sticky caramel covers the top and drips onto my fingers. I peel a section away and stuff it into my mouth. Sweet bliss explodes on my tongue, and I shiver. "Mmmm."

Leicester laughs.

"Well, it's good," I protest.

We sit outside on a wooden bench, both of us wrapped up in enjoyment. I finish my roll, and Leicester pushes the last bit of his—the soft center—toward me. "I'm full," he says, but I know he isn't. I take it anyway, unable to resist the temptation.

"We sure have been looking forward to your help with the girls."

I jerk my head up. "I'd thought to find a job in town."

"A job?" Leicester's brow knits.

"Yes, a job. That's what people do when they strike out on their own." I straighten and wipe my fingers on the napkin like a lady instead of licking them.

"Lavina, you're fifteen."

"And?"

"Fifteen is too young for a girl to be out on her own. You'll be living with us, helping out, gathering experience with children. They've been chattering for weeks about their auntie coming. There'll be more than enough for you to do around the house with a trio of little ones."

I have no doubt about that, with all of the girls under the age of three. I'm sure it *is* an active household, but tending my nieces full time isn't what I'd planned on.

"I wouldn't be out on my own. I'd still be living with you, like a boarder."

Leicester shakes his head. "Ma and Pa put you in my care, and that means you're to mind me." His eyes soften. "You are too young to take a job. If you were a boy, I'd consider it, but you aren't. You'll stay at home and learn more about tending house and family. That's what Ma and Pa want."

"I'm not a child anymore." I stomp my foot, instantly regretting it and feel my face flush. Had he noticed, or had my skirts been enough to muffle the sound?

"No, you're not. But you aren't an adult either, and you will do as I say."

"But—"

"No buts, Lavina." His voice grows stern. "No arguments. You are not out on your own. Understood?"

I nod, the sweetness of the cinnamon rolls souring into a clump of resentment.

Seneca County, Ohio
1849

Six months into my life in Seneca County, I finally surrender to the fact that I'm not as grown-up as I'd thought. The girls humble me quickly, and I grasp I'll need a lot more experience with children before I can hope to be a teacher. Leicester and his wife, Christine, include me in their discussions, revealing I also know little about adult responsibilities. And so, I set about learning all I can, still determined to become independent but knowing Leicester has been right. I'm not ready.

By the time I turn sixteen, however, I gain confidence and earn Leicester's seal of approval. He grants me permission to test for a teaching certificate and I make plans to do so as soon as I study up. In the meantime, I decide to offer tutoring services to local students.

I stride toward the small white schoolhouse just after dismissal. The children have already run past, headlong and eager to leave their studies. Early autumn chill is in the air, and I clutch my shawl tighter around me. Though excited about the prospect of assisting students, I have more than a fair share of trepidation over approaching their severe teacher. I've never seen him so much as crack a smile. I straighten my dress and knock on the door.

"Enter." I recognize Mr. Beal's sharp voice and draw a deep breath before stepping in.

"Hello, Mr. Beal." I pause at the back of the main room, unsure if I should approach or wait for him to rise from his desk.

Intent on reading papers, he sighs and lifts his gaze. Annoyance crosses his features. "Yes?"

"I'm Lavina Day—"

"I know who you are. What do you want?"

Swallowing, I keep my head high and walk toward him, forcing a cheery smile. "I want to offer tutoring services to your students."

"*Your* services?"

"Yes, sir."

"Whatever leads you to believe you're qualified to tutor my students?" Disdain fills his haughty voice.

I shift before him, small as a mouse. "Well, you see, I've been studying for my teacher's examination and—"

Mr. Beal snorts.

Dryness fills my throat. "Sir?"

"You're a female."

I'm not sure what to do with his statement. Deny it? Obviously, I'm a girl.

I have no idea what he wants me to say. "I am," I finally state, feeling even more the fool.

He peers over the rim of his spectacles. "I don't believe females have the qualifications to teach, Miss Day."

"What?" I squawk the word before I've time to stop it. There aren't many women teachers, but it's hardly unheard of.

"Nor do I believe certificates should be awarded them."

"Oh."

He rises with another sigh and gestures toward the door. "Good day."

I step away, heat filling my face as it always seems to do. Silence lies thick in the air save for the clumping of my shoes. Halfway to the door, I stop. Had he misunderstood my intent?

I turn back.

"I'm not applying for your position. I'm offering to tutor any of your students who might need extra help."

He still stands next to his desk. "My students do not need assistance."

"They're all doing well? Even those who miss half the term due to field work?"

"They are proceeding at an acceptable rate for their situations."

"I'd work with them, in the evenings."

"They are busy in the evenings. Their families barely allow them to attend school in the first place. Do not make the mistake of thinking they will be permitted to forsake their chores to study."

"Couldn't you explore it?" Even to me, my voice sounds whiny.

"No, I couldn't. More precisely, I won't. I have exhausted my efforts in getting them into the classroom for a few months each winter, and I will not jeopardize that precarious advancement."

"But—"

"Furthermore, I don't desire your assistance." He speaks over my protest. "You have no business seeking to undertake public instruction. Go home, teach your nieces domestic skills, and keep your nose out of my classroom."

"But—"

"Good day." This time, he marches to the door and jerks it open. I step out, and he slams it behind me.

I bite my lip as the anger I'd suppressed floods through me. How dare he! I turn and reach for the doorknob.

"I wouldn't, Miss. Whatever was said between the two of you won't be advanced by you going back in."

I jump at the deep voice and drop my hand.

"Once he has his dander up, there's no negotiating. He does the same thing with the school board. Folks have learned the hard way to leave things be."

School board? I compose myself and face the man behind me.

Tall, he sits on a well-used wagon; his dirty overalls announce he's a farmer. "John Eastlick." He removes his straw hat, and a shock of black hair tumbles from it. "I'm from Eden Township."

I smooth my clothing and stand tall. "Lavina Day."

"Leicester's sister?"

"Yes, sir." I cross the school yard so we don't have to yell.

"What are you doing at the schoolhouse, Lavina Day?" He grins, showing even white teeth.

"Offering to tutor students."

"Little bird like you? You don't look much out of short skirts."

I want to take offense, but there'd been teasing in his tone. Besides, I can't afford to waste the opportunity to reach my goal via another route. "I'm sixteen and studying for my teacher's examination. Are you on the school board, Mr. Eastlick?"

The grin fades into an easy smile. "A bachelor like me? I'm afraid not. But your offer has merit, and I know some folks who would benefit from your skills. No reason why you couldn't talk to them directly, is there?" He jumps from the wagon and stands beside me, his height indeed making me feel like a bird.

Looking up at him, my pulse races. I tell myself not to get too excited.

"Folks in Eden Township?"

"The Swensons, an immigrant family. Parents don't speak much English. I'm sure the kids could use help with their lessons."

"That sounds perfect." The words come out of my mouth, but my thoughts are a world away wondering if his hair is as soft as it looks. The realization startles me.

"If you're agreeable, I can drive you over there after church on Sunday."

I agree mutely, no longer thinking about tutoring at all, only about spending more time with him.

Sunday service is intolerably long. I fidget, and Leicester frowns at me. He is less than pleased about me spending the day with John Eastlick. He made a fuss about his bachelor status and gossip, but Christine told him to hush and took up my case. His stern expression, days later, tells me he still disapproves. To be frank, I don't care. I squirm again, eager to get on with the day. I have students to acquire, after all.

John sits across the aisle, a little in back of us. I fight the urge to turn and look at him again given I've already stared at him once. His hair is combed today, but I like it better mussed, I think.

Finally, we receive the benediction, and the congregation shuffles outdoors. The day is bright and sunny, and I'm glad I don't need to cover my good Sunday dress with my shawl.

In the churchyard, Leicester approaches John, and they talk quietly before shaking hands. Christine winks at me. Then John turns to me.

"You ready, Miss Day?" he asks.

I've been ready all day but I don't say it. "I am."

"I'll have her home by supper," he tells Leicester.

"I'll be expecting it," Leicester says without a smile.

John points toward the trees, and we leave my brother and his family. I'm glad of it, as stifling as Leicester's mood has been. It's as if he doesn't want me to go talk with the Swensons.

"Your brother is protective."

"My brother doesn't want me to grow up. I can't imagine why it bothers him so that I take on tutoring in Eden Township. It didn't irk him when we talked about me tutoring here in Tiffin."

"I don't believe tutoring is the issue." John mumbles the

words as he leads me to a shiny buggy, *property of Tiffin Livery* marked on its side, and hands me up.

As he crosses round, it dawns on me. The rented buggy, his well-groomed hair, Leicester's attitude and comments about gossips. This isn't merely John being helpful. He's courting me. My telltale face heats, and I am glad he's not looking at me.

He settles onto the seat beside me. "Ready?"

We leave the churchyard, both of us silent. I'm at odds for words, of a sudden, as I work through the realization that John is attracted to me. Perhaps as much as I am to him. That insight frightens me. No one has ever courted me before, and I'm unsure of what to say, how to act.

I feel like a ship in a storm, with no heading and no control against the wind and the waves.

"The Swensons are good people," John says. For a moment, I panic, wondering if I'm wrong, if this is but a business trip after all. But I notice his grip on the reins is tight; he is as nervous as I.

"The parents don't speak much English, especially Mrs. Swenson," he continues, and I'm thankful he's found a topic for us. "There are three daughters in school, and their pa says Mr. Beal doesn't take the time to work with them."

Beal's condescension comes back to me. "It's because they're girls."

"I had it figured it was being immigrants."

"Mr. Beal doesn't much hold with educated females. When he refused my services, he said women weren't qualified. It made me mad enough to spit."

John laughs, easier with me now that we're in conversation. "That wouldn't have helped."

"I've little doubt of that."

We travel on, both of us relaxing a bit, and I glance at him. His eyes are a midnight blue, almost black. He catches my gaze and smiles. "Is that what you want to do with your life, Lavina?"

I startle a bit at the use of my given name but quiet as I interpret it as confirmation of my theory. The air seems charged, as if there is an energy quivering between us. I fight the urge to check my hair for falling tresses and focus on his question.

"I've always been of a mind to be on my own. Teaching is a way to accomplish that. And I like children."

"Most girls dream of marrying and settling down."

I ponder his words and wonder what it means that I've never thought much about love and marriage. "Maybe it's because I grew up the youngest of ten. Everyone always did for me instead of letting me do for myself. There hasn't ever been a time that I didn't want to be independent."

"Even if that means being a spinster? Teachers can't marry, you know. That's usually part of the contract."

"Why is that, do you suppose?"

"Duties of caring for a house and family, taboos against wives working outside the home, women being in a family way, favoring one's own children. I've heard all of those cited as reasons."

"That's not fair."

"Likely not, but it's the way of the world."

His agreement strikes me as significant. Unlike most men, he doesn't relegate women to lesser roles.

I'm not merely attracted to this man. *I like him.*

"Truthfully, I'd not given the marriage aspect much thought. Autonomy overshadowed all else, I guess."

We both digest my words, me with no small amount of trepidation. Was that what I wanted in life?

John turns and guides the horses down a long lane. We're almost there, and already I rue the loss of our private time.

"So you view independence only in light of having a job?" he asks.

"I . . . I guess I always have."

"Me? I see having my own land as independence."

"You own your farm?"

"Not yet. I'm saving toward buying my own place. For now, self-sufficiency is about relying on my own skills to choose what to plant, when to plant, to cultivate and bring in a good crop."

"We both have goals."

He slows the horses, pausing halfway down the lane, and looks straight at me. "Might you imagine meeting your goals in another way? As part of a team rather than on your own?"

"I've never thought about it."

At least not until today.

"Perhaps it's time you do." He reaches for my hand and covers it with his. "Because if ever there was anyone I'd like to work with, it'd be you."

Chapter Three

Laura
Jackson County, Iowa
Upon arrival, May 1848

"What do I think?" Outside the small house, I echoed William's question, unable to find the words to convey my dismay. I blinked away tears before he caught sight of them and drew a breath.

"It's twice the size of our neighbors' houses. I thought you'd like a sleeping room." Excitement filled his tone, and I knew he'd done his best to please me by providing two rooms. It was not a crude log cabin, and it was not a shack. For all its simplicity, it appeared solidly built. I vowed to look past the lack of polish and make the best of the situation. William was not a carpenter, and he'd spent time building this house, time away from clearing land.

I tried to muster enthusiasm. "I . . . uh . . . it's not what I expected."

He glanced at me and must have seen the disappointment still etched on my face. His expression softened, and he took my hand. "It's not as grand as your parents' house, but we need to start somewhere." He kissed my palm before jumping down from the wagon. "Come, look inside."

He lifted me from the wagon as Monroe rushed over to welcome us. We chatted about the trip and the sowing he'd completed. Monroe unhitched the horses while William, beaming with a pride I hadn't the heart to shatter, led me to the house. Noting the rough-shaved boards, I wished he had at least brightened the building with whitewash. The unpainted exterior spoke of poverty. I'd lived all my life in a large, painted, two-story house with clapboard siding, a wide front porch, and pretty flower boxes. This would all take adjustment, but I couldn't fault him for the basic exterior when he'd had so much else to do in clearing the land and reaping its bounty. We could make improvements. A little paint and flower beds would help considerably.

I followed him across the ground-level threshold into the house. With but two rooms, the interior would be cozy. Had he chosen cherry wood or maple for the furnishings? I hoped he'd been wise enough to stick with one for the entire house. Men seldom thought of such things, but surely the proprietor of the mercantile would have steered him when he placed the order.

The room was bare, save for a plank table, two rough, handcrafted chairs, a few crates tipped on their sides and stacked to make shelving, and a flat bench near the fireplace. Dimness dominated, with only a single window set into the opposite wall.

My throat closed.

Hard-packed dirt formed the floor, and mustiness hung in the air. Through the open doorway into the sleeping area, I viewed a few more crates and a bed, which appeared to be the only store-bought piece of furniture in the house. There was no cooking stove, just a fireplace with a crane to hold pots and swing them over the flames.

I stared first at the room, then at William, aghast. "This is the comfortable, furnished house you spoke of?"

"It's furnished." His tone was defensive.

"I've never cooked on an open fire. Never."

"You'll learn." His eyes glinted.

Hot anger flooded me at the thought of all we'd left behind in Indiana, at William's placating lies. I'd trusted him!

"My father said he'd send Mama's old Saddlebag stove, the one that's been sitting in the barn for years. You told him we had no need of it."

"We needed to travel light. A cast-iron stove would have weighed us down."

"He offered us any number of finely crafted pieces, and you told him the house was already furnished."

"It is. We have what we need, and we'll replace it when we can afford to do so. I won't take charity from your father."

My jaw dropped. "Charity? It would have been part of my dowry."

"It's my place to provide for you."

So we'd come to the meat of it. I cursed his pride along with his false pledges. "Well, you aren't doing much of a job of it, are you?"

His glare spoke volumes, but he punctuated it with further comment anyway. "Laura Duley, have you already forgotten your promise to me?"

"You deceived me in this, too, Husband."

"You will hold your tongue."

I held it, biting it until it bled. But I would not live in such a state. I would not. This shanty was not what he had promised me, and I *would* have my stove and my furnishings, if nothing else.

Honoring my end of our fragile bargain was not easy.

I covered the makeshift tables with fine crocheted doilies, tacked up cloth to provide privacy for the bedroom and to hide the stacks of dishes in the open crates, hung my lace curtains at the single window in each room, and covered the dirt floor with an abundance of rag rugs. It was a paltry effort, but the house grew homier in the process. I stitched cushions for the rough chairs and for the bench near the fire (to which William had added a back) and placed my wedding quilt on the bed. Underneath the trimmings, my furniture was still nothing but a hodge-podge of boxes and planks, but I'd no other choice but to make do.

I was not, however, able to adjust so easily to the lack of a cookstove. Cooking over an open fire was not a craft easily mastered. I did all right with the basics such as fried meat, boiled vegetables, potatoes, and stews, but biscuits and bread eluded me. Underdone, overdone, or combinations consisting of burnt crusts and mushy insides were the usual offerings.

My nausea grew worse each day and no longer confined itself to mornings. As the eldest of eight, I suspected the cause after the signs continued on a daily basis. I hid them from William, until I could be certain, choking back sour churning amid bouts of sweat. But, by the time Monroe departed a week later, I could fathom no other reason for my symptoms.

Life shifted into an endless pattern of cooking and housekeeping chores. I sowed the remaining garden vegetables, anxious to get them in before the morning sickness became more acute. William departed the house with his scythe each morning, returning for lunch before heading back to the fields. I learned to keep potatoes baking in the fire and to cook enough meat to serve it cold on laundry day when I had little or no time for anything but the clothes. Strenuous farm work meant I had to wash clothing more often than I had expected, and I now knew we hadn't the money to hire the work out to a laundress, nor for a hired girl.

I also knew the baby meant there were certain things I could not delay until harvest. We would need chickens, I decided, and a milk cow. While occasional purchases of eggs and milk at the mercantile might have worked for two bachelors, it would not do for a family. I craved butter and was already tired of tasteless bread, an added insult when it was over- or under-baked. I would need a varied diet to keep strong and healthy. And, truth be told, I did not have any idea how I was going to cope without a stove. I determined to ask William for all three items at once, for I wasn't sure I had the fortitude to argue with him three times.

I baked Johnnycakes on the day I planned to bring up the subject, having found a jug of maple syrup in the root cellar behind the house. After much experimenting, I'd finally got the timing right for them. I set the rough table with my white ironstone plates in lieu of the tin that William and Monroe had stocked. Adding a vase of wildflowers, I smiled to myself and waited for William to come in from the creek where he was washing up.

He paused as he stepped through the door, a smile lighting his face. "Something smells good."

"Johnnycakes. It took a bit of practice, but I think I got them right." I set the platter on the table, and we sat. It was a good start. "There's syrup."

"This is a nice change, a treat. You used to make such delicious cakes, while we were courting. Perhaps you might make one of those?"

I seized the opportunity, launching into the plan I'd strategized. "Husband, I know very little about raising crops, about when to sow and when to reap, what we will need to sustain us and what can be sold for profit."

"True enough."

"I would suggest that you know very little about cooking and baking and maintaining a household. Would I be correct?"

He glanced up from his plate, confused. "Monroe and I kept house."

"You and Monroe survived. From his accounts, you subsisted

on beans, bacon, and potatoes and wore your clothes until you couldn't stand the stench before taking them to a laundress."

"I guess that's a fair summary."

"And now that I am here, you prefer a more varied diet and your clothes clean?"

"You were taught those skills, so yes. I would expect that. I've been surprised that you never bake decent bread. Didn't your mother teach you to master that?"

Of course my mother taught me bread baking.

I itched to tell him exactly that but knew a moderate tone was needed. My next words would be a delicate balance between biddable and firm but must be devoid of any trace of shrewishness. "My mother taught me all of those skills, but you've tied my hands in applying them."

He looked up in earnest.

"My kitchen skills were learned on a cookstove. Baking bread over an open fire is a very different art entirely. I spend hours making dough, letting it rise, punching it down only to have it ruined because I cannot predict the heat level correctly. Green wood burns differently than dry wood, disrupting the predictions I make based on what happened the day before. I don't know whether to swing the pot over the fire or to set it in the embers, nor do I know how long to leave it there."

"Stoves are expensive."

He'd missed the point entirely, even while spooning the Johnnycake into his mouth. It was time to change tack.

"I can't prepare meals properly. I have to disrupt cooking to use the crane to heat water for the laundry, which has become an all-day process in the heating of one pot of water at a time, let alone the time it takes to do the wash itself. I can't cook a varied menu because I have only a small supply of eggs and milk, purchased on the occasions that you have time to go into Bellview. We have no butter, which further limits me."

"We can't afford—"

"It takes three times as much wood to keep the open fire going," I continued, launching into yet another line of reasoning. "A stove would use less fuel, heat the room in the winter, save me both time and effort, and allow me to provide you with foods more to your liking."

"The cost—"

"If you wish me to keep this house in the manner you expect, I require a stove, a milk cow, and chickens."

There, I'd said it. I let the words sink in. Though I had but one round of ammunition left, he had no clue how powerful it would be. "You promised me a comfortable life, William. You have not provided it. You have bound my hands so that I cannot be a good wife to you, nor a good mother."

"We've a while before we need to worry about that." And with that, he brushed my request away.

Oh, William, you still do not understand, do you? Though I'd hidden my nausea, he'd missed the changes in my body as only an unsophisticated man could. I drew a breath and fired the shot.

"No, we do not have a while. I am sick every morning and have not had my courses. There will be a baby early next year."

He paused, his spoon halfway to his mouth, then set it back on his plate. "A baby?"

"I have all the signs."

"I'm going to be a father!" He pushed from his chair, rushing to engulf me in his arms.

"Do you know much about what women go through during this time? What babies need?" I asked the question against his chest, sure he was naïve in this as well.

"I was still a kid when Monroe came along."

"Already, my chores are more difficult. In the coming weeks and months, there will be days I cannot keep food down, and, when I can eat, I will need milk and eggs to help the babe grow. I will tire easily and cry at the drop of a hat. I will be cranky, and I will grow unable to do much of what I do now. And once the baby is born, it will take more time than you can imagine."

He drew back, looked me in the eye. "I didn't know," he said softly.

"I realize we haven't much extra money. But I am not asking for luxuries nor even for all of what you promised me—"

He shook his head. "Laura, I can't satisfy your whims."

Biddable slid from my grasp, and I crossed my arms, anger seething.

He would not deny me this. Though I suspected my eyes flashed, I did not yell. "This is not a whim," I told him in clipped, no-nonsense words. "You *did* promise me comfort, Husband. What you have provided is not what I envisioned when you gave me that vow. You have supplied enough to meet my needs, but that was *not* what you pledged. For now, I will accept that we cannot afford comfort. But in asking for the stove, the cow, and the chickens, I am requesting you to meet our baby's needs, not my comfort."

"Do you understand the cost of what you're asking?"

"I do not. And I care not."

I met his troubled gaze and held it. "Even if you have to write my father and ask him to ship Mama's cast-off stove or beg him to send money to us, you will do this. This is no longer about me and my 'whims.' Your child is depending on you, and, if you fail to provide for us, I will return to Indiana."

By the end of the week, I acquired a brand new Stanley rotary-top cookstove, a dairy cow, a chicken coop and a dozen laying hens, along with Mrs. Tucker. William purchased the former; Mrs. Tucker arrived on her own.

I found her perched on a stump like one of the hens when I

emerged from the smokehouse one morning.

"You Laura Duley?" she asked. "I'm Hattie Mae Tucker. Ran into Mr. Duley over at the mercantile t'other day. I'd heard he took a bride, so I asked on about you. Got an earful, I did. Made sure your man did, too, once I heard you was having a hard time of it. Told him it weren't fair of him to leave you struggling. So here I am."

I grappled for my social graces. "Would you like to have tea?" Even to my own ears it sounded odd.

Mrs. Tucker cackled, her wrinkled jowls shaking. "Oh, lordy, girl. I ain't here to have no tea party. I'm gonna learn you what you need to know to get through what's coming." Slapping her hand against her ample thigh, she caught my gaze. "You ready?"

Relief bubbled through me. If this woman was here to make my life easier, I was ready and willing to learn anything she had to offer. "I am."

"Well then, let's get things going. You look pasty. Guess we'd best brew up some tea anyways." She stood and glanced around. "You growing any ginger root?"

Monroe had left me a nicely turned garden plot, fenced to keep the deer at bay, but I knew ginger was not growing there. It required shade, and I'd seen no other plantings. "I don't think so."

"Might be they traded for some. Got a cellar?" She stalked around, looking for evidence of a pair of wooden doors set into the ground.

"Behind the house," I told her.

She turned in her tracks. I followed like a lost sheep, drawn to her take-charge, plain-speaking personality. She was rough around the edges but would be of tremendous help to me, if I could keep up with her. My stomach turned, and I covered my mouth with my hand. She clucked, descended into the cellar, and emerged with a handful of ginger root.

"First thing, you gotta move slow-like. No popping out of bed or sprints across the yard." She thrust the ugly root into my hand. "Peel and slice, boil it up for ginger tea. Else grate a bit in a cup of boiling water. It'll calm your stomach. You know how to bake soda bread?"

"If you've a recipe, I can follow it."

She marched into the house and eyed the new stove, a shiny wonder that took up a large portion of the front room. "Turntable, is it?" She hustled over and turned the crank, rotating the top. "Hmph."

"William thought it would be easier on the baby if I didn't have to do so much lifting." I turned the cooking surface so the pot of water I kept at the back of the stove was over the heat and set about grating the root.

In truth, William had selected the model for its replaceable parts, which would eliminate the need to buy an entirely new stove should anything wear out, but I doubted it was prudent to tell Mrs. Tucker so. It was best she believe he'd provided me the benefit of cooking four pots at once, all at varying heat without the need to shuffle them around as a thoughtful gift.

"And, look, there are two fuel reservoirs." I pointed out the doors, at the bottom and side. "I can keep one hot and the other cool."

Mrs. Tucker rolled her eyes. "You can cook and bake?"

"Now that I have a stove, yes." William had received his first cake last night and spent the entire evening doting on me.

"Got the chores down-pat?" she probed. "Laundry? Milking and collecting the eggs?"

"I do." I gathered the ginger shavings into an infuser and reached for a cup, tired just listening to her rapid-fire questions.

"How 'bout butter-making and putting up the vegetables? Butchering?"

"I know how to make butter, and Mama taught me to can,

though I've never done either on my own. I've never butchered."

"Dip that there cup into the water. No need to go lifting the pot. Keep things easy. I'll sell you a butchered hog this year. Pregnancy don't go so well with that whole mess. Meantime, I'll take you under my wing. I reckon I can spend a day a week with you. Learn you on making soda bread this week, get that morning sickness battled. Lift that water for you on laundry day. See to the butter and cheese making, help you with that garden once the waddle gets bothersome. You'll need a hand with the canning when that time comes, and with the birthing."

I turned, the cup still empty in my hand. "You would do all that for me?"

"Don't mind the company, me being a widow and all. I'll take home a share of what we make, and we both get a boon."

My chin dropped. William would not take kindly to sharing our foodstuffs.

Beside me, Mrs. Tucker cackled again. "He don't know how much butter or cheese a churn of milk makes, and he don't know what comes out of that garden. The secret to managing a man is to keep him in the dark, dear. Never, ever, tell a man more than he needs to know. Now finish up brewing that tea and drink it down."

We sealed our deal, not without a share of trepidation on my part, and William was none the wiser. Mrs. Tucker visited often, providing guidance and wisdom. Well past fifty, she had raised a flock of children and advised that my constant backache was not to be feared and that some mothers did indeed remain sick to their stomachs for months, particularly with their first child.

She also kept me amused with her tales of the early days. She and Mr. Tucker had moved to the frontier early, in the 1820s, when the Sac and Fox tribes still lived in the area. Since that time, they'd given up all their lands in Iowa. The Potawatomi had ceded their lands two years ago, and only the Sioux remained, far away to the northwest.

Her stories explained why we'd seen no natives in the area, and I was glad of it. William had told me not to worry about Indians, but I had harbored fears that he had misled me in that area as well. It was good to not have to worry for our safety in addition to all the other adjustments the frontier, and my pregnancy, brought.

By the time Ellen was born in early 1849, this primitive life I had never expected to live became routine. We named her for my dear sister and found her a true blessing. Hale and robust, she was a perfect baby, sleeping through the night in no time. It seemed as if she'd spent out her difficult days in my womb and was now content to sleep and gurgle and smile. She became the center of my world. William doted on his little girl, proving himself a proud and playful father and an unexpected helpmate as we adjusted to family life.

I came to love time outdoors with Ellen, so alert was she to all that occurred around her. I enjoyed her company immensely as I again sowed my garden, the time flying past. William and I also grew in our relationship. I learned, as Ellen sat and gurgled at us, of William's desire to make his own way rather than to simply follow in the footsteps of our parents and grandparents. This new insight provided me understanding into why Iowa was so important to him. We spent our summer evenings on the porch he had added, talking about our dreams and shaping a new vision for our future.

Ellen's quick transition to sleeping full nights without need of feedings left me unexpectedly fertile, and a second child was on the way. As I grew in girth, we joined a congregation in Bellview, traveling to Sunday services each week and forging our place in the community. William handled butchering in deference to my once-again-daily morning sickness, even into the middle of pregnancy. He'd softened since our early days of marriage, no longer seeking to shape our relationship after that of his parents. Winter offered up blizzards and heavy snowfall, and he took over tending the cow and the chickens during the worst of it, as I grew larger and more cumbersome.

Emiley, named for William's mother, was born just after the new year, again with Mrs. Tucker's help, about the time Ellen took her first steps.

The two kept me busy, and I was thankful the season meant fewer outdoor chores for us. As the snows melted, they left both mud and green buds. They also left swollen rivers. William told me about Minnesota Territory, where the snows were even worse, all of the melt draining into the Mississippi. As it flowed south, a half mile distant, it roared with that run-off. Even our small Spruce Creek filled to the brim before receding and leaving us with true spring in all its green glory.

None of us suspected the storms to come.

Spring exploded into summer. Once again, I relished my outdoor chores, though my attention was now divided among my tasks and the children. Ellen was ever busy, toddling as fast as her little legs could go. Oh, how she gurgled and chattered in her baby language. Emiley was eager to sit on her own, as if she needed to keep pace with her sister, and I suspected she would tackle crawling with the same enthusiasm. I had little doubt the two of them would keep me on my toes.

Though not the life I had once envisioned, it was finally one that fulfilled me. Looking at my two little towheads, I envisioned tiny princesses who would live out their own fairy-tale lives. William and I would make sure of it. Already, we were carving a place for the girls in the community. Our church family had taken us into the assembly and William had been named an officer of the congregation. Our daughters would grow up being part of a leading family, just as William and I had.

Most Sundays, the congregation gathered along the river, a short way from the church, for a group picnic. By tradition, we met near a sandbar that blocked the busy current so that the older children could wade in the river without fear of being swept away. As the summer went on, we craved the cool breezes offered up by the water, and we spread our quilts ever nearer the shoreline. By August, the Sunday respite from the heat became the highlight of our week.

The day was glorious, perfect in its sunny splendor, and I looked forward to a few relaxing hours with William. As church ended, he hinted that he had something to discuss, something that would impact our future, and I was intrigued by the wide smile that had not left his face since he'd clustered with several other men earlier that morning.

He spread the quilt away from the shore in deference to the children's safety. Ellen had developed a habit of following the older children, and we felt it best to put distance between her and those wading in the river. Emiley had mastered sitting, though she still tumbled over from time to time, and was already scooting herself along. She would be crawling soon, which would be a further challenge to our diligence.

We spread out tin plates and jars of tea, and I set down the basket. I'd fried a chicken the evening before, and my family was eager to devour it. We ate, each of us tending to one of the children, and finished the meal off with chocolate cake and faces smeared with frosting.

As I cleaned the girls up and repacked our luncheon supplies, William suggested a walk. Minutes later, we ambled toward the river, Ellen scampering ahead while Emiley fussed in William's arms.

"I've been talking with Riling." The reference was to a leading member of the congregation and businessman who owned a flour mill located a few miles distant, where the river ran fast and steady. "He's offered to take me under his wing."

I glanced at William, curious. "In what way?"

"I'd like to learn a bit more about milling, how it all works."

"As in running the business?"

"As in the millwright trade." He shifted Emiley, who by now was squirming like a little pink piglet. He shushed her and waited for my response.

William's proposal revealed a side of him I'd not previously known. In our conversations about the future, he'd always talked of land and farming. "I had no idea you were interested in machinery."

"I'm thinking ahead. The late spring had me worried. Having trade skills would be a good hedge against the uncertainty of farming." He jostled Emiley again.

"Do you want me to take her?" Sadie, one of the girls from the congregation, approached. "I could take both girls to the river. Ellen could wade at the edge, and Emiley could dangle her feet."

William looked relieved and handed Emiley over to her.

I worried, though. I'd never surrendered them to anyone else's care. "You'll take care with them?" I narrowed my eyes, making sure the fourteen-year-old understood my concern. "They can be a handful."

"I'll keep them near." She took Ellen's hand and walked away, chatting with my excited daughter.

"Stay out of the current," I yelled after her. I shouldn't fret so much. It was the hallmark of young mothers, I guessed, and it was time I allowed the girls a bit of freedom. I stood, watching them go, until William offered a soothing rub to my back.

"Mother Hen," he teased. "They'll be fine. Sadie is good with the little ones." He took my hand and led me to a batch of cottonwood trees where the shade would provide us a measure of relief from the summer heat. “What do you think? About the mill?”

“It’s a logical thought, learning a trade,” I told him as we sat. “It would be a good thing, should the weather bring problems. That said, how would you be able to do such a thing? The fieldwork takes all your time.”

“I’d thought to spend my time with him in the winter months. He’d have to understand I’d only go to the mill on good days. It would mean leaving the three of you on your own.” He rubbed my hand. “I could milk before I left, but you would have to handle the afternoon chores.”

“We’d need to figure out how to keep the girls occupied. The last thing I need is for them to end up in the manure pile or kicked by the cow. Maybe fence off a small area in the barn for them?”

My gaze drifted toward the river. An entire gaggle of children was gathered there, but Sadie sat, as promised, at the edge of the water, Emiley beside her and Ellen within reach. Satisfied, I turned back to William.

“I could come up with something,” he said.

I scrambled to reason out the benefits and drawbacks, to catch the possibilities William might have missed in his excitement. By now, I understood he was wont to do that, and it was my responsibility to sharpen his awareness. “Would you be paying for this training?”

William smiled, appreciation for my careful thought. “I would provide my labor in return for the instruction, learning as I work. Riling’s millwright will take charge of me.”

I was pleased he’d already thought to address that point, and I marked it into my mental ledger, moving to the next item. “You would bring in the harvest and finish the butchering?”

“Of course.”

“And repairs needed on the house and outbuildings? Projects

we've agreed upon?"

"Yes, you have my word."

I paused, noting nothing more in the debit column of the ledger. "What am I not seeing, Husband?"

"I guess that we would lose the winter days together. I've enjoyed those."

He was correct in counting that as a loss. I would rue surrendering that time, but the skills he gained would be an asset. Recalling the past two winters, I found the missing factor—pregnancies. "The winters have been times of ungainliness for me."

He sighed. "There has been that."

This, then, might be the sticking point. I could tell from his scrunched shoulders that he'd not thought of this, and I knew he didn't truly understand how difficult those months were for me. I drew a breath and treaded with care. "You've eased my chores much, each of those times. Would you anticipate I do without that aid should we find ourselves expecting again?"

He started. "You're not, are you?"

"No, but you do realize babies are an inevitable outcome of our relations? Emiley's quick conception indicates I am a fertile woman. Should I conceive in the coming months and find myself in the midst of a difficult pregnancy, I would expect not to endure it alone."

"Women go through pregnancy all the time, Laura."

I'd anticipated his hackles would rise, as they did each time he didn't want to hear my concerns. It was his nature, and, though I hated battering horns with him, it was easier to do so now than after the fact. I'd learned by now that these small confrontations were simply the way it was with us.

"Yes, they do, but it is a different experience for each of us. Not all women retch for month after month, and not all women suffer excoriating back pain throughout. Emiley was easier, but you remember how difficult it was with Ellen? I would not take kindly to you being gone every day if I were to find myself in the same situation again. We are a partnership."

His jaw tightened. "My back hurts every day from sowing until harvest. I sweat until I'm drenched. My hands blister, and my stomach growls. Have you heard me complain?"

"No, and I do not minimize your hard work."

I paused, letting him digest that I understood him. "But, I also work hard. I spend days on my knees in the garden to keep it weeded so we have vegetables for the winter and extra garden truck to sell at the mercantile. Those long days give me pain at night. I milk, tend chickens, smoke meat, put up food for the winter, launder our clothes, feed you three times a day and our children far more often. Every two hours when they are infants. And when they are finally abed, I knit and mend and churn butter until I fall into our bed. At sunrise, I do it all again. Do not make the mistake of assuming all of that occurs without effort simply because you are in the field and do not witness it. We both work hard, William."

"I'm sorry, Laura. I do realize all of that."

"I don't want to have an argument later, if we make this decision now."

"Let's confront that obstacle if we encounter it. I don't want to lose the opportunity by delaying. Riling could easily take on someone else. This is a chance for me to learn a craft that could be important."

We'd not completely settled things, but at least I'd raised the points that needed to be aired. It seemed a sound idea and William had asked for my opinion, as I'd requested of him. It was more than many husbands did, and I had no reason to suspect the winter would bring any change to our circumstances anyway.

"I should go find Riling, tell him I'm his man." William stood and offered his hand. "Want to come with me?"

Shrieking sounded from the river. I glanced toward the children, my breath stuttering.

Someone's dog ran through the water, the crowd of children splashing and squealing in delight. Ellen tottered after it, then plopped on her bottom, spraying water everywhere. She wailed, startled. Sadie stood and headed over to put her back on her feet, the dog still spinning in circles amid the group.

My gaze shifted back to Emiley, anticipating her laughing appreciation for the pup's antics and her sister's sudden splat. Instead she lay in the water, face down, the dog whirling around her.

Panic surged through me, and I sprang to my feet, my legs churning amid my skirts. "Emiley!"

William sprinted ahead of me, reaching the river faster than I, and plucked her from the water. He shook her, called her name, terror in his voice. Sadie stood with Ellen in her arms, her eyes wide with alarm. I reached them just as William began pounding Emiley's limp back, and I knew.

Deep inside me, I *knew.*

Dread clawed at me, shredding every fiber of my being.

Chapter Four

Lavina
New Bedford, Illinois
A few years later, 1857

John and I married the year after we met, a month past my seventeenth birthday. My aspirations of becoming a teacher blew away with the first blizzard of the winter—and John's first kiss. I found I wanted nothing so much as to be a supportive wife. Nearly seven years and three children later, my feelings are still as strong, but being supportive has required more patience than I'd anticipated.

Our own land, John's goal for so long, continues to elude us. We struggled to make a living in Eden Township. With the boys, Merton, Frank, and Giles, born one after another, our budget grew lean. We headed west, to Indiana, but land prices there, too, were beyond our means. And so, we have come to Illinois in hope of easier purchase.

I am weary of relocation but trust in John when he says we will have our dream. Spring holds promise, and, already, John has the crops sown. We anticipate a profitable year and cross our fingers there will be no problems. If all goes well, we will purchase our own land next year.

"Lavina?"

At the sound of my friend's voice, I glance up from my mending. Sophia Ireland stands at the open door, her daughters in tow. "Do you have time to talk?"

I struggle to my feet and waddle like a duck to greet her. My thick hair swings behind me in a heavy braid. I simply have no energy to wrestle with it these days.

"You shouldn't have gotten up," she says and envelops me in a hug. Sophia and her husband Tommy are an unexpected blessing to us. Tommy, more than ten years John's senior, is a fountain of knowledge and the source of much valuable advice.

I shoo Sophia's words away with my hand. "I need to move a bit anyway. This one is kicking up a storm."

The children cluster together, chirping with ideas for play. Roseanna and Giles are both three with Ellen not too far behind. Merton and Frank, pretending to be big boys, shepherd them into the yard to meet John's new dog. Sarah, the baby, stays in Sophia's arms as she sits at my table.

We chatter about my pregnancy while I bustle around, putting water on for tea, but my mind is not on our words. It's rare that Sophia shows up in the middle of the day. Busy lives take precedence over visiting and I wonder more than a little about the unusual visit. Once the tea is ready, I set two cups on the table and ease into the chair across from her.

"Now, what is it?" I ask.

Sophia blows out a heavy breath. "Tommy wants to move."

I gawk at her.

Then I push away my panic at the possible loss of my dearest friend and absorb what this might mean for her. She is a local New Bedford girl and is not accustomed to relocations. I know how she is feeling. I cried when we left my family behind in Ohio, despite all my bluster over being on my own.

"Men talk of moving all the time," I say, not wanting to acknowledge where such talk leads.

"We argued."

Her soft admission reveals much. Tommy dotes on Sophia. She stole his widowed heart when they met, and he never has a sharp word with her. Disquiet fills me. "I thought Tommy was happy here."

"I did, too."

We stare at one another for a moment, both of us uneasy. I can't fathom what has gotten into Tommy to want to leave Illinois. Life is good here, for all of us. "Whatever is in his head to prompt talk of moving?" I finally ask.

"Land. What else?"

I don't understand. While we still lease land, the Irelands own forty acres. "But you have land."

"He says we need more, that there's nothing worth having that edges on our property." She sounds resigned, and my panic returns. I don't want to lose my friend.

"What about nearby?" I ask. There has to be a solution that won't tear them away from us. "You could sell your place and get something in the next county."

"That's what I told him." She sighs.

"And?"

"And he says it's too settled in Illinois; the best land is already claimed. He wants to go west."

West. I know that word too well.

"Where?"

"Minnesota Territory."

"The territories? He does want unsettled!"

She puts her hand to her mouth, and I regret my words.

"He says Minnesota will become a state soon, and this is our chance. The territorial government is trying to build the population. You can preempt whole sections of land. That's four times what we have now. And we can pay for it later."

If all this is true, Tommy will have told John; they will have talked about it in depth. My hand covers my womb as it dawns on me that I may be once again packing up and rocking my way west with an infant in arms.

Olmstead County, Minnesota
The following year, 1858

"Tommy says Rochester has been incorporated," John tells me. We've been in Minnesota for a year now, having left Illinois with the Irelands when Freddy was but a few weeks old. The soil is rich, and the county is filling fast. We were lucky to get here when we did.

I set a bowl of fried potatoes on the table and lurch back to the stove for the ham. The pinch in my back twinges, and I wince. "What's that mean?" I ask John as I return to the table.

"It's now bigger than a town." He grins.

"Ha ha." John is in good humor tonight, and I am glad of it.

"Put Freddy in the high chair for me, will you?"

My back pains have been low and steady, but the cramping heralds a change. I hope I can get the boys fed and settled into bed before the labor pains start in earnest. Together, John and I dish up their meals and cut meat for Freddy and Giles. As usual, by the time we get to our own meals, all is cooling. At least Freddy is eating on his own now, picking up the food with his fingers but thankfully all by himself.

I continue to pad around the kitchen rather than taking my chair, and John raises his brow in question. At baby number five, he recognizes the signs.

He keeps the boys entertained, whistling tunes and telling them how the French explorers paddled their canoes into the area nearly two hundred years ago and met the Sioux and Ojibway and Winnebago Indians. Now, this area is devoid of the natives, and the Dubuque Stage carries travelers. In all, it's a pleasant area, the land fertile and plentiful. We've made a good home here, the Irelands nearby.

Finally, our life has settled, and I believe John will be content. Prosperity and our happiness have a good start here. A contraction grasps me, and I exhale.

"Should I get Sophia?" John asks.

"In a bit." There is little sense in sending for her yet. I calculate it will be some time before I need her.

"Mama, do you need me to put the boys to bed?" Merton asks. At seven, he remembers Freddy's birth and is intuitive enough to sense what John and I have left unsaid.

I smile at my oldest, this wonderful child who is always so responsible. "Can you do the dishes for me?" I ask, knowing Giles and Frank will be likely to pout and cause him problems. "Boys, off to bed."

"But, Mama . . ." they grumble, a nightly ritual.

"Boys," John says as he takes Freddy from the high chair.

The single word is enough, and they trudge into their sleeping room. Soon, we'll need to purchase another bed. Once Freddy leaves the crib, they can sleep crosswise on the mattress, but it will be a stopgap measure, good only until they sprout in height. Merton already is tall for his age.

John tends them as I continue to pace in the other room, my hand at the small of my back where the pangs grow increasingly stronger. I get out my nightgown and change into it before spreading an oilcloth over our feather tick and stacking clean sheets and towels on it.

My back seizes, and I gasp, tears springing into my eyes. Lord, but this one is putting up a fuss.

"Lavina?" John is at my side, concern etched on his face.

"Get Sophia."

He flees out the door. Another contraction grips me, sooner than I anticipated. Hard and vise-like. Still, my water hasn't broken, and I tell myself not to worry. There's time. But my skin grows clammy as time stretches.

I am panting by the time John returns with Sophia.

She eyes me, then John. "Make sure the water's on," she says and waits for John to move away. "Are you close?" she asks.

"I don't know. This doesn't—" Pain grips me and my legs weaken. My hand flounders, seeking something to steady myself. They help me into bed as my stomach ripples. It feels like I am being sliced with a knife.

Sophia spreads my legs, checking my progress. She shakes her head. Another spasm hits me, and I finally feel the warm liquid rush of my water breaking. Again, I contract and scream against the pain.

We bury William Merton Eastlick as soon as I recover the strength to stand at his graveside. I remember very little about the night he was born, save that it seemed to last forever. His middle name honors our oldest, who, at only seven, kept his brothers occupied the entire night. I feel guilty that I somehow caused his death. Sophia tells me it wouldn't have mattered. This one, conceived so soon after Freddy was born, was too weak to survive.

The loss of the life I nurtured for these past nine months nearly chokes the life from me as they lower his tiny little casket into the dark grave. This is the first child I've lost, and, though I know it's common for children to die, it shocks me to my core.

Next to me, John is shaking.

I take his hand, and we both squeeze tightly, taking solace in our shared despair. Life leaves little time to mourn, and I'm thankful we can support one another.

Sophia has charge of my other boys and has explained things to those old enough to understand, holding them close in my stead as they grieve.

But I know that tomorrow, they will have need for me. There will be no room for my sorrow. I must cling to them instead.

Chapter Five

Laura
Jackson County, Iowa
1850, following Emiley's death

The time following Emiley's death dragged on without end. My body was leaden, and it was an effort even to rise from my bed each morning. I wanted to curl up and surrender my soul so that she would not be alone in heaven, and I would not be alone here on earth. I wanted to escape the ever-present grief that racked my body. And I wanted to go home, to my mother and to the calm safety of our family farm.

Ellen's happy chatter brought me no solace those first troubled weeks as I struggled to complete my household duties. Mrs. Tucker visited frequently, helping with laundry and meals. It was August, and William was in the fields from dawn until dusk tending to haying and beginning the harvest. Nights, he was curt and withdrawn. We each lived in our own minds, separate and angry and lost.

In September, nearly a month after Emiley was taken from us, Mrs. Tucker sat down at the table across from me. I'd been sitting in my chair, unfocused but for the handkerchief I twisted in my hands.

"Laura?"

I looked at her and sighed, the exhalation long and drawn. What did she want of me? Couldn't she see I just wanted to be left alone? I was tired, so very tired, and she'd already ousted me from my bed, as she'd begun to do each time she visited. I laid my head on the table and closed my eyes.

"Laura Duley!"

"What?" I murmured, keeping my eyes closed against the sun. Was it time for Ellen's nap soon? I'd lost track. Maybe Mrs. Tucker would let me take back to my own bed. My bones ached, and I was so tired.

"Child, you got to snap out of this." Her voice was stern, nothing like the soothing caretaker I desired her to be.

"No. No, I don't. I need to sleep."

"You need to go outside, into the sun. Jerk some carrots out of the ground. Knead some bread dough, punch it fierce-like."

My head was so heavy, how could I possibly perform chores? "It's too much."

"You don't get up, you ain't gonna get past this. You lost a child, but you got another, and she's growing as dark and melancholy as you. You owe her better'n that. You must not let go here. A mother can never let go."

"I can't."

"You can, and you will. Else you'll lose two daughters instead of one."

Panic surged through me, and I lifted my head.

"You are driving Ellen to distress. For her sake, you need to quit moping. Put your attention on that little one instead of on yourself. I got work to be done at home, and I can't be here taking care of you and her no more. It's time you get back to your life."

"You aren't going to help me?" My voice sounded pitiful, petulant.

"I am helping you," she bellowed. "Get up out of that chair and go pull carrots. Now."

I stood, wooden, haggard, and trudged outside. The sun blinded me, and I squinted against it as I plodded toward the garden. A blanket and basket awaited me. I sighed, sank to the ground, and stared at the frilly carrot tops. I'd forgotten how pretty carrot tops were.

"Go on, girl. Yank 'em out."

I glared at her brusque orders. She was a witch to make me go out into the sun and do chores when I needed so badly to sleep. Angry, I grasped the leafy top and tugged. Nothing. I cursed the dratted vegetable for its resistance. Finally, I jerked hard, nearly falling over as the carrot erupted from the ground. I slammed it into the basket and wrenched up the next one. With each hostile carrot, I cursed and rebelled until the basket was full, and tears streamed down my face.

I sobbed in that garden for nearly an hour.

True to her word, Mrs. Tucker put me back to work, brooking no argument, and I took out my despair on bread dough, butter churning, and laundry until I had no anger or misery left. Each day, living became easier. The following week, she stopped coming and left me on my own. I set about putting my life, our lives, back in order.

Ellen, who had become silent and woeful, finally received the attention she needed, and I spent every spare minute with her, cajoling her back into the happy little girl she had once been.

William, too, softened as fall wore on, and we tackled butchering and winter preparations together. His eyes were still filled with sorrow, but we found solace in one another again, and in Ellen. We didn't talk of the day by the river.

We'd buried Emiley near the house, a quiet family service sending her off. Sadie had sent a note, full of grief, and I responded, telling her we did not hold her responsible. If anything, it was my fault for sending such a small child with her. It had been an accident, nothing more, a baby who had fallen over face-first into shallow water. But I did not return to

Sundays at church, nor did I allow William to take Ellen with him. Though I recovered from my grief, I would not be careless again with my remaining child. Here, at home, I could remain watchful for danger and keep her protected. Elsewhere, there were too many risks.

As winter descended upon us, Ellen uttered her first clear words; William spent his days at the mill, learning of the machinery vital to its operation. Ellen and I played games, sang nursery rhymes, and read fairy tales. I made a vow, during those months, that Ellen would have the life I had not received, and my mind explored how that dream might be attained.

In becoming a millwright, William was opening doors for that future. He'd be able to operate any mill; whether it be flour or lumber, the basic machinery was the same. One day, we could leave the constant toil of farming and have our own mill. We would live in town, and Ellen would enjoy calls from neighbors and teatime. She, and I, would have the life William had promised.

All we needed to do was hang on until he learned the craft, and we could set aside the money we would need to make that transition.

I could do that. I would.

Winona County, Minnesota Territory
Early 1856, six years after Emiley's death

We left Iowa six years later. Six long, interminable years.

Beaver village would be our new start, one we both desperately needed. Five-year-old Willie and two-year-old Emma rode in the wagon behind us, quietly playing. Ellen lay in a grave next to Emiley. We'd lost her when she was three, while en route home from a visit to Illinois. The raft ferry was struck by a log, heaving so suddenly that she fell and was pitched into the river, drowned like her sister before her. I'd spent months desolate, once again unable to function until Mrs. Tucker took charge and reminded me I must not let go. Leaving them had reduced me to sorrow once again, but I knew our new home would be safer for our remaining children as well as the one kicking inside my womb.

We'd made the decision to move in the year following Ellen's death. I refused to cross that river ever again and feared even nearing its rushing waters or what might happen should it flood. William promised me he would find us a less dangerous home and had staked a claim on farmland in Minnesota Territory two years ago. While there, he'd met several other pioneers. With them, and with my full support, he'd made plans to form a town. The children and I had taken advantage of the break in winter weather to move before the baby came, taking the stage from Dubuque to Rochester, where William met us with the wagon. A freighter would bring our household goods—those that William was not purchasing new.

Now, as the wagon lumbered on, negotiating the rugged hills of Whitewater County, I felt optimistic for the first time in years. With the income from the sale of our land in Iowa, William had built a mercantile, and we planned to live above it. He was also negotiating with two brothers to partner in building a sawmill. I was happy we were going to be in business rather than living by the uncertainties of farming. William would rent out our farmland as the area settled. Life, for once, was going to be good, and I anticipated the comforts we would finally have as William fulfilled the promise he'd made (then broken) eight years ago. I looked forward to achieving our place among respected town leaders.

"There it is!" William's excited voice broke my thoughts.

We'd crested a hill, and Beaver lay in the narrow valley below, Beaver Creek running through it. Just outside of the settlement, the creek flowed into the Whitewater River. The Mississippi, with its violent waters, lay to the northeast, close enough for commerce but not so close as to endanger the community.

I stared at the town. Or lack thereof. "Six buildings?"

"Now, Laura, don't raise a fuss."

I ignored his playful wink. "You told me there was a town. A real town."

"It's not much to speak of now, but it'll grow. We only just platted it. Now that we have the lots laid out, we can advertise and bring in others."

"I thought it would be bigger." The baby kicked in my womb, and I winced.

"It will be. We platted out twenty blocks. If it were already a populated town, we'd hardly be among the founders, now would we?"

I shook my head at his teasing. I'd gotten ahead of myself again. Our grandparents had created Ripley County from nothing. Beaver would be *our* legacy. I spied the stakes as we drew into town and, with them, the ambitious plans the men envisioned for the village. We stopped, and William helped us from the wagon.

"Well, it's good you're safely back." An older man with graying hair approached and slapped William on the back. "This must be your family."

"It is. My wife, Laura. The little ones are Willie and Emma. Laura, this is Mr. Covey. He built the first house here two years ago."

I shook Covey's hand as other residents poured out to greet us, clustering like a gaggle of geese.

Maggie Knowles, like me, was heavily pregnant. She caught my arm and steered me toward a building. "Let's leave these men to catch up. I'd wager you're more interested in this."

"Ours?" I asked, making an assumption. It was the only two-story structure in town.

"Yep. Went up last week."

It was small, fourteen by twenty feet, and was built of logs—not the large frame building I had envisioned from William's description. Of course, he'd never said it was anything but a two-story structure. I'd visualized the size and building materials all on my own. That I had even expected anything more was my own fault.

I loved William, admired his hard work and determination, his teasing and his caring ways with the children. It wasn't so much that his dreams were always bigger than reality (though they often were) but that our dreams were different.

I pushed open the front door, devoid of a lock, and entered. The front room was light and airy. I glanced at the windows along three sides. "William built this?"

"The Malindy Brothers. They've built most of the town."

I recognized the name of the duo who were partnering with William in the sawmill business. Until the mill went up, I realized, there would be no frame structures. Those would come later, and William would be part of making it happen.

The interior space was designed to be heated by the open fireplace at the center of the longer wall. I pictured a cozy area near it to beckon customers. Stairs at the rear led to the second floor, where we would live. The room was small, and the store would be cluttered, but at least it would be light. "I'm pleased they thought to put in so many windows. There's nothing worse than a dim store."

"Most men wouldn't appreciate that, but the Malindys have good heads on their shoulders; they're building our house. We've been doubled up with my brother-in-law."

Maggie showed me the back room and the living quarters upstairs. The sleeping rooms would be tight, but at least there were two of them, and the main room should accommodate the new cookstove with no problem. A tingle of anticipation surfaced as I wondered what model William had decided on and when it would be delivered. Below, we heard the men carrying in our temporary supplies and the new feather ticks William had purchased in Rochester.

The two of us shuffled down the stairs, and Maggie departed for home, leaving me to survey the mess in the middle of the room. The children chased one another around the main room of the store while William spread the ticks on the floor.

"We'll need to sleep down here next to the fireplace until the freighter arrives with the furniture and stove."

I turned to him, trepidation rising. "The freighter from Iowa is stopping to pick up the new stove?"

"What new stove?"

Now, the anger surged. "You didn't buy a stove?"

William's face grew puzzled. "Why would I do that? We have a perfectly good stove. Brand new just eight years ago."

I bit back my dander. Had he completely forgotten our discussion? "We *had* a perfectly good stove. You told me it was too heavy to freight and was best left behind."

"Now, Laura, you knew I was only grumbling."

Good lord how I hated it when he "now, Laured" me. Fury bubbled up, and I let it spew. "No, I didn't know! You did nothing but harp about how much it would cost to transport it here. Over and over again, you said we ought to leave it."

I glared at him, infuriated. "I sold that stove!"

Two days later, the store inventory arrived. I watched it being unloaded, crate by crate and barrel by barrel. There would be a decision to be made once the wagon was empty. With inventory now in hand, were we to unpack it and open for business or continue to live in the store space? The single fireplace heated the main floor. To my knowledge, William had done nothing about purchasing a stove for our living quarters.

I, in turn, cooked him nothing but potatoes and stew, beans and ham.

Burning with resentment that I'd felt forced to sell my wonderful turntable stove, I bristled constantly. I'd barely spoken to William since discovering he'd not meant his emphatic statements and blamed myself for assuming he'd truly meant for me to leave the stove behind. To compound the situation, our household goods were past due for delivery. Without a bed, I struggled in getting up and down from the floor with my huge belly and aching back. My ankles were swollen and my feet so large I could no longer put on shoes. My toes were like ice. The women of Beaver, God bless them, brought me knitted slippers and baked goods, which I fed to the children, leaving William to go without. If I could not have my belongings, he would not have bread and cookies—not if I had anything to do with it.

As the wagon left, I surveyed the pile of mercantile inventory now in the middle of the store. William was nowhere in sight, no doubt working on the dam for the mill. In the short time we'd been here I learned he enjoyed playing politics with the other town founders more than he was wont to be a storekeeper. Every minute he wasn't working on the mill, he was meeting with the men. Unless the store was to remain this hopeless pile of inventory, I would have to organize it.

"What are we gonna do with it, Mama?" Willie asked.

I hugged my boy close and smoothed the cowlick in his hair. Though only five, he had a heart of gold and was ever helpful to me.

"I suppose there's nothing to be done but to start prying the crates open." I eyed the crowbar that had been left atop the largest crate.

"You gonna do it?" Willie's eyes widened.

"You do, Mama?" Emma echoed from the corner where she

sat with her doll.

"I don't see anyone else around," I muttered.

Reaching for the tool, I slid the flattened section beneath the lid and pressed the other end down. Nothing. I drew a breath and pushed harder. Pain cramped my abdomen, and I dropped the crowbar.

"Run," I told Willie. "Get your father and the doctor."

Jefferson was born less than two hours later, coming faster than any of my other children. But he arrived healthy, despite his early appearance, thank heavens.

Now alone with William, the doctor gone and the other children with Maggie, my body slumped with weariness. Jefferson wailed in the crate we'd hastily converted for a cradle. Still waiting for the household freight and our trunks of clothing, we'd borrowed diapers and gowns for him.

Frustrated, I scolded my husband from my bed on the floor. "We should have been settled before this baby arrived. Full and completely settled."

He scooped Jefferson up and rocked him gently. "I know."

Though William's voice was full of remorse, my irritation still simmered.

"I should not have had to birth him on the floor."

"I know that, Laura." He laid the baby in my arms. "But what was there to be done about it? Babies come early sometimes."

Babies come early sometimes.

Oh, of all the infuriating platitudes. I opened my nightgown and helped Jefferson latch to my breast. I drew a breath and leveled my voice. It would do little good to provoke an argument. "They especially come early when their mothers are trying to pry open crates."

William started. "You were trying to open crates? My god,

Laura! What possessed you to do that in your condition?"

"It needed doing, and you were nowhere to be found. We own a business, and the sooner we get that business into operation, the sooner we have income."

To me, this was obvious, but I knew after all this time that obvious to one of us did not always equate to clarity for both.

"It could have waited a few days, for heaven's sake." And there was the gist of it. He didn't view it as I did.

"No, it couldn't. Those goods needed to be unpacked, recorded in an inventory log, arranged, and made ready for sale. I figured I had only a few weeks to get that done before the baby came."

He offered a small smile and shook his head. "Well, that didn't work out, did it?"

"No, it didn't." I kissed our little one on the head and caught his father's gaze. "I could have lost this child. Do you understand that?"

He swallowed. "I was so scared when Willie came for me. You took a big risk, Wife."

I knew his words were true. I had no business trying to open that crate in my condition. But William needed to understand his role in events as well, past *and* future. "You put me at risk, Husband. You put both of us at risk. And you have left me once again with only a fireplace for chores and cooking."

"I never told—" he blustered, defensive.

"Yes. You did." I said the words softly, and he stopped his protest.

"I'm sorry, Laura."

"Then fix it. For Jefferson's sake, if not mine."

Once again, focusing on a baby convinced William to put others' needs first. He spent two days unpacking mercantile inventory. On the third, he traveled to Rochester to find out where our household goods were and purchase me a stove. That same night, the new stove was installed upstairs with our other household items, which had been sitting at the freight station in Rochester. I recovered from childbirth to face the arranging of both our living quarters and the store.

As was usual between us, the incident led to discussion and new commitments from William. He was tender and caring with me, clearly sorry for his actions. I found it difficult to remain angry with him. This husband of mine so often simply didn't comprehend that the rest of us didn't march to the same drummer as did he.

William was a fine, affectionate man, but there were times he became so wrapped up in his own ambitions and his own way of doing things that it became his sole focus. He forgot details and often didn't understand how his actions impacted others. My mother had warned me that was the way of men, and I resolved to be more patient with him. It was my job to stay one step ahead of William, to anticipate him and counter his missteps before they occurred.

He'd done an admirable job of prying off lids and removing items but left the contents in the middle of the floor. I knew he had little idea what to do with all of it, and we determined I would be the one to organize the store. After all, he had little skill in such matters, while I excelled in creating order from chaos. And chaos it was, with piles scattered throughout the building, upstairs and down.

What a mess! With hard work and minimal interruptions from Willie and Emma, I suspected it would take me at least a week to put it all in its place.

I focused first on the household upstairs, which took precedence. I'd packed carefully, crating like goods together, and discovered my planning was a boon. Putting things away took far less time than anticipated.

The store was another matter entirely.

It appeared William had purchased nearly every item necessary for building a town. Hammers, axes, saws, and screwdrivers abounded. I discovered tinned foods, winter jackets, and men's boots. There were barrels of flour and sugar, crackers and pickles, all creating a strange mixture of smells that mingled with the leather goods like every mercantile I'd ever entered. But there was not a pot or pan or women's item in the lot.

There also were no shelves.

I rocked on my heels and shook my head. How on earth could he have neglected to order shelving? Or had he assumed the Malindy brothers would tend to it? I pondered out his thought process, determining he'd likely thought it more prudent to order shelves built once there was a clear idea of need. That was my husband through and through.

The items women would need never entered his mind.

I set off to locate William, children in tow, so he could order the necessary goods. I found him in Dr. Brooks's front office with several other men, all of them poring over a plat of the town.

"Laura!" he said as we entered. "I didn't expect you up and out."

I watched Willie and Emma rush into the living quarters to locate their new playmates as I shifted the baby in my arms. "I have a list for you," I told him. "Shelves and more inventory."

He grinned, but I saw his embarrassment under the action. "My busy little wife."

The men chuckled, but I sensed their disapproval that I'd interrupted their business.

"We're discussing where to locate houses," he told me. "Most folks have been doubled up, and they're ready to buy lots. I've been elected to handle the sales, land agent if you will, and I wanted to make sure we were in agreement on business and residential areas."

"I knew it must be something like that." I handed him the list. "I'll need you to attend to these items today."

One of the men punched William on the arm. "She's a bossy one, Duley."

"She keeps me focused." He glanced at the list. "All of this?"

"All of that."

He drew me into the entryway and spoke softly. "I'll get the shelves built, but I don't believe we need those types of items."

I held his gaze. "You are trying to grow a town. That means women and children will be here, and they will have needs. You can stock the things they'll need, or they can buy them in Rochester. Every time a husband needs to do that, he will buy the other items there as well."

William's jaw dropped. "Do you think so?"

"Wouldn't you?"

Comprehension dawned in his eyes. "What would I do without you!" He embraced me. "You are a gem."

I glowed at the praise. "Just trying to catch all the details."

"Well, you have a head for business. More so than I realized." He smiled, thoughtful. "Perhaps I ought to put the entire store into your hands."

Run a store *and* care for my family? "Well, I don't think—"

"It will free me to get the mill up and operating and focus on selling lots. I'll need to get our land rented out, too. The men have even talked of me running for County Commissioner."

"But—"

"The store is yours." He smiled, the decision setting well with him.

I digested what it would mean for me. Even with tending house and the children, it would be far easier than chasing William all over town. But, to do it effectively, I would need full control.

"You'll put me on the account, so I can order inventory?" I ventured.

He shook his head. "There's no need for that. I can place the orders for you."

Beaver, Minnesota
1858, two years later

Over the next two years, I built a thriving business of the mercantile. It took but a month after putting me in charge for William to grow tired of my constant interruptions and lists to fill when he traveled to Winona for commission meetings. I'd had to make a lot of extra trips to bother him that much, but it was well worth it. He placed my name on the account, and I was able to run the store without his interference. Or his resistance.

Willie started off to school, and William and the Malindy brothers converted the sawmill to a gristmill, once area farming began in earnest. William continued in politics, serving on the Republican delegation to the Constitutional Convention the year Minnesota achieved statehood. Our lives were comfortable and secure. Secure enough that we'd borrowed against the mill toward enlarging the store.

The spring had been unusually wet, delaying our plans. Three days of dry weather had prompted William to seize the chance for travel, and he'd left for Winona, promising to return with construction materials. Looking outside at the downpour that had returned today, I hoped he'd had the sense to delay the trip home. He'd take pneumonia or ague if he hadn't.

The bell on the door tinkled, and I looked up, eager to visit. There'd not been a customer all afternoon. Nor morning, for that matter.

Maggie bustled into the store, dripping wet. "Goodness, will this rain never stop?" She shook her umbrella and propped it near the door.

"Where are the children?" I asked her.

"At home. I figured it was the better choice in this downpour." She glanced down at her muddy boots.

"Leave them. Emma can sweep it up. She'll be happy for something to do. The children were so bored at being inside yet again that I didn't have a bit of protest when I suggested a nap."

Nonetheless, Maggie wiped her feet on the rug before tiptoeing to the counter. "Did the mail make it through?"

I grinned at her. "Is that what brought you out in this weather?"

"I'm desperate for news."

She was lucky. The mail carrier had come yesterday, taking full advantage of the pause in rain. I guessed he wasn't likely to return for a week or more, given how hard it was now pouring. The ground was saturated. I turned to the mail slots and took a newspaper from the one marked as theirs. "Just the *Herald.*"

She grabbed the paper and spread it out on the counter. "Let's see what's going on in Wabashaw." She perused the front page, chirping out tidbits of gossip as they caught her eye. Her face soured. "There's another ad for the Dakota Land Company."

I groaned. "Everyone in three counties is talking about moving west. From the sound of it, towns are springing up left and right. This part of the state is hardly settled. I can't for the life of me imagine why anyone would want to go even farther west."

"William hasn't gotten Dakota Fever yet, has he?"

"No. And he would do well not to." Surely he wouldn't, not with all we'd built here. We'd finally caught our dream. I couldn't imagine him giving any of it up for the frontier.

"John has brought it up twice."

"Oh, Maggie, no!"

"I've managed to dissuade him, but it's a battle every time he reads one of these ads." She sighed. "I'm tempted to leave the paper here."

"If you like. You can read it when you stop by." I'd find a place for it behind the counter. Maggie was too good a friend to lose.

"I'd best put it away for today and get back."

We chatted on as I walked her to the door and watched her hustle away into the rain. Water stood in puddles, the ground too wet to absorb any more. I shook my head and closed the door.

Seconds later, it swung back open, slamming against the wall. I turned as one of the Malindy brothers burst into the store. "Is William back?"

"Heavens, Mr. Malindy! Whatever is the matter?"

"The mill! The dam broke, and the mill's sliding down the creek bank. We're gonna lose it all."

Chapter Six

Almena

Caton, New York

During the same period, 1850

Almena Hamm picked up the carpetbag and reached down to take her brother Seneca's hand. Seneca clutched it tightly and edged closer to her.

Scared to death, poor little man.

She was too, for that matter. Maybe not scared to death but more than a little frightened and uncertain. And resentful. She kicked at a rock, sending it flying. Too bad it wouldn't hit her stepmother in the head.

If Ma were still alive, she'd never stand for this. But, then, if Ma were still alive, they'd still be living in Pennsylvania, and Pa wouldn't be married to that horrid woman.

Tears swelled behind Almena's eyes. She fought them back, refusing to cry over spilt milk. What's done was done. But no matter what, for as long as she lived, she would always put *her* children first—if she ever had any. For now, Seneca came first. In that, too, tears would be of little use.

It was a gloomy day, clouds casting pallor over the usual vibrancy of the small farms that dotted Steuben County's green hills.

Appropriate, given our inauspicious mission.

"Slow down, Almena," Seneca whined. He'd never been able to pronounce her given name, Alomina. He knew her by nothing else, and she'd left Alomina behind with the rest of her childhood.

She forced herself to slow her steps so Seneca could keep up. The boy was just five years old, for heaven's sake. Five years old and farmed out to strangers.

"You doing all right?" she asked him.

He nodded, not truly understanding. "Where're we going?"

"We're going to live with the Miniers, down the road."

"With Miss Marilla?" His voice brightened a little.

"Mm hmm." Childless, Christian and Marilla had offered to adopt Seneca. They seemed like good folk, and Almena knew he'd have an easier life with them. At nearly fourteen, Almena was too old to be adopted, but they'd agreed to have her join the household as a hired girl. She was glad of it. Having her there would ease things for Seneca. For them both, really; they'd cope with the change together.

"Why d'we gotta go there?"

Oh, Seneca. How in heaven's name did you explain something like this to a child? "Twelve is too many for a little house like ours."

It was the truth. And a little tyke like Seneca was better off not knowing the whole of it . . . that Pa was willing to split up his family and farm out his kids to make more room for his new wife's brood. Almena understood there'd been a need to remarry. But she'd never expected her new step-siblings to come before Pa's own children. Already, Pa was seeking homes for some of the others. Since his remarriage, the family had doubled in size, and they barely scraped by.

He should have picked a single lady, instead of a widow with a passel of little ones.

He *should* have put his own children first.

Almena huffed and guided Seneca onto the stoop of the Minier house.

Marilla met them at the door, opening it in welcome. The scents of cinnamon and vanilla wafted out.

Almena's stomach growled as she tried to identify the source. She couldn't remember the last time she'd had baked sweets. Not since before Ma passed, and that was more than four years now.

"Well, will you look who's here!" Marilla knelt and drew Seneca into her arms. He stiffened, unaccustomed to such affection. Marilla laughed and drew back. "I have cookies," she announced, gesturing toward the kitchen at the back of the house.

Seneca's face brightened, and he sniffed the air. "Cookies? I don't never get cookies."

"Well, you do now. Come on in and have a couple before I show you your room. We've purchased you a hobby horse."

Seneca's eyes grew wide, and he rushed down the hallway, leaving Almena on the stoop.

Marilla eyed her, her chilly glance moving from head to toe.

Almena stood straighter and wished she'd taken the time to re-braid her ash-blonde hair.

"You going to stand there all day?" Marilla finally said.

Almena swallowed. "No, ma'am." She stepped into the house, and Marilla released the door. It swung shut with a bang.

Halfway down the hall, Marilla stopped and grasped a loop of rope hanging from the ceiling. A trap door dropped open, revealing a set of folded stairs. She drew them down and faced Almena. "Your bed's in the attic." She turned and whisked away into the kitchen.

Almena stood abandoned, shaking and bewildered and completely alone.

Caton, New York
1852

By their second year together, Almena and Marilla had settled into a more comfortable relationship. Still, Almena had been relegated the manual aspects of housework for too long. She hungered to move past the tedious chores of potato peeling, dishwashing, and laundry scrubbing. She wanted to learn the secrets of "housecraft." Secrets Marilla guarded as if she believed Almena would somehow use the knowledge against her. These skills would make the difference in mastering a household and making life better for the family she envisioned in her future.

Almena wanted to be a full-fledged baker, to discover the methods of sweetening preserves so that each fruit tasted the best it could, and to learn how Marilla made such mouth-watering butter. These were the secrets that made Marilla's bread, jams, and dairy products popular enough to sell to others. If Almena could do something like that, she'd have the means to make sure her children never had to be farmed out to others.

She and Seneca had been lucky. Not all her siblings had been able to stay together as they had. And life was good with the Miniers. Seneca now had parents who loved him, an education, and a bright future. Though she hadn't attended school, Almena had learned mathematics and grammar from the primers Seneca brought home, Seneca taking great pleasure in teaching his older sister. And Christian had allowed her use of his library so she could practice her reading and broaden her knowledge. They'd not wanted for anything.

But today, she was determined to stretch that knowledge further.

She hefted the plunger of the butter churn up and down a few more times, working out her strategy before she paused to check her progress.

"Is it ready for me?" Marilla asked

Almena lifted the lid from the churn instead of waiting for Marilla to do so, eager to prove she'd paid attention when she'd watched Marilla do the task. Small granules had begun to form within the cream. But had she churned enough? Were the granules the right size? Almena shushed her insecurities and examined the mixture more closely.

"It's come," she said.

Marilla approached, one eyebrow raised, and looked for herself.

"Sure enough. Good job." Marilla squeezed Almena's shoulder.

Pride surged within her. She'd never truly known how uneducated she'd been, without a mother to teach her. And her stepmother sure hadn't bothered. Almena took a breath and turned to Marilla.

"I was thinking, maybe today would be a good time for me to learn what you do after I finish the churning." There, she'd said it.

Marilla stared at her. "You were?"

"Yes."

"I guard my butter-making, Almena. You know that."

"I'm not trying to steal your secrets."

She shrugged. "Still, they are my secrets. I bring in good money making the best dairy goods in the county."

"I'm nearly sixteen. One day, I'll have my own family. It would serve me well to know how to do the same."

Sighing, Marilla digested her argument. "And how do I know you won't rush out and compete with me?" she finally said.

"In two years you don't know me well enough to recognize that's not my way?" It hurt that Marilla didn't trust her.

"No, I suppose it's not. But if you move out of this house,

that could all change in a minute. A girl on her own is going to do what she has to do."

That made sense. The world was not easy, but she needed to make Marilla understand. "I'm not seeking a way to support myself on my own. I want to be able to assure I can always keep my family together. I don't want my children to ever face being turned out or neglected."

"Oh, Almena . . ."

"Please? I'll give you my word. I promise not to go into competition with you. I'll even sign my name to it."

"Here." Marilla thrust a jar of cold water into her hands. "Toss this in with the cream."

Almena did as instructed, watching the water seep into the crystalizing cream.

"Now put the lid back on and churn the water in a bit. If you can show me you have a talent for it, I'll teach you."

Almena fitted the top on the churn and plunged the agitator up and down.

After a few minutes, Marilla stilled her hand. "That should be enough. Let's go ahead and drain off the buttermilk."

Together, they lifted the heavy churn and poured the liquid into a pail for later use.

Once the churn was back on the floor, Marilla handed Almena a bucket of clean cold water. "Pour it in."

"Why do you add the water?"

"You have to 'wash' the butter. Fill up the churn and let it settle." The answer was terse.

Almena emptied the water into the churn, wishing Marilla had provided more information. It was clear she was ill-at-ease with the situation. The water rested a moment before she and Marilla lifted the churn a second time and drained it off. The liquid flowed out, leaving a mound of butter sitting in the bottom.

"What's next?"

"Wash it again, in the butter-worker." Marilla handed Almena a small scoop and indicated the odd-looking wooden contraption at the edge of the room. The shallow wooden trough, mounted on legs, reminded her of a sawhorse. On either end, the trough was open, with pails set on the floor below.

Nervous, she placed glob after glob of the butter into the butter worker. "I never even imagined such a thing as washing butter."

"If you don't, it won't keep. The better you wash it, the longer it lasts and the better the flavor. You can always tell a butter that isn't washed well. It tastes off."

Almena brightened, glad Marilla had finally relaxed enough to explain the reasoning behind the task. She knew it was vital knowledge, one of the keys to Marilla's success.

"More water?"

"That's right. Then roll it."

Almena poured more water atop the butter and let it soak in. She took the handled roller from its hook on the side of the butter-maker and moved it across the butter until the mound spread out in the trough like thick piecrust. "Like this?"

"Harder. You want to squeeze out the water with it."

She pressed hard, throwing her weight into the effort. Milky water ran off the edges of the trough, caught by the pails beneath.

Marilla handed her another jar of water. "Again. Keep repeating until the water runs off clear instead of cloudy."

Almena continued to repeat the wash and roll sequence, thankful for Marilla's tutelage, reluctant as it was. She glanced down at the butter, watching for the liquid to clear. When it was no longer filmy, she did one more wash, just to be sure.

Marilla smiled. "Good instinct. Mix in salt, to help preserve it, and put it in the crocks."

Warmth filled Almena as she gathered salt and several earthenware crocks. After salting and mixing the butter, she began to place butter into the first crock.

Marilla lifted an eyebrow and shook her head.

Almena paused, a handful of soft butter in her hand, oozing a bit between her fingers.

"Fling it into the crock."

"Fling it?"

"Throw it. Hard. That helps force out the air and any leftover water."

Almena tossed it as hard as she could into the crock. It smacked against the bottom, and Marilla chuckled. A small amount of water oozed to the top, and she drained it off before flinging in the next handful. Once the crock was full enough, Marilla handed her the butter press.

Almena took the stem of the mushroom shaped tool and pushed the rounded top into the butter.

"Ram it down. This is your last chance to get all the water and air out so it won't go rancid."

Almena pressed until her arms ached, draining out liquid each time it appeared. When it finally seemed dry, she stopped.

Marilla smiled at her. "That's it. Put on the lid, and we'll set it in the springhouse."

Almena sat on a three-legged stool, pride warming her. "That was a lot more work than churning."

"You'll soon get strong enough that it won't be so bad. It'll be one of the most important skills you learn."

"How's that?"

"Families who rely on farming alone are often poor. Skilled wives can make extra money. Being a good laundress is one way, but a laundress will work non-stop, ruin her hands, and break her back doing it. If a woman can make good butter and cheese, she can use her time and effort more wisely and still contribute to the household income—all for the cost of a callus or two. Not everyone has milk cows. Women who do can trade their butter and cheese for necessities or sell it at the mercantile."

"How come my stepmother didn't do that?" Extra money for so large a family might have made it possible for the family to stay together.

"Because she's a ninny."

Almena laughed. She hadn't liked the woman anyway, or her passel of kids. Life was better with the Miniers, for her and for Seneca.

"With such a large family, it could be your stepmother never had enough extra milk to make extra butter and cheese."

"We did only have one cow."

"So you see?"

"I'll make sure I have more than one. Thank you, Marilla." Almena jumped from the stool and hugged Marilla tight.

Marilla tensed, withdrawing for a moment before she hugged Almena back. As she pulled away, she caught Almena's gaze.

"Make sure you own milk cows before you marry. Or purchase them in your own right once you do. That way, should your husband be too poor, a lazy cad, or a gambler, you will always have the means to support yourself. If you have a good man, you'll be able to bring even more money into the household. A woman with cows is never a poor woman, as long as she knows what to do with her cream, and her children will never want."

Marilla's gaze softened. "If you continue to do well with this, we'll keep a heifer calf back and you can raise it as yours. What you produce from it will be profit to you. If you learn your craft well, you'll gain a reputation and outsell those who don't wash their butter or pitch their cheese well."

"Truly? You'd give me a cow of my own? And the profits?"

"Under three conditions. You make it your goal to excel at

what I teach you—what you produce will reflect on me. For the first three years, you apprentice; you will produce for the family only." She paused, staring hard at Almena. "And, once you start selling, you don't sell your products to any business that buys from me."

Almena offered her hand. She wasn't sure that left her any options for selling her goods, but she'd always have the skills to preserve her family.

Caton, New York
Three years later, 1855

Almena squared her shoulders and opened the door to Finch's Mercantile. The bell above her tinkled as she stepped in and closed the door behind her. The Miniers marketed with the store at the other end of town, and she'd never stepped inside Finch's establishment. It was the only store in town that didn't buy from Marilla.

"Morning, miss," the man behind the counter said, his amber eyes brightening noticeably. "What can I help you with?"

She approached, fighting trepidation, and set her large basket atop the counter. She was nearly nineteen years old, for heaven's sake, and she could handle this. It was too important to her future to let a little fear impede her. She needed to learn this one last skill—selling—and she'd know her family would always be secure.

"I'm Almena Hamm," she said, her voice strong and confident despite her nerves. "Are you Mr. Finch?"

The clerk appeared to be in his mid-twenties, his rich chestnut hair groomed and a neat apron covering his vest. He looked professional enough to be the owner, but his young age gave her pause.

"Just a clerk. Phineas B. Hurd at your service." He offered his hand.

She shook it and withdrew, enjoying his warm, lingering grasp far too much. She fussed at the callus on her right palm for a moment, wishing she'd put cream on it earlier, then stopped as if it had burst into flame. Lord, she hoped he hadn't noticed!

"Do you have the authority to purchase goods for Mr. Finch?"

He grinned at her. "It depends on what it is."

"I've bread, preserves, cheeses, and butter for sale." She removed the cloth and revealed her assortment of products.

Hurd peeked at them. "They look real good, Miss, but we've got a healthy stock of those type of items already."

She offered him a broad smile. "Not like these, you don't."

He hesitated. "This is a case of me having my hands tied. Mr. Finch has been buying from the same ladies for years and—"

"And I'm sure they keep him well-supplied. You'll find my goods are superior." As Marilla had advised, she gave him no time to turn her down.

"What he offers is good," Hurd protested. But a slim thread of hesitation was wound into the words.

Seizing the opportunity, she plunged ahead, her confidence building. "Not as good as what I have in this basket, Mr. Hurd."

"You're a tenacious woman, Miss Hamm," he said. "I like that." He winked at her.

Almena swallowed. Good heavens but those amber eyes were arresting! "Have you had your lunch yet today?"

"Not yet." He leaned his elbows on the counter, chin in his hands, and stared at her.

Oh, my! She tore her gaze away, wondering if there was a Mrs. Hurd. "Well, get a plate, knife, and napkin." She extracted items from the basket, arranging an assortment on the counter, trying to keep her mind on the sale.

Hurd disappeared into the back, whistling, and reappeared a few moments later, utensils in hand. He eyed the display, then Almena. "Gracious," he said, pausing in his tracks. "That's enough to make a man's mouth water."

Her face heated, and she bustled with the items. She'd brought only one type of bread, basic sourdough, but her preserves included a sampling of different berries. Her butter was stamped with a distinctive floral pattern she'd designed herself and had carved onto a roller. A fine, sharp aged cheddar (her specialty) sat next to several soft and semi-soft varieties.

"Help yourself," she told him.

He sliced off a slab of bread, breaking it, and spread one half with blackberry jam. The other, he slathered with butter. He cut into the cheddar and took a bite. His eyes lit, and he smiled. Setting the cheese down, he took the bread and bit into the buttered slice.

"Good, huh?" she asked, knowing it was.

"Are you joking? This is the best butter I've ever had."

Hah! "I told you so."

"That you did."

"Let's negotiate an order. I can supply daily or weekly per your choice. My preference is cash on delivery, but I am willing to work with you on consignment, if that is an issue."

Hurd's mouth dropped open. "I wish I dared, Miss Hamm, more than you can possibly know. But the ladies Finch buys from now are Mrs. Finch's sisters, and I don't see any way to keep my job if I buy from you instead."

Almena paused for only a second. If she knew anything, she knew Phineas B. Hurd had little chance of holding out for long. She leaned her elbows on the counter, mimicking his earlier pose. "Do you own a cow, Mr. Hurd?"

Corning, New York
Two years later, 1857

Almena and Phin stood on the New York & Erie Rail Road platform along with Seneca and the Miniers. The large broad-gauge locomotive spewed occasional hot cinders from its tall smokestack, and Almena was glad of the numerous cars of cut wood separating it from the passenger cars that lined the platform. Though there was a screen to trap large cinders, small ones still managed to escape, most burning out before they hit the ground. At least they wouldn't have to breathe in coal fumes the entire way.

The cow Phin had gifted her on their wedding day had already been loaded in a stock car, along with the now-grown heifer Marilla had given her two years ago. Only the good-byes remained.

And, the new life ahead of them. They had high hopes, both of them. Phin had secured a position at a mercantile owned by Finch's brother way out west in Wisconsin, where they hoped to buy all the land they could. The storekeeper had agreed to take on Seneca as well, as soon as he was old enough. Almena, well, she planned to make butter—the best butter La Crosse had to offer.

She chased the thoughts away and turned to Christian. "Thank you. For everything."

Christian's face reddened, and he squeezed her shoulders. "You take care of yourself, Mrs. Hurd."

"I will. We will." A week into marriage, she still forgot.

Beside her, Phin laughed. "We'll be fine."

"I know, son." Christian turned and shook Phin's hand.

Almena faced Marilla. *Ah, Marilla . . .* what could she possibly say to Marilla?

"You have a good man," Marilla said, "and cows of your own. There's nothing more you need." Her smile faltered.

Almena slipped into Marilla's arms, hugging her tight.

"You remember everything I taught you, honey, and you will never want."

"I love you, Marilla."

"Oh, girl, I love you, too."

Almena slipped from the embrace and quickly hugged each of Marilla's small daughters. She turned to smile at Seneca. "You ready?"

At twelve, he was in the midst of a growth spurt, arms and legs long and gangly. His face was no longer that of a boy but not yet that of a man. He swallowed.

Phin checked his new gold pocket watch, Almena's wedding gift, and caught her gaze.

"Seneca?" Almena said. "We'll need to board in a few minutes."

His head dipped, and he kicked at a stone. "I'm staying."

Staying? The word tumbled through her, landing in a hard clump. "St—staying?"

Seneca's face was full of anguish. "I can't leave. This is home, Almena."

He was right, and she knew his decision had not been made lightly. Christian and Marilla were his parents. Her lips trembled. "You'll write? And come visit?" she said. The words felt hollow.

"I will."

"You know I love you? That I'm not just leaving you?"

"Aw, I know that. You ain't getting rid of me that easy."

"Ain't?"

"Aren't."

"That's better. I love you."

"I love you, too." He hugged her, crushing her until the whistle sounded. "Better get on there."

She chucked him under the chin and turned away as Phin

bid him farewell. They mounted the steps and made their way into the passenger car. Tears streaked down her cheeks.

Phin wiped them with his finger as they took their seat. "You're sure? You didn't plan on leaving him."

"It's time to start our life together."

"We can do that here . . . wait a few years to leave."

"No. This is what we planned. A couple years working for Finch, and we'll have enough saved to buy that farm and a good idea of where to do it. Besides, I . . ." her voice broke, "I suspected that might happen. He wasn't enthusiastic, just pretending for my sake. This is for the best."

Phin hugged her tight and kissed her on the forehead. "I wish it weren't so far. I hate taking you from him."

"He'll visit. He has a family that loves him, and that's what's important." She peered out the window, found them, and waved. They waved back, adults with long faces, the little girls with excitement, Seneca with choked resignation. Choosing had been difficult for him, but he'd know love in the choice he made. She waved again as the train lurched and left the station.

She'd said good-byes, too, to her other siblings . . . those who still lived in Caton. The Hamm household had given up some children only to be crowded again with five new babies. She'd bitten back her resentment and done her duty, bidding her father farewell. But she'd shed no tears. They'd been shed years ago.

The train rolled through the green hills of central New York, making its way west. Almena slept, lulled by the rocking of the train, her head on Phin's shoulder. At a jerk, she woke, startled. Ahead of them, the gray waters of Lake Erie stretched as far as the eye could see.

"We'll get off, spend the night here," Phin told her. "I telegraphed ahead to reserve a room at the Loder House. I figured you'd want to sleep in a bed instead of sleeping on the train all night." He grinned. "But maybe that wouldn't have been an issue for you."

She smiled back. "Oh, you!"

They gathered their things and disembarked. The city was busy, travelers rushing to and fro. Between the railroads and the boat traffic, the bustle was hectic, and Almena was glad Phin had made hotel arrangements in advance. A few yards past the depot, someone called their names. They stopped and turned.

"Oh, I'm so glad I caught you." A small rotund man approached. "I'm the station master. I'm afraid I have a bit of bad news."

"What is it?" Almena asked.

"It's the cows. We've lost your cows."

Chapter Seven

Christina
New Ulm, Minnesota
The year before, 1856

It is a stupid idea my husband has, and I don't like it one bit. Why should we leave New Ulm? It is a good German town where the old ways are still kept. We are at home here. There are German bakers and beer makers. Everywhere, it looks like Germany, and I can think of no reasons for us to leave.

"You are crazy to even think it," I tell him.

"It is a chance for us, Christina," he says. Like me, he is trying to practice the strange English words but his accent is still so thick. *Ach,* no one will even understand him if we leave here.

"It is stupid." I stomp my foot to make sure he knows I am serious.

"That man Brink, he will pay us to hold the land for him."

Brink again. He has been in the beer hall, drinking with the men, talking about the lands to the west. He is *ein Scheisser,* that one, trying to claim two pieces of land. I want no part of it.

I hold my tongue and do not say the foul word aloud. "He is breaking the law."

Andreas sighs. He is fed up with me, I think. He did not know his wife was so stubborn. But that is how it is. He will have to get used to it.

"What is wrong with trying to get more land? There is more than enough."

His voice is softer, and I know he is trying now to sweet-talk me. He will use those blue eyes of his like he is a puppy, and I will not be able to resist.

"*Nein.* That cabin is in the middle of nowhere, and I will not go." I turn away and start to put dishes in the cupboard so he will know it is my final word.

"It is not so far from New Ulm."

I think again that he is stupid, but he is not. He is trying to trick me.

I slam the tankard on the counter and swing to face him. My blond braid whips with the movement, it is so fast. "I am not such a *Dummkopf,* Andreas Koch. I know what's what. That cabin is a two-day ride from New Ulm. Alma Schmidt told me so."

"And what does Alma Schmidt know of it?"

"A good plenty. She heard from her cousin that a man named Myers lives out there in a village called Saratoga, and he says Brink is miles from it, all alone on that prairie."

All the women in New Ulm know this. We have been spreading the word since we learned Brink was in town.

"He is in the Walnut Grove," Andreas insists, like it is a town. But the women know better and have spread the word about that, too.

"*Ja.* And the Walnut Grove is *nein* but trees in the middle of the prairie." I turn back to the dishes and slam them onto the shelves.

"All in the territory are trees in the prairies. And the lakes. This Walnut Grove will be no different. It is not so important where it is. What matters is that there is already a cabin there that we will not have to build. Brink will pay us to live there, so it is a way to make money for doing nothing. And we can farm the land and sell what we don't need. Think of what that could mean for us. Money to start our lives."

He still does not understand.

"I did not come to *Amerika* to live all alone. We should stay in New Ulm, like the other Germans, where we can buy *bier* and *schnitzel* and pumpernickel. Here we can celebrate a *Richtfest* when we build our own home."

"I am a farmer. You know this. I do not want to spend my life in a town. You knew this before we married."

His reminder hits me in the gut. I did know this. When we came to New Ulm and rented this little house, I knew it would only be for a time, that we would one day move onto land. But I didn't think it would be so far from a town.

Andreas wraps me in his strong arms. "I can make the *bier,* and you can make the *schnitzel* and the pumpernickel. I will build our own *Haus,* and you will make a wreath to hang on it. I will even say a poem to bless it. It will still be a *Richtfest* even if it is only us two. You will honor me as a good *Hausfrau* there as much as you would in New Ulm."

"There will be no one for miles and miles," I say, my head on his chest.

"I will keep you safe. And is it such a bad thing to be all alone? Are you so tired of your husband already that you do not want to be with him?"

"*Ach!* You make fun of me." I step back and slap him playfully.

He smiles. *"Nein, mein Frau. Du bist mein Ein und Alles."*

You are everything to me, my one and only. I sigh and let those blue puppy eyes draw me in.

Cottonwood County, Minnesota
May 1858

Ja, the Walnut Grove is *nein* but a grove of trees on the prairie. We live here now for almost two years. Andreas does not mind so much the loneliness, but I am tired of it and wish so much to visit New Ulm. It is not good to live so far from people. Our closest neighbors even are too far to visit by walking, and the trappers who occasionally live at Lake Shetek are at least twelve miles from us.

I have not talked to another woman for two years. Today, I will ask Andreas if I can travel with Mr. Renicker on his trip to New Ulm for supplies.

Renicker is a single man. He lives in Saratoga, a town with a name and not much else. This is about thirty miles from us, along the Nobles Trail. There, Aaron Myers also lives with a wife and children, and a widower with four little girls. But I have never met them. Only Aaron Myers, who takes turns with Renicker to go for supplies at New Ulm. They trade for us, too, and sell our crops, so that Andreas does not have to leave me alone on the prairie.

It is not good, to live like this. The prairie has much to love, with grasses waving and bright flowers, but the winters have a cold that bites and snow so deep that sometimes we cannot walk. When the winds come, we must be careful not to get lost. Those are the times I miss having other women to visit. When we are done at Brink's cabin and ready to have our own land, I will insist we settle near others.

Andreas is lonely, too, even if he refuses to say so. He is always glad when Renicker comes through, for they sit and speak *Deutsch* together. Today, Renicker is much on my mind. It is time for him to go to New Ulm for supplies and make the stop here. I have cleaned until the *Haus* is spotless and do not allow Andreas to wear his shoes inside. Even though the floor is dirt, I have laid down rugs, freshly beaten, and they must be spotless when guests arrive.

I look forward to each visit with excitement. It is good to see someone besides my Andreas. Much as I love him, we get tired and cranky of each other. That is the German in us, I think. It is no good without friends to share the *bier und kaffee.*

All is ready. I have even coiled my braid atop my head for his visit. It is time to talk to Andreas before Renicker is here. I know I should have done this days ago but I do not know what Andreas will say. Now, it is the last minute, and I am even more nervous.

"Andreas?" I call from the *Haus* yard. I know he is near and did not go to the fields today.

"*Ja,* what is it?" In his mouth, he shifts the small sliver of wood he chews on. "Does he come?"

"*Nein,* but I need to talk with you."

"I am busy, trying to clean the stable before he arrives. The stalls for his horses have a need to be mucked."

"I would like to go to New Ulm with Mr. Renicker."

"We cannot go to New Ulm," he says. "We must finish the planting. There is much left in the grain fields. It cannot wait until we go to New Ulm and come back. That is four days it would wait."

"I have sowed my garden and am free to go."

He spits out the toothpick. "You mean to go alone with Renicker to New Ulm?"

"*Ja,* if you will not come."

"*Nein.* It would not be proper."

"*Ach,* it is only riding on the seat of a wagon."

"But you will stop for the night."

"That is at Brown's Cabin. There is a whole family there. It is not like I would be alone with Renicker."

"It is not seemly." He turns and goes back to the stable, leaving me alone in the yard with no answer. I will have to ask again, but it is better not to nag him now. It is always better not to provoke a German temper. I sigh and return to the *Haus* but am not long there before Andreas shouts from the yard.

"Christina! He comes."

I rush to shoo out the cat, who has wandered in through the open door, and straighten the quilt on the bed. As I step outside, Renicker is nearing with his wagon.

"Hello, the house!" he calls, though I know he can see us fine standing in front of it.

Andreas goes to shake his hand and release the horses.

Renicker greets me. "Mrs. Koch, it's good to see you. Mrs. Myers sends her regards," he says in German, thrusting a jar of preserves into my hands from the wife of Aaron Myers. I have not met her, but her husband speaks of her when he travels through.

"Danke," I say, then remember to practice my English. "Thank you."

The men care for the animals while I finish with the meal. As usual, Renicker will go on to Brown's Cabin in the morning. Today is for visiting. I am eager for the news of the other settlers and rush to get supper on the table.

Once we are seated, I wait for news to start, my knee almost bouncing with pent up anticipation.

"Well," Renicker begins, "the widower left."

I think about him, all the way in the middle of nowhere with those four little girls and am glad to hear it. "Where did he go?" I ask.

"He said they were going to head up toward Leavenworth. That's the second family that's left now."

"So Saratoga is *kaput.*" Andreas punctuates the words with finality.

"Just me and the Myers family now. All those houses built by the government are sitting there empty. You sure you two don't want to move up there and join us?"

I look to Andreas, my pulse skipping.

"Nein. We are doing *gut* here."

But I am not doing so *gut.* I am afraid if I do not talk to another woman soon, I will dry up from the loneliness. I will have to ask again, but I have waited too long and now must do so in front of Renicker. Andreas will not be pleased.

"He wasn't happy there, anyway," Renicker continues in German. The whole of our conversation has become a mix of languages. "Came up from the lake when his wife died while back East. He didn't understand how hard it would be to raise those girls. That first winter was pretty hard."

"In Minnesota, all the winters are hard." Andreas shrugs, as if this is not important.

"Some harder. Myers almost went back that year. They ran out of flour and had to live on milk until the weather broke. That was right before you arrived."

"*Ja,* in New Ulm, the snow was deep that year," I say. "It would be good to visit with my old friends there to hear of life since."

I hope that my mention of New Ulm will remind Andreas of my desire to go, but the observation leads to nowhere but a stony glare and awkward silence.

After a while, Renicker finds a new topic. "Parmlee, from Lake Shetek, came through and said there is a new family there. Wat Smith and his wife built a cabin at the end of last year. Took over where Bennet had his shack and added on to that." He turned to me. "I bet Mrs. Smith would be glad to see another woman, if you're inclined to go visiting."

I have not been to the lake, but I know it is large. I wonder how far away this Mrs. Smith is. "Where at on the lake?"

Renicker dips a finger into the leftover gravy on his plate and traces a crude outline of the lake. On the southeast side, he makes an *X*. "Right about here, between Lake Shetek and Beauty Lake."

"How far?"

"That part of the lake, maybe fourteen miles. Oh, and a German named Charley Zierke has settled between here and Brown's Cabin. They call him Dutch Zierke. It will be another place to stop on the way to New Ulm."

Andreas looks to me. I shrug and give him a tiny up-turn of my mouth. He will want to go and visit there, to speak German with someone besides me. We will have a negotiation, I think.

"Maybe Andreas can take a day off tomorrow, and we can travel with you to meet this Dutch Zierke."

"I have field work," Andreas says.

"It could wait one day," I say, "so I could travel on to New Ulm with Mr. Renicker and have a visit with Alma Schmidt?"

Andreas's face hardens. "No, Christina, you will not go to New Ulm with Renicker. This will not be, and you will not ask me again."

Cottonwood County, Minnesota
June 1858

We wait, but Renicker does not return with the supplies. It is one week, and he is not back. "He should have been here two days ago," Andreas says for the third time.

"Maybe he had too much *bier* in New Ulm," I joke.

But Andreas does not laugh. "He is a good man, not a drunk, a man who does his business and returns."

"Maybe he stayed more time at Dutch Zierke's or Brown's Cabin."

"It is possible. But if he does not come by Friday, we will go to look. He would not visit longer than that. If a wheel has broken and he is walking back, we must find him."

I think about him out on the prairie and know Andreas is right. "We will go tomorrow," I say, "if he does not come in today."

It is less than an hour later that two men ride into our yard. I rush out, and they are already talking with Andreas. They quiet as I approach.

"Renicker?" I ask, my stomach in a knot.

"Ja," Andreas says. Just *ja*.

I see in his eyes that the news is not good.

"This is Parmlee and Hammer, from Shetek. They found Renicker between Plum Creek and here."

"What happened?" I ask. Only a few more miles and he would have been safe to the Walnut Grove.

Parmlee turns to me. "Real sorry, ma'am. I know you knew him." He does not answer my question.

The worry builds. Why do they not tell me? "Andreas?"

"He was killed by the Indians," my husband says, his voice soft as be breaks the news.

And now the worry becomes fear. My heart thumps. "Indians? But there has never been trouble with the Indians." I think how close Plum Creek is to us. "We never even see the Indians here."

"They plundered the wagon," Parmlee continues. "Took most of what was in it, from the looks of it. And the team."

"Why would they do that?" I ask.

Then I remember how I had wanted to go with him. I shiver. I would be dead beside him, I think. Or maybe worse. I have heard the stories of Indian attacks in other places.

"They get hungry. Especially if the annuity goods from the government don't get to the reservation on time." This time it is Hammer who answers.

I wonder why they didn't simply take what they wanted rather than kill him.

Parmlee shifts his feet. "Or it was the whiskey."

"The whiskey?" Andreas asks.

"Renicker has been trading whiskey with the Indians. The

keg was still in the wagon but it was empty. Could be they were drunk and fought."

I glance at Andreas, who looks surprised. We did not know that he was selling whiskey.

"Or they wanted more and there was no more. Or they had nothing to trade and Renicker wouldn't give up the goods." Hammer shrugs. "Could have been any of a number of things that led to it. We'll never know."

I clutch Andreas's arm, shaking. "Did they . . . scalp him?" My other hand goes to my coil of blond hair and I think again how I would have been with him if Andreas had not refused to let me go.

Parmlee looks uncomfortable. "No, ma'am. They left him on the side of the road, partly covered in a gopher hole. We buried him proper."

"Do you want to come in? I have *kaffee*."

"We'd best get on, back to the lake and let the others know," says Hammer.

"I'll ride up to Saratoga and tell Myers," Parmlee adds.

Andreas watches them get on their horses, his face a mix of emotions, and I realize he is afraid.

I have never seen him fear anything, and my skin prickles.

"You tell them we must have a meeting," he says. "We must talk about this attack and what we should do."

When they have gone, Andreas turns to me. "Maybe now is the time to leave this place."

We meet at the home of Wat Smith. It is so crowded that we spill into the yard. The cabin is a few hundred feet from the west shore of Beauty Lake, which sparkles in the summer sun and gives the name. The Myers children play along the top of the bank.

Lake Shetek is further west, perhaps a half mile. Smith takes the group to look at it while we wait for the last bachelor trappers to arrive. I am surprised. I have not seen such a big lake in all the time I have been in *Amerika.* It stretches for miles with pelicans everywhere. Smith says Shetek is an Indian word for pelican. His words bring us back to why we have come here, and we look at each other, all of us quiet. My stomach has churned these last few days, and I want nothing more than to return to New Ulm and leave this isolated place. *Ach,* we should have done so as soon as we heard the news.

I walk with Mrs. Smith and Mrs. Myers, excited to finally visit with other women. Mrs. Myers's oldest keeps watch on the children. The men are ahead, and we hang back, since it is not so proper for women to offer opinions. But we itch to do so.

"We shouldn't have even come here," Mrs. Smith says. "It isn't natural to be so alone and unprotected."

Mrs. Myers chimes in. "We are alone in Saratoga now. I told Aaron we are too far away from others, and I won't stay there all alone. We have four children to protect."

"I told Andreas this, too."

In fact, I have told him this non-stop since Renicker was found. I tell him we must return to New Ulm. He has grown tired of my nagging, I think.

"How much danger do you think there is?" Mrs. Smith asks. She is a quiet woman, plain in her patched dress.

"I do not know," I say. "We have not had any Indian trouble. We do not even see Indians. But the killing was not far from our house, and that is not good." I am careful of my words and hide my worry.

Mrs. Myers stops near the house and looks to make sure her brood is safe. We cluster together. The men sit in a group on logs, deep in their talking.

"They've been very friendly with us. Aaron does herb remedies and is good with injuries. He treats them if they come for help and we trade food with them. But, now that Renicker has been killed, we would be out there all alone."

"Parmlee says he was selling whiskey to them," I say.

"Never a good thing. Aaron says trading whiskey to Indians creates problems. So many of them get crazy from it. If we had known Renicker was doing that, we would have had words with him."

"What brought you to Saratoga?" I ask her.

She snorts. "Dakota Fever."

I do not know what this is, and I look at her with my brow raised.

She laughs at my confusion. "We were living in Wisconsin, and the Dakota Land Company plastered handbills all over town telling about new settlements. Aaron went to a meeting, and we ended up coming west with eleven other families, bound for Yankton, in Dakota Territory. When we got to the Cottonwood River, near here, we met a group on their way back East. They said the Indians farther west in Dakota were too wild. Some of our party turned back East with them, others went south to Sioux City, and we claimed land near Saratoga. There were houses already there. It was supposed to be a town."

"My husband heard there was a town here, Cornwell City. We were surprised to find nothing but empty land. But we like the lakes, and he is determined this is the place for us."

We turn to watch the men and send nervous glances to one another. I am a good German woman and know my place, but I do not like that we are not included. I want to know what they are saying.

Mrs. Smith sighs and says, "That's enough, ladies. I'm going over, whether they like it or not." She strides away toward the men. She is stronger than she looks, I think.

Mrs. Myers and I follow.

Andreas frowns at me but does not say anything as we sit on

the logs with them. The men look at each other, their talk at a stall.

Aaron Myers speaks. “Here’s where we’re at, ladies. None of us have had any problems with the Indians, and we all agree Renicker wouldn’t have had any either, if he hadn’t been trading whiskey.”

“We are farmers,” Andreas adds. “We came to plow the lands. We do not want to live in towns where we cannot do this.”

I want to scream at him. “We must return to New Ulm,” I say. “I do not want to live alone on the prairie.”

“Me, either,” says Aaron’s wife.

“Nor I,” Mrs. Smith adds.

“We’ve talked about that,” Smith says. “We agree that we shouldn’t be so isolated, miles away from others.”

This is good. It means we will go back to places east. We can make our farms near Mankato and New Ulm.

Aaron Myers continues. “We’ve talked about the lake. The soil is good here, and land is available for the taking. If we spread out our farms along one side of the lake, we can all have what we need for farming but be close enough that we can get to one another easily.”

“Since we have already settled here, it makes sense for everyone else to settle on up the lakeshore,” says Smith.

“Most of the trappers have small shacks where they stay when we are at the lake. They’re in a group, about a mile to the north,” Parmlee adds. “My place is a mile or so north of them.”

“When we came down from Saratoga, we traveled the length of the lake,” Myers says. “There are good spots all along it. I’m thinking we could settle at the north end, the Kochs in between. At most, we would be two to three miles apart, able to walk to our nearest neighbors within an hour’s time.”

“What?” I stand, gaping at Andreas. “We will not return to New Ulm?”

"I can farm, Christina, and you would not be so alone."

"It's not such a bad idea," Mrs. Myers says. "We would be a community if not a town. We could visit with no problem, and we can get together easily."

Ach, she is right. I know this. New Ulm is not for us anymore. It is time for me to let go of that place and take hold of this new community we will form. "But, will it be safe?" I ask. If it will be safe, I will try this.

Smith smiles at me. "None but Renicker have had problems with the Indians. Myers doctors them, and they regard him as a friend. We'll need to keep on guard if others settle here so whiskey doesn't become an issue."

"Other than that one instance, the Sioux here are friendly and eager to trade with us peacefully," Myers adds. "What other problems could we have?"

Chapter Eight

Julia
La Crosse, Wisconsin
During the same period, July 1856

Reality kicked Julia Wright in the head within days of her ill-considered marriage.

And it ached. It ached something fierce.

She slunk down in the chair and laid her head on the table, trying to block out the ruckus across the room, where Jack and two other men passed a jug of home-brewed corn liquor from hand to hand, all three bragging about their grand plans to sell watered-down whiskey to unsuspecting customers.

Hot anger sent spikes through her throbbing head. She'd thought him an ethical man!

Well . . . she'd be damned if she'd let him drag her good name through the mud. Julia Silsby had character, by God, and she would not be undone by the likes of Jack Wright.

Served her right, leaping without looking, like her sister had warned her she was doing. Jack had wooed her, told her he adored her too-plump curves, treated her like she was the most special woman in the world. He and his dimples and that glorious blond hair combed just so, looking so distinguished and worldly. Well, he wasn't distinguished now, not by any means.

Lord, why hadn't she listened? It had taken less than one week to discover Jack Wright the husband was not at all the same man as the charmer who had pressed his suit.

Stupid, stupid, stupid. With no one else to blame but herself.

How on earth was she going to manage being married to a man without an ounce of integrity? But she was stuck now, completely and thoroughly stuck. Wedded and bedded and bound for life to a dishonorable drunk who had no qualms about hoodwinking others. She'd have to figure out a way to keep him under control, for both their sakes.

She lifted her head and observed the trio in the far corner. Clearly, the whiskey in that jug was not watered. Jack was bleary eyed. His companions, neither of whom she'd seen before this evening, were pretty near in their cups. They'd stretched out, their dirty stockings and smelly feet mucking up the brand-new woven rug her parents had sent as a wedding gift. Their muddy boots were piled in the corner where they'd reluctantly shed them after she'd protested them wearing the detestable things into her clean cabin.

"So, how many d'ya think we hid away today?" Jack asked. It was the third time he'd asked the question, but she still wasn't sure what he was talking about because their drunken rambling had jumped from one topic to another.

"Ten, fifteen, m'be," the stinkiest one answered. He shifted his legs and the nauseous stench of his feet wafted through the close quarters.

I should have kept my mouth shut about their boots.

It would have been easy to shake the dried mud out later but oh, no, she'd insisted, nagged at them until they'd shed their footwear. Now, with so few windows, the stench of their dirty feet hung in the close quarters and would haunt the room until the heat of the day dissipated.

Egad, when was the last time they'd bathed?

Jack hadn't washed more than *his* hands and face since the morning they wed, a week before, despite unloading wagon-loads of furs into his uncle's mercantile these past few days.

Last night, his sweat-soaked skin had turned her stomach as he climbed into bed and started pawing at her. She'd washed the sheets this morning, along with his clothing. He'd been mad as a bear when he'd noticed that she'd grabbed them from the hook on the wall, insisting it was wasteful to wash them before the job was finished.

But the deed had already been done, praise heaven. Jack Wright would learn he hadn't married a weak-kneed woman, no matter how much wool he thought he'd pulled over her eyes.

"Ya hear me?" Stinky shouted. "Ten or fifteen of 'em."

"That ain't much," Jack mumbled.

"S'bout fifty, all t'gether," Stinky countered.

Fifty what? She thought they'd been working all day. Julia put her hand to her nose and focused on their conversation.

"Ought to bring good money." The groggy man in the corner mumbled the question then keeled over.

"They beaver?" Jack asked.

Beaver? Good heavens, they'd been stealing furs. From his uncle! Stealing and selling watered-down whiskey. Oh, she'd married a winner, all right.

"Uh huh."

"Where're they?"

"The shed. Gimme that jug."

But Jack had passed out. Stinky reached for the whiskey and collapsed atop Jack, his mouth gaping open.

Julia shook her head and rose from the table. She pushed up the single window as far as it would go and strode to the door. She threw it open and inhaled the clean air. Evening had settled, and it was cooling. She propped the door open and prayed for a cross breeze. Not that she intended to stay. She'd spend tonight at her sister's house.

But first, she needed to get those beaver pelts back to Uncle's store.

She laid down ground rules the following day, while nursing Jack's scrapes and bruises. Lorenza had advised her it was better done sooner than later, and this time she'd listen to her sister's wisdom.

When they'd discovered the missing pelts, there'd been a whopper of a fistfight among the three men, each one sure the other two had stolen the furs away. None had been able to remember a thing about the night before, which Julia counted a blessing.

"Ow!" Jack flinched as she dabbed at the bloody knot on his head.

"Sit still and be quiet." She eased the pressure of her touch. "I know it hurts, but it's your own fault."

"My fault?"

Julia exhaled, shaking her head. "You brought them here." She wiped the last trace of blood from his hair and dropped the cloth into a bucket of cold water to soak.

"Thought I could trust them," Jack mumbled.

Trust a crook? *Oh, Jack.*

She returned to the table and sat down across from him. "Do you have any idea how badly you stink? I don't know how you lived when you were single, but you're married now, and I share this cabin with you. Don't you ever come in here smelling like that again."

"Aw, Julia." He smiled at her, flashing his dimples—that same beguiling expression that had caught her in the first place.

Her heart stuttered.

She silenced it and concentrated on the task at hand. "You bathed when you were courting me, and you'll bathe now or I'll leave you. I won't live with a man who smells." She said the words firmly, praying he wouldn't call her bluff. She'd vowed to live in sickness and in health, and the Lord likely lumped smelliness into the same bucket.

"You won't." He cast his deep-brown eyes on her.

"Why would you think that I wouldn't? You stink."

"I guess I am a little ripe."

Julia snorted. "You smell like you're rotting."

"Okay, okay."

She leaned forward, vowing to get him a bath as soon as possible. But first, there were things that needed saying. She caught his gaze and chose her words with care. "You are not the same man who courted me. I've been swindled, and I don't like it. Not one bit."

"It was a bad week."

"It's a side of you I don't like. Where did the gentleman go? The one who swept me off my feet?"

"He's still here."

"I haven't seen him since the wedding. All the tenderness, the gentle loving stopped. You started drinking and turned mean and surly without an ounce of consideration for me."

"Whiskey does that to me."

"Then I expect you to stop drinking whiskey."

"Stop drinking? Good lord, Julia. That ain't right."

She drew back, considering. He had a point . . . sainthood wasn't necessary. "At the very least, I expect you to control it." Still, she wanted no more of what happened this week. "I didn't agree to marry a drunk. I agreed to marry an attentive, kind, responsible man. This week, that man disappeared."

"I'm sorry. I'll do better."

"I don't want those men here again." She punctuated the words so he would understand it was not negotiable.

"I'm done with them. Never want to see the thieves again."

"What you did with them, stealing those furs, can't happen

again. Or watering down whiskey to make a profit."

His eyes widened. "You heard all that?"

"Couldn't much help it the way you were all blathering. You're lucky half the town didn't hear."

He grinned, looking abashed. "I got caught up in their plans."

"Plans like that aren't right, Jack. I won't abide dishonesty."

"I—"

She continued, knowing she had to say the words. "I married you with the belief that you were a man of integrity. If you're not that man, you have bound me under false pretenses."

"Well, we're married now." He said the words, swallowed, a bit of shock on his face. But he offered no modifier, and the statement stood like a barricade.

Oh lord. She'd hoped not to have to spell it out completely.

She gathered her courage. "I'll divorce you if you force me."

"You can't do that."

She stared at him, knowing she couldn't back down from the bluff now. She had to make him believe she could and would.

"Then you had best return to being the man you were. The one I've seen this past week is not the one I agreed to marry. That makes our marriage a false contract and contestable. You will not push me, Jack, or we are done."

La Crosse, Wisconsin
Two years later, 1858

Julia stood with her hands deep in dishwater. Her oldest sister, Lorenza, sat in a rocking chair nursing her baby girl while Lorenza's other children played on the floor with Julia's little Dora. The men had escaped to the peace and quiet of Lorenza's front porch.

She'd not visited with her sister enough these past two years and was glad Lorenza had seen fit to set things right between them. It was well past time they repaired their relationship.

Life since marrying Jack had been an up and down journey. Lorenza and Jack butted heads often, with Lorenza seeing right through all Jack's blustering and Jack resenting her interference. Eventually, Julia had found it easier to keep distant and focus on keeping Jack out of trouble.

"I'm not used to others doing my work for me," Lorenza said.

"Hush. You tend to the baby and let me worry about the chores. It was enough that you cooked supper for us." She'd do dishes all day if it meant a visit with Lorenza.

"It's good to have you here, finally."

"With us both having children, it's hard." Julia knew she was prevaricating, but it was easier to hedge than talk about the obvious.

Lorenza shook her head and raised the baby to burp her. "It's not so hard, and you know it. You hide."

Julia looked away. "I do no such thing."

"You do, too."

Lorenza was right—always was, it seemed.

Julia blew out a breath. They'd best talk about it and get it done with. "It's easier," she said.

"I don't like that man of yours, but I love you to death. You are my little sister, and I hate that we don't talk like we used to."

Nostalgia wrung Julia's heart. Lorenza had been so helpful with advice when she'd first wed Jack. Now, they'd lost so much of that closeness. Growing up wasn't easy. At her feet, Dora whimpered, and she scooped her daughter up, jostling her. "Keeping Jack in line takes all my energy."

"I don't doubt that."

Julia crossed the room and hugged her sister, provoking squawks from both little ones. "I'm glad you asked us over. I've missed you, too, Lorenza."

"Is he treating you all right?" Lorenza whispered the words, as if saying them aloud might make the concern valid.

"We have our ups and downs. But he doesn't hit me, if that's what you mean."

"Does he treat you right?" This time, the question was more forceful.

Julia put Dora back on the floor with her cousins and sat down with them, absently stacking blocks to keep them entertained. "I don't know what you want me to say. He's the same man he's always been. At times, he dotes on me. But there's always another wild plan he gets caught up in. He goes off on a tangent, and we fight. He's never yelled at me or talked bad to me. It's such a constant battle trying to keep him out of trouble. He always wants to take the easy way to profit rather than the most ethical."

"Do you love him?"

She caught Lorenza's gaze and sighed. "There are times he makes my pulse pound with excitement, when I look at him and melt. He gets out that jaw harp of his and acts the clown with it until I laugh my head off at him. He knows so many things but has no common sense at all." She paused.

"It was a mistake to marry him, but, as long as he treats me with kindness and respect, provides for us, and keeps out of trouble, it doesn't matter much whether there's love between us. We're happy enough. What's more, I'm bound to him."

"He didn't want to come here, did he?"

"You slapped him on the face the last time we visited."

They laughed uneasily. It had been more than a year ago, and they'd done well enough together today, at least.

"He and George seem to get on," Lorenza said.

"He likes George."

They watched the children, both silent.

"Do you think he can come to tolerate me?"

Julia grinned. "As long as you don't hit him again." *And you don't tell him what to do.*

"How is he with Dora?"

"He's good with her. I don't have any complaints there. And he provides well." What was Lorenza up to?

"He's staying out of trouble?"

"For the most part. His uncle watches him like a hawk at the store. From time to time, he comes up with an idea that's a little on the shady side, and we have words."

"And that works?"

"I told him I would divorce him if he didn't live by my rules. I remind him, and he falls back in line."

Lorenza sucked in a breath. "Would you? Divorce him?"

"I don't think there would be true legal grounds, not for a woman. Besides, I made vows. Before God, for better or worse. I won't break them."

"But he doesn't know that?"

"I think he believes I'd make true on the threat. It always works. He forgets about his schemes, and life becomes normal for a while. Until the next time."

It wasn't the easiest way to make a marriage, but it worked. Jack stayed out of trouble, the family stayed whole, and she was able to keep her own reputation intact.

"Do you think there would be less temptation if he started fresh, in a less populated area where there's not so much to lead him astray?"

"Lorenza Lamb, what are you getting at? Just spit it out."

"George brought home a handbill about the Dakota Land Company. They've had posters up all over advertising they've started a couple towns in the western part of Minnesota near Lake Shetek. We've been talking about going."

Julia stood, already at a loss. "Oh, Lorenza, so far?"

"George loves trapping, and there's land there for the grabbing."

"There's trapping in Wisconsin. Why in the world would he want to traipse into the far reaches? Especially with a family in tow!"

"It's a solid idea, Julia. The fur is playing out here; farmland has been grabbed up. Moving west makes sense, to both of us. I've never shied away from adventure."

So, they'd knit their relationship only to say good-bye. "You've already decided."

"We have."

Julia swallowed. How would she survive without her big sister there to talk her through things? Heavens, Lorenza was her confidant, her strength, the only one she could talk to about Jack.

"What will I do without you?"

"George and I have talked . . ." Lorenza drew a breath. "We'd like you and Jack to come with us."

★ ★ ★ ★ ★

Part Two: Gathering

★ ★ ★ ★ ★

Chapter Nine

Laura

Beaver, Minnesota

The same year, spring 1858

Our future washed down Beaver Creek along with the quagmire that had once been a hillside. The mill broke apart, walls and flooring rushing away with the muddy floodwaters. Helpless in the pouring torrent, I watched the turbulent crest erode and destroy one more part of my life. We would have to wait until the water subsided to determine whether the heavy mill works had survived at the bottom of the creek.

Would we chase our dreams forever without being quite able to grasp them?

I prayed the loan against the mill had been denied, and we wouldn't have to pay for the useless devastation, but I doubted we'd be so lucky. We would have a loan to pay back as well as a new mill to construct. My head ached as I calculated the profits we would need to achieve at the store in order to accomplish so much. Once again, a river had wreaked havoc with our lives.

How I hated that roiling flux. Memories of the Mississippi and the horrid deaths of my little girls flowed within those cursed waters. I shut my eyes against the images and tried to take solace in that my three other children were all safe at home and that our only loss was the mill.

William returned a few days later. Along with the building

materials to expand the store.

We settled the children into bed early. Though we hated facing our options, we needed to determine our course. He sat on the small horsehair-stuffed settee he'd purchased last year—an attempt to win me over when he announced he'd been elected to the statehood convention.

I wished his diverted attention were still my only worry.

"I think we should rebuild the mill instead of expanding the store," he said.

I'd expected him to take that tack but wasn't sure it was the best choice. I perched next to him, determined to express my opinion in a quiet, non-confrontational manner, as I'd done each time I'd needed him to hear my words. I'd learned with that first stove discussion that I had to take care lest he become defensive and stop listening to what I had to say.

"We make more money from the store. It makes more sense to expand the mercantile." I'd carefully summed the returns from each and was prepared to show him the account books, if needed.

"The Malindys are going west. We'd own the entire mill ourselves." Despite the announcement, he looked less pleased about being the sole owner than I would have expected. Worry lines etched his face.

"That means the entire rebuilding cost would be ours."

"So would the profits."

"And who's going to operate it?" I asked. "In the past year, you've been so involved with politics, you've barely been at the mill. You said you intended to run for statehouse."

"I'll have to find a new partner." His voice held little enthusiasm, and I ached for him. Much as I hated it when he had unrealistic dreams, I did not want him to give up entirely.

I chose my words with care, so that I didn't defeat him. "Taking on a partner would eliminate the potential profit. Maybe the mill should wait a few years, until we are back on solid financial footing."

He slumped in the chair. "I guess I should take the building materials back to Winona, return the money to the bank, and get the mortgage released. We wouldn't be able to expand the store, but at least we'd have no debt."

Poor William. I knew what it was like to let loose of one's desire.

"That would be an option." The best, I thought, but I was uncomfortable with his dismay. This was not my usually assertive husband, and it gave me pause. "Or we add on as we planned and double the size of the store."

We would be stretched tightly, but Beaver's residents would bring us steady profit if they were able to purchase more goods locally. With a careful watch on our expenditures, we might be able to rebuild the mill sooner this way.

"Or we could go west." He dropped the suggestion so softly that it failed to register at first. "We can sell the farm property and the store, and take the recovered mill works with us."

My dander rose. "Move? Again?"

What new fantasy had he seized upon that he would disrupt our lives once more? That he would take away *my* dreams? We were part and parcel of this town, leading citizens, with a host of friends and the respect of those who arrived each month to expand the community. He had finally given me what he had promised me more than a decade past and now he wanted to take it away? I bit my tongue, aghast.

"I could go back to farming, partner in milling."

"We have land here. We have lives here. The lives we always dreamed about. How can you possibly think of taking us away from this?"

"Minnesota is being settled faster than ever. There were a lot of new precincts out west that registered during the statehood vote. And that was nearly a year ago. Those towns have been growing ever since."

How could he even ask this of me? I shook my head. "I can't."

We sat there, silent. I was baffled, unable to understand why he wanted to leave here. We'd need to recover financially, yes, but we had everything else we'd envisioned.

"I promise we'll take the stove this time, and everything else you deem necessary."

His offer, so sincere, almost broke my heart. That he would very nearly beg this of me confused me. My thoughts churned trying to fathom his reasons.

"Why, William? We have the means to make a go of things. We may have a few tight years, but we can flourish here."

"Look at this, Laura." He rose and strode to the kitchen area. When he returned, he held Maggie's copy of the *Wabashaw Herald* in his hand.

Lord, why had I not hidden that thing away?

He opened it and pointed to the Dakota Land Company ad. "See . . ."

"What I see is a land company greedy for profit."

"Now, Laura—"

I rose and poked at his chest with my finger. "Don't you dare 'Now, Laura' me. You can't spend your entire life chasing pipe dreams."

"I'm not chasing a dream this time."

I barely heard his words, so intent was I on arguing. "You can't just follow whims, taking us hither and whither. Not when it involves me and our children. It's reckless."

My hand drifted to my again-growing abdomen.

"I won't uproot us and take us there sight unseen. I can scout, find the perfect town, good land."

"I've experienced your scouting results already. Each time, you have settled us where there is fine farmland. But you also like places with fast running rivers that have stolen our children and our livelihood. I cannot abide that happening again. I will die myself if we lose another child."

He caught my hand, stilled it in his, and embraced me.

"I'm scared, Laura." His voice broke as he uttered the words.

"Oh, Husband." This was not a man who expressed trepidation. I wrapped my arms around him, held him.

"I thought this would be the place for us, but the way those hillsides slid away frightens me. Folks in Winona said the town should never have been built here, that the river rages often and consumes the entire valley. I don't want to expand the store only to lose that, too, if the creek floods the town. I never imagined that happening. I avoided the Mississippi, but I didn't think about possible flooding here. I made a mistake in settling us in this place."

He grew quiet. "I don't want to lose another child, either."

My throat tightened. "I don't know that I would be able to do that. Not again."

"It's the ravines. They're too narrow. People in Winona said both the Whitewater and the Beaver flood often. They're such small waterways that I assumed there was no threat. In truth, there's nowhere for the water to go but up."

We held each other as it dawned on me that he was right. Those hillsides had crumbled like they were made of cake batter. A little more rain, and the water would have crested the banks and poured into town. And it hadn't been unusually wet for spring, just a violent, prolonged rain. I shivered.

There truly was danger here, and that it had William worried was significant.

"Where would we go?" I finally asked.

"I don't know yet." He withdrew, his gaze catching mine. "I'll pay back the loan immediately, salvage the mill works, and try to find out what's available out West. I can look at the Dakota

Land Company offerings, visit the towns. I'll find us a place where we won't need to worry about the fickleness of a strong river. I'll spend whatever time we need to find it and avoid hills and ravines that collect water in heavy rains. I can find us a place where it's flat and there are no threats."

I agreed, even as I wondered if there really was such a place.

Lavina
Olmstead County, Minnesota
Summer 1858

I return to household duties and my living children the day after we bury William Merton. Though grief still chokes me, I have to concentrate on the four who remain. It's the way of life.

As summer advances and life returns to normal, Tommy and Sophia Ireland invite us to picnic with them, and we gather, the children running amok, our dog loping with them. It's good to return to normal life, and I'm content in Olmstead County. It feels like home, and I'm glad our family is taking root here.

"Who's up for a stroll?" Tommy asks. It's his usual activity after a meal, and we've come to anticipate the brisk walks. Tommy Ireland has never "strolled" in his entire life.

Sophia laughs at him. "Shall we walk through the woods? It would be cool there."

I look toward the copse of trees lining the small creek where the children are playing hide and seek. My head perspires beneath my hair, piled as it is atop my head like a fur hat. Walking in the shade would be a welcome respite.

"I've a mind to check on the corn," Tommy says.

I eye the trees again and let the desire go.

Tommy marches off, a ball of energy. Sophia, John, and I follow as best we can. Though in his mid-forties, Tommy remains more spry than men half his age. He leads us with a fast pace.

Thank heavens I'm not wearing a corset, or I would faint in my effort to keep up.

Ahead, the corn is already past knee high, a good sign. If we get no hail, if we have no drought, if we do not receive too much rain, the yield will be good. The green stalks stretch for acres. Beyond lie grain fields.

"We managed to get all the land into production." Sophia beams at her husband.

John looks at me. Like us, the Irelands claimed the largest parcels available by the time we got there. Tommy, able to work twice as hard as anyone else, cleared his quickly. We still labor to break ours.

"All forty acres?" John asks. There is a flash of envy in his eyes, but it is soon gone. Even John cannot keep up with Tommy, and there is no sense begrudging his vigor.

"All except the home site and the little batch of trees." Tommy grins at her. He steps among the stalks, peeling away a bit of one husk to check the progress of the ear, and smiles.

"It's good soil," John says. He pokes at the dirt with his boot. "Produces well, like ours."

Tommy glances at him. "Trouble is, it's like Illinois all over again."

Sophia looks at me and rolls her eyes. This, too, is typical Tommy.

"I sense it, too," John says.

Familiar dread fills me at this. *Not again.* I wonder if my husband will ever be content where he is.

"But the land is good," I insist. "It will be years before it's tired and worn. That's why we left Illinois."

Tommy returns to us, his expression unreadable. "That's true. The land here is more fertile. The problem is that we were only able to preempt forty acres. When we came, we anticipated whole sections being available to us. We got here too late."

I looked from him to John, confused.

"What Tommy's saying is that forty acres is not going to be enough," John says.

"But we're doing well." Sophia's voice holds a note of panic, and I know we now both understand this is more than our men grumbling. They are serious. Lunch leaps in my stomach.

Tommy shrugs. "We are surviving. Olmstead County has filled in. With so much land in production, there will be a surplus of crops. Prices will go down, our profits along with them."

"Can't we buy more land?" I take up the cause in earnest and hear the plea in my voice.

"Who will sell it to us? It's like Tommy said. We're boxed in, like Illinois."

"But if we sold our land, others would pay well for it," Tommy says. "We can head farther west, claim more land. But we need to do it before others do or we'll face the same situation all over again."

"Where are you thinking?" Sophia's mouth gapes.

"We saw an ad in the paper. The Dakota Land Company is settling in the western part of the state and beyond, in Dakota Territory."

Now it's my turn to gawk. We? They have already discussed this. The two of them have hashed it out already, and, once again, Sophia and I are the last to know. Though I understand the reasoning, anger stirs.

"They've platted towns in Murray County," Tommy says. "And the company is offering one hundred sixty acres to those who help settle the surrounding area."

"Where's that, now?" she says angrily.

"Western Minnesota, out near Dakota Territory. According to last year's census, there's a community taken hold there." John chimes in like they are a team of tinkers trying to sell their wares.

"So, you're thinking to just pack us up and go?" Sophia's voice already holds resignation.

I look to John. We are partners, and I know he awaits my opinion. Olmstead County has become home, but the points the men raise are valid. Forty acres is enough to support a family but provides little profit to set aside for lean years. That lack of cushion could bring ruin during drought or overly wet years. Even one good hailstorm could wipe a family out.

Still, I'm uncomfortable with the notion of moving to such unsettled areas. An undercurrent of fear has taken the place of my anger. I don't know how wild that part of the state remains.

"I think we need to learn more before we make this decision," I say.

"I think we have time yet," Tommy says, "but we do need to start thinking about it, looking into what's out there."

"While we don't need to be in a hurry, we do need to make plans, before we lose our chance," John adds.

Tommy nods. "We could travel out there once harvest is in, take a look, find the right place."

"After that, we can plan the timing." John holds my gaze, waiting for me to accede.

I look to him, know the men are right. Leasing land, farming small plots, is not part of what we envisioned in our dreams. Independence, true security, still eludes us. I dig into my worry, seeking the cause of my unsettled alarm and remember news accounts of Indian attacks from last year. If we can find our dream, grasp it without putting the family in danger, I will go.

"There were Indian attacks on the frontier. I do not want to settle anywhere near Spirit Lake."

"That was in Iowa. This area is miles from there. We'll find a safe settlement. I can't promise there will be no Indians, but we will make sure any in the area have a reputation of being peaceful."

Almena
La Crosse, Wisconsin
Summer 1858

In the springhouse, Almena covered the milk she'd left to cool and stood. Her back twinged, and she winced. Not even five months into the process, and, already, she couldn't wait for this baby to be born. Hand at her back, she padded to the house and into the small kitchen.

Phin sat at the table, the advertisement Almena had given him in hand. He picked up his spectacles and adjusted the oil lamp until the glow brightened. He peered at the ad.

"It's a good opportunity," she told him. "The land company is offering quarter sections. Do you think we're ready?" She sat across from him and rubbed a dab of homemade hand cream into her callous.

"We've got a good nest egg, between my four years of clerking and your three of selling to my employers."

She grinned. He'd risked his job, back in Ohio, introducing her goods little by little, until customers demanded more and more of them. Once they replaced the lost cows, she'd done well here, too. They'd built their wealth, saving everything they could. He hated clerking, but it was a means to his land-ownership dream.

"The Dakota Land Company is on the frontier, Almena. Are you sure you want to live in the middle of nowhere?"

"The article says they have several settlements. This one is in Murray County, Minnesota. Farther west, yes, but not in the territories. There's a community there already, Cornwell City. The '57 census recorded ninety-two residents. There's a blacksmith, millwrights, a grocer, even a physician. It must be way past a hundred by now."

"But it's still miles away from settled cities."

"But the land! We can pre-empt on one hundred sixty acres of the company land, sign a sales contract, and pay on installments. That'd leave our money for improvements and stock."

"I agree. But is it a safe place to raise a family?"

A prickle of fear needled her. It *would* be isolated.

"I think we need to take care," he said. "Minnesota's only recently become a state. I expect the unsettled areas are still pretty wild."

But the opportunity . . . they had to look at the opportunity. *Surely people wouldn't settle there if it wasn't safe.* She opened her mouth to tell Phin that but paused. He was right—they didn't know about the potential dangers.

"You're right."

"So are you. It's a chance to grab what we want from life." He removed his pocket watch. Opening it, he read the inscription aloud, "Time to follow our dreams."

"It's a big step. We don't have to rush, Phin. There will be other prospects."

"I want us to be safe, but I also want us to provide a good life for our family." He eyed her growing midsection. "Does it say if there's a school? I want our children to be educated."

"I don't know. I guess if there were twenty-three children listed on the census, there should be one, or will be soon."

"Indians?"

Almena drew a sharp breath. *I didn't think about Indians!*

"The Chippewa around here are peaceful, but I don't know a thing about the tribes out West. Sioux? Aren't they more warlike?"

Almena's shoulders slumped. "I think so. If I recall, there have been reservations for a number of years."

"Well, that would make a difference. If they're on reservations, there shouldn't be problems for folks in settled towns. You said there was a doctor in Cornwell City? A hundred people? It sounds no different than La Crosse but for the size. If you're not worried—"

"I'm a pregnant woman. I worry about everything." She covered Phin's hand with hers. "You're tired of working for other people—you come home frustrated. You're not a shopkeeper, Phin; you never wanted to be one. It's time to start on our dream. I looked at a map . . . there's a large lake northeast of the town. We could settle up that direction. The soil ought to be good and the water table high enough to supply a well."

"It sounds perfect. Too perfect."

"Let's do this: let's wait until summer to decide, after the baby is born. We can gather our facts. Find out if anyone has been out that direction and ask them about it."

"A good idea." He grasped her fingers. "I think Bill Jones, at the store, lived near Mankato for a while. Maybe he can offer up more details." Phin's chair scraped across the floorboards. He stepped behind her and circled her with his arms, leaning his head atop hers. "That should give us what we need to make a solid decision."

She pondered the dangers he'd mentioned, the isolation, the unknowns. They'd twisted into a heavy knot that now lay in her stomach, souring her original enthusiasm.

Christina
Lake Shetek, Minnesota
Summer 1858

Andreas and I, we move to the lake as soon as possible, in the same week the Myers also come. We do not want to be alone on the prairie so close to where Renicker was killed. The lake is farther from that place, and there will be others nearby. This will be safer, especially since the Indians are friends with Aaron Myers.

We choose a fine spot for our cabin. It is a small parcel of land that sits between the big lake, Shetek, and a smaller lake that is called Bloody. Parmlee tells us the willow roots surface every few years and turn bright red, which makes the water look like blood. It is not such a good name, I think, but it was not mine to choose. Our cabin is south of it, in a grove among many trees. I will ask Andreas to buy lilac seedlings in New Ulm. These I will plant by the door.

I have never watched a cabin being built before. It is not so easy. Andreas sweats in the summer heat. Even with his chest bare, the sweat runs from his dark hair. I regret he must work so hard, but I do not mind so much seeing his muscles ripple.

"Christina?" he calls.

"*Ja?* What is it?"

"Will you go to Myers now?"

Andreas has all the logs ready. We have chopped off the branches and made chinks where the logs will fit together, working hard for many days. Now, it is time to lift the logs. Myers will come to help, and Andreas will do the same for him.

I do not take my bonnet. It is too hot, and I have been working hard with my husband to prepare. Our house will be seventeen by thirteen feet, big enough for our bed, a table and chairs, and a cabinet or two. That is all we need. We will add another room later. With hard work, Andreas and Myers should raise the walls today.

I tidy my braid and set off to the north. Myers has a spot at the end of a small lake called Fremont that connects into Shetek. It is about two miles from us. I take the shortcut between Lake Shetek and Bloody Lake that Andreas told me about.

As I leave our cabin site, the land becomes mushy, and I am glad I am wearing my old boots. The ground squishes beneath me, and I lift my skirts so they will not get wet. Around me, birds chatter, some trilling complicated songs, others scolding in sharp tones. Pelicans lift from the water and leave ripples that cast sunlit rings. The smell of fish fills the air as I pass the remains of some animal's meal. There is life here, more than on the bare prairie around the Walnut Grove, and I am glad.

I leave the swampy stretch of land and continue around Fremont Lake, waving as I near the Myerses' home site. There, Myers and his wife are preparing their logs. Their older children help while the youngsters play in the grass.

"Mrs. Koch!" Mrs. Myers rushes to me and stops, unsure. We are strangers still.

I take her hands in mine. "You must call me Christina. We are neighbors now." The Smiths are at the south end of Lake Shetek, four miles from us with the bachelor Parmlee half-way between, and so I am the Myerses' closest neighbor. We should not be formal.

"And you can call us Mary and Aaron," she says.

"Are you ready?" Aaron asks. Andreas has already warned him that today will be the day.

"*Ja,*" I tell him and see that his walls will soon be ready to raise, too.

Aaron has a yoke of oxen, and he makes them ready as I chat with Mary. The oxen will ease the work, so that the men do not have to lift all the weight of the logs.

"I'm so glad we've moved from Saratoga. The prospect of living there all alone was dreadful," Mary says.

"*Ja.* I have been lonely at the Walnut Grove. I think the men do not understand." I think about how Mary and I will become friends and visit. I will put up my braid, and we will call on each other like the women did in New Ulm.

"Men understand very little about women, sometimes." Mary leans close and lowers her voice. "I birthed Fred with only Aaron there. He's a good doctor, but I missed having a woman with me."

For a moment, I do not know what to say. I cannot imagine such a thing as having a baby without another woman there. I think about the rest of her words. "Aaron is a doctor?"

This will be a good thing, to have a doctor.

Mary raises her hands and makes a motion as if to shoo the words away. "Not a real one. But he has a gift with herbs and healing."

"That is good to know, if we have need."

"Do you have family, Christina?"

A pang of sadness swarms me. "I came to *Amerika* from Germany with them, but only my brother came West. He did not like it and went back to the others."

"You stayed alone?" She sounded surprised, and I know I must explain.

"I met Andreas and was married."

"Christina?" Aaron calls out.

I turn and see he has the team ready. I say my good-byes to Mary, and we depart in his wagon, filled with rope and tools he says will ease the work. At Bloody Lake, he veers east, to take the oxen around the inlet. It will be longer, but he says the oxen will drive easier that way. We cover the four miles quickly.

Andreas is waiting for us.

But, with him are three other men. They are dressed in wool trousers tucked into leather leggings. Long dark hair, tamed by leather bands, flows down their backs.

Indians.

Julia
St. Peter, Minnesota
Fall 1858

"So, what do you think?"

Julia stared at Jack. Had she heard him right? What did *she* think? It was more than a little late to ask, given the way he'd just announced his new hare-brained idea. Good lord, he was about to destroy the strategy she and Lorenza had so carefully crafted to keep him out of trouble.

He was supposed to fur trap with George, clear land in the middle of nowhere, and keep his nose clean!

"You've decided already, that's what I think." She'd folded up the newspaper she'd laid in her lap when he started talking.

Jack paced the shabby hotel room, his pent-up energy ready to burst. "Aw, Julia, you know it's a good plan."

A good plan? Was he crazy? And where ever had he come up with such an idea? She forced herself to stay calm and concentrate on the why of it and not the how.

"What in heaven's name makes you think you would be a good Indian trader? I thought we were going to farm."

Jack took the rickety chair on the opposite side of the tiny side table. It creaked as it absorbed his weight. He had insisted on the "best" room in the establishment, and, if this was it, Julia shuddered to think what the other rooms were like. They should have picked a better place.

"I'll farm, too," he said.

She suspected he meant what he said. Still, if she knew anything, it was that Jack was easily led astray. She let out a heavy breath. "We planned this all out, before we left Wisconsin."

"Plans can change."

The way his eyes lit told her she hadn't much chance of changing his mind, but she'd do her best. Letting Jack run amok was best avoided when at all possible.

She crossed her arms and settled against the back of the chair. This might take a while. "Where did you come up with this idea, anyway?"

"The other day, when George and I were in the saloon."

Well, that made things a lot clearer. The saloon, Jack, and whiskey—that explained most of it.

"George thinks it's a good idea."

"Oh, he does, does he?" Wouldn't Lorenza be delighted to hear that? "When did you and George end up on the same side of things?"

"We had a few drinks." Jack had the good grace to look sheepish, at least. "George doesn't want to farm, either, you know."

She leaned forward, elbows on the arms of the chair. "Really?"

Jack shrugged, his enthusiasm dampening the way it usually did once he caught on that she wasn't buying what he was selling. "He's a trapper at heart. Always has been."

Julia suspected that much was true. But she also knew George Lamb was a responsible man who recognized what was what. "And now he has a family," she said. "George knows trapping won't support them. He said as much to Lorenza. Even Minnesota will get trapped out before long."

"But if we work the land together, it'll be less farming for both of us. Trapping and trading will supplement our income and decrease the risk if we have a bad crop year."

Heaven help her, he had a point. Still, this was Jack, and she didn't see the scheme working. "You've worked in a mercantile. That's not the same thing as being a trader."

"Uncle traded for furs all the time."

"Your uncle did, not you."

"Yeah, but I know their worth." He stood and walked to her, crouching in front of her. "And you know Indians."

Her mother had descended from a long line of trappers, many of whom had intermarried with Iroquois and the Chippewa.

Probably with others she didn't even know about. "Just because my uncle has an Ojibwa wife doesn't mean I know anything about the Dakota. It's a different tribe that lives out here."

"You pick up languages easy enough. You can do the same with the Sioux."

Julia sighed. "They prefer to be called Dakota. Sioux is a white man's word." In fact, the Dakota defined themselves by their bands, but she didn't want to try to explain all that to Jack. He'd never understand, and she wasn't sure she even had a firm grasp on the differences.

"See! You already have insight." He jumped up and paced again. "Think about it: with George spreading the word that we'll buy their furs, why wouldn't they sell to us? We'd be right there, with trade goods on hand to pay them. With you to help me communicate, it will be simple to do this in addition to the farming. Hell, they won't be there much of the time."

"Are you sure it's wise to create reasons to attract the Dakota to the settlement?" She'd heard stories. The Dakota had not adjusted well to the recent infusion of whites. Farmers were not trappers. They treated the Indians differently.

"They'll be attracted anyway. That's human nature. Curiosity, food, and things they need. We might as well take advantage of it and have goods for them. Otherwise, they'll just steal what they want."

"Jack!" She rose. "That's hardly fair. In their world, people share with those in need, no questions asked. Hospitality is a given. They don't regard it as stealing."

"So, are the customs the same across tribes?"

She shifted, unsure how to answer. "Some."

"We'll do fine."

She sighed. "I'll think about it. For now, let's stick with the original plan, pick out land, and get settled. We can decide later on the trading idea."

"All right." Jack headed for the door.

"There is one other thing," Julia said.

He turned. "Now what?"

She'd not wanted to tell him this way, but it might have bearing on the issue. Besides, it was time, and he certainly hadn't been observant enough to figure it out on his own. "I'm expecting."

"We're having another baby?" His voice grew quiet with the slightest trace of awe.

"I think it will be March or so."

"That's wonderful!" He drew her into his arms and kissed her on the mouth. "Damn!"

"Jack . . . I don't want to go until the baby is born. I want to stay where there's a doctor."

He drew back, piecing it together. "But—"

"I am not having this child out in the middle of nowhere. I agreed to settle out there, despite learning the advertised towns don't exist but I am *not* having this baby there."

"We can't stay here all this time. Good heavens, it would cost a fortune."

Even in this dump. "George has relatives in Mankato. We can stay with them."

"That will be one whole trapping season we miss."

"Then we will just need to miss it."

"But Charley Wambau and Bill Clark said—"

"Who?" Inexplicable unease rippled up and down her spine. Nothing good ever came from Jack quoting people he'd recently met. Generally, it boded ill.

"Wambau and Clark. I met them the other night, after George left the saloon. They had this great idea. Did you know there's hardly anywhere out there that sells whiskey?"

Oh, Jack, no!

Of all the things she didn't need right now! Easy money

always caught Jack's attention, usually leading him in the wrong direction. And whiskey and Indian trading was definitely the wrong direction. If this Wambau and Clark were introducing temptations like that, she needed to get Jack away from them as soon as possible.

"How about you and Lorenza and George head out to Shetek ahead of me?" she said, grasping at the first solution that came to mind.

His eyes brightened with enthusiasm. "That might work. You'll think about the trading idea?"

"I'll think about it. You and George go ahead and make plans to travel. I'll talk to Lorenza about me staying in Mankato until spring."

"I love you, Julia."

"And, Jack?"

"Yeah?"

"No whiskey, no Wambau, and no Clark. No matter what I decide on the trading."

Chapter Ten

Lavina
Olmstead County, Minnesota
March 1859

The harvest is a good one, giving pause to the idea that this land will not support us. But I know all years will not be so bountiful and accept we don't have enough land. The birth of any more children will strain our resources. The men are right; the future lies to the west.

We've wintered well, but it will soon be time to plant, and a decision must be made. I don't relish it, for the thought of living in such a wild place is unnerving, no matter how necessary it might be. I hold on to the knowledge that this town, Cornwell City, holds over a hundred souls and that we will be safe among such a number.

I clear the supper dishes and wash them as Merton and Frank dry, both of them whistling as John so often does. Merton's pitch is off key; Frank's, as true as his father. The cat folds back its ears at the lack of harmony and slinks outdoors as the boys get louder and seek to outdo one another in volume.

The time has come to make firm plans and set a date for our departure. We've eaten early, and the Irelands will be here soon. Poor tabby will not be pleased about relocating, and I wonder if we would be better to leave her here with whomever buys the property.

I'm tucking stray pieces of hair back into my bun when the Irelands arrive with their brood. John welcomes them as Merton and Frank change into their nightclothes. Sophia ushers her girls inside and settles them with my boys in the bedroom. Merton will once again take charge of them. I have been blessed in this child and his remarkable sense of responsibility. He is my bedrock.

The adults arrange our chairs near the fire, for the early spring evenings remain chilly. John stirs the logs, and they pop, the sound sharp in the quiet of the room. He tosses an evergreen sprig on the flames, and its scent fills the air.

"We made a good profit last year," my husband says.

"Us, too, but not all years will be that way."

"I don't want us to jump the gun."

"But, if we wait too long, the best land will be taken there, too. I'm tired of arriving too late. I think we need to get there soon," Tommy replies to him.

Sophia and I remain quiet, listening to their back-and-forth.

"Have you heard any more about Cornwell City? How many are there now? If we can gauge how fast it's growing, we can better judge whether we need to get there this year."

"I haven't. But it must be growing. The latest Dakota Land Company ads say the company-owned land around the town is going fast, and that worries me. We'll need to buy from the company if we want to take advantage of the time payments."

"Lavina, get that paper, will you?" John says. "The one we got yesterday. Let's check to see if there's any news on it."

I rise and retrieve the newspaper I had tucked away until we had time to read it in detail. "The front page is a story about election fraud. You'll likely need to page through it." I hand it to John, check on the children, and return to my chair next to Sophia.

John pages through, refolds the paper. "Nothing."

He hands the paper to Sophia. She takes it to the kitchen table, pausing as something catches her eye.

"I think we need to head out there in April or May," Tommy says. "If we arrive early, we'll have time to get gardens in and cut a couple crops of wild hay to support livestock through the winter. The first year will be tight, but that would get us through until we can break more land."

"We'd need to put in a big garden if we're going to rely on its produce all winter." John's lips move as he calculates in his head. "April might be best, given we'll have to break ground."

"April?" I say. I'd not thought we would leave that soon. I fight to hold my argument, knowing it must be. "That gives us only a few weeks to pack."

John puts his hand on mine. "If we're not putting in crops here, Tommy and I can help you."

"We'll sell the livestock before we go, buy new once we get near, maybe Mankato or New Ulm. That'll make travel faster."

"Tommy . . . look at this." Sophia rushes over and hands him the paper. "The article on the election."

"I'll read it later."

"You'd best read it now." Her voice is stern.

Tommy blows out an exasperated breath and takes the paper. "What? Fake precincts in an election two years ago?"

"You didn't read it all." She points to a section in the middle of the page. "Oasis Precinct is among them. It doesn't exist. Never did."

"What's that got to do with anything?"

"It's in Murray County, where we're going. For Pete's sake, read the article, will you?"

Tommy reddens, and I recall John saying he doesn't read well. Whatever is in the article, it has Sophia rattled to the point that she's forgotten it entirely. I take the paper from him and read the section Sophia pointed at. My breath catches. Cornwell

City does not exist?

I read it again to make sure.

"I'm confused. It says Oasis Precinct was never legally formed and that it was mistakenly listed in Murray County instead of Cottonwood County. The next bit is unclear, where it talks about Cornwell City. It claims no one has lived there since the middle of '57. I can't tell if they mean no one has lived in the real Oasis Precinct or in Cornwell City."

"*No one* lives there?" Sophia's skin has gone white. "You said there were two hundred people!"

I sense I'm also pale. "I don't know," I say, "But we'd darn well better find out before we pack up and go there, now hadn't we?"

Julia
Lake Shetek, Minnesota
April 1859

Julia settled baby George on her lap and buttoned her bodice. She cast a glance into the wagon bed, where Dora lay asleep, lulled by the constant rocking. Ahead of them, endless spring prairie stretched.

"It's pretty empty."

Compared to the lush woods of Wisconsin and the Minnesota River valley near St. Peter and Mankato, the land looked barren. Oh, there were hills, endless rises and falls of nothing but prairie grass, already green and growing. She suspected there'd be flowers but saw precious few of them yet.

"You'll love the lake," Jack said. "The sun glints off the surface, all sparkles and colors, and you should hear all the birds."

Whatever it was like, she'd make do. She always did. You couldn't change what life brought, only what you did with it. At least, she and Lorenza would be together. That was the blessing in all of this, one she anticipated beyond measure.

But, still, please let it be as nice as Jack described.

The road was rough, barely worthy of being called a road at all, but at least it was a clear trail. "You said this is a mail route?" she asked Jack.

"Runs from New Ulm to Sioux Falls, in Dakota Territory. Spot, the mail carrier, goes through once a week or so."

"Then we aren't entirely cut off from the world."

Jack laughed. "Not quite."

They topped a rise, and she spied the lake with a scattering of trees to the west. The waters stretched forever. They'd never want for fish, that was for sure.

"That big house, just off the trail—that's ours."

She followed his gesture. A large cabin sat on an open patch of land.

"Two stories?" Julia gaped. "Whatever do we need such a big house for?"

"Second floor's only a half story. Your sister and family are living there for now. Once they get a place of their own, we'll move up and use the first floor mostly for business—it's one big room with a small one we can use for storage. Maybe we can turn it into a full-fledged store."

"Are there enough people out here to support that?" Somehow, she doubted it. She hadn't noted another cabin anywhere.

"I'm hoping for a steady trade with the Dakota, and we'll need space for the trade goods and the furs. Or, maybe we'll fill it up with kids." He smiled at little George. "I sure wouldn't mind a few more boys."

Then maybe you ought to pay a bit more attention to me.

Or not. All the fine loving she'd expected during their courtship had never come to fruition, and she'd long since tired of his all-too-routine ministrations. The babies were blessings, but Jack's baby making she could live without. That, too, was what life had brought.

Even so, she'd not trade the children for anything. She nestled George on her shoulder, burped him, and wiped his curds of spittle with a rag.

"The trail runs right by the place. I thought we might get travelers, once the area starts attracting more folks. Easier for bringing in supplies, too."

She looked up, a bit surprised Jack had thought ahead so much. Maybe there was hope for him as a trader after all.

"Tell me about the settlement," she asked. "There are *some* families here, aren't there?"

"There are a handful of trappers who stay here part time. The Smiths, no children, live about a mile north. The trappers have temporary shacks a mile farther on; one of them, Rhodes, puts up a tepee when he's at the lake. There's the bachelor Parmlee, the Kochs—another couple—and the Myers family. It's about a seven-mile stretch all together."

"Five families." That was pretty sparse. When folks said there was no Cornwell City, they didn't say it was this unsettled. Julia bit her lip. More making do. At least it would keep Jack out of trouble. Nobody to get into trouble *with*.

"Julia!" Lorenza ran from the house, a smile stretching across her pretty face.

Julia fought to keep from leaping from the wagon. "Lorenza!" She leaned forward, waving. "We're here!"

As they neared, Julia noticed her sister's plump belly. She was glad she'd stayed in Mankato to have George. Lorenza better be planning to do the same.

Jack set the brake, and Lorenza rushed forward. "Let me hold that darling little boy."

Julia handed George down to her sister's eager arms and

climbed off the wagon. Jack was already halfway to the house.

Dora roused. "Are we here?" Her tiny voice was still sleepy.

"Yes, pet." Julia bussed her head and lifted her from the wagon.

Once on the ground, Dora wobbled a bit, searching for her land legs. She spied Jack on his way to the house and ran off after him. "Papa, wait for me."

Jack stopped and held out his arms for her, smothering her with kisses when she tumbled into them.

At least, he's good with the children.

Julia scolded herself. Jack was never unkind to them, always tender. He just . . . well, he just hadn't lived up to her expectations.

"The birth went well? Is he a good baby?"

"Yes and most of the time." Julia laughed. It was good to be with Lorenza again. "How's your brood? Growing, it would appear."

Lorenza patted her belly. "That happens."

"You aren't having it here, are you?"

Lorenza shook her head. "When I get close, we'll go to Mankato. If you'll tend the other children."

"I will." They walked, Lorenza veering toward the lake rather than the house. They skirted through the trees toward the bank, where she stopped. Sun glinted off the surface of the water, golden ripples forming as waves undulated. A trio of geese honked and splashed at one another, their noise punctuating the gurgle of the waves.

"It's bigger than I thought it'd be."

Lorenza sat on a log, looking out on the water. "Big enough so every settler here can claim a quarter-section of land, if they're inclined to want that much."

"A hundred sixty acres?" Julia asked, finding her own spot on the log.

"Jack claimed three hundred twenty."

"He what?" Had she heard right? Julia looked at her sister, but Lorenza kept her eyes on the water. "I thought there was a limit."

"There is."

"Then how . . . ?"

Lorenza pointed to a piece of land across the lake. "That peninsula is the abandoned Brown claim. Jack jumped it and filed as his father. The land we're on is filed in Jack's name."

"Oh, good lord." Julia shook her head in disbelief.

"My George isn't too happy with him."

"I imagine not. Jack plays far too loosely with the law." She sighed. "Why in the world would he want that much land, anyway?"

"It's not the land so much as it is *that* land."

Julia looked across the lake again. "What's so special about that peninsula? All the way across the lake, how can he even think it would be practical?"

"It's not. It's isolated and tough to get to."

"What's the point of filing on it?"

Even as she asked the question, worry knotted her stomach. There were few reasons a man would want to own an isolated peninsula of land full of trees. It'd be no good for farming, completely inconvenient, hard to get to . . .

Oh, no! What on earth are you planning, Jack?

"Rumor has it that two brothers use the woods over there to hide stolen horses."

No, no, no. "Is that true?"

"One of the settlers helped them put up hay one year. For their cows, they said. They never did bring any cows, but folks say there've been some nice looking horses there from time to time."

"So, a rumor."

"Yes, but one I thought you'd want to know about, Jack being Jack and all."

Julia watched the waves lap against the shore. They made soft slapping sounds, and the smells of algae and fish drifted through the air. Peaceful . . . except for Jack. She was only fooling herself, dismissing the rumor as simple gossip. Where there was smoke, there was usually fire.

"It didn't take him long, did it?"

"There's nothing to suggest he's involved with them," Lorenza said, "other than claiming the land."

No, but it implied Jack knew about the place. And that meant he was anticipating a way to make money from it, legal or not. Putting the welfare of the family and her own reputation at risk and leaving it up to her to find a way to prevent both before it was too late.

"Do he and George argue?"

"Frequently."

"I worried about that." George was too ethical not to get upset.

"Julia . . ." Lorenza paused. "Has Jack said anything to you about a man named Clark? Or Wambau?"

The knot in her stomach clenched tight. "They're one of the reasons I suggested you all go on ahead. They met in the saloon, and Jack had a suspicious gleam in his eyes when he mentioned them. I thought it best to get him away before they started scheming in earnest. Why?"

"Clark is a thief. They're the sort that would be in league with the Jacques brothers. George is worried they could show up here, hiding loot on the island."

No, there would be no peace here, despite the tranquility of the lake.

"I'll keep an eye on Jack."

"I think you'll need to." Sadness filled her sister's eyes.

"I'm sorry, Lorenza."

"Me, too, sweetie. I'd hoped this would be a new beginning." She offered a wavering smile, drowned away by glistening tears. "You need to know that if Jack brings trouble to us, George and I will not be staying."

Laura
Beaver, Minnesota
May 1859

It's been a year since baby Isabelle (Bell, as William called her) made her appearance, not long after our mill floated away in the turbulent waters of Beaver Creek. The turmoil of those waters remained with me, churning my fears. Within days of Bell's arrival, I became paralyzed with fear.

I was convinced life was conspiring against us. I couldn't stop thinking that those same waters would find a way to claim Bell as the Mississippi had her two sisters. I feared we would be unable to meet our financial obligations and that William would lose everything. But I was also frightened about moving yet again, especially farther west, where I'd heard the Sioux were still wild and untamed. I wanted a life free from all such dangers.

Each day, I became more and more despondent. It was an effort to rise from the bed and nurse Bell, let alone make my way down the stairs to tend the store. I drew my curtains closed against the bright sun and slept long endless hours. My body grew heavier and heavier with the need to sleep. Emma, just four, pleaded with me to rise and care for Bell as well as for toddler Jefferson. Seven-year-old Willie finally laid Bell with me in the bed, opening my nightgown so she could suckle. When I no longer rose to change diapers, it was Willie who went to his father.

My poor William. He didn't know what to do, as plain-spoken

Mrs. Tucker had back in Iowa. We struggled for months. He tended the store, the children, and me, with occasional relief from Maggie, who said I had the "baby blues." But Maggie's own little ones needed her, and she could offer little respite.

At long last, William wrote to Mrs. Tucker and received her response. The next day, he turned me from my bed and sent me out into the blinding sun to pull weeds. The warmth nurtured me, though I found no relief in the physical work. There was no grief, no anger, only an all-encompassing worry. But the children . . . running and laughing and playing without a care in the world . . . that's what finally turned me around. I knew I must hold on for them.

My recovery took nearly an entire year before life returned to normal. William had taken over the store during my illness and claimed to enjoy it. I began to hope we would remain in Beaver after all, without the worry of the mill, and convinced myself the town would never flood.

"Laura?"

"I'm here. In the side yard."

"We have visitors. Can you mind the store for a bit while we handle some business?"

I rose from the garden and brushed the dirt from my work-dress. Visitors, not customers. I set aside my tools and entered the store, giving my eyes time to adjust at the doorway. Two men stood at the counter, men I didn't know.

"Laura, this is Thomas Ireland and John Eastlick. They've come from Olmstead County."

"Good afternoon," I told them and stepped behind the counter. With no one shopping, I picked up a feather duster and busied myself with straightening and dusting goods. William and the two men took seats on the benches I'd asked William to install near the fireplace, a place for the children when I needed to bring them with me. I eyed the men. The one called

Ireland was tall and hale with a full beard and a shock of graying hair. Eastlick was dark, trim. I wondered what they wanted of William.

"Gentlemen, what brings you to Beaver?"

Eastlick drew out a newspaper and handed it to William. "We read this article, about the election fraud."

"It isn't very clear," Ireland said. "Since you're the nearest member of the Constitutional Congress, we're hoping you might be able to shed some light on the matter."

I narrowed my eyes, confused. The congress had dissolved over a year ago, after approval of the state constitution. Curious, I moved to a closer shelf where I could better eavesdrop.

"I was indeed a member of the congress. Honored to have been elected, proud to serve."

I dusted around a display of whitestone dinnerware. I knew how much pride he took in that service, and, though I couldn't see his chest from where I stood, it was likely puffed out like a rooster.

William continued on. "This fraud you're referring to is a matter related to the election itself. The congress certainly wasn't involved in that. I'm sorry, gentlemen, but I had no part in either the election or the fraud. I don't think I can help here."

Ireland raised a finger to stop him. "We're not concerned about who committed the fraud. We have a question about the fake precincts and thought a person like you might know about the places mentioned."

"Well, now, let me take a moment. My wife has been ill, and I haven't kept up with the news."

I stepped to the right and watched William peruse the paper, his face growing paler by the minute.

"My God," he said, his eyes seeking the two men. "I had heard there were issues with voter registration fraud, but I had no idea entire precincts had been created out of thin air."

Eastlick rose and pointed to the article. "It's this paragraph here we're concerned about. We need to know if this means no one resided in Oasis Precinct, which was registered in the wrong county, or if no one resided in Cornwell City."

"We figured you might have the answer, or at least know who to ask," Ireland added.

"Well, as you can see, I didn't even know about the details." William looked uncomfortable. He was not a man who favored being the last to know anything. I knew he was stalling them while he thought about how to respond. He reviewed the news again. "Hmm. The article makes several errors with names of towns. It's going to take research."

"Can you get to the bottom of it?" Eastlick asked, reclaiming his seat.

"I'm not sure. Do you men have a particular interest in this Cornwell City?"

Ireland sighed. "We were going to settle there."

"But if it doesn't exist . . ."

William lowered the paper. "Maybe the best thing would be to go and look."

"We heard the town's not too far from Lake Shetek," Ireland said. "If there is one."

I picked up a cup and rubbed at a smudge of dirt. It would be foolhardy to take families out to the middle of nowhere if no towns existed, but I resented them coming here. They should have simply gone and looked for themselves. William had no responsibility for solving their problems.

The men rose and shook hands, the matter settled.

"I'll make it an official expedition," William announced. "I'll set off as soon as I make arrangements here. If the land's good, I've a mind to relocate there myself. If three families went, we wouldn't need a town."

Relocate? Just three families on their own in the middle of nowhere?

I dropped the cup I'd been dusting, and it shattered on the floor.

Almena
South Bend Township, Minnesota
June 1859

Almena relaxed her shawl, enjoying the unexpected heat of the June afternoon. They'd left La Crosse behind, with Phin's storekeeping. His friend, Bill, had been enthusiastic about Minnesota. After weeks of discussion, they'd agreed to pursue the opportunity, claim their land, and make their home in Cornwell City. Bill had jumped at the chance to come with them. Together, they'd signed a contract with the Dakota Land Company agent and preempted 160 acres of land on Lake Shetek.

She liked the prairie and its colorful palette of wildflowers. Already, she looked forward to their new life and all the openness. The cloudless blue sky stretched forever, and the air smelled fresher.

Of course, Phin and Bill might not think so, shepherding livestock as they were, back behind the double-box wagon. Her two best milk cows were tied securely to the wagon—there'd be no losing them this time. Along with them, the two friends tended three new cows and ten pigs. Phin's new dog nipped at the livestock's heels when they strayed; Bill's aging canine trailed behind. Crates of chickens hung on the wagon box, their clucking erupting with each lurch. Even with a baby to tend to, she had the easiest of the responsibilities. Minding William Henry and driving the team had to be better than walking behind a passel of animals.

She wrinkled her nose and grinned. Nope, she wouldn't want

to be trailing pigs and cows.

Phin had rigged up a hammock for William Henry, and he'd taken to it right off. The bumps and jars of the ill-made roads hardly bothered him. This last short trek from Mankato to South Bend had taken awhile, though, and he'd soon be awake and demanding her breast. She was glad they'd waited to purchase most of what they needed in Mankato rather than bringing everything from Wisconsin. As it was, they'd be trailing pigs and cows for the next hundred miles or so. Between the animals and the now heavily-loaded wagon, progress would be slow. They had one more stop to make, at Bill's old farmstead, to pick up the few belongings he'd left there when he'd gone back east to La Crosse. From there on, they'd be sleeping under the wagon, which was now full to the brim with farming implements and household goods.

She looked forward to spending a peaceful, comfortable night in the farmhouse. Tomorrow, they'd launch the final leg of their journey. With luck, they'd be in Cornwell City this time next week.

"Swing right," Bill shouted.

Almena spotted an overgrown lane ahead, a small dwelling at its end. Finally.

She guided the horses down the path, and they neared the house. Smoke rose from the chimney, and a riot of flowers bloomed in a tended garden along the foundation.

What in the world?

Bill had said the place was abandoned. Apprehension filled her at the unexpected sign of occupation. Who was here?

She stopped the wagon and waited for Bill and Phin to catch up.

A tall, severe woman emerged from inside. Almena thought she'd once been pretty. Her eyes were a beautiful blue but were now overshadowed by tired lines, and her mouth was set in a resentful scowl. She lifted the shotgun in her hand and pointed it at Bill. "You!" she shouted. "You no good, dirty piece of scum."

As Almena shifted in the seat, placing herself between William Henry and the woman, she told herself not to panic. It was obvious the woman knew Bill. Things would be straightened out in a minute. Phin circled the wagon and laid his hand on Almena's leg. An unspoken question filled his eyes.

She lowered her gaze to the floorboard.

He grasped the rifle and slid it off, holding it in his hand, out of the woman's line of sight.

"Agnes." Bill stood along the other side of the wagon, his stance firm and protective. Whoever the woman was, he didn't care much for her. "I didn't expect to find you here."

"Obviously not." She barked the words out, angry and hostile, jerked the barrel of the gun toward the wagon. "Who's this with you? Your paramour?"

Almena stiffened in her seat.

Next to her, Phin raised the rifle and trained it on the woman. "If you're speaking of my wife, I'd advise you to keep a civil tongue in your mouth."

The woman's eyes narrowed. "Being your wife don't make her any less what she is." She shifted her attention back to Bill, and Almena released the breath she'd been holding. "I heard all about your little threesome. Gossip travels fast from Mankato."

Almena sucked in a breath. "How dare you! That's a ludicrous implication. You don't know a thing about me."

"Put the gun down, Agnes," Bill said. "This is Mr. and Mrs. Hurd, my traveling partners. Phin and Almena, this is my wife, who seems to have returned after all these years."

His wife? He'd told them nothing about a wife. A wife? Oh, dear lord, he didn't expect to bring her along, did he? She wasn't about to expand their group to include this lying shrew.

Agnes lowered the gun but continued to glare at all of them. "You're not welcome here, none of you. Get out."

"I came for my things. I'll get them, and we'll be on our way."

Thank goodness.

"What things?" Agnes demanded.

"My trunk, my tools . . . household things." Bill approached the door and grabbed the gun from her hands, leaning it against the house a few feet away from her.

"You mean my things?"

"I assumed you took what you wanted when you hightailed it back east to your mother."

Almena shifted in her seat and looked at Phin. It didn't feel right, sitting there listening to their personal conversation. Should she get down? Stay where she was?

Phin shrugged, looking as uncomfortable as she felt. They hadn't much choice.

Almena turned and looked in on William Henry. At least, she wouldn't sit there staring, even if she couldn't block their words.

"Well, you didn't appear to want them much. You left them behind. Guess that makes them mine."

"What are you doing here?" Bill's voice dropped.

"Mother died. I had nowhere else to go."

"You can't stay here."

"I can, and I will."

Their conversation shifted into a calmer vein, no longer loud enough to hear. William Henry stirred, and Almena reached for him, eager to keep him quiet and avoid Agnes's attention. Phin took him from her and moved behind the wagon as Almena climbed down, taking care to keep silent. She joined Phin, and they sat, sheltered. She opened her bodice and took the baby, guiding him to suckle.

"The bank owns it!" Bill shouted, his voice full of frustration.

Almena winced. So much for letting them discuss things in private. She sighed, and Phin shook his head.

"You sold it out from under me?" Agnes nearly screeched the words.

"Sold it? They foreclosed on it. It's been sitting here empty for nigh onto three years."

"What am I going to do?"

"I don't know, and I don't much care. You left me."

"You can't just turn me out."

"We were divorced six months after you left."

"Don't matter none."

Almena turned to Phin, rising. "Let's get him out of here."

Phin stood with her. "Stay here." He stepped toward the horses.

"I just want my things, and I'll be on my way. I don't have any responsibility for you." Bill turned and headed toward the stable.

Agnes jerked his arm. "Can't have 'em."

He stopped. "What do you mean?"

"Burned what was in the trunk. Sold the tools. Things in the house are mine." The bitterness in her tone was like a slap.

Phin circled the horses and coughed. Neither Bill nor Agnes paid any attention.

"You burned my things?"

"I sure didn't want them."

"Damn, Agnes."

"Bill," Phin called, "let's be on our way."

Bill sighed. He turned and walked toward the wagon.

Phin threw a smile in Almena's direction. She waited for him to return to help her into the wagon. With William Henry, she couldn't do it alone. She loosened him from her nipple, hoping he wouldn't bellow. The sooner they were out of here, the better.

"Heard you're headed to Cornwell City," Agnes called out, baiting.

"What business is that of yours?" Bill muttered.

"That where you're going?" she continued to taunt. "Good luck to you."

Almost at the wagon, Bill turned. "We don't need your luck."

"Do, too. There ain't no Cornwell City." She spat out the words, then cackled, *cackled*, at them.

Like a witch.

Almena had no other word to describe her. William Henry squawked, and Phin hastened to get them into the wagon. She set the baby in the hammock without burping him and reached for the reins.

Bill took off at a run, storming past Agnes into the house. Moments later, he returned with a small trunk in his hands. Phin took it from him and found a place for it in the wagon as Bill rushed into the small stable. Phin ran after him.

Agnes eyed Almena. "I ain't lying, you know. That town was all made up."

Almena froze, William Henry hollering like the dickens. She should turn the wagon around. The woman was only making trouble; that was all. She'd proven herself a liar, and there was no reason to put stock in any of her words.

"You sleeping with both of them?"

Almena's mouth dropped open. "You *are* a witch." She spat the words out and flicked the reins.

Phin and Bill emerged from the stable, each carrying a box of tools. Without words, they loaded them in. "Let's go."

They herded the animals together, and Almena led them back down the lane.

"Serve you all right to go all the way out there and find nothing," Agnes called from behind them.

At the intersection, Almena paused.

"Head back to Mankato," Phin advised. "She's more than likely messing with us, but we need to find out if there's anything to what she said and what to do about it before we go all the way out there."

Almena turned the team to the left, the woman's words about Cornwell City ricocheting in her head. They'd already signed the contract! Had their dream just turned into a nightmare?

Christina
Lake Shetek, Minnesota
August 1859

One of the Indians who came when we built our cabin is called Inkpadutah. For a moment, when I heard the name, I panicked, but Aaron Myers, who knows the Indians here, said he was Inkpadutah the son and not Inkpadutah the father, who killed so many in Iowa a few years ago. For this, I am glad. Aaron says the Indians do not understand Andreas's English and have named my husband "Yappee Seicha" which means "Bad Talker."

A year later, I know them better, and I no longer fear so much when Indians come to the door. We are careful whenever any of them visit so we do not disturb the peace between our groups. In the winter, they grow hungry, and the women offer us goose down for vegetables. It is a good bargain for us because we trade weight for weight, and they are happy with it. Imagine, having a feather bed out on the prairie for the cost of a few vegetables.

Our settlement is growing. Last year, the Browns built a house on the peninsula across the lake from the trappers but did not stay long. In the fall, Mr. Lamb and his family along with Jack Wright, who is a brother in some way, took a claim southeast of the Smiths. I have also heard that Wright jumped Brown's claim. In April, Julia Wright and her children joined them; their house has a second story, and Andreas says Jack Wright is trading with the Indians, grains and supplies for furs. This is a good thing, I think, for the Indians don't like Andreas so much; perhaps they will stay at that end of the lake and not visit us.

A family named Everett has built a cabin near the traders' shacks, and a man named William Duley was here in July. He set stakes to land south of Wright where the lake flows into a creek. Duley will build a mill there when he returns with his wife, Laura, and their children. The houses will be in a string along the east side of the lake, about a mile apart.

"Christina?" Andreas calls from the yard. "A wagon is coming."

I rush out of the *Haus,* anxious to see who has come.

There *is* a wagon, cows and pigs trailing behind it. I smooth my apron so I do not look so messy and think I should have put up my braid. Andreas waves, his wooden toothpick still in his mouth. I wish he would spit it out.

When the wagon nears, it is a woman driving it, and my heart sings. Two men walk behind, with the animals.

"Hello," I say. "I am Mrs. Koch. Christina. This is my husband, Andreas."

The woman smiles, looking as glad to see me as I am to see her. She is plain of face, but her smile draws me in. She is a good woman, I think.

"I'm Almena Hurd," she says. "My husband, Phineas, and his partner, Bill Jones." She climbs down as the men all begin talking about land and farming.

She shakes her head, and I want to laugh.

"Have you come far?" I ask her.

"From La Crosse, with a stop in South Bend. We were coming to Cornwell City but learned there was no such place."

I have heard of this Cornwell City, but it was never built.

One of the trappers told us it was to be a few miles south of the lake. "*Nein.* There is no town here, only settlers along the lake."

"So we learned. But we already signed the contract to buy the land, so, when we heard there was a settlement starting after all in such a beautiful place, we decided to come anyway. We traveled along the New Ulm Road and stopped at the Wrights."

"*Ja,* they are not long here, either." I have not had much chance to visit with Julia Wright all the way down there at the end of the lake. Perhaps once the harvest is in, we will have time to take the wagon there.

"Wright showed us a map he'd drawn of the lake. We're headed a little farther north, about halfway between you and the Myers family. The men have their eyes on the land east of Fremont Lake."

"That will be a good spot, a mile or two from here. But you will have to travel around the inlet. Andreas will show you. There is a shortcut, but the land there is too mushy for the wagon. We will be able to walk to visit if you build near the big lake."

She leans close, whispering to me. "There are Indian tepees near the Wright place. We weren't expecting that."

I think maybe she does not wish her husband to know she is afraid, but I hear it in her voice.

"*Ja,* Wright is a trader. He will get you feathers for a bed if you have vegetables to offer them." I know I should say more, let her know they are not violent. "There was trouble a little ways east last year, with drunken Indians." I do not tell her Renicker was murdered. "But these at the lake have been peaceful. In the old days, they had ceremonies in this place, and now they come to hunt. The one called Old Pawn has been friendly with the whites, and the others listen to him."

"That's good to hear. I worried." She brightens again.

Just in case, though, I must tell her they come to this part of the lake, too. "Aaron Myers, who is at the north end, is an herb doctor. There are sometimes Indians camped near him, but he has no trouble with them."

"Good."

We pause in our talking, still too new with one another for our words to come easily. I point to her animals. "You have cows and pigs and chickens already. This is good."

"I make excellent butter and cheese." She blushes, and I see she is not a braggart but a modest woman. That, too, is good.

"Then we will trade, too," I tell her. "I'm not so skilled at that."

She glances toward the cabin. "Do you have children?"

"*Nein.* Not yet. You?"

"William Henry, sleeping in the hammock. He's only a few months old."

I look at the little one in the clever swing they have made. He is chubby and perfect, sleeping soundly. His milky baby smell drifts to me, and I wonder if Andreas and I will ever have one like him. We are married now for several years, and still there is no baby.

"Almena?" her husband calls. "It's time we head on. Parmlee said he'd come up in the morning and help us start on a cabin, so we'd best figure out where we want to put it."

She climbs back onto the wagon and makes sure the baby is secure. "I look forward to seeing you again soon."

"*Ja.* It will be good to have someone near."

I watch the wagon turn and head east, as Andreas told them. In the distance, there is a man on a horse, watching.

I hope I have told Almena the truth about our Indians being friendly.

Chapter Eleven

Laura
Beaver, Minnesota
February 1860

I'd not been happy with William since he returned from that blasted trip west to tell me he filed on one hundred sixty acres of land in the midst of nowhere. A fifth child was on the way, and I was once again shuffling with my dress stretched tight and my feet unseen. Cranky, I resented it that he'd left me alone so much these past few miserable months.

Like my first pregnancies, this one was nearly unbearable. Sick from the first month, I cursed William more than one can imagine and looked forward to being delivered. I persuaded myself that the months of morning sickness and backaches were good omens. If William was determined to take us to the ends of the earth, I wanted this infant as healthy as possible. Still, my handkerchief was in shreds from all the wringing I'd put it through.

The bell on the door of the mercantile chimed, and a woman entered. She wore no bonnet, and her lush, thick hair shimmered in the sunlight that streamed through the windows. Oh, to have such hair!

"Laura Duley?" she asked. Confidence filled her voice.

"Yes?" I answered. I was sure I sounded far less self-assured, and unwelcome envy tinged at me.

"I'm Lavina Eastlick. I came over from Rochester with my husband, John. It sounds as if we and our good friends Tommy and Sophia Ireland are going to be traveling west together with you. I wanted to stop and introduce myself."

She looked about my age, thirty-two, or perhaps a few years younger, and moved with determination. I suspected she was a woman who could deal with anything that came her way. As she neared the counter, I wondered what she thought of all this. Was she as worried as I was? With so much conviction in her carriage, I doubted it.

Perhaps I'd once again overreacted to William's moving plans.

Lavina paused, and a smile warmed her face. "John said you had little ones but he didn't mention the one on the way."

"Men tend not to think about such things." I bit my tongue, hoping I hadn't sounded waspish.

"Travel will be more difficult for you." Genuine concern filled her tone, but her words reminded me of how, once again, my husband had made decisions without regard for my comfort.

"William has decided we'll go this summer, so we'll go. He's paying off the last of our land and has located buyers. That makes things about as firm as they can get." My face heated.

Heavens, had I just talked about finances to a complete stranger? I'd completely forgotten my social skills. What she must think of me!

She laughed, though surely she must have been uncomfortable, plunging through the awkwardness without pause. "John and I have boys: Merton, Frank, Giles, and Freddy. The Irelands have four girls."

"We have a mix," I said, glad for the shift in topic. "Willie, as well as Emma, Jefferson, and Bell."

"It will be a lively trip."

With so many children, there was little doubt it would be difficult as well. We would have need to band together. "Did your husband stake a claim?" I asked.

"No. John hasn't been to Shetek yet. Tommy Ireland went with your husband on his second trip. We'll select land near the Irelands, I suppose. We've known Tommy and his wife for years—since back in Illinois—and they're like family."

I'd be the outsider, traveling without the support they would provide one another. Jealousy nipped at me, and I shooed it away, hating that I'd become so negative. "They put up thirty tons of wild hay, William said."

"Tommy said the grass had never been mowed there. It'll be good, these first years, to rely on the prairie grasses instead of having to sow our own hay."

"William went back a third time." The words sprang from my mouth, and our conversation paused.

Lavina blinked, regrouped. "He did?"

"He took cows and oxen, wintering them with the Wrights, one of the families already there." There, I'd established a new thread.

"Goodness, he's eager to get settled, isn't he?" She laughed, the sound tinkling and carefree.

"Chasing his dream," I muttered. *Oh, dear lord!*

"What?"

"William. He's chasing his dream."

"I suppose that's what we're all doing. Looking for a better life."

"I have a good life here, Mrs. Eastlick. This settlement on the lake, it's not my dream. My dream vanished a long time ago."

She peered at me, quite uncertain, I was sure, what to make of me.

I knew my words must have sounded bitter. But they were true; I no longer had a dream. There was no safe future here, and I'd agreed to go west, but it was not to chase my dream. A few years ago, I might have grieved the loss of the excited young woman I had once been, looking for my happily-ever-after in each new place. Now, I simply accepted that my castle in the sky had vanished like a cloud in the wind.

"Mrs. Duley? Laura?"

I stared back at her.

"I think I'd best run for the doctor." She pointed to the floor.

Numb, I glanced down at the liquid pool beneath my feet and swayed.

Julia
Lake Shetek
June 1860

Dusk was falling as Julia lit the lamps. In the kitchen, Lorenza finished up the dishes, the children reading stories at the table. It was a peaceful night, crickets chirping and a breeze drifting off the lake. With chores nearly done, they could all walk down to the shore and catch the wonderful orange and purple sky and its glistening reflection as the sun sank behind the lake.

The front door of the house flew open, and Julia jumped. What now?

Panting, Charley Wambau rushed in and slammed the door.

Julia groaned.

Two months ago, Wambau and Clark had shown up, ready to re-instigate whatever scheme they'd hatched out with Jack at the saloon in St. Peter. She'd stomached them for as long as she could and finally managed to get them out of her house by suggesting they hire on to complete odd jobs around the settlement. She'd thought Wambau was nicely settled at the north end of the lake, digging a cellar.

"I thought you were at Aaron Myers's place."

"I was. But Clark showed up drunk. Says he's gonna kill me."

"Oh, good heavens." Julia hustled toward the back door.

Lorenza stood in the doorway to the kitchen, concern etched on her face.

"There's trouble," Julia said. "Take the kids down to the lake."

She opened the back door and stuck her head out. "George? Jack?"

The men turned at her yell.

"Finish with the fence later. Wambau's here, and Clark's threatening him again. This time, he's drunk."

She shut the door and strode back to Wambau. It was always something with these two, and she was sick to death of dealing with them. "What is it this time?"

"He wants the stuff." Wambau's hands flew in the air in a strange gesture she didn't understand. In fact, she understood very little about him except that he was an irksome little man who'd showed up as if he had an engraved invitation, and she wanted him gone.

"What stuff?"

"The stuff we took in St. Peter." As if that explained anything.

"What's going on?" Jack asked, coming into the house. George and Mr. Annadon, the attorney from Sioux Falls who'd come to check on the condition of the mail route, trailed him.

"Clark's gonna leave. He wants his share," Wambau said.

"Share of what?" George said.

Stuff they took.

The words finally dawned on her. Hot anger roiled, and she marched toward the little weasel. "You didn't bring stolen goods onto this property, did you?"

"Julia!"

She turned at Jack's shout. Good lord, he sounded stricken. She leveled a glare on him. "I told you no good would come of those two being here."

George looked at Wambau, disbelief etched on his face. "You stole things and came here?"

"Get your clothes and get out," Julia said.

She turned back to Jack. "I want them out, right now, and away from here, or I swear I will walk out with the kids and never come back."

"It's only a few trinkets, a bit of ammunition." Wambau nearly squeaked the words.

Julia shook her head and charged past lawyer Annadon to fetch Wambau's things from behind the stairs. She shoved his knapsack into his hands and pointed to the door. "Get out!"

George pointed to the rifle in his hand. "That your gun, Wambau?"

"Belongs to Myers. I told his wife I was going hunting."

"Myers didn't take it with him?" Jack asked. "Why would he and Jones head off to New Ulm without a gun?"

"Spare."

Julia shook her head. *Good god, Jack, who cares about Jones and Myers right now?*

"Just leave it here." She took the gun from Wambau, handed it to Annadon, and yanked the door open.

Bill Clark stood in the yard, raising his own gun. A blast sounded, the shot hitting the doorframe.

Inside, everyone ducked.

Julia's chest pounded. She lifted her head and looked outside. Clark waved the gun around, wobbling on his feet.

"Damn it," George muttered. He strode into the yard and grabbed the gun Clark was now leaning on. "Give me the damn thing."

The two tussled with it, and George wrenched it from Clark's hands. Clark stumbled away.

"Best listen to my missus, Wambau," Jack said. "I'll go grab your horse from the stable."

Jack tramped out the back door, Julia alongside him. "Gone. Away. Both of them. And don't you dare bring people like that here again."

"I didn't exactly bring them this time."

"You told them where you were headed. Did you actually think they'd fail to show up? Don't you think, Jack?"

"I—"

"Jack!" George yelled. "We've got more problems! Clark's on his way back."

Jack dropped the halter and ran for the front yard, Julia on his heels.

As they neared the corner of the house, a shot rang out. They skidded to a stop and peered around the side. Wambau lay in the dirt, hands around his head. Clark and George struggled over Clark's second gun. At the edge of the tree line around Beauty Lake, the neighbors Smith and Parmlee stood clutching their sides and breathing heavily. Annadon stood in the doorway, his eyes wide.

George shoved Clark to the ground and jerked the gun away. "Get out."

Clark scuttled to his feet and wiped drool from his mouth with his hand. "You'll be sorry. All a'you are gonna be sorry. I'm a' go up t'the Redwood Agency an' bring a bunch of 'em renegade Sioux down here. They'll kill Wambau, and they'll kill all a'you. Ever' single one."

He stumbled up the trail.

George strode back to Jack and Julia. "Good God, Jack. You got no sense letting men like this come here."

"You reckon we ought to follow him?" Jack asked. "Make sure he doesn't go up to the reservation?"

"Yeah, we got no choice. Get our guns. He's so drunk it won't be hard to trail him, but it'll be dark soon."

Julia hastened into the house to get the guns. *So much for a peaceful, quiet evening.*

She just hoped George and her idiot husband could find a way to control this senseless mess.

Christina
Lake Shetek
June 1860

I have had a good visit with Almena and am on my way down the shortcut. It has grown dark, and I think I should have come home sooner, but we were having such a fun time. It is a good thing, having people so close, and I think it will be even better when the new families come with William Duley. I think maybe tomorrow we should plan something with our neighbors to the south. We do not know them well enough.

There are voices as I near the edge of the trees, from around our cabin, and I stop. A chill embraces me. Who would be at our house at night? Indians have never come after dark, but perhaps this is an attack. I do not know their ways. I strain my eyes to make out who is here and wish I had a shotgun with me. Lord, where is Andreas?

There is a group of men . . . the men from the south end of the lake. My heart settles a bit.

Wright, Lamb, Parmlee, Smith, Wambau, and a man I do not know are clustered together, whispering in that loud way of men, thinking they are being quiet. I stay in the shadows, waiting until I know what is happening. It is strange for them to be here like this, and I do not know these men as well as I should.

"What should we do?" Smith asks. "Clark's shooting his mouth off pretty good in there."

"Koch'll get fed up with him soon and kick him out," Lamb tells them.

I hear Andreas speak, calm, in control but can't make out his words. But Lamb is right, Andreas will tire of the ranting and tell the man to leave.

Smith looks at my house, then back at the men. "Clark still drunk?"

Hah, I think. *Of course he is drunk. If he were sober, he would hear you out here talking about him!*

Clark is nearly shouting, his words slurred enough that I cannot follow what he is saying from where I am hiding.

Parmlee laughs. "He's angry."

There was something off about his laughter. A chill creeps up my spine. This is not good, and I should check on Andreas, tell them all to go home. But fear freezes me where I am.

The man inside stops yelling. Wright strides to the window and cocks his head, then returns to the group.

"What's he saying?" Smith asks.

"He's still ranting on about inciting the Indians but sounds more serious. He's threatening to bring them here."

Inciting Indians? The chill in my spine becomes a shudder. Who would do such a thing?

Lamb looks at the group. "He's drunk off his rocker. For whatever reason, he's fixated on causing the settlement problems, and, if he remembers Koch has a horse, he'll be halfway to Redwood before we can mount a chase."

I think about how many Indians live at the Redwood Agency and what would happen if they were to come here. My pulse sounds in my ears like a drum. Why are they just standing there?

"Do we take that chance?" Smith says.

"We can't." Wright gestures, frustrated. "Even if we stop him tonight, how do we know he won't go later?"

The man I do not know points at the house. "I say we storm the cabin."

Wright shakes his head. "Not all of us. He's sitting by the stove and likely to grab Koch's gun before we get through the door. Let's split up, provide cover from the windows."

"Do we shoot him?" Smith asks.

"Wing him," says Lamb.

I pray Andreas has the sense to drop to the floor. I do not want them to shoot a man inside my house, but I know he must be stopped.

The men move to the cabin and separate, Wright and Wambau to the west window, the others circling the cabin toward the door and the other window. I follow, ready to run to Andreas and make sure he is safe.

At the window, Wambau raises his gun.

"Go on, give it to him," Wright urges.

Wambau fires. Acrid smoke fills the air. Inside, the cabin there is a commotion, and I hear Andreas shout that Clark has been murdered.

I exhale a heavy breath as I grasp my Andreas is safe.

But I remember Wright's words. *Go on, give it to him.*

Ja, I think, Andreas is right. It *is* murder, and Jack Wright is as much to blame as Wambau.

Almena
Lake Shetek
July, 1860

Cresting the hill on the trail, Almena spied the Wright place ahead. Five tepees nestled in the meadow beyond, and the camp bustled with activity. The remains of several deer hung in a nearby tree, women trimming strips from the meat. Scattered campfires fed smoke beneath racks of drying meat. Everywhere, women were busy with butchering, cooking, or tanning hides. Julia Wright moved among the visitors, chatting with several of them.

Almena's lips lifted. It sure didn't look like there was anything to be feared from these people, despite all Clark's bluster. But, if there was nothing to fear, then the shooting had been groundless, just like Andreas maintained. Her smile faltered. Neither scenario set well.

She clicked the reins and urged the horses on. Up at the north end of the lake, Aaron Myers and Andreas Koch had been sharply critical of the killing, refusing to interact with the men who had been involved. She and Phin were caught in the middle, and it was high time someone bridged the chasm that yawned in their close settlement.

That meant it would be up to the women. She needed Julia's perspective.

Julia spotted her and strode toward the house, waving as she approached. "I sure hope you brought butter."

"And cheese." Almena set the brake and looped the leather around it, then climbed down. "How much are you needing?"

"We're pretty much out." She peered into the wagon. "I can take everything you brought. Between those who live here and our visitors, we always manage to trade well."

They hoisted boxes from the wagon bed and carried them to the cabin, chatting along the way. Once inside, they set their loads on the counter.

Julia gestured toward the trade goods. "Have a look around; stack what you need here while I tackle your list."

Almena left her notes on the counter and began exploring the shelves. She always enjoyed Julia's direct, open personality. What a shame such a pleasant woman was saddled with the likes of Jack Wright.

"There was a census taker through at the beginning of the month," Julia said. "A prissy little man. He made it clear he'd anticipated a town and didn't want to 'cavort around the lake,' looking for everyone's cabins."

"Since we didn't see him, I assume he flat-out refused to do so."

"Exactly. Jack gave him everyone's names and the ages from that list he keeps. We weren't sure if Phin's mother was still visiting or not so he included her. I hope that was all right."

"Either way. She's gone home, thankfully."

Julia laughed. "I take it she didn't realize you're expecting."

Almena's cheeks heated. How on earth did Julia know? She was barely showing.

"You've put your hands on your womb twice already. I do that when I'm carrying."

Perceptive, as usual. "I didn't even realize it." She took supplies and carried them to the counter. "Phin's mother is a good woman, but far too fussy to stand for too long at a time. And you're right, she didn't know. Otherwise, she'd have nested with us for the entire time."

"In-laws can be a trial." Julia measured coffee beans from a large wooden barrel and tied off the bag. "Things are strained between Jack and my sister and her husband."

"The Clark business?" Almena asked. Knowing Jack, there would be more to it, but it was an opening to discuss what had happened. And to determine if there was a cause for alarm.

"Among other things."

"What happened with Clark has divided the entire community."

"It was a disaster, from start to finish."

Julia set a bag of flour on the counter and began to factor the total but said no more, and Almena wondered how much Jack had told her. Likely the barest of details. Jack talked a lot, but only when it suited his interests.

"I helped Christina scour the blood from the floorboards of her cabin. The wood sucked every drop of it in. The stain wouldn't yield until we poured lye on it."

"I saw the lye on your supply list and wondered if that wasn't the case. I'm sorry it came to that."

"You know Christina was there?"

Julia's eyes widened. "In the cabin?"

"No, outside. She'd been at our place and was just returning. She was in the trees."

"Dear lord."

"She told me the details. I'm glad Phin wasn't with them."

"Jack didn't say much. Just that Clark was so drunk, and they'd feared he would ride up to the agency and incite the Dakota."

That was the story all the men had told, as well, and what they'd put on the witness affidavit they'd signed. All but Andreas.

"He was drunk, but Christina swears it was mostly ranting, that he'd have passed out soon."

Julia put down her pencil and sighed. "Do you think they shot him without reason?"

"I don't know. I imagine it was a difficult decision, and it would be best if we all move past it. Andreas and Christina will always see it differently than the men who were outside."

"Different experiences. They didn't fight with Clark earlier, didn't chase him up the lakeshore, didn't know him as well. He was a despicable man, a thief, and worse, I suspect. I'm not sorry to see him gone, but I wish our men hadn't killed him." Her voice held regret. "But I've no doubt he would have brought ruin to us. If not that night, another."

"Wambau's gone?"

"He hightailed it as soon as the judge in New Ulm cleared him. Thank God. Jack should never have gotten involved with either of them. But, then, Jack's not too good at doing what he should."

They shared gazes, understanding what went unsaid.

"Would the Indians have turned on us?" Almena asked.

"I don't know. I don't know those who live up at the agency, the ones Clark threatened to involve." Julia placed the supplies in the empty box as she spoke. "I think there are many there who hate whites. They survive almost entirely on annuities, and, most years, the supplies are either late to arrive or the supply is short. The Indian agents cheat them. It's not a good situation."

"I never have any problems with those who come to our place to trade."

"Nor do we. And Aaron Myers has a long history with some of them. When he lived up at Saratoga, the year the winter was so bitter, he often let them sleep inside his place. And he treated their medical needs . . . still does."

"He told us an old woman named Teeny broke another woman's arm, and he set it for her. Her brother gave him a buffalo robe in appreciation."

"I think that's true. There's a special bond in Dakota culture between brothers and sisters, a unique relationship. The tribe values kinship in all its forms."

"What about those who camp here?"

"It's a steady group. Old Pawn seems to be the leader among them."

"I've heard Myers mention him."

"Over six feet tall. You'd know him if you saw him. Fierce looking, but he's never been anything but friendly with us. I think his real name is Across the Water. His first wife is related to old Sleepy Eye."

Almena recognized the reference. Though now dead, the chief had befriended whites, and a town near New Ulm had taken his name. His nephew of the same name, rumor had it, was not so friendly.

"Are they here much? Are you ever afraid?" she asked Julia.

"They bring their tepees a few at a time, mostly to hunt,

sometimes to trade. They stay a few days, move on. It's fascinating, really. There are bands of them that live together, some on the reservation and some in villages. But there are larger divisions, I guess you'd call them sub-tribes, and the larger tribes. Sort of like how Norwegians and Swedes and Danes are all Scandinavian, and Scandinavians are all European."

"Goodness. However did you learn all that?" Almena had never suspected Indian society was that complicated.

"I talk with them, listen. Everything I learn makes understanding them easier."

"I suppose that's good for all of us."

Julia set the last bag of beans in the box. "Their ways are very different from ours, and as complex. There are even different language groups and identifications based on geographical areas. I can hardly keep track."

"Goodness, if we fail to understand that much about Indian society, no wonder there are problems between us."

"We're done here—works out as an even trade for me if that works for you?"

At Almena's nod, Julia continued. "Come with me, then, and I'll give you a little glimpse." She grabbed Almena's hand and led her outside, veering toward the small encampment.

"We're visiting them?"

"Of course, we are. How else are you going to learn?"

She steered Almena to a woman who sat on the ground, her legs tucked primly to one side. In front of her lay a stretched hide. As they approached, she looked up from scraping it and said something to Julia.

Julia greeted her with a few words, then turned to Almena.

"This is Dances in Water. She is second wife to Pawn and is glad to meet you. She has heard of the woman who makes butter."

Almena nodded, flattered but uncertain. "Tell her I am

pleased to meet her."

Julia translated then waited for the woman's response. "Will you sit?" she relayed. "There is stew in the pot, and she offers to share it with you."

"I'm not hungry."

"It's a custom—hospitality. To be polite, you should have some."

They sat while Dances in Water rose and fetched wooden bowls. The woman dipped them into the pot hanging over the fire and extended a bowl to each of them before returning to her place on the ground.

Almena accepted the bowl, watching Julia, and sipped from it as her friend did. It was good, an artful blend of venison and wild vegetables.

"This is a hunting trip; only a few couples have come. The men bring in the meat, and the women prepare it to take back to the village. That's why you see all the meat drying. They work on the hides, too, scraping them for later use."

Almena glanced around. The industry was clear, as was a pride in doing it well. Christina would appreciate their diligence. The savory soup would reap her praise as well. "Tell Dances in Water the stew is very good."

"She is pleased to honor you with it."

Almena smiled at the woman, thinking about the men who stopped by her cabin on occasion.

"The men who visit us, who ask for food . . . I thought it was because they were hungry or because they wanted to trade. But maybe they're visiting and expect us to know the hospitality custom?"

"Sometimes, they come to trade and will make an offer to you for food. In those cases, it may be hunger that drives them or maybe a desire for your butter and cheese. But they may also come to visit; I don't know. Hospitality is always offered to guests."

Almena thought of Bad Ox's visits. The tall Indian often came, asking in English to trade for cheese. But he sometimes came into the cabin and sat at her table, as if waiting for food. She'd never viewed one as any different from the other.

"When I provide a meal, they always give something to me. I thought it was a trade."

"They are returning the honor you gave them with your hospitality. I think trading is different. They offer the trade goods first."

I need to return the honor to Dances in Water.

Almena searched her apron, wishing she had brought a cheese with her. Deep in her pocket, her fingers latched onto a tin of her homemade hand cream. She drew it out and extended it to the woman.

"Tell her this is for her, to soften her hands."

Julia spoke, and Dances in Water smiled. She opened the tin and smelled the cream, then dabbed a bit on her palm. She worked it into her skin and spoke.

"She thanks you and says it smells much better than grease."

Almena laughed. "Tell her to mix rosehip into the grease." It wouldn't be quite the same as mixing dried flowers into her unsalted butter, but it would be better than smelling like an animal. "Tell her I will always have more for her."

She and Julia stayed a few minutes longer, then returned to the house.

"See?" Julia prompted. "More complicated than you thought."

"Much more. I had no idea."

"We would do well to understand the differences in our cultures and not to slap our own interpretations on actions."

"So, do you think there is any basis for fear?"

"I trust the Dakota who camp here, Pawn and the others we've come to know."

"But if Clark had gone to the agency, would there have been violence?"

Julia shrugged. "Just because certain Dakota have become our friends does not dictate what other Dakota do. Those who don't know us misinterpret us as much as we do them. We are all too much in our own worlds. Problems are created by some; assumptions are made; entire groups are blamed. Both our cultures do that."

They quieted, digesting the complexities. Then Julia turned to her again.

"We're friends with the few small groups who visit the lake. But many others are angry that whites have settled in the area. It wouldn't take much to stir them. I think the men were right to fear what might have happened if Clark had gone to them.

"We're isolated here, but what happens in one place impacts what happens everywhere else, isolated or not."

Lavina
Olmstead County, Minnesota
Fall 1860

John enters the house without his usual whistling, sheds his overcoat, and kicks off his boots. He doesn't say a thing, and I cast an inquiring glance his direction. He shrugs.

My stomach tumbles a bit. We are to start toward western Minnesota next week, and John has been in Rochester, attending to final details. Our land has been sold, the house along with it. Most of our goods are packed. We are already months behind our original schedule. Now is not the time for things to go amiss.

I tuck up a tress of fallen hair and finish frosting the cake while I wait. He will tell me in his own time. I wipe up a dollop of frosting that has dripped onto the table and lick it off my finger. John sits in the chair near the fire and slumps his head into his hands.

With that, I can hold back no longer. "John?"

"They aren't going." The words drop like lead.

"What?" For a moment, I wonder if I have heard him correctly. But his hunched shoulders say otherwise. "Who?" I ask.

He lifts his head and faces me. "William and Laura Duley are not going. Not this year, anyway."

He says nothing of the Irelands, forcing me to ask. "Tommy and Sophia?"

"They've decided to wait as well."

Resentment churns in large, rumbling waves. "What do you mean, they're not going? How can they simply say they're not going?" At the last minute? I'm unable to believe everyone has simply decided not to go. My mouth hangs open, and I blink several times.

John swallows. "Rachael, one of the new Duley babies, died."

"Oh, John, no." Memories of my dead baby flood back, and my hand hugs my womb. "Just now?"

"Early June. She was three months old."

In June, four months ago. It surprises me that no one sent word. But why would they? We're not family, after all, or even close friends. Babies die. Life goes on. It is a harsh way to think, but that is the way of it. The living remain. We must hold on for their sake.

John rises and takes me in his arms. We embrace one another, remembering our pain.

Eventually my thoughts shift to the tiny little twin girls born the day I stopped to visit Laura in the store. "They were so small, so weak."

"William didn't say what took the baby, only that Laura took to her bed with melancholy when it happened. She's still not healthy and refuses to risk the surviving baby."

I've known other women to suffer long periods of despondence but have never experienced it myself. I try to imagine what she must be feeling, but my brain doesn't allow it. Though I know she is grieving and that each woman does so in her own way, I am unable to glimpse such surrender in my mind's eye, not when other children would have need of me. But I do understand her refusal to travel when the other babe is not yet strong.

John releases me and paces the room, worry clouding his eyes. "Duley thought she'd be all right by now, that the other baby, Frances, would be stronger. That's why he didn't send word earlier."

I pity Laura, struggling so with both grief and worry. "Oh . . ."

I'm unable to say anything more.

"So, Tommy and I talked about it. Given the time of year, Tommy wants to wait until spring."

My thoughts come back to the move, unease accompanying them. Tommy has not yet sold his land; of course he has no problem waiting until spring. But we've already sold. I glance at John. Will we even be able to stay?

The answer is etched on his face without me even needing to voice the question.

Anxiety surges. "When do we have to be out?"

"The buyer will give us until November first."

Two weeks. Two weeks in which to head off to an unknown place on our own or find a place to rent, spending what we'd intended to use to start out at Lake Shetek. Neither choice is appealing, and I grow afraid.

I do not mention the baby I suspect I am carrying. Not today, when death and despair hang in the air, piercing me with memories. I will need to push it away, chase away the fear before it takes root.

We will have too much to do in this next handful of days, and others will have need of me.

Chapter Twelve

Julia
Spring 1861

The rich aroma of buffalo roast filled the house. Julia figured she'd need to head out to LaBousche's tepee and let him know the meal would be ready soon. She'd kept the last roast back, to share with the half-breed trapper when he returned to the area, inviting him over from the peninsula across the lake especially for that reason. LaBousche had shot it before Christmas, claiming it might well be the last buffalo in the area. Even the elk and moose had moved on to less settled areas. Oh, the deer and waterfowl were still plentiful, but the big game—that was a thing of the past.

She glanced into the other room, where Dora was singing to baby George. Happy as larks, those two. The community was once again at peace, and Jack had taken on Will Everett as a partner. For a return on profits, he was allowing Jack to store goods in one of the abandoned trapper shacks on his property, two miles north. Everett was a solid man, a positive influence on Jack. It was about time her husband settled into being an honest man. Finally, they could operate this business the way it should be run.

Julia smiled to herself, prideful of her good fortune. Until guilt surfaced. The Lambs had not been so lucky, after all. She'd best remember that pride goeth before a fall.

Her sister's baby had not survived, born too early at the lake, despite Lorenza's intentions of going to Mankato, and George's fur trapping had not gone well this year. Those animals, too, were moving on. Truth be told, she worried George and Lorenza would be leaving the lake. Neither was too pleased with Jack, and they talked of settling a ways east, near the town of Iberia.

Julia held back a sigh. She didn't have to like it.

"Lorenza?" she called up the stairs. "I'm headed out to let LaBousche know what time to expect supper. I'm leaving Dora and George here."

"I'll keep an eye on them, if you're willing to risk Frank teaching her to pass gas on command."

Julia laughed. Leave it to Lorenza's little ruffian! At eleven, he thought farts were hilarious.

"I'll hold my nose when I get back."

Hearing Lorenza descend, Julia grabbed her shawl and swung it across her too plump shoulders. She opened the door and strode across the yard to LaBousche's tepee. She'd grown used to having them in the yard, a few at a time, when the Dakota came. This time, it was just the trapper, but the lodge was the same. The structures fascinated her—easily transported, well-insulated, and surprisingly roomy. There were times she found them more comfortable than the log house she lived in, where air grew sultry in the summer and icy in the winter.

"Hello," she called, alerting LaBousche to her arrival before she lifted the flap and stuck her head in. Warm heat poured out, filled with the scent of sage. "Supper will be ready in about an hour."

Once the smokiness cleared, she realized Will Everett sat next to the trapper.

"Well, hello, Will. I didn't notice your horse."

Everett offered a wan smile. "Tied it up next to your barn. Jack isn't around?"

Julia's skin prickled. Something was off. "He went up to Smiths'."

"Ah."

Everett's response fueled her unease. She'd learned to trust her instincts, and his reserve was unusual. Normally, he'd be chatting a mile a minute.

"*Madame* Wright, *entrez-vous, s'il vous plaît.* There is something we must speak about."

"With me?"

"Oui."

"It's a thing you need to know."

She stepped into the tepee and adjusted the flap to keep the heat in. She circled left as Dakota women did and sat. "Something that involves me?"

"Unfortunately, yes." Everett shifted.

"That doesn't sound good." She looked from one man to the other. Nervous, both of them.

"*Madame,* there are rumors."

"It's not good, Julia."

Men. "Oh for heaven's sake, just tell me what it is."

LaBousche leaned forward. "When I was at Yellow Medicine, Tizzie Tonka, who has camped here before, he was there. He said the Sioux, they are buying whiskey *ici.* From your husband."

"Here? But Jack doesn't stock whiskey. I won't allow it."

"He claimed they bought it at my place," Everett said.

She looked at him, trepidation knocking like an impatient child. "Your place?"

"Made me mad as hell when LaBousche told me, pardon my language." Everett's face grew beet red.

Julia waved the language issue away with a gesture. She was used to worse than that. It was the whiskey rumor that was important. "Is it true?"

"I found four barrels in the cellar of one of the shacks. They were hidden under the stairs, behind a stack of crates."

"Oh, Will, no."

Not again, Jack, not again.

"It was rot-gut swill. Homemade, I think. There were a bunch of bottles there with fancy labels. I suspect he's been filling them and selling by the bottle, passing it off as good stuff."

"C'est dangereux to trade whiskey with the Sioux. And to cheat them. You *comprendez* this, *oui?"*

"I do." She understood all right. Selling whiskey in any form to the Dakota was a bad idea. Many of them handled alcohol—especially moonshine—less well than whites. Not that drunks of any sort were easy to deal with. Bad enough on its own, but to add deception . . .

She shuddered to think what they must consider Jack. No wonder the Dakota had taken to calling him *Tonka Tensena.* Big Liar. It fit, all right.

"You, they trust, but not your husband." LaBousche's words warmed her. She'd worked hard to establish a good relationship with the bands that visited the lake, allowing them to camp in the yard, interacting with them. That Jack was sabotaging all her goodwill was infuriating.

It was dangerous, it made them distrust whites, and it made the Dakota suspect *her* word.

Didn't Jack know this?

"Two of the barrels were empty, so I think he's had this side business for a while." Everett's gaze met hers. "Mira and I won't be involved in it. It's dishonest, and it's dangerous. He's apt to get himself or the rest of us killed."

The incessant foreboding hammered harder. "What is he thinking?"

"If he got the idea anywhere, it was likely from Clark and Wambau. It's the sort of scheme they'd promote. I drained the barrels, Julia, every drop. I'm dissolving the partnership, and he'll need to move the legitimate goods from the other shack."

Of course he'd dissolve the partnership.

One step forward, two steps back—the story of her life ever since she'd had the misfortune of meeting Jack Wright. She drew a breath, already exploring solutions. For the trade goods, at least.

"We'll move things to our barn again. Can you give us a few days?"

"I can do that."

"*Je suis désolé* to bring such news to you."

She smiled at the trapper's concern. "It's not your fault, LaBousche. It needed to be done."

Everett began to stand. "Julia, I was going to come up to the house, tell Jack what I told you—"

"Sit, Will. I'll tell him when he returns." She rose and straightened her skirt. "I have a few other things to say to him, and it's best you not have to hear them."

"Perhaps I should bring my plate here?" Again, LaBousche and his concern for others.

"That might be best." She circled to the door flap and pushed it away.

"Merci, Madame."

Turning, she caught both their gazes. "*Non, merci* to you, both of you."

Julia left the tepee and trod back to the house, worry chasing her with every step.

Almena

Summer 1861

Almena tucked the hair that had escaped from her limp braid behind her ears. The summer afternoon heat bore down with burning intensity, and humidity hung heavy in the air. She glanced at the group of Sioux men—Dakota, Julia said they called themselves—that were mounting their horses. *Titonhah Seachah,* Bad Ox, and two others she didn't know, had traded her six geese for two rounds of cheddar.

She smiled and waved to the group. She still wasn't too sure she cared for Bad Ox, but he liked cheddar cheese and showed up every three or four weeks to restock his supply, and occasionally to visit and enjoy her hospitality. They'd established a routine relationship, and she no longer felt threatened when Bad Ox and his friends rode up to the cabin. It was funny, how she'd thought the Indians would be the worst part of living here.

She'd never in a thousand years anticipated the biggest problem would be blackbirds.

She and Phin had selected a beautiful place for the cabin, with Bloody Lake to the south and the waters that connected Lake Shetek and Lake Fremont to the north. The cabin sat in a grove of oak trees, and their farmland lay in the open prairie to the east. In all, it was a protected spot, isolated, with glistening waters nearly everywhere they looked. This year, Bloody Lake had borne true to its name, the willow roots at its edge turning deep red in the shallow water, casting a blood-red glow all along the shoreline.

But the blackbirds.

Lord help them, she and Phin hadn't reckoned on the blackbirds. She had no idea what attracted them like flies, but she aimed to get rid of them once and for all. Shooting them didn't work. Every day, she killed a few; every day there were more of them. Though they occasionally sang in harsh-sounding melody, it was the screeching call of the males that drove her most crazy. Two short notes then that long screech.

Propping the new scarecrow up against the makeshift pole, Almena fished a hank of rope from her pocket and tied the straw-stuffed thing to the post. It flopped a bit, bending at the waist, and she sighed. He'd need rope around his neck, too.

"Almena?"

She turned to Phin's voice and lifted her braid to cool her neck. "Over here."

He wiped his dirty hands on his pants as he approached—the mark of a farmer, for sure.

"Phineas B. Hurd," she chastised.

"Sorry." He had the good grace to look abashed, at least, and she couldn't find it within her to be mad at him. "The boys in the house?"

"Napping, both of them. Though I expect Frank will be waking soon for a feeding."

Phin grinned at her. "He's a hungry one. More so than William Henry."

"William Henry's going to be our easy one, I suspect."

Together, they walked toward the house and settled on a shaded log they used as a bench. Phin mopped sweat from his face. "The birds have been at the grain again."

"Oh, Phin, no." The birds had become the bane of their existence this summer. Though they'd mostly flocked in the trees around the house last summer, they'd now discovered the fields were an easy food source.

"They're at the fields, they're in the trees, they're on the ground. I hate the things."

"I'm hoping the scarecrow helps."

"The one in the field hasn't done a lick of good," he pointed out. "I don't understand why we're the only ones plagued like this."

"I hear the blasted things in bed at night and can't tell whether it's real or if I'm having a nightmare."

Conk-a-lee! Conk-a-lee! Except the *lee* was more like a

leeeeeeeee. And it wasn't just a solo, it was a whole choir of them.

"I'm thinking I might have to move the fields farther out," Phin said. "It might be the water or maybe the acorns from the oak trees. We might have to move the cabin, too."

Almena scrunched her face at him. "I like this spot. Except for the noise and the feathers and the bird droppings."

"Maybe this isn't the right place for us."

She shivered. The way he said that didn't sound good. "Phin?"

"Maybe it's a sign. Maybe we should have moved into Dakota Territory."

She stood and faced him, hands on her hips. He hadn't just said what she thought he had? "Phineas."

"Bill and I have been talking. Maybe we ought to explore farther west. Maybe near Yankton—a real town, not an imaginary one."

"Oh, no, you don't! I don't want to move farther west." They'd been misled about the size of this settlement, and they'd take no more chances.

"I know. But at least we wouldn't lose anything more if we left before I pay up on the rest of the claim."

She shook her head. "We'd lose what we put into this place."

"Mostly logs and hard work."

"No." *No, no, no, no, no.* "Look at the livestock we have. We have crops in. We have too much invested here."

"We take the animals along, or sell them."

"I don't like the idea." Almena's mouth tightened into a thin, hard line. She hated the idea.

"All I want is for you to think about it. It's an idea, that's all. Not anything we'd do right now."

"I'll give it consideration, but don't raise your hopes." Her voice was brittle, but she didn't care.

"I'm not hoping anything, except to be rid of these darn

blackbirds." Phin stood and wrapped his arms around her. "I like it here, Almena. The neighbors are friendly, the land is fertile, the weather is tolerable—except for scorchers like today and the three-day blizzards." He dropped a kiss on her forehead.

"All I'm saying is that if the blackbirds keep at our crops, we might not have any choice."

Christina
October 1861

In the fall, we have another German at the lake, another Koch.

Though I wish it were a child, instead it is an immigrant, fresh from the Old Country. Ernst Koch shares our name—one that is common in Germany—but is not a relation, at least not that we know. Of course, when he arrives, he comes to us.

Andreas is glad of it. They spend hours speaking German to each other, and I think I am again in Dresden. Ernst brings *beir* from New Ulm and the two sit together like old friends. The only other German in the area is Charles Zierke, whom everyone calls Dutch Zierke, but he lives twenty miles away, on the road to New Ulm.

It is an interesting thing, about Ernst. Even though he is newly to this country, he speaks English better than my Andreas. We have a good laugh about that.

Ernst has a partner named Voigt, who will come to us soon. They are making plans to open a trading house; it sounds like they will have many goods for the settlers. Wright, who trades at the south end of the lake, has mostly things to trade to the trappers and the Indians. The settlers, we must still make trips to New Ulm for all but the basics. We will be glad if we do not have to do this so much. We also hear Wright does not give the trappers a fair price, so Ernst may have their business, too.

I invite Phin and Almena Hurd to dinner, to help welcome

Ernst and hear the news he brings of the southern rebellion. He will also need to find a place for his cabin, and I think it will be a good thing if Andreas and Phin can offer advice. We are much like a family at this end of the lake, and I look forward to many years of the same.

Bright leaves have all fallen from the trees and have become a crunchy rust and ochre carpet. There is a chill in the air that stings when the wind blows, as it does nearly every day now. Snow will come to us soon.

Crackling leaves and chattering children catch my attention. I jump and dash from the house. If my braid were not coiled up, it would fly behind me like a rope.

"Almena!" I rush to my friend and hug her. Little Frank wriggles in her arms. He is growing and not so little any more.

William Henry jumps up and down and tugs at my skirt. "Aunt Christina," he says. His young voice mangles my name, but I do not care. I scoop him up, and we walk together to the house, Phin and his partner, Bill Jones, trailing behind us.

Andreas and Ernst welcome us at the door, and we make introductions.

"Come into the house," Andreas says. "It is too nippy out here. We have a good fire and *beir.* And Christina made us strudel."

"Beer," Phin says. "I haven't had a beer since we left La Crosse. Show me the way."

We all laugh and enter the small cabin, tossing wraps on the bed. The men move chairs and sit by the window while Almena and I settle the boys on the bed. Almena gives them small stuffed animals to keep them occupied. The two of us go to my small stove behind the table. We are crowded, but we make do.

"Ernst will bring bolts of cloth for his trading house," I tell her.

"I can supply him all the cheese and butter he wants, bread

and preserves, too." Almena has five milk cows and makes the best butter and cheeses.

"I have told him already."

She mouths a silent thank you to me and blows kisses to her boys. William Henry has made a parade with the animals, all but the one Frank chews on. Almena laughs before going to my cupboard to gather dishes and silverware for the table. I am glad she is my neighbor—she has a joyful spirit and is such a good mother.

"Where will you locate?" Phin asks.

"I have not decided." Ernst gestures with his hands. "I will look when Voigt gets here so we can decide together."

"Voigt is his partner," Andreas says. "Another German." He raises his *beir* in a toast. *Ach.*

"Are you planning to trade with the Indians?" Jones asks.

"More with the settlers, I think. Voigt does not like Indians much, and Wright already has that trade."

I think this is a good decision. Germans and Indians are not a good mix. The Germans, we are stubborn and set in our ways. And the Sioux, they cannot understand the German accent.

"Did you hear they killed one of Wright's oxen?" Phin asks.

We, the Kochs, stare at him. We did not know.

Almena sets the plates on the table. "Old Pawn told Julia it was because Wright cheated them, and they were owed."

"*Ja,* I don't doubt that." Andreas has a bitter tone in his voice; his dislike for Wright is still strong.

But I think about other things than Wright. I think about the Sioux killing an animal that belongs to a settler. "Should we be worried?" I ask.

Phin scowls. "No, I'm sure Wright had it coming. He's not an honest man."

"We haven't had a lick of trouble with them," Almena says. "I trade cheeses to Bad Ox all the time."

"The squaws trade us feathers for our mattresses," I tell Ernst. Too late, I remember that Julia says we should not use that term, that it is demeaning. But I have said it already. She is the only person I know who worries about it anyway. Julia is like that. I think I will not worry so much. Even the Sioux men call them that, after all.

"If you locate at the north end of the lake, you wouldn't be in direct competition with Wright or need to worry about so many Indians around," Jones says and drains the last of the *beir* from his stoneware bottle.

"But Andreas says most of the north end land has been claimed."

"True enough. But you might be able to buy from someone," says Phin.

Beside me, Almena drops the silverware, and it clatters on the table.

Laura
November 1861

The wind grew bitter on the road to Lake Shetek, biting into our skin, and we were forced to stop for days to wait out snowstorms. It was cold, constantly cold, and I didn't think I would ever forgive William for waiting so long into the fall to make the journey. But the Irelands had needed to bring in their harvest and complete the sale of their property, and John said they changed their plans for us last year, when we lost Rachael. So we had waited. It had been a difficult trip for me, filled with constant worry, and I wanted so much to finally be at our new home and settle into a warm, comfortable cabin.

Traveling with two other families grated upon me. I was easily provoked and grew snappy without warning. Always, children demanded attention, taxing my patience. Oh, to be in our home with a bit of privacy.

"Laura?"

I turned to William, trying to muster a bit of enthusiasm. "Yes, Husband?"

"Are you all right?"

I winced. He kept asking this. For months, now, he'd asked it.

I was as good as I was going to get.

I was not abed, and I was caring for the children. I cooked his meals and did what needed doing. He always wanted more, tried to cajole smiles and laughter where there were none to be had.

"Yes," I answered. "I'm fine."

"I just wond—"

"I said I'm fine. Leave it be."

We sat in silence again, the wagon rocking.

William had made several trips to Lake Shetek. He'd cleared land, mowed hay, and taken the remains of the mill works on ahead. Business had dwindled at the store, but we'd managed to locate a buyer for it as well as for our land, turning a decent profit. I was glad to have the responsibility out from under us and looked forward to a quiet life as a farmer's wife.

I no longer yearned for leading roles in the community, where William would be tempted to become involved with politics and spend hours serving others. I wanted nothing but a peaceful existence. A private existence where no one bothered me.

"We're almost there."

Good. I was tired of this bump-filled mail road. Up and down hills it went, the frozen ground refusing to yield, stuck as it was in a churned up mess from the last rain of the season. We cleared yet another hill, and I spied a building in the distance.

"Wright's place," William said.

We rolled in, the Irelands and Eastlicks behind us, and

stopped near the house. It was a story-and-a-half high or perhaps even two stories, and larger than any cabin we'd seen on the cold, brown prairie.

A woman rushed out of the house. Bright eyed and a little plump, she possessed a degree of excitement I simply could not dredge from myself. A blond man and two young children followed.

"Welcome to Lake Shetek."

I sat on the wagon seat as the others clustered together, chattering like magpies. My own children clambered out the back of the wagon—all except Frances, who was asleep under mounds of blankets. Finally, William came to lift me down. I went, albeit grudgingly. I was tired and had little tolerance for an extended welcome.

We made introductions, and I shook hands with the woman, Julia.

"We're so glad to have you here. Three more families!"

"Is it always this cold here?" I winced at the rudeness of my words.

Julia laughed. "Not always. But the air off the lake holds a lot of moisture, so it can be pretty biting. You'll learn to live with it."

I doubted so, but I nodded anyway.

Julia offered a brilliant smile before moving to welcome the other women. "The Everetts are expecting the lot of you up at their place, so we'd best let you head on up."

"We'll see you soon," I heard Lavina say in that confident way of hers.

Shivering, we loaded back up and drove the two miles north, gusts blowing off the lake. Gray waves rushed across its surface each time I spied it through the trees, turbulent and inhospitable. William turned and headed straight into the gale, up a small strip of land. Ahead was a small, two-room cabin, twelve by sixteen at the best. In the distance stood two less solid buildings I could only call shacks.

My heart plummeted.

The wagons ground to a halt, and the whole bunch climbed out. This time, I went with them. It seemed we had reached our destination.

A family emerged from the log cabin, and I met the Everetts: Will and Mira and their children Lillie, Willie, and the baby, Little Charlie. Mira's brother Charlie, the baby's namesake, was to arrive after the first of the year.

Again, the entire group babbled on, until Mira Everett announced, "Let's get everyone settled. Make yourselves at home, folks." Taking armfuls of belongings, the Eastlicks made for one of the shacks, the Irelands for the other, as if it had been prearranged.

Of course it had.

And William had not informed me once again. Where in heaven's name were we going to live?

William smiled at me. "I figured you wouldn't want to make do in one of the trappers' shacks," he said.

The words warmed me, and a tiny spark of eagerness ignited. He must have already built our cabin. A small, timorous smile rose. "Shall I get the children back on the wagon?"

"What for?" He looked puzzled.

"To go to our cabin."

"Oh, we don't have a cabin yet. I'll build that in the spring." He guided me forward. "I figured, since Will and I plan to partner in the mill, we'll live with the Everetts this winter."

Lavina
November 1861

Without words, the men lead us down a travois trail through

the mature trees, created by the trappers who used to live here, and we neared the shacks. Dear lord, when John told me there would be a place for us to live, I never imagined such a dilapidated place. No wonder he's not whistling.

Though my journey to Lake Shetek has been made with far less enthusiasm than my first journey out into the world all those years ago with my brother Leicester, I'm determined to make this an adventure as well. Even though it is early winter, and our first months will be filled with cold and snow, I've observed the beauty of this place as well as its possibilities. The lake is huge, full of geese and loons most of the year, we're told. Though the water is choppy now, it reflects the sun with a glittering brilliance. The place is raw and wild and will certainly test our independence, but I resolve to maintain a positive outlook and forge a happy home here.

The shack gives my resolution pause.

I enter, Johnnie in my arms. Inside, it's dim. Though there is a window, it is oiled paper rather than glass, and the muted light is less pure, less brilliant. It's also chilly. I'm glad to note the stone fireplace at one end, but wind blows through the spaces between the logs. And through the roof.

The children scamper in and hop onto a pile of bedding stacked in one corner. Straw ticks, I imagine.

John enters behind me and stops.

"Did you see the roof?" I ask.

"I see it."

"And the walls?"

"Mm hmm."

"We can't live here, John. Not during this season. Johnnie's six months old, for heaven's sake. We'll freeze in here."

"It was supposed to be habitable. William Duley said he'd make sure of it while he was out here cutting hay."

"Well, he evidently didn't. I suspect he was too busy boasting about his accomplishments to think about it."

I bite my tongue at my uncharitable comment. Duley isn't all bad, but he does tend to puff up like a rooster more often than not. He'd served on the state constitution committee, he'd founded a town, he'd owned two businesses, he'd—

"I'll go talk to Everett about it. Will you be all right? Do you want me to start a fire first?"

"No, we can do that. At least there's been wood stacked."

I lay Johnnie on the mattresses. Goodness, they're stuffed with feathers. Feather ticks way out here! I remove my bonnet from atop my thick bun and start assigning chores.

"Merton, fetch in wood and lay a fire. Frank and Giles, start bringing in what you can carry from the wagon. Start with quilts and foodstuffs. Fred, you mind Johnnie."

I spy a broom in the corner and sweep the hardened dirt floor to clear the scattered bits of mud and leaves that have blown in. Already, I understand we will have to live here; there is nowhere else for us. My mind whirls, exploring ways to make the shack more habitable. I wonder if the Irelands are encountering the same conditions. I think about the Duleys crowded into that one-room cabin with the Everetts. None of us are too satisfied right now, I suspect.

John reenters the shack with Uncle Tommy, another man behind them.

"Lavina, this is Parmlee, another of the settlers here."

"Mr. Parmlee." I shake his hand and hope the men can come up with an idea. We can't all move in with the Everetts, after all.

"Good to meet you, Mrs. Eastlick," he says. He looks around the cabin, his gaze lingering on the ceiling.

"See what I mean?" John says.

"Yep. Didn't know it had gotten this bad."

"What do we do about it?" I ask, eager to press the issue.

Parmlee's brow knits. "My place is about a mile and a half

from here. I cut blocks of sod over the summer, was going to build a stable with them. Looks like a new roof here is more important right now. Those last few windstorms we had must have shredded the roofs. They weren't much to start with, but they were better than this. I can haul them up tomorrow, but you'll have to cut them."

"I don't have anything to trade you for it." I know John's pride prickles with the admission.

"Not to worry. I've pretty much decided I'm headed back east in the spring anyway. Whoever takes over my place will have to worry about his own stable."

"We can use the canvas from the wagon for tonight, and I can work on the roof tomorrow." John looks to me for agreement.

"I can tack up quilts on the walls for now, but the logs will need to be chinked."

"We'll pitch in and give a hand to get that done," Tommy says.

John catches my gaze. "The other shack is even worse. I've told Tommy to let it be for now. We'll get this one weatherproofed first, and they can stay with us until we can do theirs."

"I know it will be crowded, Lavina," says Tommy, "and I hate imposing but—"

"Nonsense. What's another six people?" If nothing else, the body heat will keep us warm.

Chapter Thirteen

Laura
January 1862

I snapped the quilt atop the sole bed in the cramped room the Everetts had provided for our use. The colorful patchwork lent cheer to the dull gray of the morning. Emma and Jefferson shoved the spare feather tick—the one the children slept upon—under the bed, giggling as they struggled with the ungainly mattress. The experience of so many living under one roof was an adventure to them, and I was glad of it. Even so, I envisioned a time when we would move into our own cabin and planned to raise the issue with William.

"Everyone dressed and ready for breakfast?"

A chorus of yesses sounded, and we headed in a group for the main room of the cabin, knocking to alert the others before we opened the door.

Mira Everett stood at the small stove, cracking eggs into a frying pan. "Good morning, all you little sleepyheads." She turned and beamed at the children.

They chimed replies and scrambled to chat with their playmates. Emma had become fast friends with Lillie Everett; Jefferson and Bell played nicely with their Charlie. Our William typically sought out Frank Eastlick, the two being of an age.

I neared the kitchen area and grabbed plates and silverware from the shelf. With so little room and too small a table, we had become accustomed to eating picnic style.

"Thought we'd have the last of the bacon." Mira indicated a pan on the back of the stove.

The winter had come hard and fast, and supplies had thinned. Yesterday, William and Mr. Parmlee had left for New Ulm to purchase a wagonload of foodstuffs for the settlement. Mira said it was common practice during the winter, but she thought there might be two trips this year, given how many of us there were.

"I think William volunteered for the trip just to have a break from the monotony," I said.

Mira laughed. "Too bad we don't get that luxury."

She dished up plates of bacon and eggs, and we handed them off to the children. They assembled in a group upon a quilt the girls had spread on the wooden floor. Mira and I sat at the table.

"Where's Will?" I asked.

With "William" being such a popular name in the settlement, I was glad Mira's husband preferred the shortened nickname. It was hard enough dealing with three boys called "Willie" without confusion in referring to our men.

"He ate early, went out to do chores. I think he likes the barn better than the house, once everyone is up and at it."

I laughed. "That's not a surprise. We're packed pretty tightly. I suspect the Eastlicks are much relieved the Irelands have moved out of the shack and into their own cabin."

"I have no doubt. Despite their long friendship, fourteen in one room would be far too many to abide. The Irelands must have jumped at Parmlee's offer."

A few days after our arrival, Tommy Ireland had negotiated a purchase of Parmlee's land and cabin. The entire family had moved two miles northeast immediately, with Parmlee to remain there as well until his move back East in the spring.

"When is your brother arriving?"

Mira's face lit with a smile. "I think Charlie plans to be here in the next month or two."

We finished eating and gathered plates for washing, my thoughts drifting forward. By March, we would have one more soul in a cabin that was already packed to the gills. "Where are we going to put everyone?" I asked.

"If we're fortunate, spring will come early and allow the men to get a cabin built on your land. If not, we'll figure it out."

"I imagine we will, though it'll be left to the two of us, I'm sure." The men would simply escape to the barn or clear land or other tasks to take them from the house.

We finished stacking the dishes, and Mira set the coffee on. We pulled out our mending, taking chairs near the stove, while the children scattered throughout the two rooms in play.

"I keep thinking about Charlie and where he'll claim land. John Eastlick said they plan to take their claim between here and the Irelands. That means the only available land near us is to the east, away from the lake, out on the prairie. I worry that he'll be more vulnerable out there all alone."

"He's a grown man."

"But he's my little brother, and I worry about him."

"I know. I worry about my sisters, too."

Mira rose and fetched two cups of steaming black coffee for us, setting a small container of precious sugar on the table for me, along with a spoon, before sitting back down. "Has William taken you to your claim?"

"Our first week here."

I stirred a tiny bit of the sweetener into my cup, careful not to take too much. Steam rose from the surface, and I set it back on the table to cool a bit so I wouldn't scald my tongue.

"Did you decide where to put the house, Laura?"

"In truth, no. William wants to locate near the Des Moines

River." I paused, wondering if I should share my concern. "We argued about it. Rivers have not been good to my family."

I left it at that, not telling her about my two drowned girls or the ruin of the mill.

"I didn't think you were too enthused about it."

"And it's so far away from most of the settlement. The Wrights and Lambs would be our only neighbors." And if the Lambs leave like they're planning, there would be only one family. "Neither William nor I am keen on the Indians who camp on the Wright place."

Mira waved a hand in dismissal. "Oh, the Indians have never been a problem. There's usually not more than two or three tepees there at a time and not too often at that. It's the hard winter that's had them here more these last months. We've gotten to know a few of them pretty well."

"They've come begging for food?"

"They're hungry; game's scarce. Julia said they're supposed to get annuity supplies on the reservation, but Mr. Lincoln's war has delayed delivery."

I shook my head. "I'd just as soon not have them here."

"Just be glad they're a friendly bunch."

I glanced out the window, musing. "This must be a beautiful spot in the summer months."

"It is. We set the cabin here, smack in the middle of the peninsula, for that very reason. The lake is close enough to get to, but far enough that the kids aren't tempted all the time. Lots of trees, calm water, gorgeous sunsets. But it is off the main trail. I think Will would prefer it weren't so quiet."

As for me, I thought the Everett place was one of the most picturesque cabin sites, set far back from the water, among a grove of fully matured trees. A few of the others favored the Ireland place, but this cabin's distance from the lake held special appeal for me.

I lifted the coffee and breathed in the aroma before taking a sip. It warmed my mouth and slid down my throat, a treat I'd not had for days. Coffee, too, was in short supply. I savored each sip and watched Mira do the same. We might not agree on what made a perfect location for a house, but we did both agree that coffee was a pleasure to be enjoyed.

An idea popped into my head so suddenly that I nearly spilled the treasure. "Mira? What if we traded claims?"

"Traded?"

"There's lots of land around the southern side of the lake, and it's near the New Ulm Trail. Charlie could take a claim right next to you, and Will wouldn't feel so isolated."

"Oh, my! And you would be nearer people you know, farther from the Indian encampment."

"I do like it here."

"And if we lived on the river, Will and Charlie could take on running the mill more easily. Your William could be a silent partner, the way he's been saying he wants. It's a perfect idea."

I thought so, too. Now, I just had to convince William.

Julia
April 1862

Dora rushed into the house, breathless. "Mama! Old Pawn is back again."

"Is he now?" Julia ruffled her daughter's head. Five-year-old Dora was fascinated with the huge Dakota man, despite his fierce appearance. In fact, other settlers called him the ugliest Indian they'd ever seen. To her way of thinking, Julia found him a big—very big, given his height—pussycat, but she wasn't about to tell anyone else that. The last thing she wanted to do was insult the man. "And what did he have to say?"

"He and the others have come to hunt again."

Lake Shetek remained a valued hunting ground and ceremonial area, even now, after many of the Dakota had moved onto the reservation. But, hunting here was more than their tradition now. Folks all said food was scarce at the agency. Their farming didn't support them, and the annuities ran out far too soon. And the situation had worsened since the fighting between the states.

She supposed life on the reservation could be pretty miserable.

The Sioux were a complicated people, with three different dialects (Dakota being one of them), two major geographic divisions, and seven tribes or bands. It still confused her, trying to sort it all out, but she'd at least learned the Dakota dialect and made efforts to understand and respect them. Jack sure as goodness didn't.

The first thing she'd learned was that they disliked being called Sioux, which was an Ojibwa word meaning "little snakes." Dakota was preferred, because it meant "ally." Others called themselves Santee, which referred to any of the eastern tribes.

"One of the men wanted to know if Papa had any more whiskey for sale," Dora said.

"Oh, for heaven's sake." Julia sighed and grabbed her shawl. "You stay here and watch George."

She strode out the front door, crunching across the new spring grass and ruing the day she'd met Jack Wright. What in the world was that man doing this time? She neared Pawn's tepee and paused to alert him of her presence. "Pawn? It's Julia Wright."

Pawn lifted the flap. "*Hau.* It is *waste* to see you. Do you wish to enter?"

Julia spoke to him in his own language. "It is good to see you, too. I don't need to come in. I wanted to tell you that Jack isn't selling whiskey any longer. One of the men asked Dora."

Pawn shrugged his shoulders. "There are rumors there *is* whiskey again, sold from the barn."

She closed her eyes and drew a slow breath. A year of compliance from Jack and peace of mind for her seemed to be Jack's limit. She needed to take care of the issue before it went too far.

"Tell your men I am sorry," she said. "If there is whiskey, it is no longer for sale."

"I will tell them." The way in which his mouth thinned told Julia he understood the situation completely. "You are well?"

"I am. And you?"

"Yes, my friend. I will come later to talk, to tell you of the news among my people."

Julia returned to the house, slammed the door, and marched toward the area that had been curtained off as a bedroom. Jack lay abed, snoring heavily. She yanked the blanket from him and kicked the bed.

"Get up, you louse!"

Jack jumped, glared at her with bleary eyes. "Damn it, Julia, I was sleeping."

Sleeping it off, maybe. Now, she knew why he'd gone to check on the livestock last night. "It's time to get up. It was time two hours ago."

He crumpled back to a prone position and drew the blanket back up over his head. "What d'ya want, anyway?"

"Do you have whiskey hidden in the barn?"

"What?" he mumbled.

She jerked the quilt off and let it fall to the floor. "Do. You. Have. Whiskey. In. The. Barn?"

"Don't know what you're talking about." He attempted naiveté but failed miserably. He'd never been a good liar, ought to not even try.

Still, it was a saving grace that she could always see through him. Lord help her if he ever learned to lie well.

"I will go out there myself and tear that barn apart."

This time he sat up, sighing. "Aw, Julia, why does it matter so much?"

"Why? Because you promised me you wouldn't. Because it drags my reputation through the mud along with yours. Because it's dangerous."

He reached for his pants and tugged them on. "A little whiskey never hurt anybody."

"A little whiskey gets the Dakota drunk, especially if it's that rotgut stuff you were selling before. It got Renicker killed a few years ago."

"Nobody's gonna kill us."

Julia stared at him. Did he truly believe there was no danger in what he was doing?

Of course he did. Arguing that point would get her nowhere. She crossed her arms and glared. "I will not have it here."

"Ain't that much anyway."

"Where is it, Jack?" Her foot tapped the wooden floor, tapping out a rhythm of growing impatience.

"It's my business."

"You already drove away George and Lorenza with your foolish whiskey business. Don't you realize they were afraid? That the other families are concerned? Selling whiskey impacts all of us. It's everyone's business."

"Stay out of it, will you?"

"No, Jack, I won't. Finish getting your lazy butt dressed, go out to the barn, and show me where those bottles are hidden. And any barrels, too, inside the barn or out of it."

He glanced up. "And if I don't?"

"I will pack up the kids and take them to Iberia, and we'll live with George and Lorenza. You're putting lives in danger, and I will not be a part of that. Not now, not ever."

Christina
May 1862
I am glad the spring has finally come. My lilac bushes have buds, and I look forward to the scent of the purple flowers filling the air. I think, maybe, the turn of season will brighten our moods. The winter was long, and we had to make two supply runs to New Ulm. The second trip, Andreas and William Duley went. It was not a good trip, and it lingers on like a bad taste in Andreas's mouth.

"He is a loud-mouth know-it-all," Andreas says.

All the way, Duley kept trying to tell Andreas how to drive the team. I think my husband knows how to drive a team! But Duley thought he knew better. If there is one thing I know, it is that telling Andreas how he should do something is not a good thing. Telling any German such a thing is not good.

Ach, I can see them in my mind: Duley all puffed up like he is a peacock and Andreas stubborn as a kicking mule. A stubborn German, though, can cut off his nose to spite his face, and my husband did exactly that. He drove straight into a patch of quicksand at the Cottonwood River. Oh, and didn't Duley have a great time preaching how he should have more sense? Andreas says they almost came to blows, and he will never go anywhere with the man again.

Ja, I am glad we are past the winter, and my husband can work out his anger in the field instead of telling me over and over about it.

"Hello?"

Almena! I stop kneading my bread and rush to the door to hug my friend, and little Frank who is on her hip.

"I brought butter." She hands me a basket, and I peek into it, my mouth already watering. Almena's butter is a treat, and our mouths will have pleasure tonight at suppertime.

She removes her shoes at the door and reminds William

Henry to do the same. Only then do they enter my tidy cabin. How well she knows me. She is the only one I do not have to remind of this. As usual, I have swept every spot of dirt outside. A good *Hausfrau* keeps everything clean.

Almena sets Frank down on the rug to play with his brother. The two boys are charmers, that is sure, and I am proud the rug is freshly beaten and a good spot for them. Their blond heads bob as they play with carved animals together—William Henry takes them everywhere with him. These boys are darlings, and they bring me such happiness.

I motion for Almena to sit as I return to the bread dough. "How are you?" I ask.

"Fine, fine," she says, but I am not sure she tells the truth.

Silence stretches with only the boys babbling and me punching dough. "Were there many Indians at your place this winter?"

"More than usual. I fed them as often as I could." I know we are both thinking about how cold and hungry they were this winter. "Julia Wright said there were problems getting food on the reservation. Were there many here?"

"*Nein,* not so much. Andreas and Voigt saw to that." Andreas has never wanted to trade with them, and, in the fall, Voigt became angry when they came to trade for food and shot at their feet to make them leave. It was not good, because they were only women and children. Now, the Sioux regard Voigt as an enemy. Me, I do not mind helping them when they are hungry. "Old Scalpie came a few times, when the men were not here." I shape the dough into loaves, which I put on the back of the stove to rise.

"I wish we knew her true name," Almena says. My friend has a softness that wants to avoid this awful nickname, but I have no answer for her. The woman has been called this name ever since being attacked and nearly scalped by hostile Indians.

"Even the Indians call her that," I finally say. "Is there any other gossip?"

Almena laughs at my question. She knows I will only ask this of her. "You heard about Hatch and Bentley arriving?"

"Charlie Hatch is Mira Everett's brother, I know. Who is Bentley?"

"He came with Charlie. He's staying with the Myerses for now but plans to take a claim south of the Everetts. He's a millwright. Looks like the mill operation is growing."

"Isn't Duley a millwright?" I think of the man and his bragging about his skills. He will not like it that Charlie has brought another.

Almena laughs again, understanding. "He's likely a bit put out, but Bentley's already here; what can he do? I guess they plan to start on the mill this summer. Oh, and the Eastlicks have a cabin up. It's not quite finished, but they've moved into it. They built at the edge of the timber near that small slough southeast of the Irelands. Everett moved the trapper shack the Eastlicks were in down to the Des Moines River as temporary quarters until he can build a bigger place."

She pauses, and I glance at her. I know her. She is making small talk with me instead of talking like sisters as we usually do.

"You have heard much news," I say.

She shrugs. "Phin has been up and down the lake."

I raise my brow. This is not usual for him, and I wonder if it is linked to what bothers her. I probe a little. "Just to gather news?"

"No. He went out with Ernst when he was looking at land." Almena's mouth trembles, and I rush to crouch next to her.

"What is it?"

"Phin and Bill Jones have made a provisional sale of our place to Ernst and Voigt. They are back there at our cabin now, working out the details. I couldn't stay there another minute."

"No!" I put my hand to my mouth. It cannot be. "You are not leaving us?"

"Phin and Bill want to go west, to Dakota Territory. They've been talking about it for months." Her tone is wooden, resigned.

"But why? I thought you were happy here."

"It's the blackbirds. We can't get rid of them, and they've taken over the crops."

Ach, I know about their blackbirds but to let the pesky birds push them away from here? This I do not understand. "But there's plenty of land. Can't you take another claim?"

Almena's face tightened. "I tried to tell Phin that, but he and Bill have heard about a settlement called Yankton, in Dakota Territory. And with the new Homestead Act, the land will be free."

Ja, this I do understand. It is difficult to sway a man when he has heard about something that seems to answer all his hopes.

"So far?" I am not sure even where this Yankton is, but I think it is on the Missouri River far to the west. Days and days of travel.

"I'm afraid so. The two of them will go out to look things over before we move. We don't want any surprises this time. If Yankton isn't the right place, they'll scout other areas."

"What will you do while they go?"

"The sale includes an agreement that I can stay in the cabin until they return and we pack up the place. Voigt will come up and stay in the second room to keep the place in order while they are gone. And watch over the boys and me."

I sigh. "Voigt and Ernst don't care about the blackbirds?"

"Not so much, no. They plan to make the place into a trading house."

I think Ernst will be a good trader but Voigt, not so much, not as an enemy to the Sioux. "How will Voigt handle it when Bad Ox comes to trade for cheese?"

Almena's eyes close for a moment, and I know she feels bad. "There won't be any cheese for him, I suppose. I'll warn Bad Ox about the change, if I have the chance. In the meantime, Voigt will need to keep his opinions under control."

Almena
July 1862

Almena placed the boys down for their naps and sank into the kitchen chair. She dropped her head into her hands.

Where were they?

Phin and Bill had been gone for six weeks, two weeks longer than they'd said they would be. Phin had *promised* her they'd be back by Independence Day. Instead, she'd picnicked with the other families in the wooded area between the Duleys and Smiths, pretending to be as happy and joyous as the rest of the settlers. She'd watched Frank totter after William Henry, laughing at their antics while worry battered her head. She'd eaten green peas and spring chicken, licking her fingers and chatting with the other women. But, all the time, she'd been anxious and fretting.

And every day since, the trepidation had grown, growling and churning so that she could barely eat. She'd fought to hide it from the boys, feigning that life was normal. But Phin was never late, had never broken his word. She'd been fighting the thought that wouldn't stop roiling in her stomach.

What if he doesn't come back?

Lord help her, for the boys' sake, she needed to make plans.

"Almena?" Julia Wright's voice sounded from outside.

Gracious, what was Julia doing all the way up here?

Almena patted her cheeks, stepped over Bill's near-deaf dog, and rushed to the door. She pasted on a bright smile she didn't feel. "You're about the last person I expected to ride into my yard."

"I suppose I am." Jumping from the wagon, Julia looped the reins around one of the oak trees. She swatted an errant blackbird away. "You do have a lot of them here, don't you?"

"We're infested with the damn things." Almena put a hand to her mouth as soon as the curse came out, but it was too late. She flushed. What must Julia think of her?

But Julia only laughed.

Relieved, Almena relaxed a bit. "At times, they're so thick we fire off the shotgun to scatter them. I don't know why . . . they just come back." She glanced at the wagon. "Do you want me to get Voigt to tend the horses?"

"No, no, don't drag him in from the fields. He looked busy when I passed him. I won't be too long. They can stay in their braces."

"Come on in." Almena tipped her head toward the house.

"Are the boys inside?"

A strange question. Unease crept up Almena's spine, and she kneaded her callus. "Asleep," she said, "but we can chat."

Julia shook her head. "Let's sit out here. How about on the log?" She pointed to a spot about halfway between the cabin and Bloody Lake. "The shade looks refreshing." She strode away and lowered herself onto the fallen oak.

Almena followed, apprehension growing. This was odd, Julia not wanting to come in, being worried about the boys. "What is it? Something about Phin?" She whispered the words and sank down next to Julia. Tension coiled through her.

Julia drew a breath. "The New Ulm postmaster sent word that there was a letter from Fort Pierre."

"Fort Pierre?"

"It's in Dakota Territory, about two hundred miles north of Yankton, on the Missouri River. There's a trading post there."

Dakota Territory. Almena's pulse stuttered. "Phin?"

"The letter was from a trader, who had received goods in trade from a group of Dakota." She paused and reached for Almena's hand.

No, no, no, no, no.

"—horses, a wagon, and a gold watch with an inscription."

Air whooshed from Almena, and she swayed. "Phin's watch." The words were so softly uttered, she wasn't sure she'd said them aloud until Julia answered.

"It appears so, yes. It was his name, and an inscription."

Almena's head fell back, and she scrambled to suck air into her mouth. She gulped once, twice, and squeezed her eyes shut. But the implication wouldn't be blocked out so easily. She clutched at Julia's hand.

"I gave him that watch," she croaked out before her voice broke and she could say no more.

Julia gripped her hand, grasping it until she breathed more evenly.

Almena composed herself. Emotional breakdown would do her no good, not now. She sensed Julia knew her anguish, but they were not familiars. With Christina, she would share her tears. Right now, she needed to hold herself together.

"From what the trader gathered from the Dakota, he reasoned they'd had the items since early June, maybe as early as June third."

One day after he'd left.

Almena tamped the anguish. "Maybe they found it. Or stole it."

"Maybe."

But neither of them believed it. She certainly didn't, and she spied the doubt in Julia's eyes, heard it in her voice. There was only one scenario that made sense.

"Or maybe not," Almena conceded. She removed her hand

and smoothed her skirt. Realizing what she was doing, she stilled the errant motion and stood. She needed to move, to get away from this spot.

"What do you want to do?" Julia asked, rising to join her.

"Could we . . . do you think the men would . . . ?"

"I think we could get a search party together."

Almena strode toward the lake. "Phin said they'd go to Sioux Falls first—they wouldn't have even gotten that far."

From behind, Julia caught her arm, stalling her escape.

"Almena, if they search, are you ready for what they might find?"

If they found his body, she would be ready. But until that time, he was still alive in her heart.

Lavina
August 17, 1862

The summer is hot and humid. Thunderhead clouds roll through the sky in the late afternoons, bringing streaks of lightning and threatening hail. We watch carefully for any telltale swirling that might form tornados. Something ominous weighs on me, and I'm not sure what it is. I tell myself it's only the weather and return to the field with Merton and the dog to check the crops.

Perhaps it's only that John has been away so much this summer. I'm pleased he is due home today from his trip east to work the harvest there.

Despite our house still needing a bit of work, he went with the search party in July with Everett, Wright, Duley, and Smith. Estimating where Phin Hurd and Bill Jones might have been on their second day out, the group rode to Split Rock, on the Rock River, and spent time scouting the area. Though they found traces of the men's trail, it led them no further. The search party itself became separated and returned in two groups. John told me his group thought there were Indians in the area and thought it best to come home immediately.

We laughed about it when the lost members of the search party straggled in late that same day, having found the note John had left for them after they got lost. John said nothing to the others about his Indian fears, and we dismissed it as errant worry. After all, small groups of Sioux camped along the lake all winter, begging for food. They played with our children, teaching them their language. We'd all gotten on well together. In late spring, they'd left, and we've glimpsed little of them since. It is hard to imagine violence coming from any of them.

"Mother?" Merton asks, rousing me from my thoughts.

"Yes, my boy?" I'm proud of him. Now eleven, he has a keen sense of what's needed around the farm. He and Frank complete their chores without fuss, whistling all the while. Even Giles steps up to help, Merton supervising them.

"Will you look at this corn? I'm thinking we may need to bring it in soon."

He's pulled back a portion of the husk on one ear, and I examine it with him. It looks ripe, ready to be picked. "The corn first," I say. "Then the potatoes. We can start tomorrow."

Merton looks pleased. His father taught him well.

The dog leaps off, barking, and we follow him to the house, Merton chattering about who will do what in the morning. As we near, I notice John's horse in the yard, along with one I don't recognize, and rush to locate him. I find him in the barn, hefting the saddle onto a rail.

"John!"

He turns and opens his arms. I run into them, and we share a kiss in the dimness. At someone's throat clearing, we draw apart. When I turn to see a strange man, my face heats and I'm glad for the darkness. I tuck in stray locks of hair and wait for

John to introduce him.

"Lavina, this is Mr. Rhodes. We met in Olmstead County, and he's decided to settle here at the lake. I told him he could stay with us until he settles on a claim."

I welcome Rhodes, shaking hands and ask, "How was Olmstead County?"

"Full of work. I was glad Wright suggested hiring out back there. The money will help, with the limited crops I got in this first year."

"Merton and the boys will bring the corn in tomorrow."

As the men finish with the tack and the horses, we chat about their work, the progress of our crops, the thunderstorms, and the news from back East. They met sixteen Indians on the way back, in traditional loincloths and red face paint, but found them friendly and talked with them. As well, Lincoln's war continues, and Minnesota men are leaving their farms to enlist. Rhodes hands me a pile of newspapers so that I may read about the details. We walk together to the house.

"Have the Indians been around?" John asks, a hint of disquiet in his voice.

"Not at all," I answer, waiting for him to say more.

"That's good. Good," is all he says, and I wonder what has prompted him to ask, what has made him uneasy.

"Should I be worried?"

"No, no. I just wondered." He looks at Rhodes, and something passes between them. "Wright stayed in New Ulm for a couple days. He thought he spotted Phin Hurd's dog with an Indian yesterday. He was going to dig into it a little, try to find out more."

"That's not a good sign."

"No, it's not." He pauses but says no more about it. "You go ahead in, get washed up, my little field hand. We'll be in soon."

I roll my eyes at the strange endearment and enter the house.

I wonder if the stew will feed an extra mouth and begin setting the table. Outside, John and Rhodes speak in low tones, and I catch only a few words here and there.

". . . good idea to build a fort, don't you think?"

I stop, my heart racing. A fort? I rush to the doorway.

"Why do we need a fort? What have you heard? Are we in danger?"

John glances toward me, and I swear his eyes hold distress. Rhodes shifts his feet.

"John?"

"Nothing to worry about. Phin disappearing, seeing his dog, it got us talking about how the settlement was growing. With more of us, it wouldn't hurt to explore the idea of a fort."

I don't believe him, but he will say no more.

★ ★ ★ ★ ★

Part Three: Ordeal

★ ★ ★ ★ ★

Chapter Fourteen
August 20, 1862
It Begins

Almena

5:00–6:00 a.m.

Almena crept from the house, taking care to keep as silent as possible. William Henry and Frank were still asleep in the bed they'd shared since Voigt had taken over the second room of the cabin. If she was to get her five cows milked, it was to her advantage that the children stay asleep. Hungry toddlers usually made for uncomfortable delays for the cows. Besides, this was the day Charlie Hatch planned to borrow Voigt's oxen, and he'd likely be here around sunrise.

Outside, the pre-dawn air held a chill she hadn't anticipated. She debated returning for her shawl but shrugged the idea off. It would only get in the way, and she'd warm up once she started milking. She fetched her milking stool from the barn and headed to the paddock.

"Good morning, ladies," she called, patting each of the cows with affection as they gathered around her. Hungry girls, she thought. She dumped feed into the trough and eyed the cows. Their udders were heavy; there would be a lot of milk today. Maybe she'd make an extra sharp cheddar this time, have it waiting for Phin when he returned.

When he returned.

She'd denied reality for so long now that such thoughts were almost a given. *When he returned.* But he was now months late, and she had to accept that hope was useless.

A soft neigh reached her ears. Charlie already. She sighed at the poor timing, with feed already in the trough. The cows would be less cooperative later, and they wouldn't be happy at the lack of relief for their full udders.

"Be right there," she said. Maybe Charlie would round up the oxen by himself and be on his way so she could finish milking. She turned to suggest just that, but it wasn't Charlie after all.

Ten Dakota men were in the yard, one of her trading partners, Iltimony, among them. He scratched the dog's ears as another group reined in a distance away. *"Hau,"* he said, raising a hand.

Almena sucked in a breath. Goodness, they'd come in quietly. She'd not even heard them arrive, and Bill's old dog had long since gone deaf. Her patience prickled at the inconvenient arrival—she'd need to offer breakfast. She acknowledged him and several others she recognized. Most had been at the cabin before but had never caused any problems.

"Have you come for cheeses?" she asked, hoping to send them on their way with just a trade this time.

Iltimony slid from his mount in that fluid way of their people. "We come to hunt buffalo, but we will visit with you."

Sighing, she patted the cows in apology and strode toward the house. She shouldn't be so resentful with her hospitality.

The group in the yard dismounted and followed her into the cabin.

Inside, Voigt stood near the stove. The heavy aroma of coffee filled the room. It was their usual habit, Almena laying the fire before the milking, Voigt starting the coffee. He glanced at them, a scowl forming as the Indians filed in.

Almena mouthed a silent "shh" to him, hoping he'd keep his

mouth shut. There was enough bad blood between Voigt and the Dakota, and the last thing she needed was an altercation. Thankfully, he moved to the corner of the room and remained silent.

She went to the stove, gathered a frypan, and carved ham from the hock she'd brought in from the smokehouse late last night. There were only a few potatoes. It wouldn't go far, not with the four of them and the Dakota men, but it would have to do.

The men took out pipes and lit them. Fragrant tobacco smoke wafted through the air. Voigt exaggerated a cough.

"So do you think you'll find buffalo?" she asked, hoping to distract them from Voigt's antagonism.

They conversed in the Dakota language. Over the past few months, she'd become more skilled at understanding it. What she didn't grasp, or was unable to say, was translated by Iltimony and the half-breed among the group. They chatted, mostly about the wildlife and late annuities until little Frank woke, fussing. Almena supposed it was the sight of so many Indians all at once.

She glanced toward the bed. William Henry was stirring, wide eyed. Frank was frantic.

"I will tend him," Voigt said and scooped Frank up. He headed toward the door.

Almena breathed easier. She knew Dakota children were brought up not to cry, and the men were likely judging her. Taking Frank outside would calm him and avoid the men's displeasure. One of the men she didn't know rose and followed them outside.

Seconds later, a shot rang out, and the dog began frenzied barking.

Almena dropped the fork, her pulse thundering. Frank! She raced for the door.

Voigt lay on the ground, blood pooling beneath him, Frank still in his arms.

Almena sank to the ground and met Frank's wide, startled eyes. The moment he saw her, he wailed. She grabbed him, pulling him from Voigt's limp arms. The German's lifeless eyes stared up at her, and she gagged.

Nearby, the dog squealed. Then silenced.

She heard only the sounds of horses and people running, shouting in Dakota. She turned. The dog lay still on its leash. The other group of Indians had ridden into the yard, and a host of women emerged from behind trees. They rushed into the house.

Almena followed, desperate to rescue William Henry. He was still on the bed, his mouth gaping as women rummaged through their belongings, shattering china and ripping window curtains from their anchors. One of the women yanked on the handle of the largest trunk, edging it toward the door in staccato movements. Another rustled through a second trunk, flinging belongings far and wide.

Almena shoved her way past them, and William Henry scampered into her arms. She turned and fled the cabin, a child on each hip. She turned away from Voigt, so that the boys would not catch sight of his dead and bloody body, lying there on the ground with a hole in his chest.

Outside, one of the women piled up cheeses and cakes of butter. Months of hard work sat before her—twenty-three cheeses and nearly three hundred pounds of butter. Someone had hauled a feather tick from the house and another woman sliced it open. The crash of furniture being tipped over rang out.

Horses pranced among the havoc, and Almena scrambled to avoid being trampled. She glanced back.

Oh dear lord, that's Phin's horse!

A few feet from it pranced one of the dogs Phin and Jones had taken with them.

Almena gulped, panic racing through her veins. At that moment, she *knew.*

Someone grabbed her arm and swung her around.

She cried out and clutched the boys close.

"If you go, we will not kill you," the man said.

The words were rough, and she barely heard them.

"We have no quarrel with you. Go to your mother." The Indian pointed eastward.

To her mother?

William Henry struggled in her arms, whimpering in his nightclothes. He had wet himself and shivered in the cool air.

"All . . . all right," she said. "Let me get my boys dressed."

The man shook his head. "No. You go."

"But they need clothing, and their shoes."

"If you wish to live, you will take them now and go. Otherwise, you will all die."

Still dazed, Almena stood silent.

The Indian grabbed her again. He shoved her and she began walking.

"Be quiet, William Henry, be quiet," she told the wriggling boy.

Usually argumentative, he must have heard the urgency in her voice. He gulped back sobs and clung to her as she headed east, accompanied by seven Dakota men.

Christina
5:30–6:20 a.m.

The sun is peeking into the day when I hear the hoofbeats of a horse.

"*Ja,* that will be Charlie Hatch," says Andreas. He is pulling on his boots and does not yet have his shirt buttoned. "He is going up to borrow Voigt's ox to raise the mill today. I told him he should leave the horse here so he will not have to worry about it when he is leading the oxen down the shortcut."

We hear a distant shot and glance at one another, grinning. Almena and the blackbirds.

I think she has it in her mind to shoot them all before Phin returns. I sober, and my heart is in pieces for her because I know he will never return, no matter how much she hopes. Before I choke up, I turn to Andreas and make conversation.

"Are you going to the lower end?" I ask. The mill will be built south of the lake, where the Des Moines River flows out, about four miles from us.

"*Nein,* there is much to get done here."

I am glad of it, for both corn and wheat are ready for harvest and should be brought in before we are hit with a hailstorm. When we finish our chores, we will work in the fields. This is the way of things, hard work and good weather. That is how we survive.

Andreas comes to the table, and I set his plate of bacon and eggs before him before I sit with my own.

"The Indians are back," he says. "Old Pawn is camping by the Wrights."

"*Ja,* Julia says he is a good man."

"He is ugly."

I laugh. Andreas does not like the Indians any more than they like him. They do not bother me so much. We finish breakfast, and Andreas heads outside to tend the livestock before we go to the fields. There is time, I think, to sweep out the *Haus,* and I make use of it. I do not like the dirt that has gathered on the floor. No matter how many times I sweep each day, the dirt comes back, blowing in with the breeze and clinging to our clothes.

I hear more horses and step out of the cabin, wondering if visitors have come.

Andreas is talking to a group of Indians. One of the men asks him for water. He grabs a pail, and they dismount to follow him around the *Haus* to the well at the bottom of the hill near the lake. It is not long before I hear shots. We will not get to the fields so early now, if they are having a shooting competition. I think perhaps Andreas should not have set up the targets for that, but it is a harmless thing.

The shooting stops after only a few shots, as if the contest has halted too soon.

Worry snakes through me, and I drop the broom. I rush around the house, my heart thumping. Charlie Hatch's horse is spooked, loose in the yard, and the Indians are chasing it. I do not see Andreas.

My gaze darts to the barn, and I notice him on the ground in the stockyard. He does not move.

Mein Gott! They've shot Andreas!

I dart forward, Indians scurrying all around. Not my Andreas, not like this! The horse thrashes in front of me, its hooves flying. I screech to a halt, quivering.

In that moment, I realize Andreas is dead and that I will very likely be next.

Almena

6:15–7:15 a.m.

The seven men took Almena to a little used trail, escorting her on horseback as she walked. The sun had emerged, its brightness and warmth in stark contrast with the brutality that had just ripped her world apart.

William Henry's weight grew heavy, and Almena stumbled, landing on her knees. She bit back a sob, wondered how she could keep carrying both boys. Despair crowded her soul. Phin was dead, despite how she'd tried to avoid accepting it, and she yearned to curl into a ball and cry until the loss was numbed. And, if the Dakota didn't like it, it would matter little if they killed her, too.

And, while she gave in to the grief, the Dakota would take the boys away from the only family they had left. Or worse.

She gulped a breath and dredged up a smile for William Henry.

"How about you walk a little bit?" she asked him, filling the suggestion with as much enthusiasm as she could muster.

The toddler shook his head, defiant.

The half-breed tugged on her arm. "Go. Now." He spoke Dakota now, not English as he had in the cabin, and glared at her.

Get up, Almena, get up and go. It's all up to you, now.

She made her way to her feet, adjusted Frank, and took William Henry's hand. He tugged it away, and his mouth scrunched into an angry pout.

"We need to go, my little man. We must." She pulled, and he trudged along, plodding his way across the still-dewy grass in his bare feet.

"It's wet, Mama."

She squeezed his hand. "I know, Sweet. It's all right."

"I don't want to go nowhere. I want to go home." He looked back, tugging away.

"We have to go this way. Let's have a game of it, like we're on an adventure."

"I don't want to." His lip trembled.

One of the men pushed at her.

"We must go." She grasped William Henry's arm, dragging him behind her. Her eyes burned. *Walk, William Henry, walk.*

In the distance, two shots rang out, and Almena jumped.

Christina!

She faltered, stumbling in panic. Christina would need her.

The clawing fear gave way to reality as she stood, her son clinging to her legs. "I'm scared, Mama. I want to go home."

There was no home. Christina was likely already dead.

The men grunted, and Almena took William Henry's hand again. If they did not go, they would be killed. All of them. Being allowed to leave with their lives was a gift. Though she had no clue of the reasons behind it, they needed to take what was offered and *go.*

She caught her son's gaze and forced a stern tone. "You will do as I say. You will take my hand, and you will come with me. Now. You will not let go."

He cried, wailing, then hiccupped as his sobs became whimpers. But he no longer resisted her confusing orders.

They'd gone about two or three miles when the men reined in their horses. "Go straight to the east to your mother, to your people. Do not stray. Do not come back. If you come back, if you go to the others, we will kill you."

Almena nodded. Her husband was surely dead, her home destroyed, and her friends being killed. Ahead of her were seventy-five miles of open prairie. Her children had no clothing, and there was no food. But she would go, and she would not turn back.

She clutched William Henry's hand and strode away.

Lavina

7:00–8:00 a.m.

The house is crowded, now that Rhodes is boarding with us. We don't have an extra feather tick for him, and he's forced to sleep on a pallet in the side room where the five boys have their bed. There are no extra chairs, either, and it takes two rounds at the table to feed everyone. The oldest boys have eaten and are doing their chores. Only Johnnie sits at the table with us, boosted upon a wooden box so he can reach his breakfast.

The extra furniture will need to wait until winter. Getting settled is taking more time than we anticipated, but, eventually, we will carve out a comfortable home. For now, we make do. I long ago learned to be practical about life. Events do not go as expected; when they don't, we do what we must.

I serve Rhodes and my husband and set a small bowl in front of Johnnie, giving him a spoon so he can eat his porridge. The children awoke so early that I haven't even had time to put on my shoes yet and have no idea if the boys have donned theirs.

It will be good to sit and have a few moments of peace before we start our busy day.

"Ma!" Merton calls from outside, the dog barking along with him. "Ma!"

I sigh and hustle to the doorway, my few moments of quiet and my breakfast both delayed. "What is it?" I ask.

"Charlie Hatch is coming, as fast as he can run!"

I glance across the yard and spy Charlie emerging from the waist-high grass. He is panting and can barely catch his breath by the time he reaches me. I wonder if there has been an accident in raising the mill. But he has come from the wrong direction.

I shiver. "What is it?"

"The . . . Indians are . . . upon us."

Our Indians? I'm unable to believe our friendly group has turned on us. My mind doesn't want to accept his words. "That can't be," I say.

"They've shot Voigt, and Hurd's household is strewn across the yard. Mrs. Hurd and the children are missing. When I got back to Koch's, I saw them shoot Andreas. I'm pretty sure he's dead, too."

Now, my heart thunders in earnest, but I stand paralyzed. "What about Christina?" I ask as Merton rushes into the house.

"I don't know. I didn't see her. My horse—the wild colt—was tied up there, and he spooked when they shot Andreas. They were busy chasing him. I figured I'd better run while I had the chance. I came down Stump Pass to the Irelands."

Stump Pass—the marshy shortcut between the lake proper and a water-filled slough. The shortcut saved miles and precious time. Thank God it existed!

Oh, dear Lord, an Indian attack. Of all the things I have imagined might go wrong here, this was not one of them. I turn around, looking for John. In my panic, I don't know what to do.

"Tommy said we should all meet at the Smith cabin," Charlie says, as if he recognizes my dilemma. "I came here while the Irelands went there."

"Have you warned the others?" John asks. He has Johnnie in one arm and guns in the other. I don't know when he came from the house or how long he has been standing there.

"Not yet. Can I take a horse?"

"I'll grab a saddle," Rhodes calls out and veers to the barn.

"No time. Just a bridle," Charlie says.

I stare at him, still numb with shock. "How far away are they?"

"The bridle?" he asks again, and the request finally breaks through my haze. I remember Rhodes was working on the leather last night and rush into the house. Where is it? I check the table, run to the side room.

John calls out, "Merton, get the boys together."

I grab the bridle from next to the bedroll, hasten outside, and hand it to Rhodes.

John catches my gaze. "We've got to go."

The children are barely dressed. "I'll gather our clothes."

"There isn't time." Now, John's tone is urgent, and my skin

crawls. I tell myself to focus. Do what needs to be done.

I am barefoot, the boys as well. "Our shoes?" We cannot leave without shoes.

"There's no time. Let's go." He tugs at me and sets off. I forget the shoes.

Charlie rides out of the yard, toward the Duley cabin. I turn, count the boys, and start to follow John.

"For God's sake, at least take ammunition with you!" Rhodes yells.

Rhodes is right. The shoes can be left, but we will need the ammunition. "Go," I tell the boys, "to the Smiths' as fast as you can."

I turn back and lift the front of my skirt. Rhodes dumps powder, shot, and lead into it, and I dash after John and the boys, weighed down by the heavy lead. Rhodes follows, carrying more guns. He flashes past us to the front of our scattered group. The dog trails us, ever faithful.

I run as fast as I am able with the extra weight, my feet striking the hard ground without cushion, the grass cutting my feet. Lead jounces out of my skirt, and I stop again and again to scoop it up. Panting, I call out to John, and he trots back to me, urging the boys to continue on.

"The lead—"

"We don't have time. Leave what spilled, and hike your skirt up further. Maybe that will keep the remainder secure."

I run after him, the load still heavy. I lurch on the uneven ground and flounder. "I can't keep up, John."

He rushes back to me, his face knotted with anxiety. "Grab my coat."

I imagine us both being caught. "No, go ahead."

"I won't go without you," he says. "I don't care how hard it is. You can't give up. The boys need you. I need you."

I swallow. He's right. I can't give in to the pain or the fatigue.

We rush on. My side pinches, and the rocks cut my tender feet. We run the two miles to the Smith place only to find it closed up tight.

"Smith? You here?" John calls out.

"Wright's." I gasp for breath. "They must have gone to Wright's." We race past the end of Beauty Lake. The boys, Rhodes, and the Smiths are ahead of us.

Winded and panting, we crest a hill. The Wright house is below, several Indians gathered around it.

Julia

7:30–8:30 a.m.

Julia had just finished dressing Dora and George when she heard the horse. Before she could open the door, Charlie Hatch burst into the house.

He appeared a wild man, his hair windblown, his shirt drenched with sweat. "The Sioux are attacking. We have to arm."

"What do you mean, attacking? There are three tepees in the meadow, and the whole bunch of eight was up here for coffee not more than a half hour ago."

"Voigt's dead, shot through the chest, and Mrs. Hurd and the kids are missing; household contents scattered. I saw them shoot Koch and headed out to warn everyone. They seem to be headed from the north, and we don't have much time."

His panic was real. Old Pawn and his group might be having coffee with her, but that didn't mean squat about any others.

"I'll get our guns," she told Charlie.

His eyes filled worry. "I still need to warn my sister."

"Go. Send them here." Theirs was the biggest house, nearest the Sioux Falls Trail. It made sense that they gather here.

He ran out the door, and she turned to the children. "Go

upstairs," she told them. "I want you to stay there until I tell you to come back down."

"But, Ma . . ."

"Go."

They trudged up the staircase as Julia assembled guns and ammunition from the trade stock. There wasn't as much as she'd hoped. Jack had planned to purchase more in New Ulm, on his way back from working the harvest.

New Ulm . . . he was likely there now. She offered a small prayer for his safety as she piled the arms on the kitchen table. What else needed doing?

She thought of Pawn and the lodges outside. She'd need to determine if they would stand with the settlers. She drew a breath and rushed outside.

"Pawn?" she called.

He stepped from the group he'd been talking with and approached. "The rider had urgent news?" he asked. His was even, without panic.

Julia weighed his tone. "He said an attack has been made on the settlement. Do you know about this?" She watched his face, searching for any sign that he already knew of the events.

"I do not."

A note of surprise. Easy enough to fake, but it sounded sincere. Still Julia pressed further, needing to be sure. "He said it was Dakota warriors."

"Sisseton?" he asked, referring to his band, one of seven among the Sioux people.

"I don't know."

Pawn's brow knit, worry evident.

Julia weighed his response, unwilling to distrust her friend.

"We will fight with you, if they come here. You have been friends to us, and we wish to keep you safe."

His words held the ring of truth, and her gut told her to trust him. The additional defense would be valuable, and a go-between might prove of benefit.

"Make plans. We will need you."

She ran toward the house, her mind flying to the other tasks necessary for a possible siege. In the distance, a group of people approached, and she recognized the Smiths. She waved them on, told them about the weapons, and rushed back to the yard. Rhodes was sprinting down the hill, followed by the Eastlick children.

"Merton, take the boys into the house and upstairs," she directed. "I will need you to keep them there until we call you down."

The boy straightened to his full height. "I can help shoot, ma'am."

Poor kid. He'd be a solid defender and wanted to prove himself a man.

"I know," Julia answered, putting her hand on his arm, "but we'll need assurance the children are all safe, and that will be your responsibility. If necessary, we will arm you, but I think it best if we keep the little ones away from that so they don't panic. I need you and Frank and Willie Duley to take charge of it. You three are the oldest. Can you do that?"

"We'll do it. Come on, boys. We need to get set, find ways to keep 'em all busy. There's gonna be a hoard of kids up there." The five boys disappeared into the house.

Julia glanced around, realizing three Eastlicks were missing. "Where are John and Lavina and the baby?" she asked Rhodes.

"On their way."

She mentally tallied the group. "Charlie didn't mention the Myerses. Are they coming?"

"No one knows. Charlie had to make a choice. He came south."

She thought of the Myerses, alone at the north end of the

lake, and lifted a silent prayer for them. It made sense for Charlie to have come this way instead—more families to be warned in doing so—but she hoped the remaining family had found a way to escape.

Rhodes shifted, uneasy. "You haven't been attacked?" He waved toward the tepees.

Julia eyed him. Rhodes was new to the settlement, and she'd yet to take his measure. "Old Pawn and a few others, set to head south to hunt buffalo. They've given us their allegiance."

Rhodes's eyes held skepticism. He pointed to the north. "Here come the Eastlicks. And Tommy Ireland. Looks like William Duley is with him."

Good heavens, Lavina was on her last legs. Julia rushed forward as they came down the hill, and Lavina collapsed in her arms.

"She barely made it," John said.

And no wonder. She smothered a gasp as she caught sight of Lavina's bloodied feet. "Someone take that lead from her, get her up to the house, and see if any of my shoes fit her." She turned her friend over to John and watched him usher her toward the house.

Rhodes still stood beside her, as if waiting to be told what to do. *Idiot.*

He had to be in shock, much like the others, even if he didn't appear as stupefied. "You. Gather up buckets of water from the well out back and get them inside the house. Use the pails on the shelves. The Smiths can help you."

In her mind, she knew she should be just as traumatized, but if her years cleaning up after Jack had taught her anything, it was that there was little time for panic when things needed doing, and, right now, she might well be the only person thinking clearly at all. She could fall apart later.

"Where are the rest?" she called out to Duley and Ireland.

Tommy raced to her. "They attacked before we got out of the yard. We were trying to load up supplies. They chased me while Sophia led the kids into the woods. We don't have much time."

"Laura's in the woods, too, hiding with the kids," William Duley confessed. "She couldn't keep up."

"We will go." Pawn stepped forward. Dances in Water and another Dakota woman stood behind him. "We will find them and bring them here. You make things ready."

Laura
8:00–8:30 a.m.

I huddled in the bushes, shaking, my children clustered around me. Their eyes were nearly bursting with fear. My heart pulsated with more trepidation than I'd ever known. We were going to die here, in this isolated place, and no one would ever know.

We should never have come to Shetek.

Already we have suffered so much loss and now this. We should have stayed in Ripley County or even in Iowa. Or kept the store in Beaver. A thousand regrets filled my head, and still I stood quaking, knowing none of it mattered. It would not change where we were nor what we would likely encounter.

Emma held four-year-old Bell in her arms, comforting her. Willie and Jefferson were likewise embraced. I carried Frances. The minutes stretched on, and I wondered if William were still alive, or if savages had already murdered him. Would that be our fate? Had he abandoned us here in the scrub, leaving us to perish?

I couldn't move, didn't know if I should take us onward or remain hidden. Tears streamed down my cheeks, and I remained frozen in place.

The sound of rustling leaves broke through the heavy silence of our hiding. I clutched Frances closer and stifled a scream.

The brush parted, and a haggard Christina Koch stood there. "Laura, is that you?"

"You're alive!" The words fell from my mouth, so astounded was I that she had survived.

"*Ja,* I got away, but my Andreas has been killed." Grief filled her voice, but she didn't waver as she stepped closer to us. Her dress was torn from the brush, its hem wet and muddy. Her blond hair had escaped her usually tidy braid and hung about her face, full of sticks.

"William?" she asked, seeking my husband.

"He went ahead. To Wright's."

"He should not have left you. We must go on. I saw the Indians at the Irelands. They barely escaped. We cannot stay here, or they will come upon us."

I shrank at the accusation in her words and did not respond to them. William *had* left us, and I could not refute it. Still, I did not want to leave our refuge. I didn't want to emerge from the forest to cross the open ground.

"William said to stay in hiding," I protested.

"If we stay here, we will be murdered for sure." Christina was firm, resolute.

I envied her courage and shrank smaller into my green nest. I glanced at each one of my children. "No."

"*Ach,* you do as you want, but I am going on. I will not be killed hiding in the woods."

She stood and stepped out of the bushes just as three Indians appeared on the trail.

Julia
8:30–9:00 a.m.

Julia thanked the two Dakota women who ushered the Irelands, Duleys, and Christina Koch into the yard and urged the settlers into the house.

Lavina rushed forward to greet them and drew Christina into her arms.

"My Andreas is killed." The words were wooden. "They shot him for nothing."

"We may likely all be widows before the day ends," Lavina noted and wiped Christina's face with her thumb.

Laura Duley's chin quivered, and Julia drew a breath. The last thing anyone needed right now was a gaggle of weeping women. "Lavina, take Christina into my room and find her dry clothes. Did you find shoes?"

"None that fit these big feet." She lifted her skirt and raised one foot, then gave a short laugh that hung in the air.

"Laura, take your young ones upstairs. You, too, Sophia."

Understanding fills Sophia Ireland's eyes. "Come on along, Laura." She wrapped an arm around Laura's waist and guided her up the narrow stairs.

With the women all busy, Julia turned back to the men. Edgar Bentley had arrived. She tallied the numbers. Thirty-four of them. Only the Hurds and the Myerses were missing, along with her husband and Ernst Koch, who were both in New Ulm. She suspected the missing neighbors had been killed hours ago. This would be all of them.

Of their total number, most were children. There were eight women—all could shoot, she supposed, except maybe Laura Duley—and eight men.

She glanced at the table. Three squirrel rifles, some shotguns, a few sacks of shot, and a keg of powder. "That's all?" she asked. It was as sparse a collection as she'd ever seen.

"Some of us didn't even have a chance to grab guns," Tommy Ireland said.

"It's going to make for a difficult defense," John Eastlick noted. He held his rifle in his hand; it was the best in the community and he, the best shot.

"*Ja,* you will need these, too." A freshly dressed Christina Koch dumped a collection of butcher knives and hatchets onto the table. "I took from the shelves."

"Gather up the axes, too," Julia said.

Eastlick moved to the center of the group. "There aren't enough guns for all of us. I think it best for the men to take the guns and defend from the holes we've been notching out of the chinking. The women can take the other weapons and go upstairs. Let us know when you spot them coming."

"What about the Indians outside?" Smith asked. "I'm surprised they haven't attacked."

Julia sighed at her nearest neighbor, a man of less than keen intelligence by her reckoning. "You know as well as I do they've been camped here for the past three days without a single problem."

"That's true. They're planning to head down the Des Moines River to hunt buffalo."

"You believe them?" Duley scoffed. "I don't trust the whole bunch of 'em."

"Pawn's been a friend." *For heaven's sake, I shouldn't even have to remind them of that.* "I didn't note anything in his reaction that led me to believe his intentions are evil. He offered their help. I think we need to trust them."

"You mean give them some of our arms?" Smith shook his head.

Ireland caught Julia's gaze and rolled his eyes. "Oh for Pete's sake. If they wanted us dead, we'd be dead already."

"I'm not inclined to let them in here with us, that's for sure," Duley said.

"I think Julia is right. Let's trust them. Tizzie Tonka stopped me outside, said he'd fight for us. I gave him a small horn of powder already." Ireland shrugged his shoulders. "We don't have much to lose."

"Enough already. We're wasting time." Eastlick eyed the group. "If they prove friends, we'll have need of them. Give them powder and lead and have them take up defense from the barn. That's more tactical anyway."

"And if they do turn on us?" Lavina asked from the edge of the room. "John, you asked one of them earlier if he would fight for us, and he said he didn't know."

"Uncle Tommy is right. If they had killing in mind, we'd already be dead." Julia scooped a few bags of shot from the table and strode toward the door. Ireland followed with two of the guns.

Pawn and Tizzie Tonka stood in the yard, scanning the distance. "Will you still defend us?" she asked Pawn.

"We will."

She tossed the shot to him. "Thank you, my friend."

Ireland handed him the guns. "You can take a stand in the barn."

Tizzie Tonka motioned to the others and the Dakota moved away with guns, bows, and knives.

Pawn pointed to the northwest. Ponies circled the prairie near Beauty Lake, and war whoops began to sound.

Ireland caught Julia's gaze and drew a breath.

She swallowed. It wouldn't be long.

Lavina

9:00–9:30 a.m.

In a burst of speed, Julia and Uncle Tommy flee into the house and bar the door.

Tizzie Tonka and Old Pawn have come in with them. These are old friends. I cannot believe they would be any part of savagery, but apprehension fills me, and I can't dismiss the cloying fear. Ever since the Indian in the yard responded he was unsure he would fight for us, my pulse has raced nonstop. Everything I know about these people is now topsy-turvy.

I huddle behind the counter with Christina; the other women have gone above. She shakes, her eyes narrow, upon glimpsing the two Sioux. I can only imagine the thoughts in her mind after seeing her husband lying dead at the hands of their tribesmen. I wrap my arm around her and offer her as much strength and comfort as I can muster.

Julia stands with Pawn and Tizzie Tonka as the men in the room take notice. Suspicion hangs in the air like heavy morning fog on the lake.

"It looks like they're making camp," my Merton reports from the stairs. "The women are putting up tepees near Smith's place."

"They're coming!" Laura shouts, terror in her voice.

"Two riders only," Mira Everett clarifies.

I drag Christina with me to the nearest window, unable to stay back simply waiting for the attack. Better to know what is coming, to confront it. She draws a breath and comes with me, and I realize we are of one mind in this. There's nothing to be gained in hiding in fear.

Pawn and Tizzie Tonka are at windows, too, their guns in their hands. Seeing them, I breathe easier. I believe they remain the friends I knew them to be.

Outside, two Sioux ride to the edge of the field, fire off their guns, and return to their camp, whooping. In a moment, another surges forth, aiming at a stray cow and downing it.

"What are they doing?" Duley asks. His shoulders are tense, his face filled with panic.

"They're baiting us," Uncle Tommy says.

Pawn straightens. "They are showing their bravery by riding in front of you. They are also making you fear them."

"I've heard of this," John says.

One after another, the Indians emerge. Some moments apart, others at longer intervals. I tense at the waiting, and it stretches on and on.

Christina stands at the window, her face drawn. I clutch her hand, and she says, "It will be all right. Whatever happens, it will be all right."

I am not so sure if she believes that, or if she is trying to chase her fear away.

"What do we do?" Everett asks.

Tizzie Tonka turns from his post. "Show they do not make you afraid. If you all fire your guns, they will know this and will be frightened away."

The men whisper among themselves, gather their guns. In a group, they move to the door and lift the bar.

They're going out.

My skin grows hot with sweat even as a cold shiver creeps up my spine. When they exit, Julia Wright goes with them, her husband's gun in her hand, a shot pouch and powder horn slung over her shoulder like a warrior. The woman must know no fear. I envy her.

They line up in front of the cabin as I watch from the door. As one, they raise their guns and fire toward the attackers.

All but Pawn and Tizzie Tonka.

My knees nearly buckle, and I fear they will turn on us after all. I rush out to John. "Do not discharge further," I plead, "lest they turn on you when your guns are all empty."

"Go inside," my husband orders.

The Indians continue to taunt us. We have failed to convince them we are unafraid.

Julia

9:30–10:00 a.m.

Julia stood firm as they fired. The sound echoed in her head, her ears ringing. She blinked her eyes, coughing as the combined smoke of their multiple rifles stung her lungs. From the corner of her eye, she saw that Pawn and Tizzie Tonka had held their fire.

Strategy against the settlers? Had she made an error . . . a tremendous, horrid error?

"That did no good," Smith muttered.

"What now?" As usual, Ireland got to the meat of the matter.

Pawn grunted, low in his throat. A single note of resignation. "I will go parlay." He strode away.

Julia watched him go as Lavina and most of the men stomped back inside. She debated with herself. It was possible Pawn had seen this result coming, that he'd held his fire in order to maintain an illusion of neutrality so he could better negotiate. It made sense. But she was no longer as sure of him as she'd been before. There was too much she didn't understand.

Several Dakota rode from the field at breakneck speed, directly toward Pawn. He stopped, facing them. Julia held her breath as the riders continued on, hell-bent for him. He did not flinch, and they reined the horses to a stop. They shouted back and forth before Pawn approached the riders.

Julia glanced at Ireland, who waited outside with her. His face was etched with worry.

She shivered and realized she was afraid.

We are at their mercy, and there is no way this is going to end well.

When her pulse started racing, she tamped the thought down. Fear was her enemy, as much as that group of Dakota, and she couldn't let herself fall prey to it.

"Julia," Ireland whispered, "Pawn's coming back."

She lifted her head and watched the tall Dakota man jog toward them. “I have news,” he told them.

They clustered inside, so that all could hear.

“Grizzly Bear leads two hundred warriors and many squaws.”

Julia recognized the name as the man who had become chief after Old Sleepy Eye died a while back. Some called him Lean Bear, but she knew both were the same man. “Sisseton?” she asked, trying to sort out whether or not the group belonged to the same band as Pawn.

“Yes. White Lodge and Strike the Pawnees are with him,” Pawn said. “They wish to kill the whites.”

“I say we go out there and kill them!” someone shouted from the back of the room.

“I speak for you, tell them you have been friends. I ask them to let you leave. They say you may go, if you do not fight them. But you must hurry and take nothing, or they will burn this house with you in it.”

Julia turned and faced the men. Their faces were taut with fear. Their comments blurred together as they talked over one another.

“It doesn’t sound like much of a choice.”

“The house has green shingles, but it wouldn’t last long.”

“There’s women and children to be considered.”

“We can’t be thinking of trusting that savage, can we?”

“It’s seventy-five miles!”

She emerged from the fog, stuck her fingers in her mouth, and whistled until all was quiet. “We can’t delay this, or it will be understood as a rejection of the offer.”

“Then we go,” Eastlick said. When a majority agreed, he spoke to Pawn and Tizzie Tonka. “Tell them.”

They turned and left the house.

“Should we get supplies?” Lavina asked.

Christina stepped forward. "*Ja,* I can do that, get the blankets and food."

Julia shook her head. "They said to take nothing. We would be wise to take note of it."

"We cannot take twenty children across this prairie on foot," Everett said. "Charlie, you and Rhodes go out the back, take two horses, and ride for our place to get a wagon, blankets, and food. If we're lucky, you can get through the woods along the river without them noticing. They'll be focused on the rest of us. Meet us down the Sioux Falls Trail a bit."

"I'll get the others," Lavina said.

Julia watched her ascend the stairs.

Leave now, leave peaceably, take nothing.

She shivered again.

Chapter Fifteen

August 20, 1862
Flight Interrupted
10:00 a.m.–2:00 p.m.

Almena

10:00 a.m.

Almena trudged across the prairie, Frank limp on her hip. William Henry plodded alongside her. She blew at the strand of hair that had strayed across her face, sticking fast to her sweaty skin. Damn merciless humidity. It had to be near ninety already. She sighed and glanced at the sky, trying to factor the time. She couldn't reconcile location and the sun.

She stopped and glanced around. How had she been so careless? There was no longer any visible trail, and she had no idea how long they'd simply walked on, oblivious. Were they still going east?

Think, Almena!

Their path seemed correct, felt on course. It couldn't have been more than a few minutes since she'd last glimpsed the faint path across the prairie. It had become less distinct with each step so it wasn't difficult to imagine it had faded completely. It was but an Indian trail, after all. They had to be going east. She glanced upward and found the sun.

Was it only early morning still? No, the sun was too high. Wasn't it? She thought they'd been walking for hours, but that could be an illusion. Carrying twenty-two pounds for any length of time seemed an eternity. It was hot, more like late morning, but it was also August, and the Minnesota heat rose early.

Stupid, stupid, stupid.

Hot wetness exploded under Frank, and the smell of urine filled the air.

"Frank peed, Mama."

Almena sighed. "He sure did." She guessed she should be thankful he hadn't soiled himself yet. Wet as his diaper was, it would fail to hold that, either.

"He stinks."

They all stank, she imagined.

"My feet hurt."

"Sit a little. I need to put Frank down for a while anyway."

They both sank to the ground. She shifted Frank to the grass and pain surged down her arm and into her hand. She grimaced and shook it until the sting eased and only numbness remained. Years of butter-making had made her arms strong, but, lord above, it hadn't prepared her for this!

"I didn't get no breakfast."

"I know, sweet one. I didn't either." She reached for one of his feet and took it in her hands, wincing at the sight of the bloodied cuts from the grass. "This hurt?"

"Yes'm."

She rubbed first one, then the other, hoping to ease his pain and her own numb fingers. He lay back, sighed, and fell asleep, his thin nightclothes up around his knees.

Almena shook her head. The light cotton would be a blessing through the day, but the boys would both be cold tonight. She'd need to find a sheltered spot before nightfall.

She lay on the grass next to them. The last time she'd left her home on foot with a little one had been twelve years ago with her brother Seneca. She'd thought herself frightened and uncertain, but it had been nothing. Nothing like now. After all, there'd been another home waiting at the end of that road.

Now there was naught. There was no home. There was no money, and there were no cows to help them survive. Her eyes stung with unshed tears.

Most of all, there was no Phin, with his laughing eyes and silly teasing.

There was only her, and she had no idea how she was going to hang on.

Christina
10:00 a.m.

It is like thunder, with twenty children coming downstairs at once.

"Go, go," Mrs. Everett urges from above.

They flood down with their faces dazed. Parents rush behind them, and the cabin is thick with people.

"Bell? Where's Bell?" Laura Duley is frantic, almost wild. She spins around like a *dreidel* to find her daughter.

Gott im Himmel, I think. It is all upside down. Parents run about hysterical and the children stand in stupors.

"Go to your mothers," I tell the older ones, those who are not so shocked and are looking around with terror on their faces. They have need of something to do.

Merton Eastlick herds his brothers close and shoos them to Lavina. Lillie Everett clutches her brother's hand. Emma Duley's mouth quivers even though she tries to hold it in a frozen line, but she has Bell with her. Laura sees them, puts her hand to her chest, and exhales a long, wavering sigh. Her hands are shaking. The Ireland girls dance around their mother, and I know they are nervous, because it is not how they usually behave. Julia Wright leads Dora and George outside to the sun.

Others follow in a desperate tide.

Laura and her children seem unable to move, and I go to her.

"Will they kill us? We can't leave here; we can't. There's a cellar. Can't we hide in the cellar?" Her voice has too much alarm, and I think her terror has taken over her mind.

"Listen to me, Laura Duley. You must hold on to yourself. You must be a leader for your children." I point to Emma. "Already Emma is so afraid she might break. Your husband is too busy telling the men what to do, so it is up to you. If you let go, what will happen to them?"

"But—"

"There is no choice. You will all die in the cellar if they burn the house. I think you must hold on now and go to pieces later, when this is over."

Laura draws in a breath and steers her children to the door. It is a good thing, that she finds a way to do this.

We must all find a way to do this. I think about what Lavina said to me, that the day could end with many women alone, their husbands dead. Widows.

I am a widow.

My shoulders quiver. My good, strong Andreas lies on the ground, shot dead. He will never hold me in his arms again or call me his *Leibchen* or tell me I am his *Ein und Alles.* I will never look into his soft, blue eyes.

I choke down my grief and my own worries. It does no good to do this now. The children will need the women to be strong. Already, they have noticed Laura's alarm and heard guns and whooping. It is not good if they are so panicked that they cannot be handled. This we do not need.

It will be a long day, and we must keep everyone moving.

"Are you coming," Mrs. Smith asks. "Christina?"

"Ja."

I see I am the last one. I go out the door with one last look toward the supplies. I do not know how we will cross all the miles to New Ulm without food and blankets, but Julia is right. We cannot take the risk.

It would not be a wise thing to defy the Dakota at a time like this.

Laura
10:15 a.m.

We scrambled out onto the prairie, clutching our children close. I struggled to keep my fear at bay, glad that Christina forced me to surrender my selfishness and focus on my little ones. I'd lost too many children already. I would not, could not, lose my remaining family to those demons.

Ahead, Mira Everett began to run. Like falling dominoes, the rest of us followed suit. All but Julia Wright.

"Stop," she shouted. "We need to pace ourselves."

Everyone halted, a few running into those ahead of them.

"She's right," my William said. "Stay together. Hurry along, but don't run."

"Men, fan out around the women and children," Uncle Tommy advised.

Smith shouted, "Carry the littlest ones, and keep your kids together."

The men were full of instructions, but the women had already followed their instincts. They'd already clustered the children together and herded them as faithful sheepdogs caring for lambs.

"Mama!" someone called.

"Shhh, come along now."

A few followed along the Sioux Falls Trail, but most of us were stretched out on the prairie so we were not so bunched up. Older children parted the tall prairie grasses for their siblings, and we rushed forward. A few dogs ran among us, loyally following their masters.

I cast a look back. The eight Indians who had given their word to protect us remained at the cabin. The other group had now moved in and were plundering the house. A few had climbed onto the roof to watch our progress.

Tommy Ireland was pointing in that direction. "They're keeping watch."

"Move on! Don't look back," my William directed. "Don't give them cause."

We moved as quickly as we were able, more than thirty of us streaming forth. The uneven ground beside the trail dipped, and our party undulated down, then up as we encountered a rise. Though the hills were not high, the route was difficult, and we soon tired, not even a half mile from the cabin.

"The wagon!" Merton shouted.

We surged forward, over the crest.

Hatch and Rhodes were approaching, driving two horses and a wagon as fast as possible. They halted. The horses were lathered, their sides heaving.

"Up. Get them up."

We loaded the children in, bidding them to crowd together. Charlie Hatch began handing women up, and Rhodes followed suit.

As he lifted me into the wagon bed, I glanced west one final time. More Indians had clustered on the roof, gesturing at us with sharp, hostile movements. I could almost feel the intensity of their anger.

A chill flashed up my spine.

Julia
10:30 a.m.

Julia set George into the wagon and bent to pick up Dora.

"Sit and hang on tightly, little ones. I love you."

"Aren't you coming up?"

Julia eyed the wagon and the two horses. The poor animals were already tired, and it would be a heavy load. "I'll walk for a while."

Next to her, Lavina was handing up her own children. "I'll do the same," she said. "Merton, Frank . . . you two can stay with me."

Julia extended a smile and choked back resentment that the other women had settled in the bed of the wagon. A nip of guilt struck her, and she chided herself for being judgmental. Later, after they recovered a bit, they would walk.

"Let's go!" the men shouted.

Mrs. Smith, at the reins, gave them a slap, and the horses started off. The wagon lurched and moved forward.

Julia glanced back from the top of the rise. The Dakota had merged into one group.

What? Had she expected Pawn and Tizzie Tonka to come along?

She guessed there were thirty or forty in total, not the two hundred or more as they'd been told. A scare tactic, likely. She wasn't sure if Grizzly Bear had made the exaggeration or if Pawn had done so. In any case, it had worked.

They'd left as commanded.

But she had no doubt the Dakota lookouts on the roof had noticed that they'd taken horses, a wagon, and blankets with them.

Lavina
10:45 a.m.

The war call sounds out of nowhere when the wagon has gone a scant mile or so down the road. Laura screams. At once there is a panic in the wagon.

Julia is wide eyed with realization.

"Merton, Frank! On the wagon." I scale the front of the wagon box while the boys clamber into the back. Julia tosses her gun up, and the other women heave her into the box. The men rush aboard, crawling over children until every space is filled. Those who do not fit begin to run.

Mrs. Smith starts the horses, and we jerk forward at a crawl. Too slow! I grab the whip from its holder and fling it overhead, lashing the poor animals with all my strength. They flinch and strain but still manage no more than a walk.

"They are coming!" Christina yells.

"Move those horses faster!" William Duley shouts, as if I can do anything more. "Get a man up there."

I risk a look back. Dust plumes in the air. The Indians are chasing us, gaining on us.

"Ya!" I yell and lash the horses yet again. The shouts of the war party drown my words.

"We shouldn't have taken the wagon," Julia mutters.

"Stop!" Duley shouts. "Stop and leave the damn horses and wagon."

The men's voices converge as they all shout orders.

"Everybody out. Out now."

"Run for your lives."

"Men at the rear!"

"Do we shoot?"

"We need those horses, and I'll shoot any of them that touches them."

Women and children pour from the wagon. Merton jumps down, and I force little Johnnie into his arms. "Run, Merton, but do not let go of Johnnie. Don't let go. You are responsible for him."

He nods and rushes away.

I tumble from the wagon, stepping on the hem of my dress. The skirt rips from the waistband. I clutch it so I won't trip and rush the other children forward. Confusion and panic reign around us, and I struggle to keep them in my sight. The little ones whimper at being hurried, but the older children understand and push them forward. Women and children swarm across the prairie as the men stand firm. Julia grabs her husband's gun and takes her place with the men.

Shots fill the air but come from too far away. It won't be long until their fire will reach us. The Indians have spread out in a line, their horses rearing as they yell and whoop. They fire again.

We rush on, frantic. Children flinch as shots sound. Mothers urge them on, into the tall grass. So far, they have shot above our heads, but that could change at any moment, and we must get the children away.

Several of the Indians reach the wagon and dismount near our horses. They struggle with the harness, and one of them begins to cut through the leather with his knife.

"Grizzly Bear," Christina whispers beside me, "the chief."

Four shots ring out, and the Indian with the knife drops to the ground. The others jerk, wounded.

The shooters—Duley, Ireland, Everett, and my John—are lowering their guns to reload.

"Everyone into the slough!" Duley shouts.

We run downhill, into the tall reeds to hide. Shots rain upon us. Near me, the smallest Ireland girl stumbles and screams, her three-year-old voice shrill amid the gunfire. Two of the Duley children fall; Laura tows them into the marsh.

"Laura?" I whisper. "How bad?"

"Willie's hit in the shoulder, Emma in the arm."

On the road above, Smith and Rhodes run to the east, and the other men shout at them. One of them turns, and the Indians fire on them. They both rush down from the road into the far end of the slough.

"Julianne got it in the leg," Sophia Ireland says.

One by one, mothers report in low whispers. We keep our children still so the movement of the reeds does not give away our locations. Above, the Indians continue to fire, shots falling randomly into the quagmire.

We quiet, squatting in the wetness. My bare toes squish into the mud. The water isn't deep but creeps past my ankles, and my dress soaks it upwards. Despite the heat of the day, I shiver. Freddy's teeth chatter, and I hug him close to warm him. My little Johnnie's eyes are wide with fear, but he plops his bottom into the water and digs his hand through the mud. I make no move to chastise him, for the distraction fades his distress.

Dear lord in heaven, how can this be happening?

"Eastlick? Take a shot!" someone calls. My John has the best rifle among us and is a good marksman, so it's no wonder the other men call on him. The Indians show themselves only one or two at a time on the ridge above us, shooting before moving quickly out of range. Others pop up as the first group reloads. Each time our men fire, they reveal our places, draw more fire. Dull thuds sound as targets are found, quick gasps of pain, muted groans.

The balls fall fast, and my children flinch. I crawl through the stifling reeds, hot and sticky with sweat. Mud sucks at my hands and knees, but the children do not follow, so I halt and draw them close.

"Aaaah!" someone screams. Mira Everett, I think. "My neck."

Sharp pain explodes in my side. I bite my tongue but cannot stop the moan from escaping my lips.

"Lavina?" John calls.

"I'm hit."

"Are you much hurt?" His voice is tight.

"It feels like I'm dying."

The grasses move, and I gasp. "Stay still! There's nothing you can do, and you'll draw their fire. Just keep shooting."

White hot fire bursts in my head. I clutch my scalp with my hand. My mind clouds, throbbing. The thick, sticky blood seeps through my fingers, and at least I know I am still alive.

"They've noticed me. I'm moving," John whispers. He crawls away through the tall grass. My senses haze.

He reloads, the sounds crisp and distinct, then nothing. In the quiet, more thuds and gasps.

"John?"

He groans, so faintly I can barely hear him, and I inch toward him.

"Do not, for God's sake." Christina's plea halts me. "Stay with your children. If you stir, they will all be killed."

She whispers more, but I can no longer make out the words. In shock, I grasp for my boys.

The time stretches, and I no longer have any idea how long we have been here.

Nor how long we have yet to remain.

Christina

Late morning or early afternoon

"He is dead already, and you can do him no good. Stay put." I whisper the words to Lavina and hope she hears. I think that she does, because she no longer tries to crawl to John. She hugs her children, and I wonder if she will die, too. I think she has been shot in the head.

It is muggy in the slough. Flies and mosquitoes bite, but we dare not swat them. The mud here is stagnant and cloying. I think this will be a miserable place to die.

The sun is high in the sky, and I try to figure the time but cannot see enough. I know only that we have been here for some time. We whisper among ourselves, passing news.

"Rhodes and Smith ran," someone says. "I think they made it out the east end."

"Cowards." Tommy Ireland's voice is bitter, even in a whisper.

I am not sure I agree. A chance was there, and they took it. But I cannot imagine how Mrs. Smith must despair being left alone.

I wonder now if I should also have fled at dawn, when I had a chance. I could be safe, fleeing east on the prairie. Regret claws at me but lasts only a second. I would not have made more than a few steps before turning back. Leaving all the others to die when I had the chance to warn them, to spare them, would have plagued my soul forever. I could not have left them.

"Charlie's shot," Mira Everett says. "He's got two shotguns but can't raise them."

I hear the panic in her voice and know what she is planning. If she crawls to him, she will show where she is.

"Do not go," I tell her.

"I know. He told me already. He has the guns ready, if they come into the slough, and will fire with his other hand."

"I think Duley's shot in the wrist," someone says, passing news along the line.

"I think there are many of us shot," Mira says.

Too many.

I do not know what to say to her. "Does it hurt bad?" I finally ask.

"I can't feel much anymore." She pauses. "There's so much blood."

"Can I do anything?" Empty words, even to me.

"If I die, promise you will tell Will and the children I love them."

I shudder. "*Ja,* I will promise this, but you will not die."

I say the words to her, but I do not believe it. I think that we will all die here in this miserable swamp.

Chapter Sixteen
August 20, 1862
Difficult Choices
2:00 p.m.–4:00 p.m.

Julia

The endless day wore on as Julia sat in the mud, George and Dora on either side.

"I gotta potty," George whispered, his voice urgent.

"Me, too." Dora wriggled, and Julia halted her with a sharp glance.

"Just go." Why not add the reek of urine to the sluggish mud and stench of blood and black powder?

"Right here?" George asked.

"In our clothes?" Dora's voice held shock at the suggestion.

"Shhh . . ." Julia whispered, "we're all wet anyway."

George giggled, and Julia felt his warm urine heat against her hip. He squirmed, and a muddy cloud rose. She stilled him with the same look she'd given Dora.

Dora worried her lip, distress pulling her mouth down as she continued to hold her bladder.

Aw, hell. The poor little thing had learned her manners well.

"Go ahead," Julia encouraged. "We might as well all go." She heaved a sigh and released her own bladder into the slop so that Dora would know it was all right. Moments later, Dora made a face and peed.

Julia's attention focused on the sounds around her . . . or lack thereof. The gunfire from the slough had all but stopped. She rejoiced that shots no longer drew return rallies from the

Dakota, but only for a second.

My God, they're dead.

She shuddered. She still had Jack's gun but had long since set it aside. Thank heavens she'd had the sense to do so. There had been little hope of killing any of the Dakota, and she hadn't wanted to risk the children's lives in a useless attempt to do so. Tremors consumed her as she thought it through. She'd be as dead as the men had she not done so.

Who the hell fired anyway? And at Grizzly Bear!

If they'd gone on foot, without resisting, they might have had a chance.

It would have been much easier to kill the settlers back at the cabin, if that had been the Dakotas' intent. Instead, the group had won a concession, only to waste it away by killing the Dakota leader.

She shook as bitter anger plowed its way through her core. It wouldn't have been this way. She *knew* it. The rage ran into her grief and fear, and the emotions scattered in a thousand directions. She sucked breaths in, one after the other, and wondered if there would be any way out of this.

Pawn had risked his stature by bargaining for their lives. She knew this, even if the others didn't. And they'd brought shame upon him when they broke their word. They'd behaved with dishonor and disrespect, and she doubted there was much that would help them now.

"Are you tired of fighting?" one of the Dakota called.

"Women, come out so you will not die," said another. Pawn?

"Go to hell, you heathens!" Everett shouted back.

"Everett? You have called me friend, but now I am your enemy?" Pawn said.

"You said you would defend us."

Pawn continued, "Come out with the women, Everett, and we will talk."

"I'm wounded. I can't walk. You come to me."

"You lie. I think you can walk if you wish."

Two shots rang in the air.

"Will!" Mira shouted.

Everett whispered, "My elbow's shattered. Tell him I'm dead."

The grass moved, and Mira Everett rose from the slough, wavering on her feet. Blood soaked the side and front of her gown.

"You've killed him," she called out. "He's dead." Her voice quivered with despair.

"Come out and talk peace, and we will stop shooting," Pawn told her. "We will talk how to let the women and children live, and I will take you and Julia Wright into my tepee."

Mira glanced down at her husband.

"It might be best," he whispered. "Obey for now, escape when you can. Otherwise, I think they'll kill you."

"Lavina, will you come with me?" Mira said.

"I don't think I know enough of the language to negotiate with them. Besides, my head . . ." Lavina's words were soft, pained.

Mira turned. "Julia?"

Julia sighed. She and Mira knew the language best. She kissed her children's foreheads, hoping like hell she was making the right choice.

"I'll go, if Christina will keep George and Dora."

"I will do this."

Julia stood, her pulse loud in her head. "Do not shoot my children," she called. "They are moving to Mrs. Koch."

She waited while they crawled to her friend. Christina would have the strength to keep them safe, if things went wrong. She turned to Mira. "Are you ready?"

Julia slogged toward her, mud sucking at her feet. Her dress was heavy with water, and she shivered as the air hit her.

"You're weaving. Can you walk?" Julia asked.

Mira nodded, wincing as her neck muscles strained at the wound. "I'm faint, but the pain has mostly numbed."

"Blood loss. Try to avoid moving your head." Julia wrapped an arm around her neighbor's side, and Mira leaned into her. "Let's go."

Now that she was standing, she saw the clouds building to the west, and she prayed the storm would skirt them. That was the last thing they needed right now.

She ushered Mira forward. "Be strong and choose your words with care," she whispered. "What happens next depends upon us."

"Do you still trust Pawn?"

"We didn't keep our promises. He spoke for us, and we've brought dishonor on him. I don't know how much influence he has anymore or how he feels."

They emerged from the slough and struggled up the hill, crested the ridge.

Pawn stood just beyond, amid a pair of Dakota Julia didn't recognize. She nodded to him, an acknowledgment of his superiority.

"It is good you come to speak, Julia Wright," he said.

"We are honored you asked us to do so."

He motioned for them to sit, and the trio joined them on the ground. Pawn gestured to the others. "We will speak in Dakota so all may understand."

Mira looked at Julia. "My Dakota is not good. You will need to speak for us."

Julia knew Mira had to be part of this. It was a duty she did not want to shoulder alone. "If Mrs. Everett does not understand, I must tell her in English. If I do not understand, I must ask you to use English. We have much responsibility."

Pawn grunted an agreement. "There is much disagreement among the Santee, and the Sisseton are only a small voice. Our brothers, the Mdewakanton and Wakpekute, are much displeased with your people and have attacked many settlements in the past days."

He paused, and Julia relayed the information to Mira, explaining that these were three tribes of the eastern Sioux known collectively as Santee, whom she called Dakota because of their dialect. Pawn was a Sisseton, several villages of which populated this part of the state.

"Many whites have been killed, but some have been spared on the promise they will leave. Even among the Sisseton, there are those who wish to kill the whites rather than let them leave these lands. Even among those here today, there is disagreement. I asked my brother Grizzly Bear to let you go, but, when his terms were broken, I had no power." He stopped again, waiting to make sure the women understood.

At their assent, he continued. "Now, Grizzly Bear is dead at the hands of your men. There is a thirst for vengeance and much confusion among his followers. For now, I have been delegated to speak on behalf of all here, but my power is not strong. Because I spoke for the whites and they did not keep their word, I have been cast between your world and ours. Do you understand this?"

Shots rang out from the area of the slough, and the women jumped.

Oh God, oh God.

Mira glanced at Julia, her eyes wide with fear, and she looked ready to jump up. Julia reached for her and placed her hand on her leg, shaking her head with steady intent. Mira quieted.

Julia drew a breath and searched for the right words. "I understand what you have said and wish you to know, in the white world, women have very little voice. Our men act without consulting us and often do not have clear understanding of the impact their actions have. I am honored you are speaking with two women, but we, too, have limited power."

She halted, hoping she had worded things correctly. If she had, the Dakota would know she had integrity and had made promises in good faith. If others broke the promises she made, the Dakota would know she did not intend that to happen. This would save Pawn face among the Dakota and might help gain her family's safety, should things go wrong.

"I see that we understand one another. I have asked my brothers to spare the women and children, and this they have agreed. There must be no resistance, and all must do as they are told. If that does not happen, my brothers will view any promises to be dishonored. We will take with us those who are able, but we will take no men, and we will not take those who are unable to keep up with us."

"I understand." The survivors, women and children only, would be taken with the Dakota; the severely wounded would be left behind with the men. It was harsh, but it was more than she'd hoped for.

She didn't ask if those left behind would be killed. She didn't want to know. Either outcome was too bitter to think about.

"You must also know that there is much anger among Grizzly Bear's people. His wife and mother mourn him and wish revenge, as do the families of the others killed. I have been given power to negotiate with you, but there is much dissent among the bands here. I will do my best to honor what has been said, but it is a risk."

"I will do my best to honor the agreement we make, but there is much anger among the settlers as well, and many do not view things as I do."

"I see we understand one another."

"Let me now make sure Mrs. Everett has understood and see if she agrees."

"This you may do."

Julia faced Mira. "Did you understand what he said?"

"That the Santee tribes are attacking many settlements. Those here disagree about what to do with us. We broke the promise we made this morning when we tried to take the wagon and shot Grizzly Bear and the others. Some wish to kill us all but allowed Pawn to negotiate. We must agree to surrender without resistance. They will spare those who are able to walk. If we agree, we do so knowing there is a risk that some may still be violent."

"That's what I heard, too."

"What about those who are injured? Will they save them?"

"I don't think so. He said they will leave those who are unable to come with them."

Mira shuddered. "Will they be killed or just left here?"

Oh, Mira. Her husband would be among that group.

"I don't know. I fear to ask."

"And if we don't agree to this?" Mira blinked, hard.

Julia clutched her hand. "I think they will kill us all."

"We haven't much choice, do we?"

"I'll ask that we be allowed to confer with the others."

"That's the best we can do."

Julia asked for permission to return to the slough and consult with those there.

Pawn looked to the other men, and they spoke before he turned back to Julia. "You may do this, but you must decide soon, or my brothers will withdraw the offer. When you come back, you will bring the guns with you."

Laura

When Julia and Mira started from the slough to speak with Pawn, I crouched low, with the children still close around me. I clutched my handkerchief in my pocket, worrying it through my fist. I couldn't fathom how they could trust that vile creature yet again. Had he not already betrayed us?

"I'll shoot that son of a bitch," William muttered from beside me. "Now, while he's up there waiting for them. It's too good a chance to throw away. They're going to kill us all sooner or later, and he'll be one less to deal with." He began to rise from the slough.

"No, Husband, no!" I called, the other women chorusing the same.

Ice cold fear sliced through me. If William stood and shot, he would surely draw fire to us, and we would all perish. "If you do so, you will be shot. I beg you, stay alive! Stay alive and escape from here. Go to New Ulm and relay what has happened."

He eased back to the ground, and I sighed with relief that he had, for once, listened to me. My children would be safe. I couldn't lose any more children, not like this.

Tommy Ireland rose, shouting that the women and children must be saved. Before the words were out of his mouth, buckshot exploded. Two of the Indians had moved to the edge of the slough, shooting him at close range. Blood erupted from his chest and several other wounds.

Ireland fell. "Oh God, I am killed." The choked words were enough to quiet any others who had thoughts of rising.

Muffled screams echoed through the reeds, Mrs. Ireland's among them.

Stuttering sounds poured from my mouth, and my entire

body shook. Emma and Will, Jr. quieted me with gentle words, and I went limp.

Christina

Buckshot explodes, and I throw myself over Julia's children. Tommy Ireland calls out, and I know he was the one. I think that the men have almost all been wounded now. Why they keep making challenges I do not know.

We wait. The silence is long. In it, I hear insects buzz and children whimper. It is a strange mix, the peace of nature and the fearful cries of children. Mothers comfort, but their voices hold panic.

I hold George and Dora close. Dora is five, and she draws stuttered breaths. I know she understands more than her brother. George seems only to be bothered by having to sit still.

"*Ach,* do not worry so," I tell Dora and ruffle her blond hair. "Your mama is talking with them, and she will make sure we are safe."

"Will they kill her?"

"*Nein.* They respect her." I think of my friend, who is married to such a man as Jack Wright, who has no respect from anyone. She worries so about how we regard her. She does not know how much we think of her. I am glad of her. She will be our way out of this slough, I think, if only the men will stop their fighting.

We are quiet again, waiting. Julia and Mira return. Julia wades back into the slough to where most of us cluster. The reeds shake as she nears.

"If the women and children come out and do not resist, we will be spared to the best of Pawn's ability."

She does not say anything more but lets us discuss the offer. I hear in her words what she does not say more about: to the best of his ability. I wonder if the others have heard this, but I do not raise questions. I think that it will only lead to argument and make the men rise up again.

"Do you think they will honor their word?" someone asks.

"I think it will depend on us, how well we obey," Julia answers. "If we resist at all, I don't know what will happen."

"If we don't go, what will happen?" Laura asks.

"I think we'll all be killed," Mira says.

"This is our only chance," I say.

Julia stands tall among us. "You all need to know there is much anger among them. They've attacked many settlements, and Grizzly Bear's death makes them unstable. Pawn will do his best."

Lavina groans. "You can't still trust him?"

"I don't believe he is lying, but he's one man among many." Julia glances around. "What do you say? We don't have much time before the offer expires."

I rise. "I will go."

One by one, women agree and move out of this wet, sucking place. Each step bogs us down, and I pick up George. Dora holds my hand. Julia moves about, gathering rifles and shotguns. Three Indians wait for us at the edge of the marsh.

Lavina comes with four of her boys. Merton carries the baby, Johnnie. Frank and Giles help Lavina, who has been shot and has trouble walking. She puts her hands on their shoulders and limps along. She stops and whispers, "John."

She crumples.

As I walk past her, she is clutching her dead husband. He lies with his rifle in one hand and the other over his face. His hat is still on his head. His dog, who rushed after us, lies beside him. Lavina weeps over him and takes his hand in hers. "Oh, John." She whispers words of love and kisses him on his brow. Then she rises and continues with the boys. All of them carry sorrow on their faces but remain strong for her, I think. I do not know if she even comprehends Freddy is missing.

I pass Tommy Ireland. He is still alive, but blood and froth ooze from the hole where he is shot. I think it is his lung. His wife and children bend over him, saying good-bye. I do not think he will remain long, he gurgles so. They rise and leave him, trudging as they go.

Julia stops and picks up his gun.

"Please, Julia, end this for me. Shoot me before you go."

"Oh, Uncle Tommy . . . I wish so much I could help, but I can't kill a friend, even to ease his suffering." She bends and takes his hand. "I am so sorry."

Ireland closes his eyes, and Julia moves away to join me where we wait for her.

"Charlie Hatch lives," she whispers. "I left a gun with him. Mrs. Smith is wounded in the hip, and she can't move. Ireland's little Sarah got buckshot in the bowels."

"Dead?"

"Not quite. But her face is splotched, and she's spitting blood and foam. I think it won't be long."

I shake my head, numb. We reach solid ground and join the others. There are no men.

Six Dakota surround us and command us to sit.

The sky darkens with clouds. They build and churn, signs of a coming storm.

Almena

Almena's feet ached. Beside her, William Henry cried to be carried. Frank whimpered on her hip. She sank to the ground and sighed. She should have come to a road by now.

The air grew heavy, darkness creeping upon them. She glanced up. Heavy, gray clouds roiled overhead. The wind rose with them, its violent force building.

"I'm hungry," William Henry pleaded. "Please, Mama."

"There isn't any food. Mama has nothing to give you."

"My tummy hurts."

"Mine, too. Come on, let's go a little further."

They gained their feet and moved on, plodding at a three-year-old's pace. The wind built. Thunder cracked and lightning flashed above them, and the rain began. Sharp torrents poured down on them, stinging in their force.

William shivered against her wet skirt, his thin nightclothes drenched and dripping.

Almena gathered him up, settling his thirty-plus pounds on her left hip. Frank clung to her right hip. She shifted, trying to balance their combined weight, and trudged on, forcing one foot in front of the other.

Hold on. Hold on to them. They can't do this without you.

The boys wrapped their legs about her the best they could, struggling for purchase. Finally, they clutched each other's arms tight around her middle and fell asleep, heavy with fatigue.

She trudged on, the dead weight of their limp, sleeping bodies growing more arduous with each step. Her arms throbbed. The sodden tendrils of her hair plastered themselves against her face.

One step. Two.

She saw nothing but the rain streaming down on them amid the growing darkness.

Surely, they'd come to the road soon. Surely.

Lavina

I edge away from John, refusing to cry further. My boys have need of me, and I must be strong for them. I will grieve him later, when I am able to do so. For now, I must be strong. This is the only way to get my children through this.

The sky above is turbulent, thunder and lightning moving

fast upon us. The Indians hurry to catch their ponies. We will soon be moving away. The clouds unleash a torrent of rain, and we shiver with cold, drenched to our cores.

I emerge from the slough, dazed. One of the Indian men takes Christina Koch with him; another herds one of the Ireland girls. A third approaches me. He already has Laura Duley by one hand, and he grabs me with the other. Laura's shoulders are slumped in defeat, and I resolve to go with as much grace as possible. I will not surrender my strength.

"Laura," I whisper, "be strong."

She lifts her head. Despair fills her face.

The Indian hauls us along. I go without resistance but not in defeat. Within steps, it dawns on me that my boys are not here.

I stop, turning back to the slough. Where are my boys?

Freddy, my five year old, rises from the grass. "Mama!" he calls out and begins to run to me.

A squaw, hideous and old, runs into the slough and chases Freddy, yelling something about Lean Bear.

"Freddy!" I call, wrenching to go to him. My captor holds me tight, and I struggle to break away.

The woman reaches Freddy and knocks him on the back of the head with something, a rock, perhaps. His face fills with terror, and he slumps.

I thrash against my captor. Still, the hag beats Freddy, again and again with her weapon . . . until she doesn't.

For the first time, tears flood my eyes. *Oh, my boy!*

Somehow, Freddy rises, unsteady but alive. Blood streams from his nose, his mouth, his ears. He looks at me, glazed, and starts forward.

The woman rushes back to him and hammers at him again and again. Finally, she stops, lifts him up and dashes him upon the ground.

"Let me go," I beg and tug repeatedly but am too weak to get away.

When Freddy is still upon the ground, the squaw takes out a knife.

My captor jerks my arm and drags me along with him. He hauls us across the prairie, Laura in one hand, me in the other. At the slough, the woman leaves my Freddy and grabs Laura's four year old, Bell, who is running to catch up with us. Laura screams and wrestles with our captor. He strives to keep his hold on the two of us.

"Mother! Mother!" It is Frank's voice, and I look to him. My ten year old stands with blood streaming from his toothless mouth. His thigh and abdomen drip blood. I startle, realizing I hadn't even known when he was shot.

I wrench from my captor's grasp. He lets me fall and drags Laura away.

Pawn passes by with Julia and her children. He orders them upon a horse, sends them toward the others who are running west to the shelter of the cabins. Pawn returns to me and orders me to rise and go after Julia.

"Go," he says. "You can do them no good. That is Grizzly Bear's mother, and she takes their lives because their father killed her son."

I struggle to my feet and turn toward the slough.

"It will be worse for them if you go back."

My heart breaks into pieces and stabs into me in a thousand places. I take a step, stop. It is like Solomon telling me I must cut them in half! To leave them goes against all my instincts and rips me apart. Yet, if I go, and they are cruelly murdered . . . I collapse, unable to move.

Mira Everett runs back into the slough to her husband. An Indian pursues as another fires at her. She falls, wounded in the back.

Another shot rings out, and Laura screams. Her oldest son, wounded earlier, has fallen a few steps from her. She screams again and pleads with Pawn to spare her other children. She stands with Frances in one arm, Emma clutching her other hand. Jefferson runs toward her, desperately fleeing the slough. Bell is not with them, and I fear Lean Bear's mother has killed her as she did my Freddy. She cannot know which man fired the fatal shot, and perhaps her revenge will be upon us all.

Laura's face is pale, haunted, and filled with anguish, but her eyes are full of fierce protectiveness. I know how much this costs her, to be so strong. When Pawn tells her the others will be spared, she turns and rushes the remaining children away. Willie lies where he fell.

In that moment, I know I must leave Frank and Freddy. I can do nothing to help them. Three other boys depend on me to assure their safety.

Pawn returns and stands over me, leaning on his gun.

"What do you intend to do with me? Will you kill me, too?" I ask him.

"You must go with the others. You must hurry."

I crawl to my feet and limp after the others, refusing to look back at the boys I am leaving. Each step is full of agony. I struggle to hurry, but the distance between me and the others widens. My head has stopped throbbing where the ball settled. The wound in my side bleeds with each step; I no longer feel it. I risk a glance back and see Pawn reloading his gun. I try to hurry more. I enter a small slough and wade through it, following the others. Weakness swallows me, and I fall behind.

White-hot pain explodes in the small of my back. The ball rips through me and passes through my lower right arm. I fall to the ground, face down, and lie there, waiting. I'm on the trail and know the Indians will find me, so I crawl away from it, inching my way with my good arm, unable to use my legs at all.

Footsteps approach. I hold my breath, pretending to be dead.

From the corner of my eye, I spy a man's moccasins, the butt of a rifle. He stands, watching me. Surely he will think me dead. He must. But he doesn't. He swings his rifle up.

Blows land upon the back of my head, so hard that my head bounces on the hard ground. Again and again until I lose count and can only focus on the throbbing pain shooting through me. He strikes my right shoulder in the same way. I tell myself to hold my breath, but I can't do so. I nearly smother, my face pushed deeply into the ground. I gasp and gasp.

Finally, the blows stop, and I realize he believes me to be dying.

I'm numb with fear and don't think I will even feel it if he reaches down and cuts into my head to scalp me.

Chapter Seventeen
August 20, 1862
The Long Night
4:00 p.m. through morning

Julia

Julia rode back toward Lake Shetek, George and Dora in front of her on Pawn's horse. They shivered, rain pouring down upon them. Their lives were now in Pawn's hands, and she hoped she'd laid the groundwork for his continued respect and that she could negotiate their captivity in a way that didn't destroy it.

She tried not to think about what was happening behind her, the men and women still lying in the slough, clinging to life. Whether they would be left to suffer and die slow, agonizing deaths or whether they would be savagely killed by Dakota with anger in their hearts, she didn't want to contemplate. Neither was a vision she wanted in her head, and the definition of "mercy" was no longer clear to her.

Back in the slough, Mira Everett had said a brief silent good-bye with her solemn eyes. Then, she'd run back to her husband and certain death. Julia tried not to mourn her closest neighbor, told herself it was a choice Mira had made and that she had understood the consequences. Julia wished her a quick and peaceful end.

The killings she had witnessed lingered more strongly.

She'd looked back, seen Lavina fall, and watched the Dakota man lift his rifle and bring it down on her head.

We will not take those who are unable to keep up with us.

She hadn't watched any more than that, had kept her eyes focused ahead. But she'd been unable to keep herself from flinching as she heard the shots and screams from those who had been deemed too injured to keep up.

Julia accomplished the three miles to the Ireland cabin, where Pawn had told her the Dakota would be encamped, in a surreal haze and reined the horse to a stop. Lodges and bustling people filled the usually calm home site. The cabin had been built on a point of land surrounded by a slough on one side, the lake on another. It was one of the most idyllic areas of the settlement.

Until tonight.

Rough hands jerked the children from her, and she gasped. *No, not my children.*

In the next instant, someone grabbed her off the horse and threw her to the ground.

"White squaw too proud," said one of the women. "You now a dog."

Another woman spat at her, the glob landing square on her chest.

Julia fought the urge to stand tall and lowered her eyes instead. These people were angry, still driven by the emotion of warfare, and challenge would do her no good. Instead, she needed to draw on everything she'd learned about the Dakota these past few years.

"Pawn sent us to the camp and will follow." She used the Dakota language and kept her tone submissive, hoping the strategy of conveying she was under Pawn's protection was enough to forestall a beating.

The women glared at her, but Julia knew her words had worked. They were uncertain if she was to be a prisoner or Pawn's personal property. One of them *tsk*ed and pointed to a familiar-looking tepee. "Wait there."

She started toward his lodge, the children on either side of her. "Keep your eyes lowered," she told them.

"Julia!"

She turned and saw Christina being led into camp by one of the men.

He jerked on Christina's arm, muttered a few words, and slapped her. She recoiled, defiance in her eyes. That would not bode well for her. He dragged her to a teepee near Pawn's and dumped her on the ground.

Julia resisted the urge to help her up. Instead she told the children to wait and crossed the open area. She looked around and bent to speak to her friend before those in the camp noticed them.

"They'll come soon; there isn't much time. Stay meek, eyes down, don't talk unless spoken to, and use their language. This is war for them, and they may not treat us well."

"Will they kill us?"

"No, but they may beat us. The Dakota don't often take captives, usually only to adopt them into the tribe. This is different, fueled by anger and revenge. I sense they may not agree on what to do with us. Pawn said some of the leaders wanted to kill all the whites. Everything is in chaos, and I can't predict what will happen. Don't be defiant. Watch what they do and do things the same way. If one of the men takes you as a wife, you'll be the lowest in the tepee. Work hard and do as you are told, and you have a chance."

"*Ja,* I understand. Will . . . will the men . . . will they . . . ?"

Julia understood her unspoken words. *Will they rape us?*

She tempered her fear, knowing there was nothing she could do about the situation. "In their culture, women who are taken are welcomed as part of the family and become respected new wives, but this is war. It could change things."

"I cannot do that, I cannot."

"If that does happen and you don't submit, you risk being killed. And, if you're made a wife, it will be expected of you." Julia paused and touched her friend's cheek. "I can't make that decision for you; it's up to you. Just understand what may happen before you do so."

"*Ja,* I will think."

"I need to go back to Pawn's lodge, before the women return. Stay strong, and we'll get through this." She hugged Christina, then rushed across the small stretch of open ground to George and Dora.

Everything she did, from this point forward, would be for them.

She tapped against the side of the tepee, guessing that they were meant to wait inside, hoping they wouldn't be beaten for doing so. She'd never seen the Dakota display such anger. When there was no answer, she lifted the flap. "Come," she said, holding open the flap until the children entered, Dora grim, George curious. She slipped into the darkened tepee, lit by a low fire in the center.

Lord, how good that fire feels.

Blessedly, there was no one else inside. That would change soon. Pawn's wives were no doubt being informed about the prisoners and would come soon. She knew her moments alone with the children would be short.

Dances in Water had been a friend, but she didn't know his first wife. She hoped Dances in Water would remember their visits and speak for her.

Around the fire, sleeping robes lined the circular perimeter of the lodge. Cooking pots and other household goods were still bundled, yet to be unpacked. Julia's gaze rested on the sleeping robes, knowing that she would be taken to one of them and made Pawn's wife. She wouldn't resist, not with George and

Dora needing her. She would do what was necessary to assure they were treated well.

She settled them on a buffalo robe near the fire. "Dry near the fire, my little ones, then you can sleep."

Once the two were seated, Julia paced back and forth, letting the warmth of the fire reach her own damp clothing. Her mind was too busy to sit. She hoped she could vanquish the demons so she could deal with what was at hand.

A short time later, the flap opened, and she steeled herself. But it was Pawn who entered the lodge, not his women.

"Julia Wright, I am glad you are at my fire. Please sit."

She exhaled, relieved that they would talk rather than moving directly to the robes. Near the fire, George and Dora slept. She moved each of them to a robe and sat near the fire where Pawn had already taken his seat.

"I am honored you have asked us here," she said, keeping her voice humble and her eyes downcast.

"It has been a day with much regret."

Wasn't that the truth!

"It has," she agreed.

Pawn lifted her chin so that their gazes met. "You understand there are many bands here, many chiefs?"

She'd thought as much.

"Did you know the others were attacking?" The words she'd wanted to ask all day leaped out, and she drew a breath, hoping she'd not been too forward.

Pawn shrugged. "Attacks on settlements started several days ago. I did not think Shetek would be spared."

She ached to ask him if he had come to camp there for that reason, if he had meant to intervene, but she wasn't sure if it was her place to do so. "How many bands came here?" she asked instead, hoping to gain a sense of the bigger picture and how she was to fit into it.

"Those of White Lodge and Grizzly Bear are here. Part of Sleepy Eye's band, some from Limping Devil's two villages."

She'd heard the names, had recognized Grizzly Bear from his prior visits to Lake Shetek. They were small bands of Sisseton that chose to live away from the reservation. If she had her facts right, there were five such villages and five on the reservation. She wasn't sure how many bands comprised them.

"And these are the bands that are attacking?"

"All of the Sisseton, most of the Wahpeton and Mdewakanton and Wahpekute."

My God, nearly all of the Santee. The entire state was under attack. Had her husband been killed on the prairie between New Ulm and Lake Shetek? Was she, too, a widow? Though she hadn't loved Jack for a long time, she sent a prayer he had managed to survive.

"I belong to Grizzly Bear's band. He was the one I spoke to at your cabin."

She pushed her mind to process what he was saying, what he had not articulated. She thought he was trying to give her a renewed sense of his limitations. "So you are only one voice here, and not a chief?" she asked, to clarify.

"I am a small voice, Julia Wright. I did what I could. I will try to keep you safe. Some of the leaders wished to kill the whites. Grizzly Bear and White Lodge were at the war council when the fighting started. They were among those who wished to kill all the whites. Others said they would not kill if the whites left. Today, I reminded them you have been a friend and have treated us with respect. I did not want to see your people killed."

And there it was, her answer. He had sought to intervene, had not tricked the settlers. That knowledge would make things easier, when he claimed her.

"Am I to be your wife?" she asked. Better to know for sure.

"It will go better for you if you are a wife. There is much

anger, and I do not know if our traditions will be honored. Making you a wife will keep you under my protection."

"And the other women?"

He shrugged. "In normal times, my people would treat them well, but these are not normal times, and many say kinship should not be offered to the whites this time. White Lodge says he will keep the captives for ransom, to protect our bands from white attacks, and they will not become part of our people. There is much discontent, much disagreement. Some say they will be made slaves."

She shut her eyes, thinking it through. They would fare better as wives than property. "The children?"

"Some may be adopted in the usual Dakota way, or they may also become slaves. No one knows what should be done."

"You have two other wives?"

"Yes. You already know Dances in Water. My first wife is Speaks with Strong Tongue. They are honorable women. You will not be mistreated."

"I understand."

"I must go, now, to take part in the celebration. My wives will come and tell you what you are to do."

He rose and strode toward the door, then turned.

"Know, Julia Wright, that you must not disrespect me or my wives. If that happens, you *will* be punished. Tell your children this when they waken."

He lifted the flap and exited, leaving her to ponder what, exactly, he had meant by "disrespect."

Laura

The Indian man yanked me along with him. My feet moved of their own volition. My soul was in shreds, left behind with Willie and Bell, their lives so violently wrenched from them. Oh, to see

Bell beaten so and not be able to intervene! I could not fathom the reasons for such cruelty and was glad my William was among those who shot the men who were taking the horses. I hoped his was a kill shot, and I hoped those men's families were suffering as I was.

I would never again consider the Dakota to be friends but would instead forever view them as savages.

Frances was still in my arms, heavy and limp with sleep, her poor little body drenched. Somehow, I'd managed to hold on to her through all of this torturous day. Emma and Jefferson trotted next to me, clutching my wet skirts. They were all I had left. Grief and despair threatened, and I choked it all back. I could not let it take hold, could *not* let it paralyze me. Not now. I had to hang on for these three who were left.

The Indian jerked my arm, and I stumbled to my knees. He let go, and I realized we had entered the camp and were in front of a tepee. I'd been so involved in my thoughts that I'd not noticed. The man opened a flap and pointed inside. I crawled in, the children following. Christina Koch was huddled near the fire. Her blond hair hung about her face, her tidy braid long gone.

I rose, intent on seeking warmth and speaking to Christina. Emma and Jefferson were shivering. Once at the fire, they smiled for the first time since morning, but they said nothing, the horrors of the day likely rendering them mute.

I laid Frances on a robe and shook out my deadened arm.

"I am so sorry, my friend," Christina said. She embraced me, held me close for a few moments.

"We lost so many," I said.

It sounded inane. I thought of my husband, of Willie and Bell left at the slough. It was painfully obvious there had been severe losses and hardly needed stating. Still, I was unable to say much else and fought to keep my sobbing under control.

"Julia survives," Christina said in the vacuum of silence. "She says we must obey, that the Dakota are very angry. We may be taken as wives or become slaves."

Slaves. I shuddered at the thought. Oh, to be brought so low that women of standing should be slaves. Did these people not know we were respected leaders of our community?

A rustle sounded, and I looked toward the entrance. Two women stepped in and glared at us. I trembled at their hostility. Thank heavens their tunics were not bloodstained. I would have fainted had they been the hags who killed my precious children.

The two, both around my age, muttered together. I knew very little of their language and couldn't make out their words. One of them came to us, shoved Jefferson down, and seized Emma's hand.

No.

I stepped to them, and she slapped my face, saying something in a bitter tone. I hadn't even the chance to bring my hand to comfort my stinging cheek before she grabbed it and dragged both Emma and me toward the door. I glanced back at Jefferson. His eyes were filled with fear.

"She says to come," Christina told me. "We are to work."

I tried to scuttle away, to return to my little ones, but I was yanked out of the tepee. Outside, the woman released Emma, pointed to pots, and motioned for Emma to pick one up. She turned her bony finger on me and glared.

Pick up the pot. Just pick it up.

I nodded, and she released my hand. I glanced back to the tepee flap, fear flooding me at what might happen to Jefferson and Frances in my absence. The squaw raised her hand. I stopped, remembering the sharp sting on my cheek, and picked up the pot.

Christina already held hers.

The squaw marched away. We followed. We were near the

lake, at the Ireland cabin. The contents of the cabin were strewn about, feather ticks ripped to shreds as if their value meant nothing to these coarse beings. That they preferred to sleep on the ground rather than in comfort told me volumes. We went to the lake, gathered water, and trudged back to the tepee.

"What happens next?" I whispered to Christina.

The woman turned and spoke to us, her guttural gibberish harsh on my ears. It was hard to imagine that I had treated them with such charity, only to be repaid with murder.

Again, I hoped my William's shot had been one of those that downed her clansman.

Christina replied to her, then spoke to me. "We are not to talk, except for me to relay her words."

I looked around the camp to take my mind from the injustice of it all. There were many tepees, twenty or thirty at least. People bustled, all of them busy. The women never stopped moving, and the children played as if the events of the day were nothing out of the ordinary. The Ireland girls were ordered about, but I kept my head down and did not interact with them. Heaven only knew what might happen if I did.

The afternoon edged into evening; all the time we were kept busy with chores. Thankfully, the rain eased, though the air grew chilly, and I craved the fire once again.

A large meal had been prepared, each tepee contributing. The scent of roasting beef filled the camp. Our cows, I supposed. Our vegetables likely filled their pots, too. The heady aromas lingered, and my stomach rumbled.

Emma glanced at me once and opened her mouth to talk, but I shook my head, and she held her words. We sat where we were directed and listened to our impatient stomachs until the Sioux had all eaten before we were allowed to have our meals. We gobbled them with no regard to manners, and I wiped my greasy fingers with my handkerchief, the only napkin at hand. I glanced around, looking for the tepee where we'd left Jefferson and Frances.

"They eat. You stay." The words were barked in clipped English by a nearby woman.

I stayed, holding Emma close as we finished our meals. The camp swelled as more Indians arrived. The circle around the main campfire grew as they joined those already there.

"Pawn new chief," the woman said. "We dance."

Several Indians stood and formed a circle. Drums and chanting sounded. They jumped and twisted, their feet hammering in a strange, barbaric rhythm. The children trampled in the shadows, mimicking the adults.

Christina edged closer and whispered to me. "Did you hear her? That Pawn is to be the new chief."

"I thought he was a chief," I muttered.

"Grizzly Bear was. He was one of those shot at the wagon."

I sucked in my breath. "Our men shot the chief?"

"*Ja,* they were very angry with us."

Yes, and we were very angry that they killed our husbands and children!

One of the Indian women returned. "No white talk," she ordered. As the woman stood guard, Emma fell asleep, her head on my lap, and the evening grew ever darker and the dancing more frenzied, furious.

Later, the woman prodded us. "I take girl to tepee. You go there." She pointed to another tepee near the center of the camp. "We will see if anyone wants you as a wife."

I watched them usher a dazed Emma away while two others shoved Christina and me toward the tepee where a crowd clustered. They pushed us through the door, and we shuffled toward the center. Pawn and several other men entered behind us.

My heart began to pound.

Christina

I shudder, knowing the time has come that Julia spoke of. The time when I must decide what I will do.

The men speak, arguing about what to do with us. Their voices are hostile, their eyes angry as they look at us. I do not think Laura and I will be claimed as wives. I think we will be slaves, and it will not go well for us. I think these men intend to violate us. I understand too little of the language to figure out exactly what the disagreement is about. But I recognize the tone of vengeance.

Laura's breath is fast in her chest, and her eyes are not focused. I think she understands what will happen. She is a frail woman, not stout like me. I think she will not last long before she passes out.

Me, I am strong. For the first time, I wish I was not.

There are dogs in the tepee, and they sniff at us, wander away. A woman says something about us being unfit even for dogs.

The men still argue, but their words flow too fast for me to understand.

Women come from the shadows and lead us to the robes. Then they leave with the men, still arguing together.

Only Pawn remains. He comes to me, and I know it is the time Julia told me about.

I shudder. I do not want this.

Pawn sits on the robe. "There is much anger tonight among these men. They wish to punish the women captives for what happened today, for the killing of Grizzly Bear and the others.

Revenge is strong in their hearts, and they do not wish to respect our usual ways. I have told these men you will be my wife. It is better to do this now, before they change their minds."

He waits, but I do not say anything. I cannot agree to this.

But when I do not refuse, he lifts my skirts.

I fight to push them back down, my legs churning.

Nein, I will not do this. I will not lie with a man other than my Andreas. I will not. Even if I am killed, I will not do this.

The skirts fly back up.

"Be still, German Woman. It is better this way, so you are in my protection." He is between my legs.

I thrash and bring my knee up.

He cries out and stops. When he moves away, he is clutching himself, and I know my aim was true. He crawls to the side and glares at me.

I have shamed him, and I know I will pay the price.

Other men rush in, alerted by his cry. When they see him cradling his privates, they yell and swarm to us.

I hear Julia's words in my head. *This is war. It could change things.* I have sacrificed my chance to be respected. My defiance will make these already angry men forget their traditions. My heart seizes—I have done this to myself.

One of them slaps me and forces my knees apart.

I push at him, resisting. I turn my head and glimpse Laura nearby.

She struggles, too. Fighting and kicking like I do. The man holds her down, and she weakens. *Ja,* she is not so strong as I am. He takes her, pounding into her as she screams. She faces me, terror in her eyes, tears streaking her cheeks.

But I have my own battle.

The man slaps my face again, and someone holds my legs so I cannot fight back. I wince when he enters me, hear his hoarse grunting as he pumps and his cry when he releases.

I am shamed and I will never tell anyone of this. Never.

Almena

The afternoon slid into evening and the rain thinned, stopped. Almena glanced up, weary beyond all measure. She'd managed to keep walking, despite the deluge, but only in intervals. She knew they would need to stop soon.

"I'm cold, Mama."

"I know, William Henry. Me, too." She bent down and drew her three year old close. "But we have nowhere to go, sweet boy. Nowhere to get warm."

They'd had the same conversation every few minutes. Either that or one about hunger. She cursed the prairie, the rain, and the Dakota. Seconds later, she recanted the curse.

They could have killed us.

Thank God she'd always welcomed them, fed them, traded with them. Had she not, they might not have been spared.

"I'm tired. Carry me?"

Lord, I can't. I can't do this.

She'd transferred Frank from one hip to the other and back again as her arms had grown too numb to support him. William Henry had been forced to trudge beside them. She had to find a place for them to spend the night, now, before it became any darker.

She glanced around, searching for a dry location. Water pooled in every low spot, and the grasses dripped. Everywhere, the ground undulated. Up and down and up again. She knew that only too well, having walked its terrain for the entire day.

Finally, a small rise with no grass. *A sand hill.*

She'd be able to dig out sleeping spots for the boys.

"There." She pointed so that William Henry would see.

"That's where we're going. Can you get there before me?"

He sighed and started away from her, his tired little body managing the uneven ground in spurts. His wet nightclothes clung to him. From behind, she noted his limping gait.

Oh, William, your poor little feet.

Tears bit her eyes. Reaching him, she scooped him up, gritting her teeth at the additional weight. She struggled up the hill. Each step was a gain, each sank into the sandy ground. But she felt the difference in the movement of it. She crested it and sank down, laying Frank on the ground. Despite the aches that stung her arms, she hollowed out a small hole, avoiding too much depth so water would not fill it, and laid Frank into the nest. She did the same for William Henry, who watched her efforts with curiosity.

"Lie down, Sweetie. Sleep."

He crawled into the space and curled up.

Almena reached for one of his feet, felt the cuts on his sole. She began to rub.

William Henry jerked from her grasp. "Hurts, Mama," he said and nodded off.

Almena sat, sighed. In his spot, Frank was tossing and turning, whimpering in his sleep. He'd likely waken soon . . . he'd slept so much of the day away. She glanced at the sky again, hoping to find the stars, but the clouds hung heavy, and darkness grew thick around them. She lay down next to the boys, fatigue overwhelming her.

But when the raindrops fell again, dripping onto her face, she crawled to the boys and lay atop them, sheltering them as best as she could.

The night would be as long as the day had been.

Lavina

I hold as still as possible, but no hand reaches for me; and no cold knife slices my scalp. I remain as if dead, praying I will be spared. In my haze, I hear others moaning and crying.

"Mama? Mama, are you there?"

My heart! It's Merton. The urge to crawl to him overwhelms me. I still it and stifle my voice. If Merton is to remain alive, I cannot reveal myself. I know with dreadful certainty that he would come to me, and I can't risk the Dakota noticing him. I pray he will keep quiet. I force myself to stay strong, hating that I must deny him comfort.

Lord, how much longer will this day last?

Sounds of people moving away seep through my consciousness. Then, nothing.

I shiver, wet and cold. I open one eye, then the other. The day is still dark, the rain drenching, but the Indians have gone.

I shudder a breath and shake in earnest—I am alive.

I am alive, but I don't know when they will return.

With my good arm, I push off the ground. Pain shoots through my body, and my head feels as if it will explode. I slow my movement, inching upward little by little. Vomit rises with the agony, but I fight and finally sit.

Congealed blood cakes the hand that was under my head. That the rain did not wash the blood away from the wound, that it clotted so much among my fingers, tells me just how much it has bled. I wonder if my skull is still there, or if I have left it on the ground.

My gaze darts to where I'd lain. There's blood, a good deal of blood, but no chips of bone. I raise my arm and touch my head. Within my thick hair, there is the hole, where I was shot, but only numbness. I can't feel the damage from the beating. I turn my head from side to side.

Bone fragments grate against one another, reminding me of

the sound of teeth grinding together. The sound echoes through the back of my head. Bile rises in my throat. I'm unable to choke it back. It flows down my chin, lodges bitter and stinging in my nose.

I wait for the rain to wash it away and marvel that my brain is not lying on the ground. I can't fathom how that is possible. I touch my head again.

My hair—my long, thick hair that I have so loathed piling atop my head. Though it now hangs in a tangled mess, it must have cushioned the blows enough to keep my skin intact.

Slowly, awareness sharpens. I hear sounds around me. Children still cry at odd intervals.

Johnnie . . . is that my Johnnie?

The cries come from the slough, and I wonder if Merton still has charge of him, if he has taken him back to the men who are lying among the reeds.

Oh, my boys . . .

I push to my feet, fighting the pain of my many wounds. I take a step, stagger, holding up my torn skirt with my left hand so I do not stumble on it. Each movement stirs more pain. I remember my feet are bare, cut and blistered. The wound in my side pinches as I move, my back screams, my hip twinges. My wounded arm hangs limp, and the throbbing is unbearable, so I hold it with my good arm—the one already holding my tattered dress. I take one step, two and grit my teeth. If I can continue on, the pain will eventually numb, I think.

I hope.

The route back to the slough stirs the horrendous memories of my Freddy being so savagely murdered. Determined, I fight the visions. He is gone. I must focus on Merton and Johnnie, who are still in that bog . . . on Giles and Frank, who are missing.

The air cracks, and I duck. I squelch my panicked cry so I

don't draw more fire. Only then do I realize no one shoots.

It's just thunder.

An insane urge to laugh surges, ebbs away. I'm thankful, for there is no room for hysteria now. I must find my boys.

A child calls out for his mother. Willie Duley is somehow still alive. He calls out again.

The urge to comfort him rises, but I know I can't save him; he's injured too severely to survive. I can do nothing for him, and my own boys need me. I swallow and continue past.

Again, I think I hear Johnnie and lurch toward the sound.

It is not my Johnnie.

Little Charlie Everett, two years old, lies among the reeds. He breathes sluggishly, death imminent. His six-year-old sister, Lillie, sits next to him, sheltering him from the storm.

"Lillie?"

"Mrs. Eastlick?" She looks up at me, her face bereft. "They haven't killed us all?"

"Not quite. There are a few left."

"Will you take care of Charlie?"

Sorrow stabs at me. He will last but a few minutes longer, and I don't know how to tell her. I long to sit and wait with her, to comfort her when he slips away, but those few moments could mean death for my own boys.

"Oh, Lillie, I wish I could. But I must find my own Johnnie. He is here, crying for me. He'll surely die if I don't find him."

"I know." She is calm, resigned.

"I'm sorry, Lillie. Will you come with me?"

"I need to stay."

"I'll come back, after I find Johnnie. Maybe then you can come with me." It is all I can offer her.

"I'm thirsty. Do you have water?"

"I don't, dear." I take a moment to show her how to squeeze water from her clothing.

She swallows and scrunches her face at the muddy taste. "Is there better water in heaven, do you think?" Her clear, sweet voice sounds older than her years.

"I think there is. I think when you get to heaven, you will never suffer again and never be thirsty."

"That's good." A wavering smile crosses her face, and she lies across her little brother and closes her eyes.

Sobbing, I move on, searching. I'll return for Lillie when I can and take her with me.

I find the bodies of Mrs. Smith and my dear friend Sophia Ireland. Both are dead, their clothing disturbed. Oh, Sophia. I do my best to cover them so they have more dignity. Little Sarah Ireland lies on Sophia's chest, unmoving. I spy Mrs. Smith's heavy canvas apron. It would make a good cloak in the increasing chill. I struggle to remove it. Inching my good arm under her to unfasten it, I choke back my discomfort at touching death so closely. I discover pins in their pockets and take them to pin my skirt back to my waistband so I don't have to hold it up.

In the growing darkness, I find yet more remains, a boy. *Giles.* I lower my aching body, unable to do anything else. He's been shot through the chest and is dead. He looks peaceful. I sit with him but a moment before leaving him. He no longer needs me.

The sound of breathing draws me to another child.

Oh, God, it's Freddy, still alive after his savage beating. How many hours has he lain here? He's face down, his clothes torn to shreds. I shudder at the agony he must be suffering. But I hear the rasp in his throat and know his death will also come soon. An urge to lie down next to him and hold him, to die beside him, overwhelms me.

Then, I remember Merton and Johnnie are still out there and have need of me.

I make my choice and rise.

Mrs. Everett is close by, shot through the lungs. She breathes still, the effort creating a gurgling rattle. My skin crawls at the sound, and terror fills me. I call her name, but she doesn't respond, and I hurry away, unable to listen to that haunting sound any longer.

I call out for Merton, but there is no answer. Several times, I think I hear my husband, but the sound comes from all about me, and I know I must be imagining it. I wander in circles, fatigue overtaking me. A strange light floats atop the grass, pale red, circling round and round me.

I stumble to the ground, unable to go on, waiting for the light to consume me.

Chapter Eighteen
August 21, 1862
Christina, Julia, and Laura
Becoming Captives

Julia

"Get up, you lazy dogs." The bitter voice broke into Julia's sleep, and she forced herself to find wakefulness. Today would be the day that defined her role in Pawn's family. She opened her eyes. A Dakota woman stood over her, her dark eyes hard in the dim, pre-dawn light.

Good lord, what time was it?

Julia nudged Dora and George and rose from her buffalo robe pallet. She stood before the woman but did not lower her gaze. Pawn had made it clear she was a wife, not a servant. She'd be damned if she'd let this one lose track of the distinction.

Dances in Water stood some distance away, deferring to the other woman, the first wife. Speaks with Strong Tongue, if she recalled correctly. Wasn't that fitting?

"Tell me, sister, what I am to do." She used the Dakota language.

"Sister, bah!" Strong Tongue said. She spat at Julia's feet.

"We need water and firewood," Dances in Water said.

"And the pots need scrubbing." The older wife still glared at her.

Julia refused to flinch and met her gaze. "My name is Julia Wright. My children are called George and Dora." She gestured to the children, still abed, but sitting upright, thank goodness. "We are honored to be part of Pawn's family. I will do as you ask. Are they to help me?"

"Go yourself, Julia Wright. These two will help us pack. We have much to do before we leave this place."

She'd won this round, but she dared not push things any further. She glanced down at George and Dora. "Get up—quick now, so you do not anger these women. You must do as they tell you and help them pack."

"Are we slaves?" Dora asked.

"They are wives of Pawn, and you must obey as if they are your mothers, too. But know if you do not do as you are told, they may discipline you. Get up and go to work. *Now.*"

She gave them a stern look and exited the lodge. Lord, she hoped Dora understood all she hadn't said, that Dances in Water would protect her from Strong Tongue's bitterness.

Outside, she stirred the embers in the dying fire and added the last remaining logs. She grabbed the pots and strode toward the lake. It made most sense to wash the pots, bring water, then locate more wood. She hoped she'd chosen wisely, that she was being efficient.

The sun was barely rising. It was early but not as early as she'd thought. She'd found sleep, her fatigue saturating her. She crossed the far edge of the Irelands' yard and stepped down to the water's edge. Other captives were already there, performing similar chores. A Dakota youth stood on the bank above them. A guard, she supposed.

She waded into the water and bent to rinse out the pot. Dried stew caked the inside of it and would bear scrubbing. She tugged out a few grasses from the shoreline and lifted the hem of her skirt for use as a dishrag. Her dress was far past the ruined state, so there was little sense taking care with it at this point.

"*Ja,* a good idea," Christina whispered from beside her.

"Who claimed you?"

"Wakeska, White Lodge, gave me to Running Bear as a slave. He took me to his tepee early this morning."

Julia's gaze drifted over her friend. Christina moved stiffly, stepping with care. She'd been ill-used; rage had led some of the men to dishonor the Dakota ways.

"The others?" she asked, fighting the urge to comfort her friend with a hug.

"Laura passed out, but I heard she was taken by Sleepy Eye. The Ireland girls are with Tizzie Tonka. This is all I know."

"Enough talk. Work," the teen advised. From his tone, Julia knew they'd best obey. She moved away from Christina and scoured the pot. Eight-year-old Roseanna Ireland stepped into the lake, gathered water, and returned to shore with her eyes downcast. Julia wasn't even sure she'd noticed anyone else. No doubt Ellen, being younger, had been put to work in the tepee.

Finished scrubbing the pot, she scooped water into it and returned to Pawn's lodge without speaking to anyone else. Laura staggered from a tepee, barely able to walk, but Julia didn't pause. A Dakota woman stood nearby, and it wouldn't go well for Laura if they spoke now. Besides, it was starting to drizzle again, and she knew the fire would need nursing if the rain continued. For that, she'd need more wood.

Julia quickly gathered wood from the stack Tommy Ireland kept near the cabin. There was little left, but it would be enough to keep the fire going until they broke camp. Already, the women were tearing down tepees. Her arms loaded, she turned back to the encampment.

"Julia Wright."

Julia jumped at the familiar bitter voice of Pawn's first wife.

She hadn't even heard the woman approach. She turned and faced her.

"You have much to learn," the woman said in Dakota. "I am called Speaks with Strong Tongue and am the first wife of Across the River, whom you call Pawn. I am a daughter of old Sleepy Eye, cousin to young Sleepy Eye, who is a strong leader. I am also a favorite of White Lodge, who knew my father and treats me like a daughter. As the elder of the leaders, White Lodge is much respected by all the Sisseton and has great power. It is because of my stature that Across the River has been named to follow Grizzly Bear as chief of our village."

Julia lowered her eyes. *It may have been a mistake, challenging this one.*

"I am honored to know you, Speaks with Strong Tongue."

"You think you are important because you join Across the River's tepee, but you are much risk to him. He lost importance because of you, because he negotiated for your people. My cousin Sleepy Eye and White Lodge, who have far more influence among our people, did not like his interference. His support was not strong, and there was much dissent about him becoming leader. Last night, he took pity on another of the captives, and she brought him shame when he let her knee his manhood. Now, the people laugh at how he walks this morning, and his authority is weakened further."

"I'm sorry." She'd known yesterday that he'd taken a risk, but she'd had no idea how much it had cost him. She swallowed. Maybe she wasn't as protected as she'd thought.

Strong Tongue's gaze bore into her. "Know this. It is your fault that these things have happened. Your fault that my husband does not have the status he should, that I have lost standing. I will not extend kinship to you because of that. He has made a mistake taking you as a wife, and he will soon be forced to trade you or lose his rank. You will not work your power on him to bring him more disgrace. In my tepee, you will be a dog."

No, that wasn't right. Pawn had told her she'd be treated as a wife. His other wives were supposed to make her part of the family. "Pawn . . . Across the River . . . will decide these things," she said, but doubt stabbed at her.

Strong Tongue's hand landed against her cheek, the sound sharp, the pain instant.

Julia flinched and fought to keep from soothing her face with her hand. She would not cower before this woman.

"You are impudent, Julia Wright. The band will decide. Without their support, Across the River will lose his new position. He leads with their consent. Within his lodge, I will determine how things are to be. Without my support—my position as cousin of Sleepy Eye and favorite of White Lodge, who knew my father—Across the River is nothing."

Julia's sense of control slipped further. No, this was not a woman to be toyed with. "I will not cause trouble."

"You are nothing but trouble, and I will see you dead rather than enjoying a wife's comfort."

Christina

I have been raised to be a good German *Hausfrau* and try to hold on to that this morning. Used to rising early, I did not mind so much when I was roused to do chores before dawn. I do not mind the cooking and cleaning. I am used to such things. But I do not know the ways of these people and struggle to do as they expect. Running Bear's wife has cuffed me three times for mistakes in packing.

I will learn. I have no choice. I will learn, and I will do what I can to help the children among us.

My stomach growls, and Falling Star, the wife, glares at me.

Several gunshots sound, and I jump.

This time, Falling Star does not glare. Her dark eyes soften. "Go, sit, eat," she says, pointing to where Laura is already sitting, her surviving children with her. The Ireland girls are across the camp, helping to fold a tepee. I do not see Julia.

I scoop a portion of the remaining corn mush into my hand, as the others have done. There is not much left, after all the camp has eaten, but I remind myself to be grateful I am allowed to eat at all. I shuffle toward Laura, stiff and aching. The night was long, and I hope I will not endure such as that again. I think, now that I have been claimed, that it will be easier.

"Gutenmorgen," I say as I sit next to her.

She looks puzzled, and I remember this is my greeting to Andreas and that he is no longer here. I exhale. Is it only twenty-four hours?

"Good morning," I translate.

"Is it?" she mumbles.

"We are alive. It is good."

"You can say such a thing when your husband lies dead? When I have lost three of my family?"

"They are gone. We remain and must stay strong."

"For what? More of what they did to us last night?"

"I will not talk of that. Their wrath is spent. I think now it will be better. You must be strong for your children."

She sighs. For a moment, she smiles as she looks at the three clustered near her. Her face saddens again. This will be a difficult thing for her, I think. She will need to find strength.

A horse gallops into camp—the one that belonged to Charlie Hatch, I think. The rider eases a body to the ground. He speaks to those who greet him, but I cannot make out the words. When he rides away, I see that six-year-old Lillie Everett has been brought to us, still alive. They shove a bowl of food into her hands and push her toward us. She is wounded in her side, blood drying on her dress. Laura and I make a place for her between us, and she stumbles forward. Her eyes look empty.

"Lillie, come sit," I say.

Emma and Jefferson Duley greet her and urge her to join us. She sits.

"You are hurt?" I ask.

"It hurts, but the blood stopped, and I didn't go to heaven."

Laura hugs her close. "Oh, you darling girl. You spent the whole night out there alone?"

"I wasn't alone. I sat with Mama and baby Charlie."

I look at her. "Do they live?"

"Mama went to heaven, but Charlie was still alive. They found us when they were searching pockets and made me leave him. I think he will be with Mama soon."

"Was there anyone else left?" Laura asks.

"Mrs. Eastlick was there last night, and I heard others moving. This morning, I saw only us and one of Roseanna and Ellen's little sisters. They left her there with baby Charlie."

She eats the porridge with her fingers and looks to us for instruction.

Concern for this poor little orphan fills me, and I take her hand in mine as we stand. "You will come with me, and I will keep you safe. *Ja?*"

"I would like that," she says.

There is a shot. The bullet rips through the bottom of my dress, and we all move apart, too startled to think.

"No more talk," one of the Indians says as he lowers his gun. "This one is not yours."

"She has no mother. I will keep her," I say.

Running Bear's wife slaps my face. "Quiet, German Woman. She will go to Grizzly Bear's wife. Or, if you still want to argue, they can give her to his mother, the one who took out her rage on the children whose fathers shot her son."

Freddy Eastlick and Bell Duley, the two who were beaten to death.

I look at Lillie and weep, unwilling to risk further protest. Will Everett also fired at the chief. "I'm sorry," I say and hope she does not suffer too much.

Laura

We let them take poor little Lillie away from us. We had no alternative; we couldn't let her be turned over to that wicked woman to be beaten to death. Images of Bell flashed through my mind at the suggestion, and I am ashamed that we left Lillie with no one to care for her, but there was no choice to it—anything would be better than turning her over to such a fate. Besides, I could not risk my remaining children by disobeying.

I returned to the tepee, now lying on the ground, and gathered up the poles as instructed. They were heavy, and I struggled to lug them to the travois. My body ached beyond all measure. I could hardly walk, but I knew I had to continue on, to satisfy the shrews who commanded me.

"Do you need help?" Julia Wright asked from her campsite. "We've finished, and I haven't been given any other chores."

"Oh, that would be a boon indeed. I am so sore, my muscles enraged from sitting so many hours in the slough and then . . . last night." My face heated, and I could say no more.

Julia grabbed one end of the pole, and we carried it to the travois. "Did they hurt you?" she whispered.

I squeezed my eyes shut for a moment. I didn't want to talk about it—the night was long and torturous. I fought to keep the white-hot fury at bay but could not. "Of course they hurt me," I snapped. "How could they not, doing what they did? I tried to fight them, as Christina did, but I was too weak."

I couldn't block out the visions of what was done to me, the despicable horror of the night. The dogs sniffing at me, women cackling in snide laughter that I was so worthless not even a dog would have me, the shame of being held down, my body exposed and violated.

"I'm so sorry, Laura. This is war for them, and those who did that to you abandoned their ways."

She would defend them? I paused to let my anger dissipate, telling myself she meant only to show her concern. I finished the story, forcing myself to say it out loud this once, so that I would never have to do so again. "I just lay there and let it happen and forced my thoughts to visions of the children running about with laughter, squealing in delight. I don't know how many used me. I passed out, finally."

"Do you know where we're going?" Julia said after a while.

"No, only that we are moving. They tell me nothing, and I understand very little of what they do say."

"You'll learn." She stopped and glanced around. "Is that the last pole?"

"How are we going to survive among these heathens? Did you notice how savage they were in their celebration?" I couldn't forget how they forced me to watch their gleeful dance. One by one, they declared they had killed and danced about in reenactment of how it had happened. They jumped as if hit by bullets, staggered to the ground, groaning as the others whooped and danced around him like demons. I think they did it to torture those of us who survived.

"I think it was a ritual."

"It was horrible. It's all horrible. I would give anything to escape this."

Julia looked around, leaned close. "Would you run, if you had the chance? If you could escape, before we leave the area we know, would you do so?"

If I could flee a future of nightly violations, daily beatings, savage mockery? If I could leave behind a life of toil and despondency?

I turned and met Julia's gaze. "I would take my children and run like the wind."

Julia

"You, white women! Hitch the oxen."

Julia stepped forward, her arms tired. The early morning rains had stopped, and sun peeked through the clouds to signal it was time to start on their way. Many of the tepees had been loaded onto the settlers' wagons. Already, they'd put the available horses into harnesses, and one wagon remained.

"I will get the yoke," Christina said. She strode to the Ireland barn, where a wooden ox yoke lay.

Julia joined her. There was little reason Christina should drag it alone. Her arms were likely sore, too.

They grasped the yoke, one per side, and carried it back to the wagon.

"You know how to manage oxen?"

"*Ja.* This I know." She talked Julia through yoking the animals and looping the reins through the rings.

Julia pondered the exchange she'd had with Laura. If *she* had the chance to run, would she? In truth, she wasn't sure. Last night, she would have placed her lot entirely with Pawn, trusting that she would be kept safe. Now, she no longer had faith that was the best option. Pawn . . . Across the River . . . did not have the backing of his people, and her fortunes could turn in a minute.

Would it be better to attempt an escape?

"You, German Woman, you drive this wagon. You know the ox."

Julia trudged back to Strong Tongue and shouldered the pack

she'd been assigned earlier. Pawn lay on a travois, his face tight. Christina had done damage, that was for sure. Strong Tongue had grown tired of his lurching walk—or perhaps of the thinly suppressed laughter that followed him—and had prepared the travois. Now, Julia carried much of the bulk that would normally be transported there.

Strong Tongue glanced in her direction. "You think you are above carrying our goods, Julia Wright?"

"No, but it is a labor I haven't done before."

"Hah! You will get used to it. It is your burden now. Across the River would not need to ride like an old woman if you had not begged for lives to be spared."

"I will do it." She shifted the pack, trying to balance the weight, but was unable to stand erect. She was certain Strong Tongue had distributed it so it would rest high on her back instead of low, as fur trappers carried their loads.

Strong Tongue laughed. "Move. Can't you see we are leaving?"

Julia looked up from her hunched position and stepped forward.

As they headed north, she lagged behind. George and Dora stayed close, each shouldering their own burdens. Each step became more and more difficult, and the weight pressed down on her. The group circled around the Koch place and turned northwest toward the Hurds, crossing a narrow strip of land between two bodies of water. Under her feet, the ground grew soft, mushy, and walking became more difficult.

She glanced at the children, saw them struggling as well. Tears streamed down Dora's cheeks. George barely walked. In the next moment, he dropped to the ground.

Julia and Dora halted. As one, they shrugged from their packs and freed George. Julia glanced at the party, now quite far ahead of them. She eyed the land around them, the water, the trees.

I would take my children and run like the wind.

Chapter Nineteen
August 21–24, 1862
Almena and Lavina
Seeking Dutch Zierke's

Lavina

August 21

Dawn breaks as I lurch across the prairie. Once the strange light disappeared, I'd again crawled to my feet, trying to move as far as possible from the slough under the cover of darkness. I couldn't find Merton and Johnnie, and I tell myself they're still alive, escaped from this dreadful place. I must save myself for their sake. I will find them, no matter what.

As muted light spreads across the prairie, I stumble to a patch of tall weeds and fall to my knees, hoping the grasses will hide me from any Indians still roaming the area. I find little comfort. The drizzling rain lessens as I lie there and finally stops. The sun emerges, warming me.

Oh, what a mess I am. My thick hair droops about me. At nearly three feet long, it will warm me, once it finally dries out. My dress is in tatters, gaping open where it tore from the waistband. The pins I took from Sophia Ireland hold it here and there. Blood has stained the cloth brown.

But what does it matter? There is no one to see me. I am alone.

I staunchly refuse to let melancholy overtake me. John's dead, and I can do nothing about it. Freddy and Giles lay where they fell, all now with John. I'm glad they're free of the pain and suffering that filled their last minutes, and I pray that Frank didn't linger long. I must focus on Merton and Johnnie and hang on for them.

Time crawls. I hear children calling out and know I'm still near the slough. The cries continue throughout the day, in spurts. Sometimes, they shriek in pain. Other times, there is low whimpering. I long to crawl back and help, but I'm so weak. It's hellish to lie and do nothing, and my soul weeps.

Mid-afternoon, I hear three shots, and the wailing stops. Finally, they've been given peace.

I hold fast to the hope that Merton and Johnnie escaped.

But my mind doesn't rest. It conjures visions of Merton and Johnnie among those who suffered all day, among those now dead. I think I'll lie here and let myself die. There are enough wounds to my body, to my head, that it shouldn't take more than a few days.

Yet, what if Merton and Johnnie do live? I told Merton to never let his brother go. Merton, the man that he is despite his youth, wouldn't give up, and I must not either.

With all quiet and twilight upon me, I push myself to a sitting position and look around. I need to make my way to Dutch Zierke's. The old German is the closest settler, sixteen miles east of Lake Shetek. I spy timber on the horizon. I must be close to Buffalo Lake, which lies along the mail route a few miles from the slough, one third of the distance to Zierke's place.

I gain my feet and begin to walk to the timber as evening descends. I trudge for hours at a snail's pace, barely able to move. I dig in, drawing on every ounce of strength, until I can go no further. I lie on the damp ground, the dew seeping into my dress. I try to scoop up the moisture with my hand to quench my thirst but to no avail. My failure makes me even more aware that I've had nothing to eat or drink for two days now. Finally, I sop at the dew with the hem of my skirt and suck on the cloth.

I ease Mrs. Smith's apron over me and close my eyes. I blow onto my cold hands and shiver, my teeth chattering. Finally, as I warm, I hear footsteps approach. I keep my eyes closed and still myself, but my heart thrashes.

An animal sniffs at my head. It moves, nudging me, licking the old blood in my hair. When the wolf nears my face, I can feel its hot breath, and the stench of death bathes me as it stands over me.

I thrash at the animal, and it jumps back.

Hah, you thought me dead, did you?

Surprised the wolf didn't snap at me, I gape at it. It's too dark to see the animal's eyes; they are but a glint in the darkness. It sits a few feet away, watching me. I push to my feet, shocked it has not lunged at me, has not torn me apart. With my good arm, I snap the apron, and the wolf rises and saunters away.

There is no need for it to bother taking down a live being, even one as weak as I. As long as it knows I am alive, it will leave me alone and seek an easier meal.

The macabre reality is that the wolf will not go hungry tonight, and I will be safe because of it.

As long as I do not sleep like the dead.

Almena

August 21

That same morning, Almena woke early, still as tired as she'd been the night before. Frank had fussed most of the night, and she'd caught only snatches of troubled sleep. She stretched her aching muscles. Oh, how she wished Frank could walk. But he couldn't, and she'd best put the thought out of her head. It would do her no good. As the sun rose, around 5:30, by her reckoning, she stood and woke the boys. It was time to move on. Today, she hoped to reach Dutch Zierke's place.

Frank's diaper was both soaked and soiled. She shook it out, rubbing it in the grass to clean it as well as she could while William Henry looked on.

"It's still dirty, Mama."

"I know, little man. I can't get it any cleaner."

"Why don't you leave it?"

The idea was tempting. The cloth did little good, but it was an extra layer that might keep Frank's thin little nightgown from the soil of his waste. "We might have to, later. We'll use it as long as we can."

"Are we having breakfast today?"

Almena kissed his little head. "We have nothing, my sweet." Frank had suckled a few times, but her milk had dried. "You and I will have to be strong and go without again today. We'll eat when we get to Dutch Zierke's."

William Henry's lower lip trembled, but he didn't cry. He simply started walking.

Almena gathered Frank, settled him on her hip, and strode after her little one. His thin nightclothes flapped with each step, and he limped worse than ever. The rain had ceased during the night, but the clouds hovered, low and gray, and she knew they held more water.

Progress was slow, between William Henry's short steps and his poor little feet, and Almena had little clue how much distance they were covering. Time dragged on, and she heard shots.

"Oh, lord." She stopped and sat on the ground, her shoulders slumping as she released Frank.

"What's a matter, Mama? You got tears."

She wiped her eyes and gazed at William Henry.

"I think we're still near Lake Shetek, honey. We've been walking in circles." The shots had to have come from Shetek. There were no other settlements west of Dutch Zierke's. She sank her face into her hands and sobbed. An entire day, and they were still at the lake.

"It's okay, Mama, don't cry." William Henry wrapped his little arms around her and hugged her tight. "Maybe we can go back and get bread and milk."

"I wish we could, but we can't go near the lake. I think the Indians are still there, and we'll only be safe if we go away."

"I'm hungry, Mama."

"Me, too. Come on, let's head on." She pointed, showing him a new route, one which veered away from the direction she'd heard the shots. "This way." She stood, and they travelled on.

The day proved as wet as she'd anticipated, with the clouds dipping lower, misting at intervals.

The boys shivered, William Henry begging often for food, all of them resting frequently. Toward dark, he dropped to the ground, retching.

Almena lowered Frank and kneeled next to the three year old, rubbing his back as he vomited onto the wet prairie grass. She wiped his spittle with the edge of her skirt, and they sat while he whimpered, his head on her lap. At last, she roused them, hefting both boys as she stood, one on each hip, and trudged on again. They had another half hour before complete dark, and they needed to find a better spot for the night.

They crested a hill, and she stopped. *A road. The mail road.* She lowered the boys and glanced around, trying to get her bearings. And when she realized where they were, she plopped down with them and sobbed.

Another entire day of walking, and they were but four miles from her own cabin.

Lavina
August 22

I wake before dawn and find the wolf gone and my body still fully intact. Rising, I set my sights again on the tree line and set off. Today, I will reach Dutch Zierke's and send out word I've survived. I'll find Merton and Johnnie, and we'll strive on.

My steps this day are more painful. The numbness of yesterday is wearing off. My feet are bloody, cut by the prairie grass, and they throb with each step. I don't know what the soles look like, but the tops of my feet are lashed nearly to the bone. I enter a slough and wade in it, craving the cool caress of the mud. In seconds, I grasp it is water, not mud. I stoop and scoop it up, drinking again and again.

I slog on, parting the shoulder-high reeds and wading through two-foot-deep water. At the bottom, my feet squish, and mud sucks at me. Finally, when I think I can go no further, I emerge and find dry ground on which to rest.

As the sun edges up and light blooms, I realize I'm but a short distance from the timber. I stand, swaying with weakness. I'm light-headed and must wait before I move. I drag myself onward.

The squawk of geese startles me, and I look up. Despair crashes over me. This isn't Buffalo Lake! I'm back at Lake Shetek.

I sway on my feet. How can I have wandered for days and gotten nowhere? Dejected, I crawl into the nearest patch of weeds. Mosquitos swarm, and I cover my face with the apron and retch, my stomach protesting the lack of food. Misery claws at me as I think about lying here, where I started, dying of starvation while I hide from the Indians.

But I'll die either way. I can't lie in the weeds until dark, sacrificing another day. The risk of being discovered is less than the certainty of perishing if I fail to find food. And so I stand and push on toward the house—Tommy Ireland's, I think.

I wade through another small slough and clutch my way up the bank. The weeds are so tangled I simply stop and lie among them, too exhausted to move.

Maybe I should have gone around the slough. No, better to take the short route, isn't it? It's not so bad here, now that I'm not crawling through the weeds. I could lie here and sleep. Just a little while. The sun will be so warm. I'm shivering, after all. It would feel so nice.

A while later—an hour? a lifetime?—I drag myself up the bank, grabbing onto the underbrush with my hands until I reach the top. Uncle Tommy's cornfield is in front of me, and I stagger to it, wobbling with each step, and pluck the first ear of corn I spy. I remove the husks, wondering why it's so difficult, and strip off the corn silk. I attack the ear like a wild animal. The kernels are milky, not yet ripe, but I don't care. I eat two rows before my stomach rebels, and I retch my puny meal back up and collapse.

When I finally rise, I totter to the house. The slaughtered remains of a bull and several pigs clutter the yard. Clothing and dishes are scattered all about, feathers strewn far and wide, the mattresses emptied.

Shoes! I should search for shoes.

But I haven't the energy. I stumble to the cabin. A dog lies dead in the corner. I spy a crock on the table and rush to it, releasing the sour smell of spoilt buttermilk, mold crusting it. I vomit again, but there is nothing but spittle.

I lurch back out and take a cup of water from the spring before crawling into a plum thicket.

When I wake, it's evening, and darkness is thickening. I stand, still weak but no longer staggering. I return to the cabin, manage to catch a chicken, and kill it. I skin it. Desperate, I sink my teeth into its flesh and tear it apart. I don't remember until later that there was surely a knife at the cabin. I rip the raw meat from the bone, dip it all into the salt brine at the bottom of the pork barrel to preserve it, wrap it, and put it in a tin pail with three ears of corn.

Afterwards, I head east, to locate the mail route and the road to Uncle Charley's. It takes me all night to cover the two miles to the road. My heel, where it was shot, is swollen, and I can barely walk on it. Why didn't I look for shoes? Around eleven o'clock, I reach Buffalo Lake. The road crosses an inlet via a makeshift bridge.

Halfway across, I hear the sound of splintering wood, and the bridge breaks apart.

I fall into the inlet, water filling my nose and mouth. I sputter. My food pail bobbles, and I flounder in the water, unable to use my limbs to make my way to shore.

Almena

August 22

Almena roused herself to discover another foggy day. During the night, she'd gone back and forth between despair over having wandered about for two days and a sense of joy over having found the road at last. She'd again slept very little, and fatigue had lodged itself in the body, working its way deep into her muscles and her bones. She stretched, but it did little good.

She stood and surveyed her surroundings in the light of day. The road was marked but overgrown with grass. Still, she was no longer lost. Today, at last, they would reach civilization.

She wakened the boys and began the long trek. William Henry

lagged, and she stopped frequently to wait for him. When he collapsed, she gathered him up, as she had done much of yesterday, and staggered forward with both boys. But, today, the fifty-plus pounds wore on her, and she swayed under the weight, able to take only a few steps.

Weak, I'm so weak.

Setting the boys down, she sat next to them to catch her breath. She spied a puddle of water at the edge of the road, scooped it up, and drank, then showed the boys how to do the same. They both sipped but showed little interest in other activity.

If we don't cover these twelve miles today, we might not make it at all.

The thought hit her with enough force to make her faint. It was up to her, all up to her. She would need to dig deep if William Henry and Frank were to survive. No matter how much she wanted to sit here next to this pool of water and sleep, she couldn't.

Sighing, she tilted William Henry's face so he was looking at her. "You must listen to me. I need to leave you here, next to the water, for a little while."

"No, Mama, no! Don't leave me!"

"I'll come back."

"No, Mama."

"Mama can't carry both of you today. I can't. But I can carry one of you. I'll take Frank a little ways and set him down and come back for you."

"Promise?" His lips trembled.

"I promise. I won't leave you for long. But you must wait right where I leave you so I can find you. Can you do that?"

He lay down at the side of the road. "I'll be right here, Mama."

"Drink a little more while I'm gone."

"I will."

Almena drew a breath and picked up Frank, and headed east. Though she knew it was the only way, her heart broke leaving her boy behind. But she walked on, covering about a quarter mile. Once she found a good spot, she stopped, set Frank down, and gave him the same instructions.

Then she returned for William Henry.

The day passed, endless hours of back and forth treks that tripled her steps and the time it would have taken under normal circumstances. Almena was glad for the puddles of water that quenched their thirst and gave each of them the strength to go a little farther.

Late in the afternoon, a shout sounded from behind her. Fear catapulted through her, stalling as she realized it was a child, not an Indian. Clutching Frank close, she turned.

Merton Eastlick trudged up the road, his little brother in his arms.

"Mrs. Hurd? Is that you?"

"Oh, dear boy, it is." She waited, questions swirling in her mind, as he struggled forward.

"We didn't know where you were," Merton said as they continued together.

"The Indians killed Voigt but let me go as long as I went right away and didn't warn anyone." She paused, unsure if she wanted to ask her next question. "What happened, at the lake?"

Merton stopped. The boy wouldn't look at her. His breath came faster and faster.

At last, he settled. "They killed Andreas Koch, but Charlie Hatch escaped and gave the alarm. We all went to the Wright place. Old Pawn was there, and he said he'd help us. The other ones, the ones who killed Koch, they said we could go."

"So everyone is safe?" Almena held her breath, hoping Merton and Johnnie had simply become separated from the group.

But his eyes grew dark, haunted. "No." He paused. "Everything went wrong. They tried to take the horses, and a bunch of the men shot them. We all ran into a slough, and they started killing us. Mother told me to take Johnnie and not to ever let him go. I ran when I could."

Oh, Merton.

She set Frank down and knelt in front of him, her hand on his arm. "The others?"

"I don't know." He gulped air, swallowed. "Father's dead. Mother got shot. A lot of people got shot. I think a lot of them died. Uncle Tommy got away, but he told me to go without him. He was shot a bunch of times." The words came in a rush.

Almena hugged both boys, holding them as Merton sobbed against her shoulder. "And you made it all this way on your own?"

He freed himself of her arms. "I found the road, and we stopped at Buffalo Lake for the night. That's when Johnnie got all bit up by mosquitoes." He shifted, and Almena saw the little one's face, full of scabs where he'd scratched at the bites. "It rained all night. I tried to keep Johnnie dry. And the wolves came and howled for hours. I yelled at them, though, and they went away."

She gave him a wavering smile and picked up Frank. They walked on as he told her more about the journey. She didn't ask him any further questions about the events at the slough. He'd said enough for her to put it all together.

She pointed down the path. "There's my William Henry, waiting."

They stopped, Merton setting Johnnie down.

"Why don't you rest while I take William Henry on ahead. I'll be back for Frank."

"That'd be real good." He dropped to the ground.

After two hours more of going back and forth, as twilight

settled, they spied the cabin ahead. She pushed through her pain and fatigue in a burst, rushing to the door.

"Are we here, Mama? Is this it?" William Henry asked.

"We're here." She pounded on the door and called out. "Hello the house!"

No one answered.

Lavina
August 23

By the time I finally make it out of the inlet, I'm exhausted. I wring out my dripping hair and remove my wet clothes. After squeezing the water from them, I hang them on bushes to dry. As well, I hang strips of the salted chicken out to dry in the sun—it's too slimy for me to choke down as is. I can do no more. My body craves rest, and I again must lie in the grass and recover my strength. I'm weary of having to do this so often, but I can't go on.

When I wake, the sun is high in the sky. I dress, wrap my feet in bits of cloth I tear from my skirt, and eat a bit of corn and meat—which is improved but still slippery. I force it down anyway. I'm finishing when a crane and several ducks rise from the lake in a sudden flurry.

I dive behind a tree so the Indians won't glimpse me when they come over the hill. I lie there, waiting, hoping they will not hear my ragged breath.

But it's not Indians!

The horse draws a small cart, and I recognize the driver as Spot, our mail carrier.

I hope it's not a mirage and crawl from the grass.

"Help," I call. It comes out in a hoarse croak.

Spot reins the horse to a stop and speaks in Dakota with the strong guttural accent of the Germans.

I don't understand him but try to tell him the Indians have killed all the whites at the lake.

He speaks again, this time in English. "You look too white to be a squaw."

I finally comprehend he'd asked if I was Indian. It's no wonder, given the filth of my clothing and my undone hair flowing in the wind. "I'm Mrs. Eastlick. You've met me at the Everetts'. I'm badly wounded." I limp out of the brush.

He jumps from the wagon. "Here, now. Let's get you in the sulky."

He guides me to the small vehicle. The dam holding my despair breaks, and I sob while he holds me.

"There, there," he says. When I'm through telling him of the attack, he looks at my wounds and deems me solid enough to travel. He edges me up onto the seat and climbs aboard. It's crowded, with two of us, but I don't care. I'm safe.

We near Dutch Zierke's in the late afternoon, and Spot stops the cart. "I think you should stay here," he says, "while I check the house."

I creep down, hiding in the grasses while he goes to the cabin. Moments later, he returns.

"It is safe. There are no Indians here. Only a man who says he is from Shetek."

"Who is it?"

"I don't know him. Come, let's get you to the house."

A few minutes later, we arrive, and the door flies open.

"Uncle Tommy!" I scream.

My dear friend stands in the doorway, pale and gaunt, his eyes sunken. But he has a smile for me as I make my way from the cart. Spot helps me to him. Tommy opens his arms, and I fall into them.

"Dear Lavina, I never expected to see you again." His voice is a tired rasp, barely audible.

"Nor I you," I say. We both weave a bit on our feet, and I know we must sit. "Let's go in."

We stumble into the house and find chairs, collapsing into them.

"Merton and Johnnie escaped," Tommy says, a smile brightening his ghostly face.

Fresh tears drip down my face, and my lips tremble.

"They made it out the day of the attack. I'm thinking they may have made it here before the Zierkes left, that they're safe, maybe in New Ulm."

"Then we'll find them there."

"Will Everett made it out, and Charlie Hatch, and Bentley. They left ahead of us. I thought I was going to die there."

"But you didn't." I pat his trembling hand.

"When Merton said he was going to take Johnnie across the prairie, I'm ashamed to say I told him not to go, to stay and die with me." His voice cracks. The admission has cost him much.

"Oh, Tommy . . ." I can do nothing but hold his fingers.

"The boy would have none of it. He said he promised you he'd keep Johnnie safe, that he'd never let him go."

Pride swells. "That's my Merton."

"I decided to go with him to the road, to make sure he found it, but I only made it a half mile. I couldn't go further. I lay in the grass and prepared to die."

"Yet, here you are." I smile, realizing I shouldn't have been surprised. If I had the strength to make it out, then a hardy man like him most certainly did.

"I think I laid there for a day and a half. Far enough away the Indians didn't find me when they came back. When I didn't die, I forced myself to get up and walk. I got here last night."

"I'm so glad, Tommy. Now we've only to go on, to find my boys."

"Lavina . . . Frank . . . Frank was still alive. He tried to go with Merton, but he was hurt so bad. His thigh, his stomach, his mouth. He couldn't even make it out of the slough."

I gasp, my hand flying to my mouth.

"Merton sobbed. He couldn't take them both. I couldn't take him."

"I know. I couldn't either." *Oh, my boy.*

"He's gone now. I don't see how he could have lived."

"I know."

The door creaks, and Spot steps in. He searches the house, finds cheese for our hungry stomachs, and we rest a bit. Before we leave, I wrap up the rest of the cheese and a few turnips from the garden, and we're on our way.

The sulky is too small for all of us, and Tommy walks, his gait shaky at first. But he gains his feet and soon manages to keep up. We camp for the night, feasting on cheese and turnips, sheltered by a quilt and Spot's oilcloth blanket, which he gives to us when it begins to rain. At morning light, we continue on.

"There's someone ahead," Spot says. His voice is tense. "A group."

"Indians?" Tommy asks.

"I don't know. I think I will take us in the ravine for a while." He turns the sulky off the road. We keep quiet, looking at one another, fear evident in all our faces. Spot stops and climbs the bank. When he fails to see anyone, he returns.

"Well, what shall we do?" he asks. "We can go back the way we came, all the way to Sioux Falls."

"If you think it's safer for you," I say, "but I won't go back west. You can leave me, and I'll make my way to New Ulm."

"Same here," Tommy adds.

"I'll not leave you. If it's New Ulm you want to go to, I will go with you."

"I don't want you to risk your life for me," Tommy says.

"We'll be fine."

"*Nein,* we all go." We continue on, Spot going ahead to check for the Indians, Tommy and me following as he signals it's safe. Together, we all regain the road and travel on. But as we crest a hill, we spy them again, and Spot halts the horse.

"It's a woman," he says, "and children."

We close the distance. I think for a moment it's Laura Duley and call out for her to stop. She turns.

It's Almena Hurd.

"Almena!" We rush the horse forward and stop beside her and her two boys. "You're safe!"

She stands in shock for a few moments, shakes it off, and greets us all. Her glance settles on me, and she smiles. "Merton and Johnnie are ahead, just over the hill."

"My boys," I choke out.

Spot urges the horse forward, and suddenly we're upon them.

Merton turns and stares at us. Spot stops the cart, jumps down, and takes Johnnie from his wearied arms. He hands the little one up to me, and I kiss his poor little head and scabby face. I open my other arm, and Merton tumbles forward, his face against me. I brush his head and embrace him.

"I didn't let go, Mother. Not once."

"My brave hero," I say before my voice breaks.

"Are we safe?" he asks me.

"We're alive, and I'll keep you safe," I say as Uncle Tommy and the Hurds catch up to us. But I have no confidence this will be an easy thing. There are eight of us now, and it won't be so easy to hide nor to find enough food to sustain a group of this size. With the Zierkes having fled, I sense the Indians have been on the attack here, too, and I don't know what we'll find in the miles ahead.

Almena catches my gaze, and I know we agree. For now, we hang on and make it to where the next whites live, the Browns, halfway between Dutch Zierke's and New Ulm. The house is there, in the distance, and my heart sings.

It's but a few minutes later when we hear the bark of dogs in the distance.

Chapter Twenty
Late August 1862
Christina, Julia, and Laura
Among the Dakota

Julia

August 21

"You, Julia Wright." Speaks with Strong Tongue stood at the top of the rise. Several men on horseback joined her.

Panic seized Julia, and she jerked the children to a halt. She hadn't been fast enough, hadn't even made it into the trees.

Think, think.

"Dora," she whispered, "pretend you need to potty."

Dora's chin dipped, and Julia knew she understood the situation.

The men approached, cantering across the prairie. "Where do you go, Julia Wright?"

"To the trees. My daughter needs to relieve herself."

"She made water before we left. Do you try to escape us?"

"But I do have to go," Dora said. She gazed up at the Dakota with an innocent expression worthy of the stage, grimaced, and farted loudly.

George giggled, but Julia grasped the slim hint of hope. She sure as heaven would never chastise the children again for their uncouth abilities to expel gas on command.

"Please," Dora whimpered.

"Take her," the man told Strong Tongue. "You," he told one of the other men, "report back to Across the River."

The woman grasped Dora's arm and hauled her into the woods.

Julia prayed Dora could produce something.

"I think you lie to us," the man said. "You will not do this again."

They waited, Julia's concern rising. Would they be beaten? Killed? Her pulse thundered, but she did not show her fear to her captors.

Finally, Dora and Strong Tongue returned.

"She makes gas like a demon," Strong Tongue said, "but she does not go."

"I thought I needed to."

"Maybe. Maybe not." Strong Tongue pushed her toward Julia. "Go back to the others. Across the River will decide what must be done with you."

Christina

August 21

We stop at the Myerses' house. There is no one here, but the wagon is gone. I do not know if the family escaped or if the Dakota have taken it. But there are no bodies, and I think they may have gotten away.

"Come here," Running Bear's wife tells me. She has tied together three of the heaviest of the tepee poles, and they are raised high above. "Take one."

I grasp it, the weight catching me by surprise, but I hold firm. I must learn what is expected of me.

The wife takes another, and a third woman takes the last. "Now, go." She points, and I move away from the group until we form a triangle, the poles crossed above.

She looks at me and points again. "Go more."

I step further from them until my pole extends more than the others. It looks strange to me, but I do not argue. I push the point at the bottom into the ground as they do. We gather smaller poles, four each, and Falling Star shows me where to put the points, how to cross them on the others, all four at once. When we are done, there is a circle, but the top is not centered. I look around. Other tepees are being formed the same way. I had not noticed this before and wonder about it.

We push the poles into the ground. Falling Star takes the rope hanging from the three main poles and steps outside the ring. She walks around the ring four times, keeping the rope tight, then goes back inside. At the center, she tightens the rope and ties it to a stake.

"Come," the other woman says. She is standing at the long end of the circle with a folded bundle of hides. When I am there, she places one end of the heavy bundle in my arms. "Stretch out." She points beyond the ring. I unfold the bundle as she brings another long pole. She lays the pole next to it and attaches it to ties sewn to the largest fold. "Watch."

Falling Star and the other woman work together to raise the pole and the attached hides and prop it against the others. Falling Star turns it, and the fold falls open. Several hides are stitched together. They are scraped thin—not like the hides inside the tepee that are used for beds. "Pull out."

We move away from the fold at the pole, each hauling a section of hide that continues to unfold as we move around the tepee. I struggle under the weight but continue until we meet at the front. When we are done, Falling Star points to the back of the tepee, the long side. "Smoke hole," she says. "Above the fire. Smoke less this way."

The other woman has attached another flap of hide there. Falling Star sets a pole against a flap of hide and shows me how to open and close the smoke hole. So that is why the top is off center. The skins around the top are draped closed, and the poles will not catch fire. It is a good design, I think.

"Go in. Tie skins."

I enter the tepee and see there are ties that hang down. She follows and knots them around the poles. I do the same, and, with that, I have helped to raise my first lodge. It has taken only a few minutes. She is pleased with me, and I am glad.

Like good Germans, the Dakota seem to value industrious work. This I know how to do.

When I leave the tepee, I notice the others also working. Lillie works with Grizzly Bear's wife, and her captor does not seem so pleased. She cuffs Lillie again and again.

Guilt swarms me, and I want to go to her, to hit the woman as she hits Lillie. But I do not move. If I go to her, she will be beaten worse. I turn away, unable to watch.

Roseanna Ireland works with Redwood's wife. This woman talks to Roseanna and smiles often. I think I will not have to worry so much about her.

Then, I see Pawn with Julia. He is yelling at her. Something bad has happened, and I have a sick feeling Julia will not have so much favor as she did our first night.

Laura
August 21

Wearied and hungry, I stumbled into the tepee and dropped my load of wood onto the pile near the door. Sleepy Eye's wife glared and stalked toward me. I flinched.

"You are a useless fool," she yelled and slapped my face.

I cowered, my cheek stinging. It was the third time she had hit me since making camp, and I feared my skin would be bruised purple before long. I didn't know what I'd done wrong. Tears threatened. How could I do better if I didn't know what

I'd done wrong?

"Stack it neatly," Emma said. "Do it right and they won't be displeased with you."

I knelt next to the wood and restacked it. Who would have thought these people cared about neatness? As far as I was concerned, they were dirty as pigs, with their greasy stains on their clothing and dirty hair.

Then I remembered how I looked and sighed. I was reared a lady and never thought to be brought so low as this. I stood and walked toward the fire.

"Other side, Mama," Emma advised. "One side for women, one for men."

However did my little girl know such things? I switched directions and approached, then sat next to her. She was kneeling, some sort of tool in her hand. She was sewing hides, shoving a bone needle through them. Lord, had it taken but one day for her to become an Indian?

Frances sat on a buffalo robe, intently watching her sister. I hugged my frailest girl close. I knew I had only a short time before the old hag would force a new chore upon me. It was only the solace of having my little ones near that kept me struggling to do as I was told. I had never worked so much or so hard in my entire life, not even when on our first farm, back in Iowa.

Oh, to be back in that shoddy little cabin. I wouldn't even care about lack of a cook stove.

Jefferson bounded headlong into the tepee.

The wife yelled and cuffed him.

"Always go the other way, Jefferson," Emma said. "This is the women's side."

He hung onto me and muttered an acknowledgement. I comforted him, stroking his back. How I loved these three that were left to me. I would do whatever I had to do to protect them.

Someone rapped on the tepee skins, and the wife responded. "Enter," she said in Dakota; I was proud I'd understood her this time.

Another squaw poked her head in and said a few words before leaving. I remembered that Julia had said the word was disrespectful, but I didn't care. I did not hold much regard for these people.

"All go out," the wife said.

We stood and went outside, each of us this time minding our routes. The sun was setting, its rays casting orange and purple across quiet ripples of Fremont Lake. We were camped near the Myers farmstead, north of Lake Shetek. Tomorrow, we'd strike off across the prairie, into places unknown. I hated to leave the lakes. It was one more home I was being forced to leave behind.

Christina had whispered their plans to me earlier. She said they would move us faster in the coming days. My loins still pained with each step; I'd not even been allowed to wash the small tears I'd suffered last night, much less to treat them with any salve. My muscles ached from walking the seven miles from the Ireland cabin. I wasn't sure I'd survive more than that, but I couldn't surrender to my distress; my children needed me.

We moved to the center of the camp, where Pawn sat before a fire. Julia and her children were standing before him, as were the Ireland girls. Christina approached with Lillie Everett, and we joined them.

Lined up as we were, I could almost *feel* hostility emanating from Pawn. I twisted my handkerchief in my fingers. Emma was stiff, Jefferson clutching my dress. I looked to Christina. She was biting her lip. Julia stood firm but kept her head downcast instead of up, as she normally held it.

"I am much concerned," Pawn said in English. "This day, my

wife Speaks with Strong Tongue tells me there was an escape plan."

I gasped and glanced at Christina again. She shook her head. Julia? I couldn't believe it. Christina was the rebel, I thought. Julia had been nothing but dutiful. Then I remembered our discussion. Had someone overheard? Had someone heard me say I would run? I staggered a bit.

"I have trusted too much." His gaze bore into Julia's, and she lowered her head more.

What had she done?

"Though I wished to give my white captives comfort, my hand has been forced. As leader, I must prevent such things." He paused and looked at each one of us, his expression deadly serious.

His wife, Strong Tongue, grinned.

"Dora and George Wright. Emma Duley and the little girl, come here."

"No!" Julia and I cried out together.

"Silence!" Pawn's face reddened as he saw how we clung to our children. "Take them."

Women came forward, grabbing our little ones, holding us back as they were dragged forward. I struggled against the hands securing me as my children were taken to stand with the man who had betrayed us all so grievously yesterday.

Oh, how I hated him.

"Stop, women! I can easily kill these children."

I stopped. Julia did the same.

"Laura Duley, your boy I will leave with you. Sleepy Eye's wife has need for him. These others, I now give to other lodges."

Emma and Dora, old enough to understand, turned to look at us, their eyes full of questions, lips trembling.

"Please," Julia said, "please don't do this. I only meant to stop for a moment. It won't happen again."

"I cannot take that chance. I am the leader, and you have pushed me to take this step. From now on, these children will not live with or walk with their white mothers."

Women approached and herded the children away. The older girls struggled but were hauled apart anyway. A young squaw grabbed Frances from Emma's arms, and her cries rent the air.

"Please, do not punish all of us," I pleaded. "Please!" I fell to me knees.

"I have spoken," Pawn said. "It is this, or their death."

Julia
August 24

Evening was falling by the time the party set up camp a few miles outside the Redwood Agency. The group was smaller now—White Lodge and his followers had split off to attack Sioux Falls—and they moved faster. Julia's feet ached from the day's long march. Her legs ached, her arms ached, her back and bruised skin ached. And . . . her heart ached. The last three days had provided her new perspective, and she chided herself for having considered taking her former position for granted. And for being prideful.

From here on out, she would think before she acted.

She brushed sweat-drenched hair from her face and shrugged off the heavy pack in the spot Strong Tongue had indicated. By her reckoning, they'd covered twenty miles today. It had been the longest day thus far. She had precious little time to dump the pack and fetch the lodge poles.

Julia's muscles sighed with relief, but the respite was short lived. The minute she straightened from her hunched position, they seized up on her. With stiff steps, she returned to the wagons. A crowd of women clustered around it.

As a leader, Pawn's lodge poles were at the top of the stack, and Julia knew others were waiting. If she didn't get her poles off the wagon, the other captives might be punished for taking too long. She'd found that out the second night, at their camp on Long Lake. She'd lingered too long, and Laura had been beaten for not returning promptly with her poles.

They were all interconnected now.

Julia reached for the roll of twelve poles, grasping the rope that tied them together. She wrapped the rope around both hands, turned with the rope over her shoulder, and began to walk. The rope bit into the scabs on her hands, opening the wounds. She strained forward, wincing as the rope sliced her shoulder.

Laura stood at the edge of the group, watching her. Julia tugged harder. She didn't want to see the scowling in Laura's eyes, the blame.

In the next moment, Christina was there, grabbing the rope with her, moving the dreadful weight with her.

"How's George?" Julia asked. Thankfully, Running Bear's wife had taken George, easing Julia's worry by half.

"He cries, but he eats and does as he is told."

Julia's throat closed. Her poor little boy, too young to understand why he'd been jerked away from his mama and taken to live with a stranger. Thank heaven for Christina, that he had her there with him.

Dances in Water had told her removing the children was not a punishment but instead was a way to prevent the women from running away. Neither she nor Laura would leave children behind.

"Have you seen Dora today?" she asked.

"*Ja.* She was gathering wood and works hard."

That was Dora. At five, she knew what was expected. Old enough to obey, but hardly old enough to comprehend all this. Julia damned herself for giving in to temptation, for failing to think about consequences.

"If you get a chance, tell them I love them and that I'm sorry." Her voice broke.

"*Ja.* This they know, but I will tell them." Christina's words were soft, comforting. She was a good friend.

The logs dropped from the wagon behind them, the sudden movement ricocheting up the rope. It slapped against Julia, and she jumped. "Ouch!"

Christina shook her head. "The wife of Pawn does not help with this?"

"No." Strong Tongue helped with very little anymore. Except to berate her and hit her. And it was only when Strong Tongue wasn't watching that Dances in Water assisted. Julia envied Christina, who was aided in heavy tasks by Running Bear's wife. Then she squelched the green-eyed monster. She had no one to blame but herself. "I think she is very bitter to defy Dakota customs so much."

"I would help more, but I dare not."

"I know. It's all right. Thank you."

"*Ja.*" Christina squeezed her arm before returning to the wagon, where Running Bear's wife waited.

Julia turned and jerked the poles along behind her. When she arrived at the lodge site, she untied the logs and grouped them together, the three main poles, the three sets of four, and the extra pole. She tied the main poles together and left them for Strong Tongue and Dances in Water, who would erect the lodge. She hurried to unpack the skins so they would be ready when it was time.

"What took you so long?" Strong Tongue asked.

"I am not yet strong."

"You are lazy." Strong Tongue's eyes glinted, and she slapped Julia's face.

Julia's head dipped forward, her skin and eyes both stinging.

"I will work harder," she choked out.

Strong Tongue spat at her and walked away.

Dances in Water, Pawn's second wife, bit her lip, her gaze full of pity. But she said nothing.

It was enough, though. Julia gave her a quavering smile, letting her know she understood the hierarchy of the lodge prevented any interference. Julia turned away and started meal preparations, hoping she would do well enough to avoid another slap.

Routine filled the rest of the evening, and Julia was bone weary by the time she finished cleaning up the meal.

Full darkness had descended when Pawn approached. "Julia Wright, I would have you walk with me."

This was the first he had spoken to her since the night of the attack. "You are well?"

"Much better. German Woman is strong." He gave a wry grin, out of place on his hardened face and guided her to the bank above the Minnesota River. He motioned for her to sit and lowered himself to the ground beside her.

"I have seen you are sad. For this, I am sorry. You have been a good friend. I walk a thin line and could not let your actions go unpunished."

It was both an apology and the explanation, she realized. "I was not trying to escape," she told him—a stab in the dark. She doubted it would ease things, but she damn sure wasn't ever going to admit her guilt.

"That may be. Or may not be." He shrugged. "This I don't know, but it does not matter. It appeared you were trying to escape, and that was enough. I cannot be weak and continue to be leader of my village."

"I understand."

"Do not put me in that position again."

"I won't."

He watched her for a while, and she tried to keep her ease under the scrutiny.

"Speaks with Strong Tongue voices her displeasure with your work," he finally told her.

She looked up. She'd never please that woman, and they both knew it. "I'm trying."

He laughed, a short grunt-like sound. "I know this, but you must know she is honored as daughter of old Sleepy Eye. Her word carries weight.

"I would have you welcomed into my family in the way of the Dakota, yet my wife chooses to put herself first in this. She ignores our kinship traditions but it is her lodge and her decision." He stood and looked down at her. "Take care, Julia Wright, for I will not be able to spare you punishment if you fail to obey her."

If it came down to her words against those of Strong Tongue, it wouldn't matter whether she'd obeyed or not. Her life was now dependent upon the whim of a bitter woman who hated and resented her.

She suspected it would only be a matter of time before Pawn's warning became reality.

Chapter Twenty-One
September 1862
Almena and Lavina
Recovery

Almena
Brown's Cabin
September 2

Almena tucked the boys into bed, warmth filling her. It was good to watch them asleep so soundly, their tummies full and William Henry's little feet healing. She kissed them on their heads and prayed the night would be quiet.

"Hear anything?" she asked Lavina.

Her friend sat in a chair, bolstered by pillows, her leg propped on an empty crate so her swollen heel hung over the edge. Beside her lay one of the dogs that had so frightened them the day they'd arrived, some nine days ago now.

"Not tonight," Lavina answered.

It had become their standard exchange in the days since they'd reached this place. After the mail carrier had assured the house was safe, he'd returned with food he'd found inside and left them, headed east for help. They'd remained in hiding until dark, in case the Dakota were still around, before moving to the cabin. Those words—*hear anything?*— had been their constant refrain. Days later, they remained diligent.

"I still worry," Almena admitted.

The dog moved to lay its head in Lavina's lap, and she scratched the animal's ears. "I'm glad we figured out these fellows belonged to the Browns, or we'd still be shaking out there in the plum thicket thinking they were Indian dogs."

Now, one dog slept inside with them, the other two just outside the door.

"Do you think Spot made it to Sioux Falls yet?" The mail carrier had reached New Ulm only to discover no horses or people about, just burned buildings and Indians creeping among the ruins. After stopping to report the news, he'd left them again, this time heading west.

Lavina shrugged. Neither voiced their fear that he'd met trouble. Instead, they sat in silence, both of them weary, until Lavina dozed in the chair.

Almena shook her awake. "Go on to bed. You're going to fall off the chair. I'll wait up a while." Though dead tired herself, she knew Lavina needed the rest more than she did. When they both retired, neither of them slept. At least this way, they could trade off.

"Do you think Uncle Tommy made it?" Lavina asked, only half awake.

He, too, had left them, determined to obtain more food, even if he had to sneak past the Dakota to do so.

"Stubborn as he is, of course." She had her doubts, but she wouldn't discuss them. Though he appeared to have regained his strength, his injuries were severe, and it was hard to believe he was as well as he pretended. She hoped he wasn't lying on the prairie somewhere.

Lavina inched across the room, still nursing her inflamed heel. She crawled into the bed, and the room quieted.

Almena watched her sleep. Like Tommy, Lavina was a survivor. Her stories of the horrors at the slough, the deaths of her husband and children, proved it. And her injuries, like Tommy's, should have killed her days ago.

Thank God they let us go.

She blew out the lamp and sat in the dark, listening.

Lavina
Brown's cabin
September 3

I wake with a start. Outside, the dogs are barking fiercely. "What is it? Do you hear anything?"

"No," Almena says. She is at the window, peering into the darkness. "Maybe it's just cattle moving through." Her words are casual, but concern fills her voice.

Chills rush up my spine, and I reach for Mrs. Brown's wrapper. We'll need to gather the children.

"The dogs are frightened," she says, confirming my own thoughts. "They're running back and forth."

"I'll rouse the boys." I leave the wrapper and grab my clothing instead, throwing it on. I hurry across the room.

"My God," Almena says. "It's Koch!" She runs to the door and throws it open.

For a moment, I think she speaks of Christina, who was taken away from the slough by Indians.

"Ernst Koch, is that you?" Almena says.

"*Ja!* And Jack Wright."

I dash to the door, forgetting about my heel. The German trader who had left the lake before the attack stands there with Julia Wright's husband.

"Tommy Ireland sent us for you," Wright says. Beyond them, a group of soldiers ride in with a wagon.

The boys, stirring from their beds, appear behind us, curious. Wright fetches a lantern, and light engulfs us.

Chapter Twenty-Two
September–November 1862
Christina, Julia, and Laura
Different Routes

Laura
Encamped near Redwood Agency
Early September 1862

During the two weeks we had been encamped near the Redwood Agency, the Sioux were much unsettled, and we captives suffered dearly for it. Each day, riders brought updates of attacks and battles along the frontier. Not understanding the language, I had little grasp of the details beyond that Sioux victories brought celebrations, and defeats often led to beatings for us. Julia and Christina tried to communicate with me surreptitiously, but we were allowed little time together, and I lived isolated, enduring the travails of this new, horrifying life with no one but Jefferson to talk to.

Julia insisted she'd not tried to run, and I struggled not to blame her for causing my children to be taken from me. I couldn't, really, when all I wanted was to slip away to one of the many towns within the settled Minnesota River valley. But I dared not with two of my children in other lodges. Nor did I have any idea about what was happening in the area.

And so I hung on, for that was the only thing I could do with any certainty.

I had to find a way to be strong in this and shun any surrender to despair. There was no one here to force me from it. It would be up to me.

"Mama?"

"Hmm?" I stayed put where I was. I needed to complete the chore I'd been assigned before the Old Hag returned. She'd never told me her name, and I'd never asked. She called me Dog.

"Can we go home today?" My boy asked this each day, and each day I'd been forced to tell him no.

"Not today. If you've finished stacking the firewood, go out and tell the Old Hag you're done. Otherwise, she will hit you again."

He left the tepee, pausing to hold the flap so a woman could enter. I didn't recognize her and drew a breath, resigning myself to yet more abuse.

"Is this Sleepy Eye's lodge?" she whispered.

Her English took me by surprise, and I looked at her more closely. She was dressed as most of the women in the camp, a combination of worn white woman's clothing and Indian dress, her hair in braids.

"It is," I said, still trying to sort out who she was. "Are you Sioux?" I finally asked.

"Half. I'm a captive."

"A half-breed captive?"

"My husband and I had a farm in Renville County. He was killed three weeks ago, on August eighteen, when the attacks first started. I've been kept in Little Crow's camp."

So Pawn had told Julia the truth . . . the attacks were not isolated to our settlement. But it hadn't occurred to me Indians might turn upon one another. I considered it for a moment.

"What are you doing here?" I asked, unsure how direct I should be.

"Sleepy Eye traded a locket for me."

"A locket?" She must have been valued very little.

"We're not worth much once they tire of us." She approached me and sat. "I'm Josepha; they call me Jo."

"Laura; they call me Dog."

I grappled with the fact that she was part Sioux, wondering if she'd been sent by the Old Hag to entrap me. "Why are *you* a captive?" I finally asked, weary of trying to process it.

"We didn't live as Dakota, and we refused to join the attacks."

"Oh." I appraised her anew. A farmer Indian, I think they called those who abandoned Sioux ways. This woman might have more knowledge, and I needed to seize the opportunity.

"Do you understand Sioux? Why are they doing this?" Of all the questions I had, this remained foremost in my mind. I couldn't fathom why they'd turned on us. We had been friendly, many of us trading with them.

Jo bit her lip. "It's complicated. The Sioux on the reservation were starving. Annuities were months late. The day before the attacks, there was an argument when a group of settlers refused to give food to four young Dakota men. The Dakota killed them and fled to their village for protection. A soldiers' lodge met—leaders from all the bands—but they didn't agree. Some decided to attack; others did not. Some wanted to chase away the whites; others wanted to kill them."

"How widespread?"

"New Ulm, Fort Ridgely, all along the Minnesota River north to Fort Abercrombie. East to Acton and Hutchinson, west to Sioux Falls. All the small settlements in between."

"Oh, my stars!" I felt faint, glad I had not tried to escape. "Are there no soldiers defending?"

"General Sibley leads a force but has few men. Everyone has been sent to fight the Rebels."

I'd forgotten . . . it had been so long since I'd heard news about Lincoln's war. "There was a big celebration a few days ago, and the men brought fifty horses and a herd of cattle into camp. What was that?"

"Sibley's burial detail was attacked at Birch Coulee. It was a huge victory for the Sioux. Sibley started peace negotiations, but Little Crow refuses to surrender."

"How many are dead?"

"Hundreds or more, and hundreds are captives." She paused. "How is it here?"

I shrugged. What could I tell her?

"It's harsh. My daughters were given to others. I see little of Emma and pray she is not beaten too severely. Frances is two, but very frail. Every night, I hear her crying, wailing for hours, and I don't know why. I worry she's being tortured. They left my boy here, with me."

"They did?" She looked surprised.

I thought about it for a moment. "I think it is to keep me in line." I looked down, unsure if I should reveal more, but she was a captive, too, and she'd likely experienced similar treatment. And, if not, she should know what was ahead for her. Still, I could not look her in the eyes. "Every night," I whispered, "when Sleepy Eye has his way, the Old Hag sits beyond the fire with Jefferson. I am afraid she would burn him if I resisted."

Jo's eyes grew wide. "This does not sound like the way of a Dakota woman. Perhaps it is an illusion?"

"I wouldn't put it past the—"

Jefferson burst into the tepee. "The Old Hag says to pack up. The soldiers are coming, and we need to leave."

Jo's hand flew to her mouth, but I scrambled. There was much to gather if we were to be away. The last thing I wanted was to be in the middle of a battle.

I'd survived too much to die that way.

Christina
Ten miles north of Yellow Medicine
Early September 1862

Our camp is near the place where Sleepy Eye has his village. We fled Redwood and unpacked little at the camps along the way. I think the leaders are very afraid the soldiers will catch them. They do not look so pleased now, and their faces are angry. Sleepy Eye's wife says we will move again. That means the soldiers are close. We always move when such news comes, breaking camp very quickly.

I take the stewpot and hurry to the river to rinse it.

Around me, Dakota children play, unaware of the tenseness. The boys pretend to be hunters, the girls care for dolls. I have watched them and seen the respect they have for their elders, how the older children teach the younger ones this. When a toddler misbehaves—a rarity—the oldest sibling is disciplined with quiet reserve.

In all, they are a happy people and enjoy one another. The women laugh while they work, like good German *Hausfraus,* and the children are much loved. I do not see the Dakota even slap their children. I have learned, in normal times, captives would not be hit either. Instead, they would be taken only to be adopted into a family.

Ach, these are different times, though.

This is a large war instead of a single raid on the enemy, and there are many unexpected captives. No one knows what to do with us. There is so much hatred that it changes how the Dakota respond. I think this is a bad thing for all of us.

Julia is at the river, and I go to her, eager for a few words. This is our first chance to talk in days, since she was shot for doing chores the wrong way. I think it was because Pawn's first wife resents her. I am thankful Running Bear's wife is not so bitter. Now that I have learned my chores, she treats me well.

"How is your heel?" I ask her. I step into the river and scrub at the pot.

"Scabbed, sore, but getting better. Just a flesh wound."

So, Pawn's shot glanced off. I think he had to do something because Strong Tongue made such a ruckus, but that he did not want to hurt Julia too much. He respects her, I think.

"How is George?"

"He does as he is asked, a good boy, and is not beaten. He sleeps on my robe and cries for you but says he is glad he is with someone he knows."

"Give him hugs and kisses from me. Tell him I love him and wish we could be together."

"I will."

"Do you see Dora?" she asks.

"She works hard as well. I think she is not mistreated."

We finish and climb the bank. Julia limps and does not put much weight on the heel. I think it hurts her badly. "You are limping."

"Limping but I still have my foot, still have my life."

I know she is right. She is still the same Julia and will not let this defeat her. But when we leave the river, she moves away from me, and I know she takes care not to anger Strong Tongue. Again, I am glad I am not mistreated.

We tear down the tepee and move minutes later. I drive the wagon, as usual, and George is allowed to sit with me. It is a good thing I was given such a job and do not have to walk with heavy packs like Laura and Julia. Today, the Ireland girls herd the cattle that will be butchered for food. The herd is growing smaller all the time. Lillie Everett is still with the wife of Grizzly Bear and suffers greatly.

After about ten miles, we stop to make camp again, and the tepee goes up as fast as it went down. White Lodge and part of his group are here already. We have not been with them since before the Redwood camp. Tonight, news will be exchanged. The women in his group have already cooked the meal, and we hurry to join them in the circle.

"Sioux Falls is destroyed," White Lodge reports. He is an old man but has much power among his people. I think he has been a chief for a long time.

They speak in Dakota, and I am glad I am able to understand.

"Are there soldiers to the west?" someone asks.

"No settlements are left. The soldiers come from the forts along the Missouri River. But I've heard they're thick here, along the Minnesota River."

"They move upriver. Many of our people are weary of running from them and talk of surrender."

"I will need to ponder this, decide what will be best," White Lodge says.

The men continue to talk of recent events while the captives and Indian women clean up the camp and finish unpacking. I am putting out the sleeping robes, George at my side, when Running Bear comes to the door.

"Come," he says. "Both of you. White Lodge wishes to see the captives."

I usher George out, and we follow Running Bear across the camp. White Lodge, who is also called *Wakeska,* is the man who first took me, who gave me to Running Bear. My stomach is in knots as I wonder what this is about. Ahead, the prisoners line up in front of the leader. Their captors stand in a group. I take George by the hand, and we join the line.

White Lodge paces in front of us. He looks at us as if we are prizes. When he stops in front of me, my feet want to sidestep, but I force myself to stand firm.

"This one," he says.

I look up at his words. This one what?

Running Bear steps forward. In the distance I spy Falling

Star, who has treated me so well. She strides to him and whispers in his ear.

"Well?" says White Lodge.

I swallow.

"She is a good worker. My wife doesn't wish to trade her."

The knots in my stomach tighten. When fighting first began, White Lodge wanted to kill all the whites.

"That's the reason I want her. German Woman is sturdy, and she raises your lodge well."

"My wife—"

"She also understands Dakota, and that is important. I will offer a horse for her."

I hear Julia gasp, and I hold George close.

Running Bear exchanges glances with his wife, and her lips draw tight. She whispers to him again, and he says, "What will you give for the boy?"

"I do not need the boy."

"My wife does not want the boy without the woman. Too much work for her."

"Why should I pay for something I don't want?"

"Perhaps the woman won't be such a good worker without the boy."

White Lodge sighs. "The horse has a good bridle. You can have that. This is all I will offer."

Running Bear pushes us forward, and I choke back my fear of what will happen next. Falling Star has given a gift, sending George with me, and I must be grateful and do all I can to make sure he remains safe.

White Lodge grins at me, and I cringe.

Julia
Ten miles north of Yellow Medicine
Mid-September 1862

Camp was in an uproar, despite the misty weather. Julia held fast to her chores, trying to avoid the hullabaloo. In the past ten days, more captives had been brought into camp. Some were sold away immediately but a few half-breeds were still being traded within camp. Though originally distributed among lodges in case they were needed as bargaining chips, the captives were now being sold and traded for other reasons. Bands were constantly on the move, and food was growing scarce.

Traditional rules no longer seemed to apply, and, despite Pawn making her a wife, Julia feared Strong Tongue would offer her up in a minute.

News of soldiers came daily, and tempers were short as the men bickered about what to do. White Lodge wanted to move to his own village and rejoin those who had stayed there. Others preferred to maintain the camp where it was.

A few days earlier, young Frances Duley had wailed the entire night, dying before morning. The child had been but two years old; Laura was bereft and had taken to her buffalo robes, unable to bear the grief of losing another daughter, and Sleepy Eye's wife had beaten her severely for refusing to work. Now, she finally emerged from her lodge, her face mottled with bruises.

Julia gasped. *She must be in such pain.*

But her attention was drawn away by a woman who entered camp with Lillie Everett in her arms.

Oh, no.

Julia started forward but was stopped by Dancing in Water's grip on her arm.

"It doesn't concern you," she said. "You must not go."

"What happened to her?"

"Grizzly Bear's wife continues to beat her for being the daughter of Will Everett."

"Because Will was one of those who shot him?"

"She cannot get past the hatred. It is an eye for an eye to her."

"This hatred is very strong."

"It destroys us. We are not a hateful people, Julia Wright. We should be offering hospitality and kinship to our guests. Too many are forgetting our ways, and this will leave a bad mark on our people."

Dances in Water offered a wan smile. "I must go. Speaks with a Strong Tongue will soon return and will expect you to be at work."

Julia turned away and dropped to the ground, marveling at how different the two wives were. With a simple reminder, Dances in Water had pointed out the need to remain productive. Strong Tongue would have hit her out of spite, even though it was not the Dakota way.

She focused on scraping the hide in front of her, but her attention was on Lillie. As they passed, Julia saw it was not Grizzly Bear's wife but an old woman, familiar somehow, who carried the girl. Lillie's body was limp and drenched with blood.

Lord, will it never stop?

"She takes Lillie to her lodge," Christina said.

Julia looked up and brushed away a damp lock of hair. It was the first time she'd seen her friend since Christina had been sold to White Lodge.

"Are you safe? George?"

"We are both fine, thank *Gott.* White Lodge is old. His eyesight is not so good, and he sits a lot. Sometimes he talks to me, asking questions, but otherwise he does not bother with us. We work hard, and his wives like us."

"Grizzly Bear's wife beat Lillie."

"With a stake, I heard. Two women found her lying on the ground, the cow bellowing next to her."

Poor Lillie; thank goodness she'd been rescued. Then, she realized why the woman looked familiar. "Was that Scalpie? The Scalpie who visited Shetek?" The elderly woman was a regular, scarred from being nearly scalped by a hostile band many years ago.

"*Ja.* This is good, is it not?"

"Very good. Scalpie was a patient of Myers, and I think she worked for Lillie's mother. If she recognized her, she'll take care of her."

"Laura is up."

"Did you see her face?"

"*Ja.* But she is up, and this is good."

"German Woman!"

Julia and Christina both looked toward the voice.

One of White Lodge's wives approached. "White Lodge has need of you," she said. "He has decided to go to his village and will take you with him."

Christina
Ten miles north of Yellow Medicine
Mid-September 1862

White Lodge's sons complain about his decision. "He should not take her. It would be better to leave her here," they say again and again.

"You should not go," one of the wives says. "Here there is more food. The village has nothing to eat."

"Hah, they will eat you," says another.

I do not want to go to this place, to leave my friends and be alone, but now I am afraid, because of their words. I think the village will be a harsh place if everyone has such bad words to say.

"German Woman, I am ready. Come." White Lodge beckons.

George rushes to me, and I hug him tight. "Be good, and these women will take care of you," I say, hoping it is the truth. He is sobbing, and everything in me breaks as I join White Lodge. One of the wives picks him up and holds him as we walk away.

When we get to his horse, he hands me his gun and mounts. I start to hand the gun back to him, but he grunts and says, "You carry it."

I walk alongside the horse. The mist becomes drizzle, and the air cools. I am cold and wet, and each step takes me farther from everything and everyone I know. My insides squirm.

The gun grows heavier, and I shift it from one shoulder to the other. Though I am strong from hard work, I think if I go on, I will never be found. The powder horn hangs from the gun and bumps against my chest, and the rain becomes miserable.

On the horse, White Lodge drones on about how the whites should have all been killed.

I re-shoulder the gun, and rain runs into my eyes. Oh, how Andreas hated rain like this when he hunted with his percussion gun; he had to take such care to keep moisture out of the powder charge when reloading.

My foot catches in an animal burrow. I struggle to keep my balance and nearly drop the gun.

"Take care, German Woman," White Lodge says, "or you will shoot yourself."

I pause, regain my footing, and see he has not stopped. Now, I will need to catch up. But I do not go right away because his words sink in.

I cannot shoot myself unless the gun has already been primed to shoot.

If it has been primed with powder already, I can shoot him. Then I pause, thinking it through—this would be a risk, if I miss. But if the powder got wet . . . he would not be able to shoot me, and perhaps I can run. A plan forms in my mind.

Glancing forward, I see the horse still moves, and I start to walk in case he looks back. But I move slowly so the distance grows. When he is enough in front of me that I think he will not be able to see clearly through his old and cloudy eyes, I ease back the hammer until I can reach the percussion cap. I remove it and hold it in one hand while I shift the gun so rain runs into the hole to the barrel, where the powder is.

"You are slow, German Woman. Keep up."

"I am coming, but my ankle hurts."

"Come faster. A good woman does not let pain stop her."

"Yes, White Lodge."

He continues, slowing a bit. I do not have much time before he will stop entirely. I know he will not let me get too far behind, especially since I carry the gun. I am thankful he does not realize I know how to fire it.

I squeeze water from my hair, and it fills the tube. I put the cap back on, ease the hammer down, and catch up to him. I am careful to limp when I get near. We continue on, and I keep up the limp—not much, but enough so he will believe I slowed because of it.

"Your wives say the Sissetons in the village have little to eat," I challenge.

"This is true, but we will hunt."

"*Ja*, but game is scarce."

"Then we will move camp."

I can see he does not like me arguing, but, still I push, unable to hold back my quarrelsome German tongue. "Your sons say it is a bad idea to take me with you."

"My sons are impudent."

My heart pounds. "I don't wish to go with you."

"It does not matter what you wish. You are mine, and you will go where I say." He is angry now.

Ach! No more!

I stop and raise my voice. "I will not. I will go no further with you."

He turns, faster than I think possible, and jerks the gun away from me. "You will obey me, German Woman." He raises the gun and points it at me, and I pray the powder is wet through. Either way, I have had enough.

"*Nein,* I will not." I step back and thrust out my chest, inviting him to shoot.

Laura
Big Stone Lake
Late September 1862

White Lodge returned to the camp with Christina, deferring to her as if she had special power and causing much speculation. It was five days until the focus of gossip shifted, when the riders came with news of a large battle at Wood Lake. General Sibley's forces attacked Little Crow's men, roundly defeating them. Worried they would soon be upon us, we disassembled the tepees in haste and fled northwest.

Jo had taught me more of the Sioux language, enough to understand the Old Hag's instructions and pick up the news around camp, and I chastised myself for not learning sooner. I thought of all the beatings I might have been spared and my new security in knowing what was happening in the world. I resolved anew to remain strong for my two remaining children.

Our new camp was at a place called Big Stone Lake, a widening of the Minnesota River. The gray waves reminded us fall had descended, and the prairies stretched brown and dry beyond the lake. We'd crossed into Dakota Territory, and the remaining Indians spoke of moving farther west if the soldiers gave chase. But some had broken away, refusing to leave Yellow Medicine. They said they were tired of fighting and would surrender or join the camps of the friendly Indians who had refused to take up arms in the first place.

"Did you hear?" Jo asked.

"Hear what?"

"White Lodge didn't bring Christina when we moved."

I jerked up my head. "What?"

"He sent her and George with a group of younger men who went to the west when we left Yellow Medicine."

"He sold her away?" I was surprised. I couldn't imagine he'd sold her. She was such a good worker.

"Maybe he got tired of all her fretting about going back to the whites."

And no wonder. She'd talked of it constantly. And, with indulgence other captors did not exhibit, he'd allowed it. "Maybe so," I agreed.

It was unfortunate, for her new captors would likely not be so accommodating. In fact, if she'd gone west, her life would likely be much harsher.

Oh, Christina, what did you do?

Chapter Twenty-Three
September–November 1862
Wandering

Christina
Yellow Medicine
Late September 1862

After my trick with the gun, White Lodge is very different. My plan to run was not well thought out—I'd forgotten to consider his horse. But now, I think he believes I worked magic. He tells me I am the bravest woman he has ever seen and gives me more freedom. I am glad of the honor he gives me, and I tell him I want to go back to my people, hoping he will consent.

But this morning, he gives me to the young men, and now I do not know what to think. The men march me away, before it is even daylight.

Ach, this is not a good thing. I fear we are going back where White Lodge was headed when I did the gun trick. Perhaps I was talking too much of wanting to leave, and White Lodge decided to punish me. Now, I am all alone, except for George Wright, who was sold to these men, too.

I pick him up and carry him for a while.

The five-year-old is confused. His face is pale, and he calls for his mama. Though he did not see her often, he knew she was in the camp. Now, the camp is gone, and we are the only whites with this smaller group. George shivers and drops his head on my shoulder.

"German Woman, keep up."

I move faster. I do not know if I am stronger or if George is losing weight, but he feels lighter. I think maybe he is wasting away and hope I can keep him safe. I promised Julia I would do this and know it will be harder if we go onto the prairies in Dakota Territory. Winter is coming, and our life will be harsh. I have heard stories of how the wind blows there.

We walk into the night and stop many hours after dark comes. I have no idea where we are, and no one tells me. I am ordered to help one of the women with a lodge. Her child has a cough, and she doctors it with teas and tells me she is also a captive and was married to a white man. She says now is a good time to escape because there are fewer men in the group. She vows to do so as soon as her child is well enough. I think at least this night I will have nothing to fear.

I put George on a buffalo robe and lie next to him hoping this will be true.

When the woman wakes me, I have hardly rested.

"German Woman, get up."

The fire has died down, and I am sure she will tell me to go and fetch wood.

"It is time to go."

I stand and start to the door.

"No," she whispers. "Take the boy along but do not let him make a sound."

Only now do I realize she is whispering.

"Quick, quick," she says. "The men rode out early, and we must go, before the rest of the camp wakes."

Her words do not make sense, not unless no one is to know we are going. Hope floods me, but I dam it. I must get George and follow her. I pick him up. He stirs but settles as I put him against my shoulder.

"Hurry."

I slip out into the night, and she follows with her child, who no longer coughs. With sharp hand signals, she directs me, and we jog away into the darkness. The camp dogs stand to follow us but return to their places, not caring much that we are going. An owl hoots, and I trip, but she catches my arm and steadies me.

After about thirty minutes, I dare to speak. "Where are we going?"

"I am taking you to your people."

Hope surges within me, but I must be sure. "To White Lodge's camp?" I ask.

"Away from the Dakota."

I quicken my step, new energy flowing in my veins. We wade through water, and she tells me this will hide our tracks, and the dogs will not have our scent if the men search for us. The children sense the need for quiet and do not fuss. Through the day, we rush on, going back and forth across the Minnesota River. We say little, even when the water is deep, and we struggle for our footing. Our clothes are wet, cold in the autumn wind, but I try not to think about it. We take no roads, and my guide says this is because she cannot be seen. I trust she is right.

Near nightfall, we approach a camp. I stop, fearful she has led me into a trap.

She turns. "It is all right, German Woman. This is Red Iron's village, and they wait for the white army. They have no will to fight and will surrender. There are many whites there, waiting."

"Why do you do this?" I ask her.

"Because you have been favored."

I do not understand her meaning, and she explains no further.

We enter the camp, and she speaks to someone there, then takes me to a tent. "This a half-breed family of a Frenchman. I know them, and they will keep you safe." She pushes me forward. "I go to find my friends."

"Thank you," I say. I want to hug her but smile instead, unsure.

She smiles back. "Go. It is time." She disappears into the darkness.

A few days later, three days after the Battle of Wood Lake, General Sibley's troops arrive. He names the place "Camp Release" and accepts the surrender of friendly Indians camped there. That day, ninety-one whites and one hundred fifty mixed-blood captives are freed.

I clutch George's hand, and we walk forward to give our names. Today is a good day, and we have survived.

Julia
Big Stone Lake
Late September 1862

Julia swayed on her feet, unable to digest Laura's words. George was gone? She grabbed the tree branch to steady herself. "When?" she asked.

"Yesterday. White Lodge sent them with another group."

"Where to?" She looked from side to side, stopped herself. *Stupid thing to do—he's not here.*

"No one knows. They left camp very early."

Tears stung behind her eyelids. "Oh my God."

"I tried to get to you last night but couldn't."

"Oh my God." A sob escaped, and she wavered on her feet.

Laura held open her arms, and Julia fell into the embrace. She'd never thought she'd be brought this low. "I thought I'd escape losing them."

"I hoped you would. Just hang on to the fact that he lives, that they didn't kill him."

"Yet."

"Christina will protect him."

Julia drew a breath. It would do no good to give in to despair. None. "How did you get through the pain?"

"I haven't. But if I surrender to it, I won't be here for Emma and Jefferson. They are all I have left."

Guilt nipped at Julia. Laura had needed comfort, too, and she'd not given it. "I'm so sorry if I didn't seem to care when—"

"I know you cared. But you had your children about you, and they needed you."

"What he must be feeling, ripped away like that!" How would a boy of three even begin to understand?

"Christina will make it better for him. She'll tell him it's only for a little while. He'll be all right. Focus on Dora. She's smart as a whip, and she'll figure out what's happened. She'll need to see you being strong, even if from across camp."

"I'm usually the one offering advice."

"I know. Strange how events turn. You've taught me much about being strong. I guess it's a fair turn-about for me to help you."

Julia gave her a wavering smile. Laura was right. But it was strange, her being the strong one now. Laura Duley had been frightened of her shadow for the entire time Julia had known her, that or weeping about her fate.

"Ellen Ireland was sold, too. To Talking Spirit." Talking Spirit was young, recently married. His new bride would be much honored with the gift, but Julia doubted the teen would know what to do with the six year old. But, who knew? There could well be a baby on the way for her to tend.

"I hope they treat her well. Pawn talks of more of the main group splitting off. It'll be hard to travel in large numbers once the snow flies."

Laura shivered. "Not what I want to think about."

Julia turned, knowing she had no more time to spare before Strong Tongue came for her. She trudged back to camp, water vessels in each hand. Near the lodge, Pawn stood talking with White Lodge. She neared and set the water down.

"What is that one called?" White Lodge asked.

"Julia Wright."

"She is strong, like German Woman."

Julia sharpened her ears. White Lodge spoke of Christina.

"She is a good woman, despite what Speaks with Strong Tongue thinks."

"I have need for her to replace German Woman."

Julia held her breath. This was not good.

"I took her as a wife."

"She is not a wife, not in our old ways. She is a captive like the others. Your wishes do not matter to me, Across the River. Your stature is not secure. I will buy this Julia Wright. You may have three buffalo robes for her."

"I do not need any more buffalo robes."

"I will give you a cow."

"I will keep her, thank you."

"Robes, cows, take your pick." White Lodge shrugged his shoulders. "Either way, she comes to my lodge now. I like speaking with the white women, and I have need of her."

And, with that, White Lodge reached out, grabbed Julia's arm, and yanked her away.

Laura
Sheyenne River, Dakota Territory
October 1862

There was a rush of trading before we left Big Stone Lake, and I was sold for a blanket. At the time, it was like a slap, to be valued so little. With the first snowfall, I realized the value of blankets and rethought my assumption.

"I'm so cold," Lillie Everett mumbled. Trudging next to me,

she tightened her scrap of wool around her shoulders.

"You were lucky Old Scalpie gave that to you," I said.

My teeth chattered, and I despaired of ever being warm again. I prayed Jefferson, sold into a different lodge, was faring better than I. The wind blew bitter ice fragments into my face, stinging it red. I had no need to look into a mirror to know how chapped it had become—I could feel it burning.

"Maybe she'll give me one for you."

"It's better not to ask. It will only cause trouble." I longed for my flannel shawl, for my knitted scarf, but I'd survive. I had to. Emma and Jefferson needed me to be strong so they could be strong. I envied Lillie, but I rejoiced for her good fortune as well.

"I'm glad she rescued me."

"Me, too. You're a lucky girl." It was hard to imagine these people having the kindness and warmth the old woman had shown Lillie after rescuing her from Grizzly Bear's wife. She'd hauled the six year old on a travois, enduring chastisement from the other women. When they'd taken the travois away, Old Scalpie had carried her on her back.

"That's because my mama was good to her. She remembered."

Too bad more of them hadn't remembered the kindnesses given them by our little group of settlers. I'd never been able to understand what Julia saw, to trust Pawn as she did. In my view, he'd betrayed us, led us straight into death.

"You can use my blanket for a while, if you want."

I smiled at Lillie and shook my head. She needed it more than I. "I have my calico." I drew the piece of cotton around my shoulders. It was a remnant, full of holes, but offered extra protection to the tattered dress I'd worn for nearly two months.

"Look! The camp!"

I glanced up and followed Lillie's pointing finger. Across the wide expanse of tall, brown prairie grass ahead of us, I spotted tepees. The buffalo hunters' camp. My stomach growled.

"Tonight, we'll have meat," I told Lillie.

"Truly?"

"That's what the Indian women say." The cows had all been butchered long ago, and our only foodstuffs came from dried meats, berries, and wild game—which was too scarce to support us. Hunger became a constant companion this past week.

We neared the encampment, and a group was dispatched to secure our welcome. The buffalo hunters were not Sisseton but, rather, members of a local band. One of the men returned with word we would camp near them for a day or two.

With renewed energy, we hurried to make camp. There were forty or fifty lodges in our group, and we swamped the other group. Lillie returned to Old Scalpie, I to my new owner. This woman barked orders but had not yet hit me as did the Old Hag. She'd yet to tell me her name, so I called her Loud Talker. It seemed appropriate.

"Hurry," she said. "There will be a feast, and we do not want to be late."

"They'll feed us all?"

"We are guests, and guests are always fed."

I wondered if that applied to captives as well but didn't ask the question. I helped her pitch the lodge and put our sleeping robes inside. My feet ached, and I wished I could sink down and remove my shoes. They were worn thin, the soles full of holes, the tops torn where the grasses had cut through the leather. Some days we'd covered nearly thirty miles.

I could find no rhyme or reason to our path, save we were perhaps avoiding soldiers or trying to confuse pursuers with our zigzag route. Up until a few days ago, we'd often traveled by night, sleeping during the day. Many times, we'd camped without fires.

"Hurry, woman," Loud Talker said.

I followed her from the tepee.

"Go there. Tonight, you may all sit together." She pointed.

Across the camp, the captives were clustering together, the whites in one group, the half-breed women in another. My lodge-mate, Jo, was no longer among them, having been sold away en route west.

I rushed to my friends, and we exchanged hugs, mindful of those who watched us.

"Why do we get to sit together tonight?" I asked Julia.

"I think because they don't want to bother with us during the feast. We have no idea where we are, so there's little chance we'll escape."

"We're near the Sheyenne River," I told her, repeating what I'd heard Loud Talker say.

"As if any of us knows where that is."

We traded news about new owners, most of us now traded at least once. Only Roseanna Ireland remained with her original captors. The couple favored her and named her *Ondee,* which meant Rain. She was treated well and often released to play with the children of the camp. Julia said there might be an adoption ceremony for her, if we ever stopped fleeing.

"Mama!"

I turned at Emma's voice and took her into my arms. "My sweet girl, look at you." Her beautiful hair was in tangles and her dress a dirty mess. But she looked healthy, save for her haunted eyes. I clutched her.

Jefferson bounded into us, and I showered him with kisses. "Oh, darling! Do you stay warm? Do they treat you well? Do you eat?" The words tumbled from my mouth.

We chattered on, I with my children, Julia with her Dora, the Ireland girls and Lillie. All of us were cold, tired, and hungry, but we'd learned the way of things and how to avoid beatings.

Hard work was prized among these people, and it had become our way now, too.

"How's White Lodge?" I asked Julia.

"His wives are tolerant of me, not like Strong Tongue. He spends much time asking me about the whites."

"Have you heard where we go from here?"

"He's mentioned Elm River, wherever that is."

Like her, I was no longer familiar with the landmarks we encountered. We were hopelessly lost. "How far do you think we are from Shetek?"

"I don't have a clue. All I know is that we haven't reached the Missouri River yet."

"Do you think we'll be captives forever?" I asked, already suspecting we would.

Julia shrugged. "It gets more likely every day."

Julia
Near the Big Bend of the Missouri River
October 1862

Julia set down her pack and watched the people in the other camp. They called this place the Big Bend. It was a distinctive curve in the Missouri River, and, if she remembered correctly, Jack had said the Big Bend was due west of Lake Shetek, halfway across Dakota Territory. White Lodge had led the group north, then back south.

This other camp spoke Lakota, still Sioux but speakers of a different dialect. They were western Sioux—Tetons—the village led by Two Kettles. He was not happy about them being here; that much was obvious to everyone.

She straightened, aching from the rough use these past three nights. Her newest owner's preoccupation with her had also angered his wife, and she'd been beaten daily. Today, her ribs were sore, and she hated to think about how bruised her face must be. From across the camp, Pawn looked at her, and she thought his eyes held apology.

But they were no longer friends.

The loss should have caused her sorrow, but she was numb to it. She was on her own, and all she needed to do was hang on. She could endure anything. She had to.

White Lodge neared and stopped in front of her.

"Julia Wright, I have missed you."

Odd as it was, she had missed him—*if that's what one called it.* Though she hated him with every fiber of her being for having been among those who led the attack on Shetek, he was a tolerant captor.

"Yet you sold me," she said.

"I needed the blankets for my wives. They were cold."

Practical, matter of fact—she could relate to that as well. Didn't mean she had to like it, though. "And are they still cold?"

"They are warmer than you. But now I am much lonely, and my wives miss you. You are a good worker and a good cook."

Julia had learned straight off that work was valued in this culture. Jack had valued that, too. It'd be nice to be valued for herself sometime.

"My wives think they would like to have you back in the lodge."

"That does not involve me," she said.

"They will share blankets, so I may offer one to buy you back. You will go to my lodge again."

"Hmmpf."

"It has already been done. Come now."

Julia followed White Lodge, accepting the change with little emotion. She was beyond any mourning or celebration regarding who owned her. But she couldn't help hoping the man she was leaving preyed on his wife tonight and left *her* bruised and battered. Maybe, the wife would hit him. That would be just as good.

They neared White Lodge's tepee, and he paused. "I wish you to come with me. I go to smoke the pipe with Two Kettles. I would have him see my fine white captive so he will know I have good medicine and agree to be my ally."

Being valued simply because she was a white captive wasn't exactly what she had in mind, either.

When they entered the other camp, White Lodge led her through the circles of lodges to the center. There, he told her to sit while he met with Two Kettles. She settled outside the lodge, and a few of the women neared.

"You are White Lodge's captive?"

"One of them." She heard the hollow tone in her voice and wondered when she'd stopped caring.

"How many does he have?" another asked.

"Two white women, six white children, six half-breed women."

"So many."

The women chattered among themselves in Lakota. The words were hard to distinguish, but she understood the gist of the conversation. They spoke about the captives and disagreed about the strategy of taking white captives as well as about their treatment. They'd noticed the bruising on her face, her slow gait.

One of the women gave her a bowl of stew, and her stomach growled. She forced herself to eat it slowly so her empty stomach wouldn't rebel. She had one handful remaining when White Lodge exited the tepee. She quickly ate the last of it and handed the bowl back to the women, offering her thanks. She followed White Lodge back to his tepee.

As he'd told her, the wives were glad of her return, and White Lodge welcomed her into his own robe that night. Though he whispered he would wait until she healed instead of taking her that night, he'd not asked her to be a wife. The old traditions had become a casualty of war, and she was nothing now but a possession to be passed from one man to another.

She felt his hardness against her back as he spooned her, and she wept.

Laura
Along the Missouri River, near Beaver Creek
November 1, 1862

Winter came on with full force, dumping snow often as we traveled north. White Lodge's big plans to unite with Two Kettles failed miserably when the leader sent word his people had no quarrel with the whites and did not wish to join in the fighting. The band supplied them with food and told them to move on.

Bitter winds accosted us as we trudged north. A few days ago, we'd camped near a band of Yantonais, another band of the Teton Sioux, and White Lodge was attempting to recruit them to his cause.

I shivered as I neared the shoreline, my fabric scrap shawl no longer of much use. My shoes had gone by the wayside miles ago—I'd cut off the soles and tied them to my feet. But now, those, too, were worn beyond use. I sat on a rock to attend to my feet. My chores could wait. I'd stolen two strips of leather from the tepee. I didn't care if I was beaten. My feet were nearly frostbitten, and I could go no further in this condition.

Julia walked the bank collecting dried buffalo dung, water vessels hanging from her shoulder. I waved to her and began working on my new footwear. I untied the rag strip holding the useless sole and peeled it from the bottom of my foot, wincing as my tortured skin went with it. The cloth was in shreds. Sighing, I ripped the cotton I'd used as a shawl and used half to wrap my foot. My arms would have to go bare—there was nothing else for it. I bound the stolen leather around it, round and round, and tied it off around my ankle. From my pocket, I took strips of sinew and lashed them around my foot to help hold everything secure. Not fashionable in any sense, but much better than before.

No fairy-tale glass slippers, certainly.

With unexpected suddenness, I laughed at how my priorities in life had changed. It was the first time in months that I'd found humor in anything.

I crossed my other foot onto my lap and repeated the procedure.

Julia had disappeared to the south, but I heard a commotion from upriver. Afraid they'd come to search for me, I grabbed my own bag of buffalo dung and hastened back the way I'd come.

Treading up a low rise, I spied sails and dropped the bag in my rush up the hill. It was a Mackinaw boat! The wooden sailboat was common among fur traders.

Whites?

A group of Santee, mostly from our camp of Sisseton, were at the edge of the water, beckoning the group in the boat to shore. Three men jumped from the boat, and I recognized them as Yanktonais from the group camped north of us. They yelled for the rest of the group to move on, no matter what. Then the Santee raised their guns toward the boat.

Oh, please go on. Do not let these people take you.

I wanted to shout, but I held my tongue. I couldn't risk a warning if I was to keep Emma and Jefferson safe. But another man had already waded ashore. He *was* white, as were a number of his party in the boat.

I approached, keen to hear what was happening, but took care to stay out of sight. The Santee were arguing with the three

Yanktonais men, their voices loud.

"We must kill all of them," one of the Santee said.

"No, the woman is Yanktonais and must be spared."

I glanced at the boat, where an Indian woman sat atop a high pile of goods. She watched the man on shore closely.

"What is she hiding, there on the boat?" the Santee asked.

"Eagle Woman doesn't hide anything," the white man said. "She is with the body of our son, and we're taking him home for burial."

"Galpin tells the truth," said one of the Yanktonais. "We were on the boat, and we saw this."

"And the other men?"

"They are miners, riding with us. We mean no harm," Galpin said.

"We will spare you if you give us all you have aboard, the food and the trade goods."

Galpin agreed and beckoned to the boat. One of those still aboard tossed a rope, and the Santee hauled the boat close, wading into the water to take possession. The two groups continued to argue about what Eagle Woman might be hiding. Finally, one of the Yanktonais men became angry.

"You will let these people go or the Yanktonais will turn on the Santee."

Eagle Woman stood in the boat and screamed at her husband to come. She pointed to the shoreline. More Santee had crept through the grass. Eagle Woman cut the rope, and Galpin jumped aboard as the boat floated away. Aboard, everyone crouched low. The Santee raised their guns and fired.

I jumped at the sound, tears biting my eyes. Heaven only knew when I would again see whites. I moved back, afraid to let the Santee witness me spying, unwilling to let them glimpse my tears. My dung bag had slid down the hill. I sighed and turned back to fetch it.

In the distance, Julia ran along the shore shouting at the boat.

I held my breath.

But the boat passed her by and continued downriver.

Chapter Twenty-Four
November–December 1862
The Fool Soldiers

Julia
Along the Missouri River
November 1, 1862

Julia watched the boat pass by, disappointment squeezing every fiber of her being.

Damn, damn, and damn!

The vulgar words, foreign to her a few months before, no longer shamed her. She'd hardened. She was no longer the lady she'd been raised to be, the wife who fought to maintain her reputation, or the woman who rescued her scoundrel of a husband.

She'd fought too hard, survived too much, *allowed* too much. It was enough to make her want to curl up and die. How could they have sailed past, as if they hadn't cared one whit about there being white captives? She'd made a split-second decision, had staked her life—and Dora's—on calling out to them. And they'd gone on past.

The boat floated away, well out of earshot now, and she watched it until it disappeared. When it was gone, she picked up the water vessels and the bag of dung she'd dropped on the ground and trudged back to camp.

She supposed it was too much to ask that no one had noticed.

"Julia Wright."

She looked up at the sound of White Lodge's voice. His face was stern, his voice hard. She stopped in front of him and waited to be disciplined.

"I do not know why you keep doing these things."

"It did little good."

"And I am glad of that. Still, it cannot go unpunished. Pack up your things. I am trading you back to Across the River. Speaks with Strong Tongue will deal with you. My wives are not strict enough."

So, back to Pawn and his embittered wife. She took the buffalo dung and water vessels back to White Lodge's wives before trudging to Pawn's lodge.

"What a disgrace you are that you have to be traded to me so you stay in line." Strong Tongue kicked her, spat at her. "You are worthless."

Julia lowered her head. She knew that wasn't true. She was a good worker as well as a good cook. But she was also known for disobedience. She'd tried to be like Christina, but she guessed it wasn't in her nature.

"Well, take down the lodge. The Yanktonais withdrew their hospitality. We've been asked to leave."

Less than an hour later, the camp was packed and ready to go, back south this time, to the Grand River. Julia hefted her pack and marched forward with the rest of the band. She spotted Dora and waved.

A smile lit her daughter's face, and Julia smiled in return.

Heavens, how did I let myself forget?

She needed to count her blessings. White Lodge could easily have traded her to the Yantonais before they departed. And, though she didn't have control over what others did to her, she *did* control how she responded. She was strong, damn it, and she was done with simply enduring.

Though she had no quarrel with Pawn, he refused to interfere with Strong Tongue. Life was easier with White Lodge. She'd find a way to persuade him into buying her back. His wives liked her, he liked her, and he would have need of a white captive again when he made yet another plea to another band to join his cause and attack settlements in the spring. Then, she'd focus on finding a way to get Dora into his lodge.

Ahead, Laura slowed, and Julia caught up. The band had grown more lax, now that they were so far from civilization, and didn't bother to keep the captives separated so much. In the evenings, Julia sat with the children, making sure they were all right and offering them encouragement. There were fewer beatings now that all knew what was expected of them. Lillie was treated well by Old Scalpie, and Roseanna was a favorite of Redwood's wife.

"They didn't stop," Laura said.

"You saw?"

"I was too frightened to call to them and so proud of you. You're always the one taking risks for the rest of us, bolstering us when we need it the most."

The words warmed her. "We're pretty close to out of food, again. There will be hungry nights ahead. Maybe we should start stashing roots and berries. I've had enough of watching them eat while we starve." The only good thing about wasting away was that neither had conceived a child.

Laura lifted her tattered skirt hem. "Did you see my new shoes?"

"Very fine. White Lodge's second wife gave me her old moccasins, holes and all."

"Will we wander from camp to camp all winter, do you think?"

Julia thought for a moment. "Game is so scarce that I doubt they'll make a permanent winter camp. Besides, White Lodge is so determined to recruit among the Teton so he can renew fighting the whites in the spring."

"I hear mumblings. Not all his people agree anymore."

"Mumblings, yes, but I doubt enough to change his course. We're in for a hard winter, friend of mine."

Laura

On the Missouri River, near the mouth of the Grand River

mid-November 1862

I limped to a log and sat down, my buckshot heel paining. For reasons that bewildered me, my owner's wife had grown angry and shot at my feet, one of the balls landing in my heel. A week later, I still had no idea what had prompted her outrage. I was fortunate it had been a light wound and that they'd sold me to someone with compassion enough to dress it.

The camp was busy with chatter. A small group of men, perhaps from the Two Kettle Band where we'd camped several weeks ago, was setting up lodges a mile or so distant. The gossips were having a fine time speculating about them. Though they'd come from the direction of Bone Necklace's camp—where we'd seen the boat—everyone agreed they were from further south. Perhaps they'd broken from Two Kettle to join with White Lodge. If so, they would be the first Tetons to do so.

White Lodge paraded back and forth, preparing to welcome the young men to his cause. What that meant for us, I did not know, and I was eager to talk to Julia. She was back in White Lodge's tent again; he constantly sold her and bought her back. She joined me at the log, both of us watching him.

"Look." I pointed to two young men entering camp on horseback. They both dismounted and walked through camp.

"I recognize them," Julia said. "They *were* at Two Kettle's village. I saw them when White Lodge took me to the council there."

"What do you suppose they want? Will they join the Santee, do you think?"

"I don't know. Come on." She grabbed my hand, and I limped along with her, weaving through the tepees. I glanced around, fearing we would be observed and punished for leaving our work. I halted, out of sight, as we neared White Lodge. This was close enough.

Julia huffed but stayed beside me.

The men looked to be in their late teens or perhaps early twenties. They passed us, speaking quietly. "There are too many warriors here to fight, but they are starving. We will use that."

Fight? Who were these men? I glanced at Julia, and she shrugged.

The two approached White Lodge with the deference due an elder and leader and stopped.

"I am known as *Wa Anatan,* or Charger," said the taller.

"I am called *Wa Yaya,* or Kills Game," said the other.

White Lodge grunted. "You are from Two Kettle's band."

"Yes, there are ten of us," Charger confirmed.

"And ten more who left you and turned back." White Lodge flung out the insult, but neither young man flinched.

"They were from Bone Necklace's camp," Kills Game stated.

Though the explanation meant little to me, White Lodge nodded as if the distinction was important. "What is it you want, Charger and Kills Game? You have come a long way."

"We wish to hold council with the Santee," Charger said.

"We have little food to offer you." The admission seemed to pain White Lodge.

"We have food and will bring it to share with your people," Charger answered. "We want to speak about your captives."

I gasped and reached for Julia's hand. Her eyes were wide. She motioned for me to keep still with her finger to her lips. We stepped backward, quietly, until we were a distance from the trio.

"What do you think is going on?" My head spun with possibilities.

"I'm afraid, Laura. Very afraid. Before this night is done, some of us may well be sold away."

Julia
On the Missouri River, near the mouth of the Grand River
mid-November 1862

Julia sat at the back of the council lodge, against the outer wall, well behind the elder members of the tribe. She knew she was present only because White Lodge might need to display her. If not, she would remain unseen behind the men.

But she would be able to hear and might have at least a chance of warning the other captives about which of them were to be traded.

The two Teton men, Charger and Kills Game, boys really, sat with White Lodge. Together, they shared the pipe, until White Lodge lowered it and gestured for them to speak.

"You see us here. Our people call us crazy, but we want to do something good." Charger paused, and Julia held her breath, waiting.

At Kills Game's agreement with his words, Charger continued. "If a man owns a thing, he will not part with it for nothing. We have come here to buy the white captives."

Julia fought to draw a breath.

White Lodge grunted, stiffening at the words.

"We will give horses for them, all the horses we have. That proves we want the captives very much."

All their horses. The cost for captives had dropped from guns and horses to blankets, a pair of pants, and measly trinkets. This was a generous offer, and White Lodge might very well accept it. Julia leaned forward.

"You speak of doing a good thing. I wish to know what you mean by this."

"We wish to return the captives to their friends."

They want to ransom us? Set us free?

"Hah!" White Lodge said. "In the east, the sky is red from the fires that burn the homes of the whites. I have taken these captives after killing many of their people and can never again be considered a friend of the whites." He paused. "I have chosen my path and now must follow it, fighting until I die. I may have need of the captives so the whites will not attack and risk their lives. Or I may ransom them to the whites. I will not sell them to you."

Oh, White Lodge, no! Take the horses; please take the horses.

Charger signaled with his hand, and others in his party brought goods forward.

Julia strained for a glimpse. Bread, sugar, coffee, she thought, perhaps more.

Charger waited until the other men dropped back again. "Here is food. Eat what you want and go home, and we will take the captives and go home."

White Lodge grunted again and gestured for his tribal elders to eat. They did so, taking what was offered them. No one said a word. The tension was thick, the air heavy with lingering traces of smoke and unspoken words. Julia's pulse beat loud and fast, ringing in her ears. She prayed no one could hear it in the silence.

White Lodge stared at the two guests and finished the last of the food.

"Your people are right to call you crazy. You think you are like soldiers, coming to rescue the captives, but you are fools. The whites care nothing for you and would cut your throats in an instant. You are boys who should go home in shame rather than attempt to be men. You bring shame to the Teton and to the Santee. I spit on you."

He rose and left the council, a final insult to the two petitioners.

No, the captives would not be separated, but neither would they be rescued.

Laura
On the Missouri River, near the mouth of the Grand River
November 19, 1862

The Fool Soldiers, as everyone was calling them, returned, and the gossips had another holiday discussing whether captives would be sold. This time, White Lodge did not invite them into his lodge. He insulted them by meeting outdoors.

I snuck from my tepee and crouched behind another, as closely as I dared get. I prayed I wouldn't be discovered, but I had to learn as much as possible. Julia had not been able to get word to me about the first meeting, and I knew only what I'd gathered via the rumors—that White Lodge had refused to discuss a sale.

The young man, Charger, spoke, but I couldn't distinguish all of his words. He spoke in Lakota, which was foreign to me, enough different from Dakota that I had difficulty comprehending when he spoke rapidly.

"Go home," White Lodge said. "You are boys, and I will not sell these captives to you."

So it was true! I grasped the last shreds of my handkerchief in my fist. Who did they wish to purchase? Which of us would be sent away? Lord, please not my children.

"Again, I say to you we will offer all we have." It was the young Charger again.

"And, again, I say to you I will not sell."

Silence stretched, and I could imagine them looking at one another, White Lodge with his face stony and resolute.

"You talk big, White Lodge. You speak of killing white men who had no guns. You steal women and children and run away with them. Where is the bravery in that? If you are truly brave, why did you not fight the white soldiers instead?"

I held my breath, waiting for White Lodge to spring up and attack Charger for the insult. He'd spoken slowly, each word deliberate, and the leader must be seething with anger.

"Three times . . . we will take the captives . . . Teton will come against you . . ." This time, the words came too fast. I understood only that the captives might be stolen away, and fighting might be imminent.

My breath stalled.

We'd battled in the slough near Shetek and experienced only death and despair. For the first time since being taken, I prayed we would be sold.

White Lodge said nothing, but other men whispered of warriors riding back and forth in the distance. I remembered when they'd done that at the Wright house, before the attack at the slough, and I shivered.

A new voice joined in, a young man from White Lodge's camp. "Black Hawk, son of White Lodge, why do you not speak? Why sit so still?"

Black Hawk had been the one who had advised Christina not to go with White Lodge back at Big Stone Lake. After a few moments, he spoke. "You boys have courage in your hearts and strong intent. You bring us good food, and you are respected among your people. This I know. But my father does not know you."

Several voices mumbled.

I sat, tense, waiting.

Black Hawk continued. "It is winter, and we are starving. I have one white child that I will give up. Let the others do the same and give up their captives. It is time for them to go."

One of the Ireland girls. How in heaven's name would the girl survive alone? I struggled to hear the mumbling among the men. Many of the voices affirmed the Santee might survive better, be welcomed more easily by those who lived in the area, if the captives were not with them.

Panic crushed in on me as I realized there might be more sold, that my children might be separated from me.

White Lodge made a low grunt. "My own son believes the captives should leave us. Go, Charger, and return with all you have to trade. I will let each family who has claimed a captive decide for itself."

I limped away as fast as I could. I had to keep Emma and Jefferson with me, no matter the cost. Even if it meant offering myself as wife to one of these heathens.

Julia
On the Missouri River, near the mouth of the Grand River
November 19, 1862

"What are they doing?" Julia asked White Lodge's wife. Across the camp, a large lodge was being raised, much bigger than the lodges they lived in. She wasn't sure what it was for, though she suspected it had to do with the Fool Soldiers. She'd heard enough about what had happened that she knew they would be returning.

"Putting up the council lodge. The meeting will be large, many more than just the elders."

Julia tried to stay calm. If they needed space, the rumor about White Lodge consenting to the sale of the captives was true. She glanced at the woman who had always treated her well.

"We're being sold?"

The woman looked at Julia as if weighing her response.

Julia held her breath.

"Each family with a captive will hear what is being offered. Each may negotiate or not."

"My daughter . . ."

"There is nothing you can do, Julia Wright." She motioned to the tepee. "We have work inside—go."

Julia took a last glance at the council lodge, wondering when they would go. An hour later, when people began to move outside, Julia dropped her needlework and rushed to the door. "They're going to the lodge," she told the wife.

The woman stood behind her, both of them watching. The Ireland girls, Lillie Everett, the Duleys, and Dora were ushered in. Laura looked anxious.

Julia's pulse quickened. She glanced at the woman behind her. "Shouldn't we be going?"

"We are not going."

Julia's mouth dropped open, words clogging in her throat. Was she not to be sold? *They're selling Dora without me?* That couldn't be. She'd been sold again and again. Maybe White Lodge planned to make a production of it. That had to be it. She'd misunderstood, that was all. He was saving her for last.

"Go back inside. White Lodge does not wish to sell you."

"No!"

"It is not for you to decide."

"I won't lose Dora."

She slipped through the opening and rushed forward, toward the council lodge. Behind her, the wife yelled. Hands grasped her and lifted her from the ground. Her feet churned as she fought to get away, but it was no use.

Laura
On the Missouri River, near the mouth of the Grand River
November 20, 1862

I sat inside the big lodge, my eyes glazing with fatigue. I'd tried to stay awake through the night, to keep up with the negotiations, but had fallen asleep several times, my head jerking as I awoke. We'd been lined up in a row, whites and half-breeds. Everyone but Julia. I didn't know where she was or why she wasn't with us, and I was afraid for her.

They'd offered her daughter first, negotiations going back and forth for over an hour before agreement was reached, and Dora had been sent to sit with the Fool Soldiers. She'd sat there, looking back at us with terror in her eyes, and I'd tried to signal to her that it would be all right. But I didn't know if it would be. I didn't know what would happen.

Then they'd sold my Jefferson.

I'd screamed and raged, offered myself to his owner, been slapped into silence with a warning that Emma and Jefferson could still be killed at any time. I resigned myself and prayed I would not be left behind.

By the time late morning came, all of the children had crossed to the Fool Soldiers. Now, there was me.

There wasn't much left to offer, by my accounting. I tried to force myself to listen to the offers going back and forth, but I was so weary I could barely keep track. My gaze settled on my children, and I held on to hope. They'd offered for me, and that was a good thing.

I was jerked to my feet and shoved across the room. I rushed to my children, and they fell into my arms, all of us in tears. At least we would remain together. With that, we could survive.

"We have been told there is one more," Charger said.

Julia! In my panic, I'd forgotten about Julia.

"The last one is mine. I will not sell her," White Lodge said.

"She is a fine cook, and I will make her a wife."

Dora looked to me, her eyes filled with fear. All I could do was open my arms to her, hug her tight with my own family.

"We need to be done with these captives," one of White Lodge's sons said.

White Lodge glared at him. "I have spoken."

A heated argument broke out among White Lodge and his sons, Charger standing with them.

The other Fool Soldiers gathered us together and told us to make ourselves ready to leave. They spoke rapidly, and I had trouble understanding them. Lillie Everett explained what I failed to grasp. We stood, ready. Only Roseanna had belongings to take, a necklace of blue beads given to her by the woman who had treated her as a daughter and cried as she'd been sold away. But the necklace was hidden, under Roseanna's tunic, and there was nothing to gather.

Suddenly, one of White Lodge's sons strode from the lodge, returning with Julia as we exited. Confusion filled her eyes but vanished as she saw her daughter. The man released her and told her to go with us. He told the Fool Soldiers to go quickly while he and Charger completed the last sale.

The men ushered us away onto the snow-filled prairie, and Charger joined us soon after.

"We must hurry," he said in English. "White Lodge is not happy, and we have one hundred miles to the nearest white outpost."

We walked faster, in our threadbare clothing. I glanced around, limping and dazed by the events. There was one horse remaining, a tepee and a few blankets, two rifles. Snow began to fall.

Julia
Along the Missouri River,
Late November 1862

Julia trudged beside Charger, each step an effort in the deep snow. During the three days since leaving White Lodge's camp, they'd moved in spurts. Each time her eyes grew heavy or her legs protested, she told herself to move on. *Move on or you will die.*

The first day had been the hardest. She'd heard the Fool Soldiers' comments on the rags they wore, their emaciation. They'd hoisted Laura onto the single horse and given up their blankets. Charger had walked barefoot, giving his moccasins away. They'd carried the children most of the time and pushed a rapid pace, resting when necessary but walking into the dark of the night before the men had finally stopped and erected tepees.

Julia knew the hectic pace had been because of her. White Lodge had been angry at his sons for bringing her to the council lodge. Though her ransom had been completed, he'd threatened to follow. Indeed, he'd appeared in the distance with five Santee the next morning. They'd trailed the group, on foot, through the increasing snow until his companions had turned back. Later in the day, White Lodge had finally done the same.

"How much farther, do you think?" Julia asked Charger.

"I think today, we will reach Fort LaFramboise."

They'd stopped at the village of Bone Necklace, near the place where she and Laura had seen the boat. The Yanktonais had supplied a cart, food, and more moccasins to the group, and they'd pushed on. The snow had been heavy, but the bulk of the blizzard had been ahead of them. They'd come across the bodies of the ten men who had split off from the Fool Soldiers before arriving at White Lodge's camp, frozen in the snow a few miles from the Yanktonais village. They'd died unaware of how close they were to safety.

"Why are you doing this?"

Charger gave her a small smile and shrugged. It had been his answer each time she asked. She'd not pushed. Instead, they'd talked of Teton life and white life. But if they reached the trading post today, she might not have another chance to ask.

"Charger, I wish to know."

"Because it is the right thing."

"I saw you, at Two Kettle's village, when White Lodge asked for an alliance."

"You have keen eyes and a good memory."

"The village was divided."

"It was," he agreed. "Some of the young men had gone east, in the summer. Some were at the war council of the Santee, before the attacks."

"In Minnesota?"

"In the east, yes. There was much discussion at that council. Some wished to chase the whites away, some wished to kill them."

"Were you there?"

"I was. I did not agree to killing or taking white captives. We left that place and returned home. It is one thing to fight soldiers; it is another to kill those who cannot fight."

"And you just decided to rescue us?"

"There is no honor in harming women and children. When White Lodge bragged of his captives, we were much dismayed. We made a pact, though our people thought us fools."

"That's why you are called Fool Soldiers?"

"That is why. But we have displayed honor. We have also set the Teton apart from the Santee and hope the white soldiers will remember this."

"I will remember it."

"The woman you call Laura, does she respond today?"

"I think she's in shock. Her mind is flooded with all she couldn't think about before, when she worried about her children, about surviving."

"How long have you been captives?"

"I think about three moons."

"Look. There is Fort LaFramboise." He pointed ahead.

Not much of a fort, but solid buildings nonetheless. The small post sat across the river. Three men were at the shore, waving and calling to the group. Women stood near the buildings.

"There are the traders, LaFramboise and Dupree and LaPlant. Now you will have better clothing and more food."

Julia smiled after him as he jogged ahead. On the opposite shore, the men readied a small boat. Ice was forming on the river, and she knew the boat would have to be navigated carefully. They weren't safe yet, but a little ice was nothing.

Nothing at all.

★ ★ ★ ★ ★

Part Four: Aftermath

★ ★ ★ ★ ★

Chapter Twenty-Five
1862-1864
Decisions

Christina
Camp Release, Minnesota
Late-September, 1862

The camp is crowded though not so much as it was last week when General Sibley rode in celebrating victory. Sibley may think it was his actions, but the captives know it was the poor conditions among the Dakota that brought them here so they can surrender and have food and shelter again.

Ach, we know how it was.

The refugees, we are trickling away to make our lives again. I do not again meet the woman who helped me escape and I never make sense of her words to me. I do not know if it was good luck that put us in the same place that night or if White Lodge was swayed by my words and provided a way for me to leave.

I am thankful and that is enough. I think how it was only one month that I was a captive and I cannot believe it. It seemed a lifetime.

"Mrs. Koch?"

I poke my head out of the tent where many women are crowded together. "*Ja,* I am here."

"There are two men looking for you and the boy. They're over at the headquarters tent."

"We will come." I duck back into my tent and smile at George. "Get your things. Your father has come for you."

"Papa?"

"*Ja,* come now." We leave our blankets for the others and walk through the camp. Little George trots beside me and there is a spring in our steps. Jack Wright sent word he was alive and would come. I do not know who else is with him.

"Will Mama be there? And Dora?"

"*Nein,* I think only your papa."

George clutches my hand tight and we go on. A man waves us into the big white tent and we stop.

"George!" Jack Wright kneels and opens his arms.

"Papa!"

My face almost cracks with my smile. To see that tough little boy run to his papa so happy fills my soul.

Ernst Koch, who boarded with us at Shetek, is also here and I step into his embrace. It is not so proper but I cannot do otherwise. I thought him dead.

"*Ach,* Christina, it is good to see you."

"*Ja,* I feel the same."

He leads me to chairs and we sit to visit while George and his papa are still hugging and talking together.

"I heard about what happened at the lake," Ernst says.

"Who survived to tell?"

"Several." He hands me a newspaper with a headline *The Boy Hero of Lake Shetek.* "Merton Eastlick carried his brother out." He lists the others: Lavina, Tommy Ireland, Will Everett, Bentley, Charlie Hatch, Wat Smith, William Duley, Rhodes, and Almena Hurd and her boys. Even the Myers family, all but Mary who died of pneumonia during their escape.

"More than I thought," I say.

"*Ja,* I am surprised."

I tell him a little of my story and what I heard this week of

Frank Eastlick, who was shot in the mouth and left for dead. "There is gossip here that he somehow crawled away from the slough, to one of the houses and the half-breed trapper, LaBousche, found him there and took him west. Someone thought they went to a fort. Another said he left the boy with a friendly band of Indians. No one knows for certain."

"This is news his mother will want to hear. She is in Mankato or St. Charles, I am not sure. She's been moving around."

He tells me about the attacks on New Ulm when he and Wright were there and I tell him what I know of Julia and Laura and the children still captive. Jack hears us and comes closer with George to hear.

"She's still with them?" he says. "She didn't escape with you?"

"She did not have the chance," I say. "She was taken with the larger group." There is a tone in Wright's voice. It sounds like accusation, and I want to defend my friend. "I was lucky when George and I were sold away and there were not so many watching us."

"Thank you for bringing my boy back to me."

"*Ja,* you are welcome."

"We'll be on our way, Ernst. I want to get us back as soon as possible."

I turn to George and think I am losing a bit of myself. I squeeze him tight in my arms. "Be a good boy for your papa." I kiss his head as my eyes start to sting.

"Bye, German Woman," he says, using the name given by the Dakota.

"Good-bye, Little Man," I say, doing the same.

Wright takes his hand and leads him out of the tent. He looks back once, at the doorway, and waves. Finally, they are gone and I let the tears flow.

Ernst gives me a handkerchief.

"You'll see him again. Wright's been staying in Mankato."

I sniffle. "That is where you are?"

"*Ja,* I will stay there. Or go to New Ulm when they rebuild. It won't take Germans long to put things in order."

I think he is right. We are an orderly people. I will need to put my life in order, too. Perhaps I will go to Mankato. There is little use in wandering about—it is time for me to make plans. Mankato is civilized, a good place, safe, where a person can have a *Haus* instead of a cabin and keep it as it should be.

I think I will do this.

Julia

Fort Randall, Dakota Territory

January, 1863

Julia paced the small room. Jack and George would arrive soon and her stomach was in knots. She'd wept, hearing they both lived, her first tears since the Fool Soldiers had moved them across the river to Fort LaFramboise over a month ago. She'd rejoiced. But with reunion close at hand, she was all nerves about Jack and his sharp views.

She forced herself to stop pacing and glanced at Dora. Her clothing was still neat and tidy. As good as it's going to get, she supposed. They still looked a wreck, but there was nothing more to be done.

A knock sounded, and she jumped.

Oh, God, they're here.

She smoothed her dress and opened the door, her stomach in knots.

Jack stood there, George at his side.

Her eyes stinging, she stilled her heart. *Oh, George!*

"Mama!"

Julia knelt and scooped him into her arms, smothering him

with kisses. "I am so glad you are safe, my little man."

"German Woman took care of me."

"I'm glad she was with you." So Christina was safe, too. Julia's anxiety loosened, edged out by warmth and thanksgiving. How on earth was she ever going to thank her friend for keeping George safe?

She drew a breath and stood, George in her arms. He was heavy again, no longer the thin little boy who'd been sold away at Big Stone Lake. A good thing, along with the likelihood he'd remember little of the horror as he grew. There were blessings in being young.

Glancing at Jack, she smiled. He held Dora. Her little arms were stretched around his neck. If she was lucky, Dora, too, would forget much.

"Hello, Julia," Jack said. His tone was soft, but discomfort hid behind the words. "Your hair?"

She fingered her shorn locks, cut short at Fort Randall when they couldn't get the tangles out. "It was knotted, full of grease."

"Oh." He released Dora, and she scrambled away to play with the doll she'd been given by one of the women at the fort.

Julia set George down, and he ran to his sister. Then she drew a breath and faced Jack. "I'm glad you're safe."

He closed the door and sat in a straight-back chair as silence stretched tight between them.

Stilted, as she'd feared.

"I thanked Mrs. Koch . . . heard the story from her, at least through her escape."

"When you wired that you found George safe, I wondered what had happened." Typical of Jack, he'd supplied no details. She'd wondered for days.

"They got away, near Big Stone Lake." So, not long after they'd parted. Good.

"That's where she and George were sold away."

"I heard in October you were a captive there, with Pawn. But you were long gone when I got the news."

"In Dakota, by that time. Sold to White Lodge."

Jack's expression remained stoic.

"Where did you end up?" Julia asked. "When it started, I mean?"

"I helped with the defense of New Ulm, led a burial detail to the lake. Since, I've mostly been in the Mankato area."

It was hard to imagine him helping with the defense of New Ulm. He was more the type to run. But, perhaps he'd found his backbone. "I'm glad you weren't at Shetek," she said.

"Me, too. Dead in a slough is not the end I'd want. Imagine them attacking after all we did for them." His voice was bitter, and Julia ached to tell him about how traders like him, bent on cheating the Dakota at every turn, had laid the foundation for the hatred.

But she didn't. He wouldn't grasp it.

"It was awful, watching our friends die."

His eyes darkened. "Dirty savages."

She'd heard so many use those words. She comprehended part of it, knew women like Laura who had watched family die in brutal ways who would never get past hating. She hated, too, but she refused to label an entire people for the acts of a few.

"Not all of them. A few tried to save us."

Jack's eyes grew dark, accusatory. "They tricked you, and you fell for it."

The comment stung, though she'd expected the sentiment would come at some point. "You weren't there, Jack. You don't know."

"I know they're back-stabbing sons of bitches, and anyone who thinks otherwise has been duped. It'll do you no good to voice such opinions once we return. An Indian lover is not what you want to be."

And there it was, the core of the matter. Or at least the beginning of it. Julia's hand pressed against her abdomen, again in knots.

"If it weren't for ten Sioux men, I'd still be a captive." It seemed a better place to start. She had no idea if he'd accept the concept that there were good people and bad people within any culture, but Charger and his Fool Soldiers deserved a defense.

"The military was on its way. Another week and they would have been there."

"And there would have been a battle during which we might have been killed."

Jack shook his head. "You should have escaped when Christina Koch did. Or before you left Shetek."

"I had two children to protect."

"And did you protect them? No. You let those heathens take them on an eight-hundred-mile trek through the cold and subject them to Lord knows what."

Oh, the man! Did he actually think she just willingly went along?

"I tried to escape, Jack. The second day. They shot me and took the children away."

"You shouldn't have even let it go to the second day. From what I heard, you were the one who told the women and children to give up. You should have crawled away with them instead."

Julia glanced at the children and lowered her voice. Jack had no idea of what it had been like, none. "Crawled away? We were in a slough, at the bottom of a rise. How the hell could we have crawled anywhere?"

He leaned forward, glaring. "You didn't even try. At least Mira Everett had the sense to run back and be shot instead of surrendering to them."

"You'd rather we died?"

"You let them *have* you."

She let his words hang. This was it—the very heart of what bothered him the most. That she'd been used by Dakota men. She'd known this would stab at him, suspected he'd never get past it. That it might even end their marriage entirely.

"I didn't *let* them do anything," she said. "I endured it to keep the others alive. To keep my children alive."

"You weren't anyone's keeper, Julia."

She opened her mouth to tell him she was but shut it. She'd spent their entire marriage keeping Jack from trouble, assuring respectability for her family, fixing things in the community because she felt responsible. And, yes, she had fought to keep the other captives safe. She'd endured because her children depended on her. She'd borne it all.

Until it nearly defeated her and the only choice left was to fight for herself.

In the end, the only vow that mattered had been the one she'd made to survive, and, if Jack wanted to divorce her, she'd welcome it. He didn't define her anymore, and her vows to *him* didn't matter anymore.

"I'm my own keeper, Jack. I chose to survive, and I'll be damned it I let you take that away from me."

"I don't know if I can be with you anymore, Julia."

"Then we're agreed."

She waited for grief to rise, for the mourning of her marriage to overtake her, but it didn't. There was only serenity in the decision.

She'd found herself, and she was never letting go.

Laura
Fort Dodge, Iowa
January 1863

I glimpsed William from the window of the stagecoach as it came to a stop. He looked worn, haggard, as if he, too, had been through hell. I knew not what he'd think when he saw us.

I patted my short hair and brushed the wrinkles from my calico dress. Julia had sewn the simple garments for each of us while we rested at Fort LaFramboise. Jefferson's matched mine. He was not pleased at being in a dress rather than pants, but we'd had little time, and I'd pacified him by fastening a neckerchief for him so he wouldn't appear girlish. Emma's frock was of differing fabric but just as simple. We were glad to have them, after the rags we'd given up, and had worn them for the pictures taken at Fort Randall.

My nervous mind was wandering. I refocused and turned to the children. "Stand up, now. Your father waits." I glanced at Lillie Everett, who had traveled with us, and she readied herself, as well.

My joy in hearing William lived had brought me strength these last weeks. I'd traveled much of the way through the snow thinking we'd again been sold, moving ever farther away from civilization. We'd arrived at the trading post, and I finally accepted we *were* free, that it wasn't something Julia had latched onto as a dream.

I must confess, I took to my bed for nearly two weeks, secure in the knowledge my children were finally safe. I'd let the good women of the fort tend them and surrendered to fatigue and grief. But when word came from William, I'd risen, put myself in order, and prepared to return to life.

And here he was, at last.

He opened the door, and Emma tumbled into his embrace.

"Me, too, Papa!" Jefferson squawked.

William set Emma down and withdrew our son from the coach, kissing him soundly. He stood him next to his sister and held out his arms for me.

I stepped out with care. Though my heel was better, I remained weak, and I waited until he held my weight. He pulled me close, smothering me with kisses.

"I thought I'd lost you, Wife."

"And I, you."

We must have been a spectacle, kissing so in public, but I hardly cared. Until a week ago, I'd thought myself a widow. I rejoiced in his welcome, touching his face, my finger tracing the worry lines that hadn't been there before.

"Oh, William," I choked out.

"I can't believe I have you back. All of you." He smiled at Emma and Jefferson. He said nothing about our three missing children, and I was thankful. My eyes misted as the loss jabbed at me. I had two left, and I reminded myself to delight in them.

William let me go and helped Lillie from the stage. She'd patiently stood there, waiting while we'd said our hellos, still the fine, sweet girl she'd always been. Once she was on the ground, she walked past us.

I turned. There was Will Everett standing near a bench, leaning on a cane. We'd thought him dead, and I remembered how his wife had turned back to die with him. Shocked, I brought my hand to my mouth. I'd not expected him to be present, and warmth filled me when he drew Lillie to his breast. She clung to him, neither saying a word as tears poured down both their faces.

"Oh, William," I said, "no one knew!"

"I thought her uncle, Charlie Hatch, would come for her. I didn't know Will was coming until he showed up. Charlie's here, too, but wanted to give them a moment."

We left them with privacy, and William unloaded our meager

belongings—a basket of food sent by the women of Yankton and a valise with donated clothing. We made our way to the hotel, where we'd stay until we traveled to Mankato.

Once the children were settled down for naps, William and I retired to the sitting area. We'd been five months apart and had much to catch up on.

William told me of his return to Shetek in late October, with soldiers. He, Tommy Ireland, and Charlie Hatch had identified twelve bodies and buried them in a common grave. The two Everett boys and one Eastlick boy had not been located. I told him of Frances being taken from me and how she had cried without ceasing until she had died or been killed—I never knew which.

"And you, Laura? Did you suffer much?"

"It was not easy. That first night, I couldn't fight them off. I'm sorry."

William held me while I cried. "There is no shame, Wife. You did the best you could."

"I was much damaged. I fear there will be no more children."

"Then we will smother Emma and Jefferson with our love."

"I heard . . . you were there . . . when they hanged the Sioux." In truth, I'd been told he served as hangman.

"I was. They hanged thirty-eight. Lincoln commuted the sentences of the rest. I was asked to cut the rope." He paused. "There was so much hate in me that I said yes. I didn't know it would be so difficult. The first time, I missed the rope and had to swing the ax again."

"One rope, for thirty-eight?"

"A pretty complex scaffold. There were angry crowds there. A man offered me money to take my place. I refused. I was bitter, thought you'd all been murdered, and I wanted to get even, any way I could."

"I know. I've felt the same. Julia tries to understand, says whites treat the Indians as badly. I can't grasp it. Not anymore."

We sat in quiet, knowing our lives would never be the same, until William caught my gaze. "I'd like to join up as a scout, help track down White Lodge's band."

"Is that to be your new dream?" I thought of him being gone from me, and resentment burned.

"Not a dream, just something I have to do."

That, I did understand. But there were things that still needed to be discussed. "And after that?"

William shrugged. "I don't know."

"We've spent our entire lives chasing dreams."

"Mostly mine." The humble admission told me volumes.

"Always yours," I said in soft agreement. "I left my dreams in Indiana."

"I'm sorry, Laura. I'm not good at perceiving things from others' points of view." This, too, I knew. But I sensed his realization of it might be a turning point for us.

"We have a second chance, Husband. I think this time, we need to pursue common dreams."

He smiled, offering no argument. "I think we can do that."

"The frontier has not been good to us. We've lost all of our children but two. We've lost our property and our land. I'd like to start somewhere different. Away from farming, away from rivers, away from Indians. No more new settlements, no more being a 'first family,' no more politicking. Let's focus on us."

"That sounds like an idea I can live with. This experience, what happened at Shetek and after, has changed me."

"We're agreed?"

"We are." William smiled at me and kissed my hand. "Just as soon as I help Sibley track down and purge the Dakota who escaped justice."

Almena
St. Peter, Minnesota
April 28, 1863

"You realize many were in tears, don't you?" Almena's attorney said as they exited the room where the U.S. Indian commissioners were meeting.

She carried Frank in her arms; William Henry held Mr. Berry's hand.

"They were?" She exhaled a heavy breath. Telling her story had been the most difficult thing she'd done since living through the events, and she was glad to have it over. Besides, the crying was more likely due to the boys being there in the room than her words. Those boys could melt hearts; she doubted she could.

"Indeed." Mr. Berry patted her arm. "It was exactly what the commissioners needed to hear. I think it will help when they process the claims."

"I didn't relish telling it." She'd been shaking the whole time, more so once she'd spotted reporters taking notes.

"The damages claim has been officially filed—depredation claims, they're calling them—and is now in their hands. Once I hear on the findings, I'll notify you. I don't expect that to happen for a while. Government moves slowly."

"How does the government expect all of us to live? We lost everything we had."

Mr. Berry opened the door of the courthouse, and they exited into the crisp spring air. Almena breathed in the warmth, a blessing after the bitter winter. To her, it heralded new life.

"I don't expect you'll get the entire amount you claimed. There aren't many women who claim their own property in addition to household property."

She'd thought as much when she listed the items lost and their worth. She'd cited the highest values she could justify. It was like negotiating a sale. Start high in expectation of settling lower. That was the way of things. But her pride hadn't allowed her to dismiss that she'd owned her own property, and she'd listed it separately.

"I owned livestock in my own right. Why should I not claim that as a loss?"

"I understand that, Mrs. Hurd." He escorted her down the quiet boardwalk. "It might have been wiser to lump it all into household property, to which you are entitled as a widow. Government officials won't know what to do with this."

"Property is property, whether I claimed it as Phin's or as mine. They'll merge it, and they'll award only a portion of it, either way. That's how government operates. By the time you get your percentage, there will be little left."

"But at least there will be something," he placated as they stopped at his office door. "Will you be staying on in St. Peter?"

Almena shook her head. She'd thought about it, but this wasn't where she wanted to rebuild their lives. There was nothing left here—no land, no home, no livestock. She'd lived the last few months on the charity of others, and she refused to continue in that vein.

"It's time to leave. Minnesota has little to offer me anymore, save for the ties to my fellow survivors, and those will not support us."

"You are a strong woman, Mrs. Hurd. I suspect you could make your way." His words held encouragement, but Almena had made up her mind.

"You'll be able to reach me in La Crosse for the next few months. I have friends there."

"And after that?"

"Caton, New York." Home . . . as much home as anywhere. Her boys needed family more than ever. In truth, so did she.

"That's a long way."

"I've always sworn my children would have family. I can't

bring back their father, but I can give them an uncle." Seneca, his wife and children, the Miniers—all waited for them. And there were her other siblings, maybe even her father and step-family. "It's time those ties are renewed."

Mr. Berry smiled and offered his hand. "I think you'll do just fine."

"I'm sure we will. My brother has already bought a cow for me."

Lavina
Ellenboro, Wisconsin
1864

After dinner, I ask Leicester to stay at the table so we can have a discussion. Christine herds the children—teenagers now—out of the kitchen along with Merton and Johnnie. I face my brother, anxious to have his input.

"I've been thinking," I start.

"Not unusual." He grins at me, gray hair and wrinkles reminding me we've both aged.

"Do you remember, all those years ago, when I first came to live with you?"

"Hah! You were fifteen and thought you owned the world."

I smile at him, recalling my naiveté. "I wanted adventure, independence, and didn't think I needed anyone."

We laugh, then sober. "And now?" Leicester asks.

"Well, I've certainly had more adventure than I ever imagined and not the type I'd envisioned."

"That's true." He pats my hand. Neither of us needs to say anything more about what happened.

"And, now I'm forced to be independent and discovering it not quite what I'd imagined."

I think back to the weeks after reaching safety, scrambling for hand-outs, petitioning to the government, fighting tooth and nail to be treated fairly when so many were attempting to take advantage of my widowhood. I'd been forced to stand up for myself and the boys, even becoming a bit of a shrew at times.

"It can be a troublesome responsibility," he says.

"I've thought much about it, how I can take care of the boys. I don't want to live here with you and Christine forever."

"You know you're welcome here." His voice is warm, brotherly. My parents in Ohio said the same, but it's time I stop making the rounds of my relatives and stand on my own feet.

"I know. But it's not what I want."

"And you have an idea, I take it?"

"Remember me telling you about that man in Minnesota, the artist?"

"Mr. Stevens? The one who was painting the panorama about the uprising?"

"I had a letter from him. As planned, he's taken the paintings on tour and has had a good response. I suppose it's human nature, being drawn to tales of horrific events without having to experience them in reality."

"And?"

"I've written about the events at Lake Shetek." I lift a notebook from my lap and lay it on the table. "I'd like to get it published and sell copies."

Leicester picks up the tattered notebook and reads bits, here and there. Finally, he looks at me. "You're sure you want to do this, share this with the public? You'd have to travel around, promote it, speak about it."

"I'm sure," I say. "It will provide me a way to support the boys." I meet his gaze and draw a breath. "Besides, what happened to us there is too important to be forgotten."

EPILOGUE
Reunion

Lake Shetek,
July 1895

Charlie Hatch walked across the dry summer prairie, retracing the route he'd taken thirty-three years before. He moved slowly, images flashing through his mind . . . sun glinting off the water, mud sucking at his feet, the first distant shot that hadn't seemed at all ominous. Then, Voigt dead in front of Almena's doorway, the realization and his frantic flight down the lake to warn the others. And, finally, the taste of fear and panicked faces as they rushed for the slough and the carnage that came after. Though he'd told the story often, his skin crawled at being here again.

Five of the survivors had returned—plus the Burns Brothers who had once lived at Walnut Grove—responding to an invitation by Dr. Workman, a local man who was compiling a collection of accounts to assure future generations would know of the event. They'd told him the stories again, showed him where things had happened.

And they'd sat and talked.

"There's so much I'd pushed out of my memories," Lavina said, suddenly beside him.

Cold sweat chilled Charlie's spine. He hadn't even heard her approach. "Mine, too. Even in telling reporters over the years, it was never this sharp."

"It's odd. Johnnie and I couldn't even locate exactly where the cabin used to be. But I remember everything that happened.

As soon as I stepped out of the wagon with Uncle Tommy, it flooded back. I don't think I'll ever come here again."

She turned away, back toward where the others had gathered.

Charlie let her go. She had her own memories and was best left to deal with them on her own.

He stood alone, his gaze on the slough while the images took life in his mind, then died. In the silence, he honored them: those who had died and those who had found the strength to survive.

At length, he, too, left.

There's nothing more to be done here.

AFTERWORD ON LAKE SHETEK SURVIVORS

Laura and William Duley resided in the Mankato, Minnesota, area until some time in the 1870s. Secondary sources claim she "lost her mind" for two years after being released and spent time institutionalized. There is no record of her being a patient within the Minnesota State (psychiatric) Hospital during that time, a time during which William would also have been away from home serving as an army scout, and Lavina Eastlick reports in her 1864 booklet that Laura's children lived with Laura during William's absence. According to obituary accounts, William was discharged from military service on February 10, 1865, and, by the summer of that year, was farming eighty acres in Blue Earth County. Anecdotal accounts say William provided wood from his sawmill in Mankato to build a fence around the graves at Lake Shetek. Sometime in the 1870s, the Duleys relocated to Colbert, Alabama, where William worked as a millwright and, in 1880, was appointed as justice of the peace and notary public. Emma Duley married and moved to Texas. Around 1890, Laura and William moved to Gig Harbor, Washington, near Tacoma, where Jefferson served as chief of police. William worked as a machinist and carpenter and died there in 1898; Laura died on March 2, 1900. She was seventy-one.

Lavina Eastlick returned to Minnesota and published "A

Personal Narrative of the Indian Massacres 1862" (first printing 1864). Merton stayed briefly with John Stevens and his wife in Minnesota, touring with the panorama show, while Lavina went to visit family, and he returned to her while she was with her sister in Wisconsin. On April 1, 1865, she married widower Henry W. (Wat) Smith, who had also resided at Lake Shetek. In June of the same year, she left him. According to divorce documents, they were never compatible, Lavina complaining he did not love her or her children and Wat complaining she was away peddling books and disregarding her wifely duties. Divorce was filed for in July 1866 and granted on January 24, 1867. In the 1870 census, she is recorded under "Eastlick" as a widow with a farm of 145 acres near Mankato that she bought with the proceeds of her depredation claim award. On November 30, 1870, she married Solomon Pettibone (marriage documents list her as "Smith"). Three months later, he left her, went to Ohio to visit his sister, and disappeared. Lavina was pregnant at the time and gave birth to a daughter, Laura, in August 1871. Merton worked while Johnnie, age ten, cared for the baby and Lavina worked the fields. Merton married in 1873 and moved to Rochester, Minnesota. He died in 1875. Johnnie married in 1885 and settled one mile from Lavina. Records indicate he did not own land but operated a threshing business. Laura married Angus McDonnell in 1895. The couple farmed near Lavina, then moved to Alberta, Canada, in 1906. Lavina joined them in 1915. She died there on October 9, 1923.

Almena Hurd relocated to her former home of Canton, New York, where she married Elbridge George Woodward on August 11, 1864. Elbridge is listed as a carpenter with his own land in the 1874 census. The two had several children: John, Carrie, Albert (Bertie), Fredrick, Charles, and Seneca. They moved to

Roulette, Pennsylvania, in 1883, where they farmed and ran a boarding house. A daughter, Alice, is listed as being adopted. Almena was widowed in 1905 and died in 1922 at age eighty-six.

Christina Koch resided in Mankato, Minnesota, for the remainder of her life. By 1870, she had married Charles H. Heinze (sometimes recorded as Heinz, sometimes as Charles A. Heinze), who made his living as a baker. Property value listed in the 1870 census is sufficient to indicate he likely owned the bakery. They were listed in the 1880 census as well. Charles died in December 1883, and Christina married Carl F. W. Hohmuth (Hohmith, Holmeth) on October 15, 1884 (Oct. 16 also cited). He is identified as a laborer in the 1885 census. In 1894, Christina provided an interview to Dr. Harper Workman, who recorded her story of the events of 1862. In 1900 and 1905 censuses, Carl is listed as a small farmer. Christina died March 1, 1907 (also reported as March 5) of cancer of the liver. She never had any children. In all official records, she is listed as Christina, although Dr. Harper Workman always referred to her as Mariah in his historical accounts, as do those local to the Lake Shetek area today.

Julia Wright disappeared from history. Though Lillie Everett later thought Julia had given birth to a mixed-race baby soon after her release and that John Wright had divorced her because of it, there are no records of such a birth or of a divorce in either Minnesota or Wisconsin. On July 8, 1863, she provided sworn testimony on John's depredation claim, identifying herself as his wife. In February of 1865, daughter Eldora died in Minnesota. No record of Julia is found after that date. There are unsubstantiated reports that John married a woman from Austin, Minnesota, then left her. A marriage record for a John Wright is recorded in Winona in 1872, but there is no way to know if this is the correct John Wright—Wright was a common name. A John G. Wright shows up in the 1875 census for La Crosse, Wisconsin, but La Crosse was full of Wrights, and the state census lacks enough vital statistics to verify identity. There were also reports that Julia remarried and moved to Nebraska, but there are no census or marriage records to prove or disprove this. She shows up in an online family tree as marrying a James Cart in Alamosa, Colorado, in 1877, but the reference offers no citation of source, and Colorado records indicate Cart married Annie Julia Coal, aka Aimee Julina Kohl (died September 1880), and there is no evidence this was Julia Wright. A search of census records for Minnesota and surrounding states reveals many possible Julia Wrights and Julia Silsbys but none matching in all vital details. When Dr. Workman and Neil Currie were collecting information on the 1862 events, they attempted to contact George and John Wright (identified as living in Utah and California at that time), but there was no response.

Thomas Ireland: Thomas married Sally Haddock, and the couple lived on the Myers property at Lake Shetek. Widowed after sixteen years, Thomas then married Sarah Ridgeway and resided in Mankato. Roseanna moved to Butte, Montana, after the death of her father in 1897. She worked as a domestic before marrying Joseph R. Miller. After Miller's death, she married Samuel VanAlstine. Roseanna died in 1936. Ellen (Nellie) married Albert Hotaling and resided in Mankato until her death in 1946.

Edgar Bentley, who came to Lake Shetek with Charlie Hatch, enlisted in the army, serving until the end of the war. There is no record of him thereafter.

Frank Eastlick was never seen again, though rumors continued to surface that he survived and was taken to Dakota Territory by Joe LaFramboise. Aaron Myers claimed to have spoken to LaFramboise in 1873, at the Minnesota state fair, and that LaFramboise confirmed the story.

William Everett recovered, though he suffered pain from a ball in his leg for the rest of his life. He married Amelia Addison in 1865 and moved to Waseca, Minnesota, where he founded Eaco Mills. He died in 1892. Daughter **Lillie** (Ablillian, Lily) Everett Keeney died in 1923 in Oakland, California.

Charlie Hatch: Charlie enlisted in the Union Army in 1864. After the war, he married Hattie Bangs, and they farmed near Huntly, Minnesota. In later years, he moved to Tappen, North Dakota, and died there in 1907.

Aaron Myers and his family escaped the attack on Lake Shetek. Around 6:00 a.m., Myers spotted a Dakota tearing down his fence, yelled at him to stop, and reminded him of past friendship and medical attention. The Dakota left. Son Arthur discovered Voigt's body around 10:00 that morning, and Aaron found Andreas Koch soon thereafter. He loaded his ill wife and children (daughter Olive was boarding with the Lambs in Iberia) into a wagon, and they headed to Dutch Charley's, warning the Zierke family. The journey to New Ulm was fraught with narrow escapes, but the family did arrive safely. Mary Myers died of pneumonia a day after they reached safety. Aaron eventually settled in Garretson, South Dakota. He and son Aaron provided their stories to Workman's history.

The Fool Soldiers dispersed not long after successfully ransoming the Shetek captives and six half-breed women. Their names were Martin Charger (*Waneta*), Joseph Four Bear (*Mah to top ah*), Swift Bird (Alex Chapelle), Kills and Comes (Kills Game and Comes Home or *Waktegli*), Mad Bear (*Mato Watogla*), Red Dog, Bears Rib (Kills Enemy), Sitting Bear, Pretty Bear (*Mato Waste*), Charging Dog, Jonah One Rib, Strikes Fire, Big Head, Foolish Bear, and Black Tomahawk. Exact membership varies among sources with most sources indicating there were initially eleven members. Martin Charger is usually named as the leader. The story of the role these young Lakota men played in freeing the captives was largely lost. Nearly all official military reports fail to mention them and magnify the role of the military instead. One is reported to have been killed by the military for stealing rations. It is suspected others were part of the group rounded up in 1863 when they admitted they had been present "in the east" at the war council meeting that occurred prior to the initial Minnesota attacks (even though they voted not to participate and left the area). For many years, the only records of the Fool Soldiers were the oral stories passed down to their descendants. These oral histories are now part of the South Dakota Oral History Center collections at the University of South Dakota. The stories differ, a natural result of oral histories repeated through multiple generations and translation issues. Their history was lost until the 1970s, when interest was renewed.

AUTHOR'S NOTE ON HISTORICAL ACCURACY

As a historian as well as a novelist, I took great pains to remain true to the historical record wherever possible. However, my purpose was to make the stories of Laura, Lavina, Christina, Almena, and Julia come alive rather than to offer a scholarly reporting of events. While I was able to locate clues to their major life events, I could only surmise their personalities, their family interactions, their dreams and motivations, conversations, or what they thought and did in their daily lives. I have not changed any of the facts I was able to uncover. However, to create my story, I filled in the gaps and developed the women as characters, from my imagination, around factual events. This is a novel, not a history.

To shape each of the women's personalities, I relied on clues within census records, local histories, personal accounts, and descriptions related by others. The Workman and Currie Papers contained recollections from many of the early Shetek settlers, though there were discrepancies in dates and details.

In a few cases, I altered names to eliminate confusion due to duplication of the same name. John Wright became Jack (a common nickname), Laura Lamb became Lorenza (her middle name), Almira Everett became Mira, and variations were used to differentiate all the many Williams and Johns.

Laura Duley: Through census records, I noted that Laura's family owned more valuable property than other families in the township and that the family was one of the first in the area, which was confirmed by county histories. It made sense that she might have been used to a comfortable life and may (or may not) have expected to continue in that lifestyle upon her marriage to William, who was also from an established family. I could not verify William and Washington Monroe were brothers, since early census records do not list children's names, but their ages and parental references matched, so I made them brothers as a mechanism to launch the story. William did claim land in Iowa prior to marriage, and he and Laura moved there shortly after marrying. Online obituaries indicate two daughters drowned in the Mississippi while they lived there. Census and land records trace movement to Beaver. Local histories reveal Willian operated a mill and a mercantile. Birth and death records trace their children. Workman's collected histories provide information on the arrival at Shetek and the events there. There is no direct evidence that Laura suffered from depression other than references that she "lost her mind." Given the number of children she lost, I chose to create this as part of her personality. Other settlers reported William as pompous; I adapted from that. Laura's short account of her captivity reports being raped repeatedly on her first night of captivity. Physically, it would be unlikely she could endure the treatment as she reported. The Duleys' personal accounts were bitter and indicated they had little positive interaction with the Dakota and were likely very biased in their opinions. Still, stigma of the time would have made most women reluctant to admit being raped. Thus, I treated her account of the night as exaggerated but holding some truth, despite rape being an unacceptable behavior within Dakota culture. I chose to adapt her story, motivating the incident with anger and revenge for her husband being one of the men who fired on Grizzly (Lean) Bear.

Almena Hurd: Census records indicate Almena and her brother lived with another family—he listed as adopted, she as a laborer. Previous records list them with the Hamm family, with the change coming after her father remarried. I used this as a defining influence for Almena's character. Census records and birth records trace the Hurds' journey to Wisconsin and Lake Shetek. Accounts given to Workman and Currie indicate there was a rumor at some point about her relationship with Phin's partner, Bill Jones, but that no one who knew her believed it. Accounts also mention her great butter that was sold to others; and her own depredation claim cites the amounts of butter and cheese destroyed in the attacks. The current owner of the Hurd cabin site reports the blackbirds are still a problem. Almena did not contribute to the Workman collection but did leave a detailed account of the attack in her depredation claim. A newspaper account, printed after her testimony to the commission, relates the events with a more sensationalistic tone. Her own words reveal she was educated and practical. Because she was released and told to go east "to her mother" (in Dakota, it would mean to her people), it is likely she had a respectful relationship with them.

Lavina Eastlick: Lavina's early life events were taken from census records as well as her own personal narrative. I have no idea why she went to live with her brother at age fifteen, but I sensed, from her personal narrative, that she was not afraid of adventure despite being apprehensive about the move to Shetek. She was also practical. She had to have been to leave dying children and crawl east for the two she thought had survived. Much of the detail on the fight in the slough and her escape was taken from her account as well as the accounts in the Workman Papers.

Christina Koch: No one knows her maiden name or when she married Andreas or when she emigrated to the U.S. from Germany. Online family trees are fraught with errors and a lack of supporting citations. She provided little information about her captivity to Workman beyond a short statement that "the way Mrs. Duley and I were treated cannot be told and from what Mrs. Wright told me afterwards, she fared no better. Many of the horrible reports are not true. I was not outraged" (despite Laura Duley's statement saying otherwise). The report of her resistance to Pawn was reported by a newspaper just after her release. Those living in the Lake Shetek area always refer to her as Mariah, but I could find no documents with that name. As a German, she may have used her middle name rather than her first name. (Germans had a custom of naming children after a close relative, which made for confusion, and thus they were usually called by their middle names instead.) All vital records list her as Christina. She provided a short account to Workman about dates they settled at the Walnut Grove (and, yes, that's the same Walnut Grove that later became the town of Laura Ingalls Wilder fame) and life at Lake Shetek.

Julia Wright: Her birth and marriage as well as the births of George and Dora can be traced through vital and census records. Her ancestors may have included fur trappers who intermarried with native women. There is little clue to her personality except via the comments of other settlers that she was caring and supportive and upstanding. Remembrances provided to Workman left little doubt about her husband's reputation. The accounts of the attack all say she took on a leadership role and that she was of good character. I chose to make her a woman in conflict with her husband. As well, she became my filter through which I provided a glimpse of Dakota culture and history. An account provided by one of the men who accompanied the ransomed captives to Fort Randall referenced her discussing the displeasure she expected from her husband for having been a "wife" during captivity.

The Fool Soldiers: It was difficult to reconcile the history of these young men. White historians dismissed them, for the most part. Officers' reports from Fort Randall gave them no credit (although a lesser report clearly stated their role). The stories passed to their children and grandchildren were later recorded as oral histories. Most of them indicate the Fool Soldiers were taken prisoner and some of them were killed. No military reports claim this. However, a deeper study of military records indicates a force was dispatched in the months after the release and that some Teton were taken prisoner; one is recorded as dying in the guardhouse. There is note that several answered they had been in the "east" when the fighting started. This may have been a translation issue for members of the Fool Soldiers who had been in attendance at the War Council on August 17 and left the area without becoming involved in the fighting because they disagreed about the path of action chosen by the council. The discrepancies with the oral histories are likely due to natural corruption of details over the years and issues with the meanings of words used (example: "when the snows stopped" was translated as "spring," when it likely meant a blizzard stopped).

Dakota Culture: Within Dakota culture, there is a huge emphasis on kinship—whether family or social in nature. The Dakota were not known for taking captives and usually only did so in situations where a person reminded the raiding party of someone who had died. In those cases, they would be taken captive and soon adopted into the tribe in an official ceremony. My Dakota advisors tell me they would have been treated as social kin, a member of the tribe, and not abused. The Dakota did not hit their children nor did they beat others. Women who were taken captive were adopted or taken as wives if they consented. However, consent might be an ambiguous statement or a statement about wives that white women might not have understood. A ceremony may or may not occur. Hospitality and industry were both highly important. Adults and teens would have been expected to know this, and white women may have seemed woefully ignorant or lazy when they failed in that understanding.

In the days following the outbreak of hostilities in Minnesota, the Dakota found themselves in a position of having captives that would be used as shields or kept for ransom, and it is likely many were unsure how to treat them. Clearly, they were not being made part of the tribe, and captives as property would have been an alien idea. While the Dakota did practice "an eye for an eye" in warfare (allowing family members to be killed in revenge for a death), rape was not practiced in their culture. That some Dakota men did give testimony to having done so indicates this war was different. This was *not* part of their traditional culture. Other native testimony of the time indicates some Dakota made an effort to hide captives from groups of angry young men who would have mistreated them. This was a time of intense hostility toward the whites that blurred traditional lines of behavior, fueled by months of suffering and insult. Further, these were not captives in the usual sense, and there was an ongoing state of war that was much different from the quick raids usually practiced by the Dakota. I believe this was a time when some broke with tradition. I chose to strike a middle ground with some Dakota characters behaving outside the bounds of traditional behavior. I hope I have not been too disrespectful in doing so.

ACKNOWLEDGMENTS

As with every book I write, there is an endless list of people who contributed. Whether through inspiring me, supporting me as a writer, easing research tasks, or participating in the edit process, their roles were essential to making this project a reality.

This novel began in my head while I was still in elementary school, shaped by the knowledge and love of history shared by Bill Bolin, my ninth-grade history teacher at Tracy High School. Bill was a friend and neighbor, father of my friend Kelli. In that role and as seasonal naturalist at Lake Shetek State Park, he introduced me to the history of Lake Shetek. Later, in his class on Minnesota state history, he provided more detail, and my imagination took off. When I pursued my B.A. in history a few years later, I had no clue I would return to the story again all these years later. In 2017, when I traveled to Minnesota to re-walk in the footsteps of my characters, Bill was there to share his boxes of research materials and take me on tour of the cabin sites and Slaughter Slough, despite his struggle with cancer. His wife, Sandy, welcomed me into their home and put up with five solid days of listening to us. I wish he had lived to read the finished book.

A huge debt is owed to Dr. Harper Workman and his determination to record the Shetek history. His extensive interviews during the 1880s assured memories of the original settlers would survive. His foresight in providing a copy to the

Minnesota Historical Society all those years ago guaranteed his collection would endure. Neil Currie's dedication to pursuit of additional remembrances was an additional invaluable contribution. Without their efforts, we would not know what happened at Shetek.

In college, years before I thought of this book, I wrote my senior research paper on the duality of historical event and fiction. All those years ago, I conducted research at the Minnesota Historical Society with Dr. Alan R. Woolworth as my personal guide. Alan was a friend of my late husband, and he took care to provide me access to the Workman Papers and other information I would need for that paper—and later, for this project. I also had the opportunity to visit with author Frederick Manfred at his home near Luverne, Minnesota. His novel, *Scarlet Plume,* was inspired by the Dakota Conflict and at the heart of my study then. His insights stayed with me. Both of these men passed away years ago; their generosity remains.

During my 2017 visit to Minnesota, many old and new friends and professionals assisted me. Jeff (Jesse) James, my former English teacher, also stepped up to the plate. Knowing of Bill's ailing health, Jesse invited me to ride along on a Road Scholar tour of the Shetek area to assure I would be able to visit sites as well as obtaining more detail on them. The program, *Minnesota's Dakota Conflict,* was a great addition to my research arsenal. Jesse's passion was infectious (he lives on the Hurd site!), and I was pleased to connect with Roseann Schauer, current seasonal park naturalist at Lake Shetek State Park, and with Janet Timmerman, who coordinated the Road Scholar module. Jon Wendorff and Billie Jo Lau graciously pulled files and allowed me to access the entire collection of Lake Shetek materials at the Wheels Across the Prairie Museum in Tracy, including a copy of Christina Koch's depredation claim, which couldn't be located in the National Archives. And, to Dan Dries, my Airbnb host and his wonderful Lake Shetek cabin—within walking distance of many of the sites—thank you so much for your hospitality and allowing me to spend time in the footsteps of the settlers.

Many thanks to Dakota Conflict historians Curtis Dahlin, John Isch, and Elroy Ubl. Elroy welcomed me to his home where he and Curt shared their files and information and were available via email to answer questions as they arose. John was always ready with guidance and provided the map for the book.

Research professionals were critical to this project, and a long list of them assisted. A huge debt of gratitude is owed the Minnesota Historical Society for having digitized the entire Dakota Conflict collection and making it available online. Josh Jordan, Site Coordinator, and the End-O-Line Railroad Park & Museum in Currie, Minnesota, provided assistance in acquisition of research materials as did Rebecca J. Snyder, Director of Research & Publishing at the Dakota County Historical Society in St. Paul, Minnesota. Darla Gebhard and Dan, the volunteer whose last name I missed, provided assistance prior to and during my visit to the Brown County Historical Society in New Ulm, Minnesota. Matthew Reitzel, Manuscript Archivist at the South Dakota State Historical Society Archives/Cultural Heritage Center in Pierre, South Dakota, assisted me with review of records from Fort Randall.

There were a host of professionals who responded to my online inquiries as I tried to chase down vital records: Karen S. Myers, Deputy Director Taxpayer Services of Blue Earth County (Mankato, Minnesota); Krista Lewis, Archivist, History Center of Olmsted County (Rochester, Minnesota); Walt Bennick, Archivist, Winona History (Winona, Minnesota): thanks for all your help.

Several professionals at the National Archives and Records Administration in Washington, D.C., assisted with tracking down specific depredation claims and military documents. My thanks goes to DeAnne Blanton, Archives I Reference Section; Rose Buchanan, Archives Technician, Archives I Research Rooms Section; and Danielle Marie Eyre, Archive Technician, Archives I Reference Section.

When staff of the National Archives was unable to track down information, I was fortunate to have Ranel Capron, friend and BLM archeologist, who was in the D.C. area and willing to spend time researching my project. Ranel—your dedicated line by line reading of Fort Randall military records provided me with previously unknown/unconfirmed details about the Fool Soldiers and their ransom of the Shetek captives. I owe you!

Sam Herley, Ph.D., Curator at the South Dakota Oral History Center, University of South Dakota, also provided me access to the oral histories left by family members of the Fool Soldiers. The perspectives offered in these recordings were invaluable.

As I completed my manuscript, I found input from Dakota tribal members and experts on Dakota history and culture invaluable. To my Facebook friends—Mike Lord, Bud Johnston, Terri Bischoff, and Adrienne Zimiga . . . thanks for extending connections. Barbara Britain . . . thank you for the review of the manuscript and comments. And Breon Lake . . . your input on tribal culture, history, names, and sensitivity issues was critical. Thank you for your willingness to share it with me. I hope I have represented the culture fairly.

Of course, my critique groups and beta readers, who helped immeasurably in shaping my craft, hold my everlasting appreciation. To my home team, my RMFW Critique Group (Alice, Carla, Cate, Denee, Janet, Jessica, Kay, Peggy, Robin, Steven, and Thea): thanks for always being there and getting me through the worst of those awful early chapters! Many thanks to my WFWA Critique Group (Amanda, Debby, and Karen) for their genre insight, their input made such a difference. And, my beta readers: thank you Elke, Janet, Liz, Peggy, Sharon, and Susan for the time you took to provide me such valuable feedback on the manuscript as a whole—though I hated the edits, I appreciate you making me do them.

The support of my family means more than I can say. My parents, Dick and Vauna, fostered my imagination daily and encouraged me to pursue my dreams. My siblings and their loved ones—Judy and Dave, Mike and Brenda—couldn't be more supportive of my writing. My daughter Katrina and her family (Don, Asher, and Xander) are always there and always cheering me on as are Ilka (and Edger, Luca, Enzo, and Giulio) and Danika (and Sergio, Kathia, and Erik). Thank you all!

And then there's Ken, my love. Daily, he allowed me time closed up in my office, listened to me rant and rave about history and the story and challenges and worries, and took me in his arms when I needed to be held. He shares his life with my writing and loves me all the same. His support means the world to me, as does his love.

SOURCES

Documents, Manuscripts, and Transcripts (Including Primary Sources On-line)

1790 United States Federal Census [database on-line]. Provo, Utah, U.S.A.: Ancestry.com Operations, Inc., 2010. Images reproduced by FamilySearch.

1820 United States Federal Census [database on-line]. Provo, Utah, U.S.A.: Ancestry.com Operations, Inc., 2010. Images reproduced by FamilySearch.

1830 United States Federal Census [database on-line]. Provo, Utah, U.S.A.: Ancestry.com Operations, Inc., 2010. Images reproduced by FamilySearch.

1840 United States Federal Census [database on-line]. Provo, Utah, U.S.A.: Ancestry.com Operations, Inc., 2010. Images reproduced by FamilySearch.

1850 United States Federal Census [database on-line]. Provo, Utah, U.S.A.: Ancestry.com Operations, Inc., 2009. Images reproduced by FamilySearch.

1860 United States Federal Census [database on-line]. Provo, Utah, U.S.A.: Ancestry.com Operations, Inc., 2009. Images reproduced by FamilySearch.

1870 United States Federal Census [database on-line]. Provo, Utah, U.S.A.: Ancestry.com Operations, Inc., 2009. Images reproduced by FamilySearch.

1880 United States Federal Census [database on-line]. Provo, Utah, U.S.A.: Ancestry.com Operations, Inc., 2016. Images reproduced by FamilySearch.

1900 United States Federal Census [database on-line]. Provo, Utah, U.S.A.: Ancestry.com Operations, Inc., 2006.

1910 United States Federal Census [database on-line]. Provo, Utah, U.S.A.: Ancestry.com Operations, Inc., 2006. Images reproduced by FamilySearch.

Canada, Find A Grave Index, 1600s-Current [database on-line]. Provo, UT, U.S.A: Ancestry.com Operations, Inc., 2012.

Claim #1 (Almena Hurd), filed 4/28/1863; Box 1709; Indian Accounts (Entry 3503A); Records of the Accounting Officers of the Department of the Treasury, Record Group 217; National Archives Building, Washington, DC—copy in files of Brown County Historical Society.

Claim #2 (Henry W. Smith), filed 1863; Box 1709; Indian Accounts (Entry 3503A); Records of the Accounting Officers of the Department of the Treasury, Record Group 217; National Archives Building, Washington, DC—copy in files of Brown County Historical Society.

Claim #4 (John G. Wright/Weight), filed 8/15/1864; Box 1709; Indian Accounts (Entry 3503A); Records of the Accounting Officers of the Department of the Treasury, Record Group 217; National Archives Building, Washington, DC.

Claim #9 (William J. Duley), filed 11/12/1862; 13E2A, 35/22/2, Box 1709 (tabbed); Indian Accounts (Entry 3503A); Records of the Accounting Officers of the Department of the Treasury, Record Group 217; National Archives Building, Washington, DC.

Claim #26 (Thomas Ireland), filed 8/17/1863; 13E2A, 35/22/2, Box 1709 (tabbed); Indian Accounts (Entry 3503A); Records of the Accounting Officers of the Department of the Treasury, Record Group 217; National Archives Building, Washington, DC.

Claim #53 (Estate of John Eastlick—deceased), filed April 29, 1863; Box #1710; Indian Accounts (Entry 3503B); Records of the Accounting Officers of the Department of the Treasury, Record Group 217; National Archives Building, Washington, DC.

Claim #63 (E. G. Koch), filed July 15, 1863; 13E2A, 35/22/2,

Box 1710 (tabbed); Indian Accounts (Entry 3503B); Records of the Accounting Officers of the Department of the Treasury, Record Group 217; National Archives Building, Washington, DC.

Claim #1161 (Ernest Koch, on behalf of Christina Koch); Box 3; Record Group 75; National Archives Building, Washington, DC—partial copy in files of Wheels Across the Prairie Museum.

Currie, Neil, 1842–1921, compiler. "Information of Victims of the Lake Shetek Massacre Obtained by Correspondence and Personal Testimony," 1894, 1946. Dakota Conflict of 1862 Manuscripts Collections. Minnesota Historical Society, #1925.

Duley, William J., 1819–1898. "Notes on the Sioux Massacre of 1862," 1885. Dakota Conflict of 1862 Manuscripts Collections. Minnesota Historical Society, #4546.

Eastlick, L. (Lavina), 1833–1923. "The Lake Shetek Indian Massacre in 1862," 1890. Dakota Conflict of 1862 Manuscripts Collections. Minnesota Historical Society, #6868.

Guetzlaff, R. E., *Letter to George V. Staeburg.* June 26, 1912.

Hamm, Mary A. (Pew). *Letter to Sylvia Ham Lightzer.* Undated copy.

Hatch, C. D. "Massacre of 1862." *1897 transcript of article.* Prepared for the *Fulda Republican* and reprinted in the *Martin County Independent* (April 22, 1897). From files of Brown County Historical Society.

Hatch, Charles D., 1837–1907. "Narrative of Charles D. Hatch's Experiences in the Indian War in Minnesota in 1862," undated. Dakota Conflict of 1862 Manuscripts Collections. Minnesota Historical Society, #7817.

Illinois, State Census Collection, 1825–1865 [database on-line]. Provo, UT, USA: Ancestry.com Operations, Inc., 2008.

Indiana Marriage Index, 1800–1941 [database on-line]. Provo, UT, USA. Ancestry.com Operations, Inc., 2005.

Iowa, State Census Collection, 1836–1925 [database on-line]. Provo, UT, USA. Ancestry.com Operations, Inc., 2007.

Kansas State Census Collection, 1855–1925 [database on-line].

Provo, UT, USA: Ancestry.com Operations, Inc., 2009.

Michigan, Compiled Marriages for Select Counties, 1851–1875 [database on-line]. Provo, UT, USA: Ancestry.com Operations, Inc., 2000.

Minnesota, Births and Christenings Index, 1840–1980 [database on-line]. Provo, UT, USA. Ancestry.com Operations, Inc., 2011.

Minnesota, County Marriages, 1860–1949, database with images. FamilySearch.com. Intellectual Reserve, Inc., 2016.

Minnesota, Death Index, 1908–2002 [database on-line]. Provo, UT, USA. Ancestry.com Operations, Inc., 2001.

Minnesota, Marriages Index, 1849–1950 [database on-line]. Provo, UT, USA. Ancestry.com Operations, Inc., 2011.

Minnesota, Territorial and State Censuses, 1849–1905 [database on-line]. Provo, UT, USA. Ancestry.com Operations, Inc., 2007.

Minnesota Territorial Census, 1857, database with images. FamilySearch.com. Intellectual Reserve, Inc., 2014.

Myers, Aaron, 1825–1906. "Aaron Myers reminiscence and biographical data," 1900, 1906. Dakota Conflict of 1862 Manuscripts Collections. Minnesota Historical Society, #2048.

Myers, Aaron. Untitled transcript. Received from Rick Myers, grandson, Nov. 14, 1961. Files of Brown County Historical Society.

New York, State Census, 1855 [database on-line]. Provo, UT, USA. Ancestry.com Operations, Inc., 2013.

New York, State Census, 1875 [database on-line]. Provo, UT, USA. Ancestry.com Operations, Inc., 2014.

Ohio, County Marriages, 1774–1993 [database on-line]. Lehi, UT, USA. Ancestry.com Operations, Inc., 2016.

Pattee, Major John, 41st Iowa Infantry, Commanding, to Charles Poimeau, Esq., Fort Randall, DT, Nov. 15, 1862; 9W2; 34/8/9; Letters and Telegrams Sent (Entry 370-2, Vol. 3 of 17 Ft. Randall, SD, Post Letter Book); Record Group 393,

National Archives Building, Washington, DC.

Pattee, Major John, 41st Iowa Infantry, Commanding, to Capt. F. H. Cooper., Fort Randall, DT, Nov. 16, 1862; 9W2; 34/8/9; Letters and Telegrams Sent (Entry 370-2, Vol. 3 of 17 Ft. Randall, SD, Post Letter Book); Record Group 393, National Archives Building, Washington, DC.

Pattee, Major John, 41st Iowa Infantry, Commanding, to Major Gen. John Pope, Fort Randall, DT, Nov. 26, 1862; 9W2; 34/8/9; Letters and Telegrams Sent (Entry 370-2, Vol. 3 of 17 Ft. Randall, SD, Post Letter Book); Record Group 393, National Archives Building, Washington, DC.

Pattee, Major John, 41st Iowa Infantry, Commanding, to Brig. Gen. G. Cook, on the March from Fort Randall to Fort Pierre, Dec. 1, 1862; Part V, Entry 2, Vol. 3 of 17; Ft. Randall, SD, Post Letter Book; Record Group 393, National Archives Building, Washington, DC.

Pattee, Major John, 41st Iowa Infantry, Commanding, to Major Gen. John Pope, Fort Randall, DT, Dec. 1, 1862; 9W2; 34/8/9; Letters and Telegrams Sent (Entry 370-2, Vol. 3 of 17 Ft. Randall, SD, Post Letter Book); Record Group 393, National Archives Building, Washington, DC.

Pennsylvania, County Marriages, 1885–1950, database with images. FamilySearch.com. Intellectual Reserve, Inc., 2016.

Racou, J. C., 1st lt., Co. H, 41st Iowa Infantry, Fort Randall, DT, Jan. 13, 1863, Report of Expedition; Part V, Entry 2, Vol. 3 of 17; Post Letter Book—Ft. Randall, SD, Record Group 393, National Archives Building, Washington, DC.

Somsen, Henry N., Jr. *Letters to Mrs. Clark Kellett, New Ulm Public Museum.* Feb. 26, 1963, and May 23, 1963. Copy in files of Brown County Historical Society.

United States Bureau of Land Management. *Minnesota Land Records* [database on-line]. Provo, UT, USA: Ancestry.com Operations, Inc. 1997.

United States Bureau of Land Management. *Minnesota, Homestead and Cash Entry Patents, Pre-1908,* [database on-line]. Provo, UT, USA: Ancestry.com Operations, Inc. 1997.

United State Census of Union Veterans and Widows of the Civil War,

1890, database with images. FamilySearch.com. Intellectual Reserve, Inc., 2016.

U.S. City Directories, 1822–1995 [database on-line]. Provo, UT, USA: Ancestry.com Operations, Inc., 2011.

U.S., Find a Grave Index, 1600–Current [database on-line]. Provo, UT, USA: Ancestry.com Operations, Inc., 2012.

U.S. General Land Office Records, 1796–1907 [database on-line]. Provo, UT, USA: Ancestry.com Operations, Inc., 2008.

U.S. Returns from Regular Army Infantry Regiments, 1821–1916 [database on-line]. Provo, UT, USA: Ancestry.com Operations, Inc., 2011.

Web: International, Find a Grave Index [database on-line]. Provo, UT, USA: Ancestry.com Operations, Inc., 2013.

Wisconsin State Census, 1875, database with images. Family Search.com. Intellectual Reserve, Inc., 2016.

Workman, Harper M., 1855–?. "Early history of Lake Shetek Country," undated and 1924–30. Dakota Conflict of 1862 Manuscripts Collections. Minnesota Historical Society, #3470.

Books, Documentaries, Letters, Interviews

Anderson, Gary Clayton, and Alan R. Woolworth. *Through Dakota Eyes: Narrative Accounts of the Minnesota Indian War of 1862.* St. Paul, Minnesota: Minnesota Historical Society Press, 1988.

Barbier, Charles P. "Recollections of Ft. La Framboise in 1862 and the Rescue of Lake Chetek [sic] Captives." *South Dakota Historical Collections* (Doane Robinson, ed.), vol. XI, 1922: pp. 232–42. Digital version.

Britain, Barbara, producer. *Return to Lake Shetek: The Courage of the Fool Soldiers.* White Bear Lake, Minnesota: Barbara Britain, undated.

Bryant, Charles S., and Abel B. Murch. A History of the Great Sioux Massacre by the Sioux Indians in Minnesota. Cincinnati: Rickey & Carroll, 1864.

Carley, Kenneth. *The Sioux Uprising of 1862.* St. Paul, Minnesota: The Minnesota Historical Society, 1976.

Charger, Sam. "Biography of Martin Charger," *South Dakota Historical Collections* (Doane Robinson, ed.), vol. XXII, 1946: 1–25.

Child, James E. *Child's History of Waseca County, Minnesota.* Owatonna, Minnesota: Whiting & Luers, 1905.

Dahlin, Curtis A. *Calamity at Lake Shetek.* Roseville, Minnesota: Curtis A. Dahlin, 2015.

Deloria, Ella Cara. *Speaking of Indians.* Pickle Partner Publishing. www.pp-publishing.com, 2015; originally published 1944. Digital version.

Deloria, Ella Cara. *Waterlily.* Lincoln, Nebraska: University of Nebraska Press, 1988. Digital version.

Eastlick, Mrs. (Lavina). *A Personal Narrative of Indian Massacres 1862.* No publication data listed, 1864, 1959, 1967.

Eastman, Charles Alexander. *From the Deep Woods to Civilization: Chapters in the Autobiography of an Indian.* No location: Little Brown and Company, 1916. Digital version 2017.

Eastman, Charles Alexander. *The Collected Complete Works of Charles Alexander Eastman.* No publication data. Digital version.

Greene, Jerome A. *Fort Randall on the Missouri, 1856–1892.* Pierre, South Dakota: South Dakota State Historical Society Press, 2005.

Haymond, John A. The Dakota War Trials of 1862: Revenge, Military Law and the Judgment of History. Jefferson, North Carolina: McFarland & Company, Inc., 2016. Digital version.

Heard, Isaac V. D. *History of the Sioux War and Massacres of 1862 and 1863.* Ann Arbor, Michigan: University of Michigan Library, 2005. Digital version.

Hibschman, Harry Jacob. *The Shetek Pioneers and the Indians.* New York: Garland Pub., 1976.

History of Winona County, 1883. H. H. Hill and Company, 1883. Digital version.

Isch, John. *A Battle for Living: The Life and Experiences of Lavina Eastlick*. New Ulm, Minnesota: Brown County Historical Society, 2012.

Isch, John. *The Dakota Trials: Including the Complete Transcripts and Explanatory Notes on the Military Commission Trials in Minnesota 1862–1864*. New Ulm, Minnesota: Brown County Historical Society, 2012, 2013.

Johansson, Eric J. *Letters to Bill Bolin*. 1985–1987, from files of Bill Bolin.

Kelly, Fanny; Clark Spence and Mary Lee Spence, eds. *Narrative of my Captivity among the Sioux Indians*. New York: Barnes & Noble Books, no date.

Manfred, Frederick. Interviews with Pamela Gieser. Brookings, SD, and Luverne, MN. Jan. 9 and Mar. 9, 1983.

Manfred, Frederick. *Scarlet Plume*. New York: Frederick Feikema Manfred, 1964.

Michano, Gregory, and Susan A. Michano. *A Fate Worse than Death: Indian Captivities in the West, 1830–1885*. Caldwell, Idaho: Caxton Press, 2009. Digital version.

Morris, Lucy Leavenworth Wilder. *Old Rail Fence Corners: Frontier Tales Told by Minnesota Pioneers*. St. Paul: Minnesota Historical Society Press, 1914. Digital version.

Native South Dakota: A Guide to Tribal Lands. Pierre, South Dakota: South Dakota Department of Tourism, 2014.

Pattee, Colonel John. "Report of Colonel Pattee," *South Dakota Historical Collections* (Doane Robinson, ed.), Vol. V, 1910: 273–96.

Schwandt, Mary. *The Captivity of Mary Schwandt*. Fairfield, Washington: Ye Galleon Press, 1975.

Seymour, John. *The Forgotten Arts and Crafts*. New York: Dorling Kindersley Publishing, Inc., 2001.

Sharp, Abbie Gardner. *The Spirit Lake Massacre and Captivity of*

Miss Abbie Gardner. Big Byte Books, 2015 (original publication 1912). Digital version.

Silvernale, John A. *In Commemoration of the Sioux Uprising Aug. 20, 1862.* Tracy, Minnesota: Tracy Publishing Company and the Murray County Historical Society, 1962, 2006.

Sneve, Virginia Driving Hawk. *Betrayed.* New York: Holiday House, 1974.

Wakefield, Sarah F. *Six Weeks in the Sioux Tepees.* Guilford, Connecticut: Globe Pequot Press, 2004.

Newspapers

"125th Anniversary Set at Shetek," *Tracy Headlight Herald.* Aug. 19, 1987, p. 1.

"Arrival of Mrs. Duly [sic] and Children," *The Stillwater Messenger.* February 19, 1863, p. 1.

"Arrival of Mrs. Duly [sic] and Children," *The Wabashaw County Herald,* vol. 3, no. 24: Feb. 26, 1863, p. 1.

"Arrival of Mrs. Duly [sic] and Children," *Mankato Free Record.* Jan. 31, 1863, p. 2.

"Author Has Special Feeling for Pioneers," *Tracy Headlight Herald.* August 19, 1987, pp. 1–2.

Bolin, Bill. "Hatch Kin Still Linked to Shetek," *Southwest Sailor,* July 199?.

Bolin, Bill. "Pioneer Mothers Escaped Indian Slaughter at Shetek," *Southwest Sailor.* July 199?, pp. 12, 14.

Bolin, Bill. "Shetek's 'Paul Revere' Rides On," *Southwest Sailor,* July 199?.

Brown, Curt. "Forgotten Survivor of a Frontier War," *Minneapolis Star Tribune.* October 16, 2016, p. B4.

Brown, Curt. "Minnesota History: Image Surfaces from a Grim Chapter," *Minneapolis Star-Tribune.* November 1, 2015, p. B4.

"Dakota Conflict at Shetek: 1862–1987 Year of Reconcilation

Edition," various articles, *Tracy Headlight Herald.* August 19, 1987.

Dakota Land Company ad, *St. Paul Pioneer & Democrat.* Dec. 15, 1861, p. 1.

"Early Events Recalled: An Interesting Story Connected with the Outbreak of the Sioux," *The Mankato Review.* July 6, 1892, un-paginated copy.

"Elmira [sic] Descendants of Hurd Family Recall," *The Sunday Telegram.* Dec. 1931, un-paginated copy.

"First Settler in Lyon County Believed Found," unidentified, undated newspaper clipping. Files of Brown County Historical Society.

Golden, T. C. "The Indian War-Expedition to Lake Shetek—Letter from the Chaplain of the 25th Wisconsin," *St. Paul Pioneer.* Nov. 11, 1862.

Hatch, Charles. "A Part of the History of Murray County: Scenes of the Lake Shetek Massacre," *Southwest Minnesotian* (reprinted from the *Waseca Herald*). Weekly series April 7, 1887–June 7, 1887.

Hatch, Chas. D. "Story of Indian Massacre Told by a Survivor," *Minneapolis Tribune.* Aug. 18, 1912, clipping.

"Held by Indians for Many Weeks," *Blue Earth County Enterprise.* Jan 24, 1927, clipping.

"Heroine of War with Sioux Dies: Captive of White Lodge Passes Away at Mankato," *Mankato Review.* Mar. 6, 1907.

"Heroism of Elmira [sic]: Pioneer Saves Lives of Her Babies," *The Sunday Telegram.* Dec. 14, 1931, un-paginated copy.

"Historic Claims Paper Reveals Contents of Koch Cabin at Time of Massacre," *Tracy Headlight Herald.* July 4, 1963, p. 1.

"The Indian War—Lake Shetek Massacre—More Bodies Found," *St. Paul Pioneer-Democrat.* Sept. 10, 1862.

"The Indian War—The Massacre at Lake Shetek: Statement of Mr. Everett," *The St. Paul Pioneer.* Sept. 3, 1862.

Johnson, F. W., Mrs. "Hurd's Heart-Rending Story of Sioux Massacre," *Journal.* August 11, 1937, un-paginated copy.

"Lake Shetek Massacre Edition," *Tracy Headlight Herald.* Various articles, Aug. 16, 1962.

Lee, Zion. "The Fool Soldiers," *Pierre Capital Journal.* July 21, 2016. Digital version.

"Left for Dead: The Story of Thomas Ireland," *Mankato Free Press.* April 6, 1893, clipping.

"Mankato Woman, 80, Recalls Horror of Indian Massacre," *Mankato Free Press.* June 8, 1936, clipping.

Mathis, Tedd. "At the End, 38 Men Hanged," *Worthington Daily Globe.* Aug. 27, 1987, pp. 1, 10.

"Mrs. Hotaling Survivor of Indian Massacre," *Mankato Free Press.* Feb 2, 1946, clipping.

"Notice of Departure of Wm J. Duly and Family," *Ft. Doge Republican.* Jan 21, 1863, p. 1.

Olson, Corrinne. "Descendant Offers 'Thank You' for 1862 Rescue," *Sioux Falls Argus Leader.* Undated, un-paginated copy in Brown County Historical Society files.

"Personal," *The New York Times,* from the *St. Paul (Minn) Press.* September 28, 1862.

"Pioneer Recalls Massacre at Shetek 69 Years Ago," *Mankato Free Press.* Aug 21, 1931, clipping.

"Released Captives," *Mankato Weekly Record.* Jan. 24, 1863, clipping.

"Remembering the Battlegrounds," *Worthington Daily Globe.* August 14, 1987, p. B3.

"She Asks for a Pension," *Mankato Review.* March 2, 1898.

"Shetek Hero," *Tracy Headlight Herald.* Aug. 16, 1962; Section 1, p. 12.

"Shetek Massacre Edition," *Tracy Headlight Herald.* Various articles, Aug. 19, 1932.

"The Sioux Barbaritie [sic]-Narrative of Mrs. Phineas B. Hurd before the United States Commissioners," *Goodhue Volunteer.* Vol. 7, no. 45, June 3, 1863, p.1.

"The Sioux War—From Sibley's Camp," *Mankato Semi-Weekly*

Record. October 18, 1862, pp. 1–2.

"The Sioux War—Statement of a Released Prisoner," *Mankato Semi-Weekly Record.* October 18, 1862, pp. 1–2.

"Sudden Death of Mrs. Hohmuth," *The Mankato Review.* March 5, 1907, un-paginated copy.

"Where Are They Buried? Heroic Fool Soldiers Killed and Left in Gregory Co.," *Gregory Times-Advocate.* Vol. 110, no. 14, April 2, 2014, pp. 1, 10.

Periodicals

Britain, Barbara. "Gifts from the Fool Soldiers." *Minnesota's Heritage,* vol. 4, July 2011: 36–43.

Carpenter, Paul. "Charles Hatch, Survivor of Slaughter's Slough-Lake Shetek, Minnesota 1862," unpublished article in files of Bill Bolin.

Gray, John S. "The Santee Sioux and the Settlers at Lake Shetek," *Montana: The Magazine of Western History,* vol. XXV, no. 1; winter 1975: pp. 42–54.

Ketcham, Jim. "The Fool Soldiers." *Minnesota's Heritage,* vol. 4, July 2011: 6–19.

Laut, Agnes C. "Pioneer Women of the West II: The Heroines of Lake Shetek," *The Outing Magazine,* vol. 52, 1908: 271–86.

Nelson, Jim. "The Fool Soldiers' Story Told Many Ways." *Minnesota's Heritage,* vol. 4, July 2011: 20–35.

Oral Histories

Plummer, Stephen. "American Indian Research Project Field Notes," *Institute of American Indian Studies, South Dakota Oral History Center, University of South Dakota.* 1972. Mss. #0850, 0851, 0852, 0854, 0855, 0856, 0858, 0875.

"South Dakota Oral History Project," *Institute of American Indian Studies, South Dakota Oral History Center, University of South Dakota.* Mss. #1616, 1967, 1968.

Online Websites

"Beaver, Minnesota," *Wikipedia.* https://en.wikipedia.org/wiki/Beaver,_Minnesota: last accessed May 20, 2019.

Curtiss-Wedge, Franklyn, Editor. "History of Whitewater Township, Winona County, Minnesota," *The History of Winona County, Minnesota.* Chicago: H. C. Cooper, Jr. & Co., Publisher, 1913. http://history.rays-place.com/mn/wi-whitewater.htm: copyright 2003–2013: accessed Feb. 18, 2017.

"Dakota People," *Wikipedia.* https://en.wikipedia.org/wiki/Dakota_people: May 14, 2019. Last accessed May 21, 2019.

"During the War," *Minnesota Historical Society: The US-Dakota War of 1862.* http://www.usdakotawar.org/history/war/ during-war: Last accessed May 21, 2019.

"Early West Murray County Minnesota History," *USGW Archives.* http://www.usgwarchives.net/mn/murray/history/116-117.htm. Last accessed May 21, 2019.

Eckles, Polly, transcriber. "1854 State Census of Iowa, Jackson County, All Townships," *IAGenWeb State Census Project.* http://iagenweb.org/census/: 2008: accessed Feb. 18, 2017.

"Ferryboats," *Encyclopedia Dubuque.* From Oldt, Franklin T. *History of Dubuque County, Iowa.* Chicago: Western Historical Company, 1880. http://www.encyclopediadubuque.org/index.php?title=FERRYBOATS: Creative Commons BY-NC-SA, 15 Nov 2015: last accessed May 20, 2019.

Find a Grave www.findagrave.com

Capt Wiliam J. Duley, Sr. Memorial #59962077; Oct. 11, 2010. Cindy K. Coffin, sponsor.

Jefferson M. Duley. Memorial #56823287; Aug. 8, 2010. Nolte, Gwen, creator; maintained by Cindy K. Coffin.

Laura Terry Duley. Memorial #59962127; Oct. 11, 2010. Cindy K. Coffin, sponsor.

Lavina Day Eastlick. Memorial #61103083; Nov. 4, 2010. Bill Cox, creator.

Fool Soldiers Band Monument. Memorial #2385551; Jan. 22, 2011.

Andreas Koch. Memorial #37509095; May 25, 2009. Cindy K. Coffin, creator.

Rachel Sunman Terry. Memorial #60686252; 12/16/2016.

Almena Hamm "Alomina" Hurd Woodword. Memorial #63748588; Jan. 5, 2011. Created by Bill Cox.

Eldora Wright. Memorial #174942797; Jan. 6, 2017. Created by Candy.

"Flood of 1851," *Wikipedia*. https://en.wikipedia.org/wiki/Flood_of_1851: Feb 15, 2017.

Flora, Stephanie. "The Covered Wagon," *The Oregon Trail and Its Pioneers.* http://centralthirdgrade.weebly.com/uploads/7/3/9/0/7390012/ covered_wagon.pdf: 2007. Last accessed May 21, 2019.

Gerischer, Debbie Clough, transcriber. "Crossing the Mississippi," *IAGenWeb Project.* From Parish, John C., editor. "The Palimpsest," *Iowa History, vol. 1. no. 5.* State Historical Society of Iowa: December 1920. http://iagenweb.org/history/palimpsest/1920-Dec.htm: last accessed May 20, 2019.

Greene, William A. "The Erie Railroad," *Allegany County Historical Society Local History and Genealogy.* 2003–2012. http://www.alleganyhistory.org/culture/transportation/railroads/ erie-railroad/1060-the-erie-railroad: last accessed May 20, 2019.

Grey, Jim. "About the Road" and "Traveling the Road," *The Historic Michigan Road.* https://historicmichiganroad.org/: 1/16/2016. Last accessed May 20, 2019.

Harris, Howell. "Henry Stanley and the Rotary Stove," *A Stove Less Ordinary.* Aug. 20, 2016. https://stovehistory.blogspot.com/2016/08/ henry-stanley-and-the-rotary-stove.html: accessed Feb. 18, 2017.

Harris, Howell. "The Pioneer Cooking Stove, Indiana, Late 1830s," *A Stove Less Ordinary.* https://stovehistory.blogspot.com/2013/04/ the-pioneer-cooking-stove-indiana.html: April

2, 2013: accessed Feb. 18, 2017.

Hintz, Susan. "Roseanna Ireland Miller VanAlstine (1853–1936)," *Susan's Space.* https://sooze471.wordpress.com/2011/09/25/ rose-anna-ireland-miller-vanalstine-1853-1936/: Sept. 25-2011. Last accessed May 21, 2019.

"History of South Dakota," *Wikipedia.* https://en.wikipedia.org/wiki/History_of_South_Dakota: Feb. 20, 2019. Last accessed May 21, 2019.

"History of Weather Observations-Fort Ridgely, Minnesota 1853–1867," *MRCC.* http://mrcc.sws.uius.edu/FORTS/histories/MN_Fort_Ridgely_Boulay.pdf. Last accessed May 21, 2019.

Hubbard, Lucius F. "Wahpeton Chiefs," *Minnesota in Three Centuries.* 1908. www.archive.org/stream/minnsotainthree03bubbuoft/minnesotainthreeo3hubbuoft_djvu.txt: Dec. 28, 2009. Accessed May 21, 2019.

Iowa Land Records. https://iowalandrecords.org. Last accessed May 23, 2019.

"Ishtakhaba," *Wikipedia.* https://en.wikipedia.org/wiki/Ishtakhaba: May 2, 2019. Last accessed May 21, 2019.

"Jackson County Cemetery Directory," *IAGenWeb Project.* http://www.usgwarchives.net/al/jackson/cemetery.htm: 2008-2017: accessed Feb. 17, 2017.

Knox, Douglas, and Michael Conzen. *The Electronic Encyclopeida of Chicago.* c. 2005, from *Encyclopedia of Chicago.* Chicago: Chicago Historical Society, 1848. http://www.encyclopedia.chicagohistory.org/pages/500003.html: last accessed May 20, 2019.

Krogman, Mary Kay, transcriber. "Jackson County, Iowa," *Genealogy Trails,* from "About Bellevue, Iowa," *The History of Jackson County Iowa.* No publisher listed, November 1879. http://genealogytrails.com/iowa/jackson/towns_current.html, copyright 2017. Last accessed May 20, 2019.

Krogman, Mary Kay, transcriber (from various sources). "Murray County, Minnesota: Dakota War-Victims and Survivor Stories," *Genealogy Trails History Group.* http://genealogy

trails.com/minn/murray/history_massacre.html. Last accessed May 21, 2019.

"Lakota and Dakota Sioux Fact Sheet," Native American Facts for Kids. http://www.bigorrin.org/sioux_kids.htm: Native Languages of the Americas website, 1998—2015. Last accessed May 21, 2019.

"Lakota Phrase Archive," Akta Lakota Museum & Cultural Center. http://aktalakota.stjo.org/site/News2?page=NewsArticle&id=8577. Last accessed May 21, 2019.

"Legislators Past & Present: Duley, William J. 'W.J'," *Minnesota Legislative Reference Library*. https://www.leg.state.mn.us/legdb/fulldetail?ID=12622: last accessed May 20, 2019.

Leigh, Ray, and Kathy Leigh, "The Tragedy of Minnesota," *US-Roots*. http://www.us-roots.org/colonialamerica/ pioneer/chap26_1.html: Oct. 26, 2001. Last accessed May 21, 2019.

"Michigan Road," *Wikipedia*. https://en.wikipedia.org/w/index.php?title=Michigan_Road&p;dod=745612427: 22 Oct. 2016: last accessed May 20, 2019.

"Minnesota Weather for the Year 1862," *Climate Stations*. https://www.climatestations.com/minnesota-weather-for-1862/. Last accessed 5/21/2019.

"Mrs. Alomina Hurd: A Story of Border Suffering," *Civil War*. http://www.civilwar.com/people/21-union-women/ 148422-mrs-alomina-hurd.html: last accessed May 20, 2019.

Pridmore, Jay. " '1848: Chicago's Turning Point' Exhibition Lives Up To Its Billing," *Chicago Tribune*. Nov 6, 1998. https://www.chicagotribune.com/news/ ct-xpm-1998-11-06-9811060472-story.html: last accessed May 20, 2019.

Sherman, Bill. "Tracing the Treaties: How They Affected American Indians and Iowa," *Iowa History Journal*. http://iowahistoryjournal.com/ tracing-treaties-affected-american-indians-iowa/: last accessed May 20, 2019.

"The Start of Ripley County, Indiana," *Ripley County Historical Society Library*. http://www.rchslib.org/ripleyformed.html: accessed Feb. 17, 2017.

"Sunman, Indiana," Wikipedia. https://en.wikipedia.org/wiki/

Sunman,_Indiana: last accessed May 20, 2019.

"Sycamore Row (road)," *Wikipedia:* 12 Jan. 2016. https://en.wikipedia.org/wiki/Sycamore_Row_(road): Feb. 15, 2017.

Sykora, Jason, and Matt Robertson. "Koch Cabin Lake Shetek," *RRCNET.* http://www.rrcnet.org/~historic/kcabin.html: last accessed May 21, 2019.

"Tete Des Morts. Jackson County 1893. Iowa. 1893," *Historical Map Works Residential Genealogy.* From *Jackson County 1893, Iowa.* Northwest Publishing Company: 1893. http://www.historicmapworks.com/Map/US/54824/Tete+Des+Morts/Jackson+County+1893/Iowa/: last accessed May 20, 2019.

Weeks, John A., III. "Dubuque-Wisconsin Bridge," *Highways, Byways, and Bridge Photography.* http://www.johnweeks.com/river_mississippi/pagesA/ umissA09.html: accessed Feb. 13, 2017.

Whitaker, Beverly. "The Chicago Road and the State Road," *Road Trails: Early American Roads and Trails.* http://freepages.rootsweb.com/~gentutor/genealogy/trails.html: 2006: last accessed May 20, 2019.

BOOK CLUB DISCUSSION QUESTIONS

1. Westward expansion is a major thread in *Never Let Go.* What factors motivated the Shetek settlers to move west? Do you feel those reasons were valid? How much of a role did restlessness play? In what ways did land companies lure and manipulate settlers? Would such techniques work today?

2. Cultural misunderstandings and biases were rampant in nineteenth-century Minnesota. In what ways did white settlers fail to understand the Dakota? What parts of white culture were not understood by the Dakota? How were such biases perpetuated? Which of the Shetek women do you think displayed the most prejudice? The least? How did this impact them as events unfolded?

3. The novel takes places during a time when gender roles were defined much differently than they are today. Which of the women was most bound by these expectations? Do you think her adherence to these "rules" made her weak? Why or why not? What methods did the five women use to "work around" such expectations?

4. All of the women in the novel discovered their adult lives to be different than the expectations of their youth. Which of the women did you identify with most? Why? How did you feel

about the ways in which she adjusted? At what point in the story did she discover her strength?

5. Laura may have suffered from depression. Do you feel she was predisposed to mental illness, or did external factors shape her response? How so? If she were alive today, how might her "treatment plan" have differed from that created by Mrs. Tucker? Do you believe she was weak? In what ways did she exhibit strength?

6. Julia coped with a husband who was irresponsible, willing to break the law, and who drank heavily. Why do you feel she was willing to remain with such a man? Do you feel those reasons were valid, given the era in which she lived? Would she have behaved differently if she were alive today?

7. Christina and her husband had very strong opinions about the shooting of Clark. Based on what happened, do you think the settlers handled the threat in the best way? What other solutions might they have explored?

8. Lavina was forced to make life and death decisions concerning her children. How did you feel about what she decided? If you had been in her position, what would you have done?

9. Almena's adult life was much shaped by her early years. What traits did she exhibit that might be traced back to those events? What other paths might she have taken in her life?

10. Which woman do you feel had the largest spirit of

adventure? The most courage? Was most ill-suited for frontier life? Why?

11. What actions of the settlers, over time, contributed to the events of August 20, 1862? On the day of the attack, what decisions were made that impacted the outcome of the day? Do you think the day might have turned out differently if those decisions had not been made? Why or why not?

12. Do you believe the decision to attack white settlements was one with which all Dakota agreed? What unexpected issues did the Dakota have to deal with as a result of the decision to attack? How did the taking of captives differ in this instance? How did it complicate Dakota life?

13. Published accounts of the time (book and newspaper) told stories of atrocities. Do you believe these accounts fairly represented what occurred? Why or why not? What impact do you think these accounts had on Dakota/white relationships thereafter?

14. The Fool Soldiers did not receive credit for their role in ransoming the Shetek captives until recently. Why did the army fail to recognize these young men? Why has it been so difficult to trace the real story of events surrounding the Fool Soldiers?

15. Scars of the Dakota Conflict still remain in both white and Dakota societies today. Why do you think this the case? What role have bias and misunderstanding played? What impact have the atrocity stories played in this? What retaliatory actions occurred? Do you believe either or both cultures have avoided negative history? In what ways? How might these scars be healed?

ABOUT THE AUTHOR

Pamela (Gieser) Nowak was born and raised in southwest Minnesota. She has a B.A. in history and was a teacher, preservationist, project manager for the Fort Yuma National Historic Site, and administrator of a homeless shelter prior to her writing career. Her four historical romance novels have won numerous national awards and garnered critical acclaim for her ability to weave actual people, events, and places into her plotting. Now writing women's historical fiction with a heavy basis in fact, she's returned to her roots. The voices of these five Shetek survivors have called to her since she first learned about the Dakota Conflict and walked in their footsteps along the shores of Lake Shetek.

The employees of Five Star Publishing hope you have enjoyed this book.

Our Five Star novels explore little-known chapters from America's history, stories told from unique perspectives that will entertain a broad range of readers.

Other Five Star books are available at your local library, bookstore, all major book distributors, and directly from Five Star/Gale.

<u>Connect with Five Star Publishing</u>

Visit us on Facebook:
https://www.facebook.com/FiveStarCengage

Email:
FiveStar@cengage.com

For information about titles and placing orders:
(800) 223-1244
gale.orders@cengage.com

To share your comments, write to us:
Five Star Publishing
Attn: Publisher
10 Water St., Suite 310
Waterville, ME 04901